For Kate

Jean Renwick

THE MOURNING BROOCH

BOOK ONE

An ending. A beginning.

THE MOURNING BROOCH

BOOK ONE

An ending. A beginning.

Jean Renwick

Cover design by Sandy Bradley

Photography by Mark Astle

ISBN 978-1-7399425-0-2

For Dorothy Walker,
my godmother,
great-granddaughter of
Elizabeth Addy,
1920-1989

CONTENTS

FOREWORD

In the spring of 1989, I inherited from my godmother, Dorothy Walker, a canteen of cutlery and a mourning brooch. This curious gold brooch contains a lattice of brown and grey hair; on the back is inscribed the name of a deceased woman, her age and date of death. With help, I discovered that Elizabeth Addy, who died on 3 January 1849 aged 39, had been the wife of a Yorkshire farmer living near Doncaster. So, how did the brooch arrive into the hands of my godmother who had lived all her life in Lancashire and was a close friend of my mother?

Over a number of years delving into on-line resources, I managed to track Elizabeth's descendants. The trail down the generations eventually went cold but then I spotted a brass plate on the canteen of cutlery which revealed it to be a wedding gift from the Earl of Derby to Dorothy's parents on 6 August 1903. Working backwards, the link was made: Dorothy was Elizabeth's great-granddaughter.

Elizabeth died leaving two daughters: Mary-Ann (later Marian) aged six and Frances, known as Frannie, only six months old. And this is where the story begins. Research can be compulsive and following the lives of these two girls took me through several generations from south Yorkshire, around England and on to the United States – Philadelphia, New York, California.

Eventually over seventy people were identified as linked to the two sisters and, soon, I began to picture these people in my imagination. I had the urge to bring some of these characters to life in a novel, a family saga built upon real people and whatever facts I could unearth following key events. *The Mourning Brooch* saga encompasses the period from 1839 when Elizabeth married Joseph Addy and ends during World War II when Dorothy inherited the brooch from her mother. BOOK ONE covers 38 years as far as 1876, from Joseph's courting Elizabeth, their wedding, her death and up to the marriages of their two daughters.

Throughout the writing of this fiction-based-on-fact, I was conscious that these were real people to be treated with respect unless unwarranted. Consequently, I have vested in each character a personality, appearance, actions and spoken words that I do not claim to be true. Only a few names included in *The Mourning Brooch* were made up but many happenings were a creation of my imagination.

Jean Renwick

THE CAST OF CHARACTERS TO 1876

Doncaster Area

John Addy, a farmer in Bentley

Ann, his wife

JOSEPH ADDY, their son

ELIZABETH, Joseph's wife

MARY-ANN (later MARIAN), his elder daughter

FRANNIE, his younger daughter

George, Joseph's brother

Hannah, George's wife

Will, their son and nephew of Joseph

Godfrey, Joseph's brother

Susannah, Godfrey's wife

Nancy, Joseph's sister

William Stacey, Nancy's husband

William, their son

Dinah and Harriet, the Addys' housemaids

Thomas Hall, Elizabeth's father

Betsy, Elizabeth's mother

Mark, Elizabeth's brother

Ann, his wife

MARY, Elizabeth's sister

Sophia, Mary's daughter

John, Mary's son

Henry and John, Elizabeth's brothers

Will Barraclough, Joseph's leading farmworker

Elizabeth Vazin, midwife

Reverend John Sorsby, vicar of All Saints, Arksey

MARIA Cockin, single lady of independent means

Mary Caroline Legge, joint academy owner

Maria Catharine, her younger sister

Hutton family, where Marian works as a tutor

Sheffield

Samuel Binns, Sheffield chemist

Sophia, his wife

Mary Bray, sister of Maria Cockin

Joseph, her husband

Joe, her son

THE MOURNING BROOCH

Bradford Area

John Willey, wool merchant

Mary, his wife

Charles, John's eldest son

Matilda, his wife

Godfrey, John's second son

Sarah, his wife

John Quarmby, their son

JOHN-HENRY WILLEY, John's third son

ALFRED, JOSEPH-HENRY, HENRIETTA, ERNEST, John-Henry's children

Francis (Frank), John's fourth son

Richard Clarendon, John's fifth son

Benjamin, John's youngest son

Louisa, John's eldest daughter

Elizabeth, John's second daughter

HANNAH-MARY, John's third daughter

Betsy-Emma, John's youngest daughter

Sam Edwards, English settler in California

Other Characters

William Mellows, farmer and land agent

Joe, his son

Joseph William, Joe's first child

Jane Cavendish, Harrogate friend of Maria Cockin

CHAPTER 1

1849 Summer

In Joseph's calloused palm lies the brooch. All that remains of Elizabeth. Protected by glass, a brown tress is latticed with his own grey hair. The surrounding scrolled pattern in black lacquer contrasts with the gold of the oval casing. He turns it over to read the inscription.

Mrs Addy

Ob: Jan: 3 1849

Æl: 39

'I trust you are satisfied, sir?' The jeweller's widow is anxious to please. The approval of the Addy family is prized among Doncaster tradespeople.

'Aye. Thank you kindly, Mrs Bright. It is as I expected.' Two months earlier he had studied the various designs suggested by her son. He desired something to honour his wife's memory and finally chose the brooch. It would also look handsome as a pendant suspended from a gold chain or a black velvet ribbon. Not for some years yet, but one day it will be worn by his elder daughter, Mary-Ann.

Joseph returns the brooch to its velvet nest and the top closes over, replicating the lid of Elizabeth's coffin some seven months earlier.

On the High Street, Joseph stops before Parkinson's double-fronted sweet shop to admire the choice of confectionery displayed in the bay windows. This is where he buys Doncaster's speciality, butterscotch, greatly loved by Mary-Ann; and by his mother, truth be told. Next month, the race-goers visiting for St Leger Week will crowd into this shop to carry home a packet of its famous confectionery.

His pony and trap makes its way out of the town, crowded today for its well-regarded market, heading back to his farm on the edge of Bentley village. Joseph shrugs off his jacket in the August sunshine but the brightness of the light does little to raise his sombre mood. The sight of Elizabeth's hair, entwined with his own, awakes the memory of his mother, back in January standing beside the body of his wife freshly washed and dressed in a simple white nightgown.

'Shall I cut a piece, or will you?' Her Yorkshire practicality was tempered by a sentimentality which surprised him. 'You'll want to save something for the lasses.' In those aching hours as Elizabeth lay neatly prepared for the coming burial, it was the last thing on his mind.

He nodded though had no idea what he would do with the trimmed locks. He watched with unwilling fascination as Ann Addy gently teased hair from the nape of her dead daughter-in-law and with her sewing scissors carefully cut a generous tress some ten inches long.

'There. That should do for when you decide.' She wrapped it carefully in a white cotton handkerchief embroidered with an E.

For some months the folded handkerchief lay in the bedside drawer, still Elizabeth's bedside drawer. In late spring and on her sixth birthday, the first without her mother, Mary-Ann asked about the preserved hair, no doubt prompted by her grandmother. They were returning to the pony and trap after Sunday morning service at All Saints, the medieval church in Arksey which had been attended by generations of the Addy family. The girl was slightly built, like her mother, but a restless soul, always eager to discover. No doubt that held her in good stead with her schooling, Joseph reflected.

Before the service, she and her father had walked around to the north side of the church, to the grave of her mother on which she placed flowers cut from the garden, diligently brushing clean the inscription on the flat memorial stone.

Sacred to the memory of Elizabeth,

the beloved wife of Joseph ADDY of Bentley,

who died January 3rd 1849, aged 39 years.

Looking for that blessed hope and the glorious appearing of the Great God and our Saviour Jesus Christ. She died in peace.

Now heading home, Mary-Ann caught hold of Joseph's hand.

'Father, what will you do with Mother's hair?'

His mind had been elsewhere, albeit not unconnected with his wife's death. For some time, he had been tussling with how to raise his two daughters with only the help of his mother and his sister-in-law, Mary. For his mother, now sixty-eight and widowed, it was all becoming a struggle.

'Joseph, have you looked at our mother these days? Are you blind that you cannot see how tired she is?' Nancy, his remaining sister, spoke for the family during a recent visit. 'I've been talking to our brother and we're agreed: you need to find a full-time nursemaid for Frannie. A one-year-old is too much for Mother to cope with and Mary-Ann is a lovely child, but needs managing, else she'll grow up wilful. As for Mary, well, you shouldn't be having your deceased wife's sister in the house; folk will talk.'

He nodded his agreement. His mother was worn out with the demands of his daughters. But he relished neither the rigmarole of seeking a suitable woman to care for his girls, nor a stranger in his home. However, no matter what, his mother will remain at the farm. Neither of her other children was hastening to claim her.

As he and his daughter passed through the gate, he tugged his thoughts back to the child's question. What was he to do with the hair? He remembered the locket he gave Elizabeth on their betrothal but it already contained the curls of their two daughters. He had bought it from Bright's, the goldsmiths that had made the Gold Cup for the Doncaster races.

'I am minded to go into town to see Phillip Bright's son. Their business continues to thrive since the old man died and they've a grand reputation. I shall ask him to put the hair into a piece of jewellery, something you could wear in years to come. Something to remind you of your mother,' he ended with a weak smile.

'I shan't ever need anything to remind me of Mother,' came the emphatic response from Mary-Ann. 'I shall never forget her. Maybe Frannie should wear it. She will have no memory of our mother and probably ...' She hesitated. 'It was her being born that ...' Her voice trailed away.

'What's that you say? Is it your meaning that Frannie's birth was in some way linked with her death?' The girl remained silent, un-wishing her words. 'There's no truth in that, lass, and I'll not have you say otherwise.' Her father's face flushed with anger but he checked himself. In reality, perhaps the girl was right. He did not wish to dwell on it.

'Why don't we go into Doncaster shortly and we can look at what is now the fashion? Will you come with me?' He wanted her to share in the making of this keepsake. But he couldn't bear for her to think ill of her little sister, a baby who would never know the gentleness and love of her mother. The girl shrank back and shook her head.

*

Now some months later and with the brooch in his pocket, Joseph crosses the River Don and forks right towards Bentley. A thought occurs to him. Instead of heading on towards the village and home, he branches off towards Arksey. He urges his pony, Molly, towards the stumpy tower and steeple of All Saints, the village itself set like an island amidst the low-lying landscape. He will not be missed back at the farmstead. Will Barraclough has been left in charge of the men and they have work enough to keep them occupied for the rest of the day.

As the pony trots over the railway bridge, Joseph is relieved that no train is passing. Old Molly hates the clanking, the chuffing and the speed of the locomotives which rush wagons and carriages north and south across the flat countryside.

The Plough Inn stands warily under the spiritual gaze of the church opposite. Joseph descends from the trap and hands the pony's reins to a skinny young lad who hastened from the stables the moment he heard the clatter of hooves and wheels. In welcome, the boy runs his hand over Molly's neck and leads her to shade and water. Joseph vaguely recognises the boy as one of the numerous children of the innkeeper, his old schoolfriend, Will Trout.

Will lost his wife after the birth of her fourth child, and his elderly mother passed away only months later. Joseph sees something of his own predicament in Will's efforts to manage with only the help of his family before the innkeeper married for the second time. Tongues wagged that Charlotte Sidwell's two illegitimate children could already be his, a calumny which Will denied. Nonetheless, without hesitation, on marrying Charlotte, he took in her two children and raised them with his own four. Together they have created yet three more.

Joseph turns back across the road. The graveyard is empty of folk other than those sleeping for eternity. He strides past the grey and gold-coloured stone church to the lonely north side where Elizabeth's grave lies, the memorial stone left with space for his own name when his time comes. What would she think of his solution?

CHAPTER 2

1849 Summer

This is Joseph's first visit alone to Elizabeth's grave. Usually there are members of the family beside him which helps curb his emotions. The Addys are not given to displays of feeling. Today is different. He wants to talk to his wife, share his worries, imagine her words of common-sense.

1838-1839

It was Elizabeth's steadiness that first appealed to Joseph. A farmer's daughter, she understood the vagaries of agricultural life: the constant battle with weather and inconstancy of the markets. His own father had professed high regard for hers, Thomas Hall. Until his untimely death, he had farmed good arable land in Bentley, though on a much smaller scale than the Addy family.

From his earliest years, Joseph accepted that farming was to be his life; it was what the Addys had done for generations. Although education was imposed upon him and his older brothers, he never found it easy. As a lad, his mind would wander from the schoolroom where boys' thoughts had ever strayed since the school was built in 1683 in the days of Charles II. Already, Joseph's older brothers, Godfrey and George were labouring alongside their father and he champed at the bit to get out and join them the minute the school bell rang out the end of lessons.

Although friendly and easy-going, he was rarely seen at the village gatherings held in Arksey. Truth be told, he was weary by the end of the week and the heavy drinking of some led to wild behaviour, beyond boisterous, which he disliked intensely.

Two by two, most of the young people of the neighbourhood paired off. Joseph, buffeted by much older sisters and unused to the company of young ladies, had no sweetheart. Nor did he express any immediate interest in marrying. Yes, one day he would want a son, but at that time no lass had caught his eye. Farming was his life and quite enough for then.

Among the eligible young women was Elizabeth Hall. Middling height, brown hair, pleasant enough face, but known to be strong-minded. She was being courted by a local farmer's son, Matthew, some ten years older and due to inherit a tenancy. Joseph heard that it was a sparky relationship, with both parties loth to give way. They were not betrothed but there was an understanding and they were expected to marry ere long.

It was not to be. The man was killed while loading hay onto a wagon. The brake failed, or maybe was incorrectly engaged, the heavy load rolled back and he fell beneath a wheel. His parents lost their only child and the future of their farm. Elizabeth felt keenly what she had lost.

Face set, showing no emotion, she followed his family to the burial, rejecting the custom for only men to attend. Joseph, representing the Addy family among the mourners, respected her strength. She was twenty-five, around his own age, late for a woman to be seeking a husband. Matthew's death had other consequences. Elizabeth's mother, Betsy Hall, had struggled to manage the farm since her husband died in Doncaster's cholera epidemic, some five years back. She was left with two daughters and boys of only six and nine. Mark, her eldest boy, now nineteen, was long gone to make a living among the alehouses of Doncaster. For Widow Hall, a farmer as a son-in-law would have meant handing over the reins into competent hands.

The death raised anxieties also in the minds of Joseph's parents, John and Ann Addy. What would be the future of their own farm? Their eldest son, George, had never wanted farming, a source of disappointment and anger to his father. Instead, he sought a life as a butcher, slaughtering the beasts on the family farm. Second son, Godfrey was already away and renting his own land, building a solid farm of his own. Joseph, a farmer to his finger-tips, was already in his late twenties and not courting. If he did not find a wife soon, they could see him leading a lonely life if he were to take on their tenancy in years to come. A farmer needed a companion to share the challenges of nature through the seasons.

Ann Addy was especially concerned. With distress she noted her husband's failing eye-sight and the gloom which descended upon the household as he raged with frustration. He relied increasingly on Joseph to judge the progress of their crops and the condition of the stock. Joseph respected his father and always asked the old man's advice, so that the instructions to the men came from Mr John, the father.

Every Sunday morning at All Saints, Ann Addy would consider the suitability of the single women seated in the simple polished oak pews. Joseph took the place at her side vacated by her husband who could no longer read the hymn books, even though he knew the verses by heart. He refused to go to church for what God had brought on him.

'How fares Widow Hall's daughter, since she lost her sweetheart?' Ann Addy's question to her son as they reached home for their Sunday dinner. He removed the thick blanket from his mother's knees and helped her down from the trap.

'Hard, I imagine, and hard also for Widow Hall. Her eldest son is gone away from farming and the two younger boys are still at school, so no great help around the farm. She has Kenny Oades to manage a couple of men but I imagine poor Matthew would have answered the old lady's hopes.'

As custom, they ignored the front door of the farmhouse and entered through the warm kitchen where their young house-girl, Dinah, scurried about with steaming pots and Sunday-best dishes.

'Elizabeth Hall is around my age and can help her mother and there's a younger sister but she's probably not much use yet.' He stood thawing out by the parlour fire until the food was brought to table by Dinah. 'Maybe it's time we should talk to our own family and see what help we can offer. The Halls are good neighbours and are in need. What do you say, Father?'

John Addy was in no mood for charity but had liked Tom Hall and at one time enjoyed his company at market. Tom, like himself, had been cursed with an eldest son who refused to work the family farm alongside his father. He felt sorry for Tom's widow and nodded his consent.

'Talk to Godfrey. See if he can spare a man now and then. We can send our lad, Robert, for the odd day, but mind you keep an eye on things, else Lord knows what will become of the Halls.'

Widow Hall accepted the Addys' offer with alacrity and not a little flicker of hope. Joseph Addy was unmarried. As the son still remaining on the family farm, he could well inherit the tenancy as his older brothers had made their own way. Above all, he was known to be an honourable man with a pleasant manner and the Addys were highly regarded in the area. No wonder she lay awake that night, her imagination flying in all directions.

Joseph sent one of their lads to support the Halls' farm hands and soon called by to review work already under way and offer advice on the imminent crop sowing. Mrs Hall was grateful not only for the extra labour but also to be able to talk through day-to-day tasks. Initially, Elizabeth was indignant that it was thought that the Halls could not manage their own affairs, but soon she acknowledged that without Joseph's advice, the farm would fall behind and they would not meet the next quarter's rent.

As the seasons passed, Joseph could be found as often at the Halls' as at his father's farm. He laboured in the fields alongside the men and only once a week did he come into the farmhouse to clean up and meet with Mrs Hall. And her daughters. Young Mary would bounce into the room and dart quickly out again when she spotted Joseph's stocky figure. They were talking farm business and she preferred to disappear up to her room and her books. Elizabeth took an interest in what was being discussed and afterwards would walk Joseph back to the stable and his waiting horse.

'We have much to thank you for, Joseph. Mother's mind has been at rest in these last months, knowing we could call upon you for guidance. My brother, John, is but a child and one day will take his place at my mother's side. For now, though, it is not easy.'

In the coming months, Joseph was a regular visitor to the Hall farm and the widow was quietly satisfied to observe a growing attachment between this earnest man and her wilful daughter. She admired Joseph's way of parrying Elizabeth's robust views on life, the farm, even the politics of the day. Joseph had little truck with the wider world and took the view that as he could do little to alter things, his maxim was to keep his head down and press on.

Far from being exasperated, Elizabeth appeared amused by his conservative views and an easy friendship developed between the two. Knowing it would set tongues awagging, Ann Addy invited Elizabeth to eat with them after church, and warmed to her uncomplicated natural ways. She even viewed the girl's undoubted spirit as a positive foil to her son's easy-going manner. In Elizabeth she saw a potential daughter-in-law and was eager to set wheels in motion, fearing that Joseph would plod along happily without consideration for Elizabeth's relatively advanced years for child-bearing.

'Your father approves of Elizabeth.' Mother and son were seated by the range in the large farmhouse kitchen. John Addy had gone to his bed as soon as the light started to fade from the day. Sitting by the fire with a pipe no longer soothed him, especially when Joseph would read aloud items of news from the *Gazette* which he felt of interest to his parents. It simply reinforced his inability to see print and the alternative silence weighed heavily.

Joseph looked up from the newspaper and frowned.

'What is your meaning, Mother?' He knew exactly her intent.

'You will be thirty-one next birthday and Elizabeth not far behind. She is a good woman. She understands the life of a farmer's wife. You should marry her.' Bluntly said, but kindly meant.

Joseph made no response, smiled to himself and reflected on his mother's words.

Elizabeth did not hesitate when Joseph asked her to marry him. It was more than a year since Matthew had been killed. Her love did not die with him but she recognised that her options were diminishing. In time, her youngest brother, John, would be old enough to take over the running of the farm. Her younger sister, Mary, was prettier than she and, although a timid girl, no doubt the boys would come courting very soon. She, on the other hand, risked a future as a spinster sister, eventually living in her brother's home under the management of the woman he took for a wife. A recipe for conflict, whoever the woman might be.

Joseph Addy was a kind-spirited man, a conscientious farmer and did not frequent the alehouse. She had already seen within her own family the damage drink can bring. Although her heart did not quicken on those few occasions when they were alone, she recognised that such feelings were not essential for a good marriage.

In celebration of their betrothal, Joseph purchased from Bright's, the best jewellers in Doncaster, an oval silver locket engraved with the letters J and E entwined.

'Elizabeth. Something for you to wear until our wedding day when I place my ring on your finger.' He held it aloft by the fine silver chain and made to fasten it around her neck. Instead, she reached out to hold the locket in the palm of her hand, to see the lettering more closely. She opened the clasp and regarded the two empty shells.

'What shall we place in there, Joseph? Our hair perhaps, or maybe we should wait and preserve that of our first children?' Joseph was not normally superstitious but felt strangely uncomfortable at tempting fate. He nodded his agreement.

Both families welcomed the news of the betrothal, each recognising the assured continuation of their respective farms. Widow Hall hoped that her future son-in-law would continue to provide advice and occasional labour until young John was skilled and wise enough to take on the tenancy. Some while back, her hopes that middle son, Henry, would take on the farm had been dashed by the schoolmaster in Arksey when he persuaded her to let her brightest son train as a clerk in Doncaster.

Widow Hall knew that with her elder daughter married off, she needed then only concern herself with the future of Mary, now seventeen years old, and a more submissive version of her older sister.

At the church service following the harvest home celebrations, the couple made their announcement. They would marry early in the New Year at a quieter time when farmers struggled to get out onto the land.

'How will you feel about living with Joseph's parents? I hear his old man can be cantankerous and it can't be easy to share the household with a mother-in-law.' Mary was curious to hear how Elizabeth would cope. Within their own home, her sister tended to manage their widowed mother. Not unkindly, but with a measured intent.

'Most people have to live with family when first they marry. Why should we be any different?' Elizabeth bent over her sewing and avoided a direct answer. The two girls were mending petticoats beside the large window of the parlour. Not often used, the sparsely furnished room was kept neat and spotless and provided good light for needlework. Elizabeth, unlike Mary, had little aptitude for sewing and only agreed to help her sister while rain lacquered the slate roof of the wash-house opposite. Indeed, she had no intention of sewing her own trousseau and planned to buy what she needed in Doncaster.

'I have spoken with the wife of Joseph's brother, Godfrey, and she says the old man never used to be crabby but has turned thus since his sight waned. As for his mother, well, I shall just have to bite my tongue for Joseph's sake.' Behind Ann Addy's smiles and kind words, Elizabeth recognised someone as strong as herself and a woman who would not defer to her opinions as her own mother did.

The snow held off for their January wedding. Elizabeth was wrapped snugly in a padded cloak of pearl grey with matching bonnet as she arrived at the south door of All Saints on the arm of her older brother, Mark. To greet them, a few hardy locals huddled around the church door, unable to work the fields on this wintry weekday morning. Watery sunshine floated through the windows of the Norman church. The extended Addy family of uncles, aunts and cousins sat in the pews of the north aisle with its three round columns positioned annoyingly to restrict views of the ceremony. The smaller Hall contingent sat opposite, the south aisle wall supported by even wider octagonal columns. The congregation was swaddled against the cold striking upwards from the stone flags and people snuggled into the high collars of their cloaks, some ladies warming their numbed fingers on hot baked potatoes smuggled into their best hand-muffs.

As the couple knelt to take their vows at the chancel steps against the backdrop of the three Romanesque windows above the altar, Ann Addy allowed herself to relax against the hard back of the pew and make a prayer to the Lord to grant them a long and fruitful marriage.

Afterwards, back at the farm, guests were reinvigorated by platters laden with hot pies and roast meats and by steaming hot punch to toast the bride and groom. Joseph called for silence as people sat back with stomachs full and sufficient ale and Madeira wine to bring warmth to their cheeks.

'Friends, family, my wife and I wish to thank you for joining with us on this happy day and for all your good wishes for our future together. I am honoured that Elizabeth agreed to wed me and I am blessed indeed to have found such a spirited companion willing to be at my side through life. It is my good fortune that I wed the daughter of a fine farmer, the late and much missed Thomas Hall, and that she is well prepared for what life will bring as a farmer's wife.'

Elizabeth judged the moment and resisted the temptation to add a tart rejoinder to her new husband's speech. 'Spirited'? Was that a compliment or an admonishment? She simply smiled and raised a glass of wine in her lace-gloved hand.

That night they lay together in the bedroom set aside for them at the other end of the corridor from Joseph's parents. The housemaid had ensured as best a fire as possible in the small grate but it did little to reduce the biting cold of that January night. For warmth they held each other close. Both were tired from the day's events and more than a little anxious.

As a farmer's daughter, Elizabeth was well versed in the practicalities of coupling, but the consummation of her marriage was something different. She was grateful for Joseph's kindness and although their first night as man and wife was no great success, it was at least encouraging. She hoped that with time, and practice, at best she would come to enjoy their physical union, and at least not dread it.

CHAPTER 3

1849 Summer

'What other option is there, lass?'

Joseph stares down at the gravestone.

'Mary-Ann, Frannie, they need a mother to raise them. My mother is far too old and too much has fallen on her shoulders. Your sister, Mary helped with the girls as you lay ill and ... well, now she walks over each morning to get them up and Mary-Ann off to school. She's fond of them both and truly cares. It's not just out of duty to you.' He gazes over the surrounding headstones, seeking in vain for the right words. 'Lizzie, I can see no other solution. Would that I could.'

There is no response in this one-sided discussion. If only he could hear his Lizzie weigh up the possibilities and lead him to the only sensible conclusion. He can reach that point alone. But he needs to hear it from her.

*

1839

The union of Joseph and Elizabeth Addy was a good one, based on mutual affection and respect. The farmhouse was large enough for one of the bedrooms to be turned into a sitting room for the newly-weds. Together they chose floral wallpaper in a sunny yellow and a small sofa to make the room homely. Elizabeth and her mother-in-law recognised the need for separate space and both women worked to make their home harmonious.

During the day, Ann Addy would accompany her tormented husband as he walked the farm, reporting to him the level of water in the drainage ditches, a constant worry for farmers in this low-lying area, and hailing neighbours to come over to speak with John and counter his loneliness.

Elizabeth preferred to be out of the house while Joseph worked. She felt stifled by the presence of her parents-in-law though she knew such feelings were uncharitable. They were good people but she could never relax with them. Instead, she would walk into the centre of Bentley to buy provisions beyond their own resources. Hams hung in their larder alongside butter and cheeses, and Dinah would bring fresh milk from the cows and eggs from the hens. Fitted across the head of the stairs was shelving which by September of every year would be laden with bottled fruit and gleaming jars of jams and pickles. Ann Addy was rightly proud of her preserves which carried the family through the bleak months of winter.

Food was an important part of the Addy day and meals were taken by all four together. Joseph would be out on the farm by six o'clock, overseeing the milking of their small herd of cows, and would return by eight to eat breakfast with the family. In the winter he needed a hot meal around mid-day and Dinah spent the mornings under Ann Addy's supervision preparing a cycle of stews of various meat and vegetables. For Elizabeth the routine became monotonous but for Joseph little changed in his life and he was content.

THE MOURNING BROOCH

It was late spring following their marriage when Joseph noticed an increasing lethargy in his father. With the longer days and the warmer weather, he hoped John Addy's spirits would rise. On a bright Saturday morning, his brother, Godfrey, had ridden over with his thirteen-year-old son, ostensibly to see his parents but, in reality, to measure the health of their crops against his own, some miles distant. A tall, wiry man, Godfrey dismounted and passed the reins to his son, bidding him take both horses to the stable. He walked into the kitchen and greeted his mother, busy polishing brasses with vigour to remind them that she was still mistress in this house.

'Where's my father?' Ann Addy pursed her lips and shook her head without looking up. 'What's to do? Is he sick?'

She raised her eyes to him. Eyes that implored.

'He won't get out of bed and hasn't done so for these past three days. He hasn't eaten hardly anything and won't let me call the doctor.' She dropped the cleaning cloth and held up both hands in frustration.

Hearing horses arrive in the yard, Joseph had left his work in the barn and joined his older brother in the house. Both men nodded their welcome and Godfrey ploughed in.

'What ails Father then? Does he have fever? Does he ache? Why do you not call the doctor?'

Joseph sat down at the large, scrubbed wooden table. He loosened the kerchief around his neck and resisted the temptation to respond to Godfrey in like tone.

'Why don't you go up to see for yourself?' He would have continued but for the entrance of Elizabeth who had descended from their sitting room, glad to welcome any visitor. After an exchange of greetings, Joseph continued, his strong arms resting on the table, his grimy hands held palm upwards in a gesture of openness.

'He has none of those ailments which is why we have not insisted on the doctor visiting. It is as though he's decided that he's had enough of this world. His sight troubles him more and more. He is capable of less and less. We try our best to help him with the practicalities of life but we cannot see inside his head. He is closing in on himself.'

'Can you not find a good tonic for him from the pharmacy in Doncaster?' Godfrey clearly felt that the family was not doing sufficient. Elizabeth wanted to dispute the effectiveness of his suggested medical quackery but held her tongue.

Godfrey climbed the stairs, taking with him a bowl of broth to tempt his father. The family below sat in silence listening to the low murmur of his voice as he cajoled his father to eat. His slow steps down the creaking treads foretold that the broth had been rejected and his ministrations rebuffed. He looked shaken by the deterioration in his father's appearance.

The doctor came out to the farm the following week and pronounced that, apart from his failing eye-sight, John Addy was physically sound. As for the farmer's spirit, that needed to be addressed and he promised to send over a draught of his own concoction which, if taken twice daily, would counter the black mood that had descended. The family wished to believe him.

John Addy never again rose from his bed. Spring blossomed into summer and the rhythm of the farming year continued apace. In the evenings, Joseph would sit with his father and talk of the tasks of the past day. He and Elizabeth no longer felt it kind to leave Ann Addy alone and their little sitting room was neglected as they supported her watching her husband drift away.

John Addy died in September 1839. Sadness was tempered with frustrated relief. What else could they have done for him? Nobody had a solution. He simply gave up on life and had chosen a slow path to decline and die.

THE MOURNING BROOCH

It was the day of the funeral and Ann Addy had made it known she wished the women of the family to attend. The great and the good of Arksey, Bentley and the surrounding farming area descended on the same church where eight months earlier the Addy family had celebrated the happy union of Joseph and Elizabeth. George, as eldest son, was intent on honouring his father, the father he had feared, the father he had disappointed. He led the cortege in a carriage that also bore his wife, Hannah, his mother and his next brother, Godfrey with wife Susannah. Joseph followed on with Elizabeth and his remaining, now middle-aged sister, Nancy.

'I hadn't expected you to come.' Ann Addy broke the respectful silence within the carriage hired to take the principal members of the family to All Saints. Nobody was in any doubt at whom this comment was directed.

'Enough, Mother, not today of all days.' Godfrey's wife, Susannah smiled inwardly at his swift defence of his elder brother, George. She knew that Godfrey had wanted to lead his mother behind the coffin. After all, he was the son who remained farming alongside his father before receiving a tenancy of his own. George, on the other hand, had not exactly disgraced the family but had displayed a rebellious trait, in Godfrey's view.

George remained silent. His wife, Hannah seethed. She was fully aware that her husband was a disappointment to the family. She also felt let down by the fine-looking lad she had married, the eldest son of one of the big farming families in the district. She was a scion of the Cockin family, even more esteemed and prosperous than the Addys, and it was her family's expectation that she would marry well and be kept in the comfort to which she was accustomed. As, when they wed, the Addys' farmhouse was still crowded with George's siblings, her family had offered a modest cottage in Bentley until George found his own land to rent and farm. That dream never materialised. Now they lived in the same tiny cottage and he made a living slaughtering and butchering the beasts from local farms.

Her mother-in-law could not let it rest.

'Your father would have welcomed seeing you towards the end.'

George and Godfrey both doubted it. George knew that whatever he said now would be wrong. He remained silent and gazed out over the fields awaiting harvest, seeking an unspoken pardon from his father. Was it his fault that he had never felt at one with farming? He was not afraid of hard work. Slaughtering and cutting up carcasses required strength and stamina. Throughout the rest of the funeral and wake, mother and eldest son exchanged not a word.

The day after the funeral, as Dinah continued clearing up the house, Joseph sat in the parlour with his mother and wife. Elizabeth was conscious that the hierarchy had shifted over the last few days but was equally sensitive to her mother-in-law's feelings. Ann Addy had just lost her husband of many years. He had provided her with children and a good home. Although not a demonstrative man, John Addy had never given her cause to regret their marriage. Now, the balance of life had altered and Joseph would officially inherit the role he had assumed in recent months as his father weakened.

Both women were dressed in mourning black. Elizabeth was relieved she could still fit into the cotton gown she wore seven years earlier on the death of her own father. Joseph itched to get back into the fields and felt stifled by the propriety custom demanded. The Will was to be read this afternoon and the family would return to hear the wishes of John Addy, though few surprises were anticipated.

'Tomorrow we need to go up to the Hall to sort out the tenancy.' At the funeral, the estate manager had offered Joseph his condolences and invited him to come over to Wheatley Hall so that they could sign the papers transferring the tenancy from John to Joseph, as his father had requested.

'You should take Elizabeth with you.' His mother fussed with the tassels of the plum-coloured arm cover. 'She will need to get to know the folk up there.' Her eyes met those of her daughter-in-law. She recognised that Elizabeth would not be a passive partner in running the farm and so from now on she did not expect to be involved again in decision making. It rankled more than a little but she was wise enough to accept that such was the way of farming life.

'Of course, Mother, I am happy to go with Joseph. Many's the time I have accompanied my own mother on quarter day when she has gone up to pay the rent,' Elizabeth replied cautiously. Women who demonstrated too much enthusiasm with regard to business were viewed with suspicion and it was still early days in her marriage.

That afternoon, Widow Addy was joined around the dining table by her surviving children, apart from George, to hear the family lawyer read the simple Will, drawn up some two years earlier. It was already known that the tenancy of the farmhouse and land would pass to Joseph, given that George had long since disclaimed any such inheritance and Godfrey had built up a substantial tenancy nearby.

George had declined to attend, aware of the likely humiliation.

'Are you going to stand back and let them take your share?' his wife, Hannah had protested.

'My share of what? Whatever money there is will go to my mother. Anything else of value will go to Godfrey, I have no doubt.' George's acceptance infuriated her.

And so it was. Godfrey was to receive the gold half-hunter watch and chain which John Addy wore on his waistcoat on

Sundays and at family celebrations, the last time at Joseph and Elizabeth's wedding. Ann Addy had anticipated the announcement and rose from her seat beside the lawyer and walked round the table to hand the watch to her second son.

In the adjacent parlour, Elizabeth waited with the other female members of the family, each of them aware of her new status as wife of the head of this Addy household and the woman who would be tasked with living alongside Ann Addy.

CHAPTER 4

1849 Summer

In farewell, Joseph reaches down to scrape leaves and grass from Elizabeth's gravestone. Guiltily, he thinks of his father's gravestone nearby, rarely visited over the last ten years. Next time he will bring shears to neaten the grass.

He straightens and hitches up his breeches. Time to head back. His mother is eager to see the brooch and Mary-Ann will be equally curious. He crosses the road from the churchyard and enters the stableyard of The Plough. Will Trout has been watching for his friend's return and appears at the side door.

'How do, Joe. Bin paying respects to Elizabeth?' He guesses the reason for Joseph's unexpected mid-week visit to the church. Charlotte, his second wife, joins him in the doorway. Joseph notes her condition and despairs at his old friend's inability to curb his appetite. Another mouth to feed come New Year, a tenth child?

Joseph nods his acknowledgement and tips his hat.

'Will you step inside for some bread and cheese? It's past dinner time.' Will's invitation is tempting but Joseph has never enjoyed the pungent smells of the tap-room and excuses himself with a smile.

'Mother expects me and will have kept something for me. I'm later than planned.' He does not wish to linger and be persuaded into discussing his dilemma with the Trouts.

1839

Following John Addy's death, it was routine that helped the transition within the household. Elizabeth was careful to invite her mother-in-law's advice in planning the week's marketing. They would sit side by side and draw up a list. Initially, Elizabeth followed Ann Addy's recommendations to the letter. Within the house little changed other than the couple joined Joseph's mother in the parlour each evening and the yellow sitting-room was relegated to a quiet space where Elizabeth would withdraw when she needed solitude. Private conversations between husband and wife were restricted to their bedroom, removed some distance from Ann Addy's larger room where her children had been born and her husband died. Although their room was smaller, Elizabeth preferred the privacy it afforded not only for their discreet exchanges but also for their couplings with the revelatory creak of bedsprings.

As the months progressed, an unspoken question hung over the house, floating onwards to the wider family. When would there be a baby? Ann Addy's hidden fear centred on Elizabeth's advancing years; she would soon be thirty.

Elizabeth's own mother was not as reticent.

'How are things at home?'

Elizabeth deliberately misunderstood the question and answered: 'Joseph's mother is not easy to live with but it could be worse, a lot worse.'

Widow Hall looked up from the bowl full of flour and lard, soon to be transformed into cobble-stone scones to top the mutton stew, dinner for herself, John and Mary.

'It's not that which concerns me. I only wonder when you will present me with a grand-child.' She formed the dough into patties lined up on the scrubbed wooden table, brushed the flour from her hands and looked uncompromisingly at her daughter.

Elizabeth refused to be drawn into such personal matters and carefully overlapped the scones atop the ready-cooked stew.

'No doubt the family are all speculating, so you can tell them it's none of their business. We are very happy and what will be, will be. A child will come in God's good time, Mother.' She lifted the heavy earthenware dish and carried it over to the fireplace where her mother opened the door of the side oven. The fire was stoked up and in just over half an hour the mutton cobbler would be ready to eat.

Within her own thoughts, Elizabeth was less easy. She knew that it was part of her duty to deliver Joseph a son and heir and although he never voiced such a view, it was what all men expected from marriage. It was still early days but she yearned for a child.

1849 Summer

As Joseph leaves the Plough Inn and points the trap towards Bentley and his farm, he looks out over his neighbour's corn fields, just starting to fade from green to ochre. Please let his own crops do well and the price of grain hold up. But, whatever the outcome of the harvest, Joseph must find a solution to his predicament and certainly before the winter.

1842-1843

Joseph recalls those difficult early years of the marriage. The three of them orbiting around each other within the large farmhouse, each intent on harmony, each conscious of the passing of time. The lack of a baby was a matter of sadness to him, not only because children were needed to help run any farm but also because he sensed the unvoiced frustration of his wife.

Elizabeth had sought the advice of the family's physician and the remedies suggested had not worked. She was not surprised. She had no belief in the concoctions she smuggled to their room and which she took each night as a magic potion before she knelt in prayer.

At church, the congregation seemed constantly celebrating the birth of yet another prince or princess to the undoubtedly fecund Queen. Victoria's growing family only served to underline Elizabeth's misfortune. Rumour had it that Her Majesty was again with child.

It was late autumn after a fruitful gathering-in celebrated with a harvest-home supper, when Elizabeth and Joseph fell wearily into bed.

'I cannot be sure, Joseph, but I reckon it's happened at last.'

Joseph twisted towards her, unsure of her meaning.

'I believe I am with child.' Elizabeth's tentative smile betrayed her inner fear that this was another of the false signs which had disappointed them twice over the last three years. 'I have waited longer before telling you, until I could be certain. I feel different from past occasions and am sickly when I wake in the morning.'

Joseph held her close and kissed her forehead.

'Let us keep this our secret for a while, until we are sure. Don't think I haven't seen the looks my mother gives you when my sister brings her lads to visit.' He knew that were they to share this news with his mother, she would be hard pressed to keep it to herself, and then, if Elizabeth should lose the child ...

But Widow Addy already knew. After raising five children of her own and miscarrying yet another, she recognised the signs of pregnancy without being told. Elizabeth's pale face at breakfast, poor appetite and reluctance to cook meat, revealed all. But she was canny enough to hold her own counsel and wait for Joseph to inform her. She may be tough but she knew only too well what it was to be the subject of scrutiny by the family, by the village, right through to the confinement.

The birth came with springtide, some two weeks after the Queen had given birth to a second daughter, Alice, attended by the finest doctors in the land. For Elizabeth there was no lay-in hospital but the family's doctor reassured her that he was well versed in the latest expertise in the field of childbirth and would ensure her a safe delivery, on the understanding that he was called in good time.

Nearer to hand was Elizabeth's old friend, Elizabeth Vazin, the daughter of a midwife. She had learnt her craft alongside her mother and other wise women of the surrounding villages. She was known and respected by the local doctor and he had no qualms in leaving Joseph Addy's wife in her instinctive and scrupulously washed hands until his arrival.

The pains started early one mid-May evening and Dinah was despatched to bring Farmer Vazin's wife. Ann Addy took charge of affairs and ordered Joseph to ride and fetch the doctor. Her son was reluctant to leave his wife and wanted to send Will Barraclough instead.

'What do you think, lass?' He sought guidance from his wife who was resting between pains.

'Well, Joseph, you've helped with the birth of many a fine calf over the years but I really think that my dear friend, Elizabeth Vazin, will be more than capable until the doctor arrives.'

He touched her shoulder in a gesture of affection and encouragement and ran from the house, calling the lad to help saddle his cob. He was soon out of the farm gate and galloping the lanes towards Doncaster.

The birth of Mary-Ann Addy was slow and difficult. The midwife needed all her years of experience to help her friend who was visibly weaker by the time the doctor arrived. Ann Addy opened the door on hearing the hooves skittering to a halt in the yard. The anxiety in her face hastened the doctor up the stairs and turned Joseph's sweat to ice.

Seated alone at the kitchen table, Joseph listened in horror to the cries of pain coming from above. He was appalled. His animals bellowed, bleated or whimpered as they calved, lambed and pupped. But surely this degree of suffering should not be expected of a woman?

Dinah busied in and out of the scullery carrying pails of hot water. His mother remained upstairs offering support to the doctor and midwife. He alone sat useless, unable to move.

Then, a thin cry. He stood and waited. Another cry. Then his mother's tread as she descended the stairs.

'A girl.' She smiled a thin smile. All that pain for a girl.

'Elizabeth?' Joseph moved towards the foot of the stairs, his face horrified by the unknown.

Ann Addy put out a restraining arm.

'No lad. Leave be. She'll do. She's had a bad time, but she'll do.' She led Joseph back to the table and sat down heavily. 'Dinah! Hot tea, as quick as you like.'

1849 Summer

Mary-Ann hears the trap approaching and runs to open the gate. Her interest to see the new brooch is second only to the prospect of the Parkinson's butterscotch her father always brings from Doncaster. Joseph waves his thanks as he steers Molly into the cobbled yard. The lad appears from a loose-box and keeps the pony steady as Joseph jumps down, holding tightly to his paniers. Taking the reins, the lad leads Molly to the cart-shed to be unharnessed then fed and watered.

'Father, you're late back. We were worried.' The six-year-old scolds her father with the frown of her grandmother. 'We have already eaten but Dinah has put a dish aside for you, so come in quickly and wash up.'

Joseph aches as he hears the expressions and mannerisms of his late wife, projected back at him through their child. He nods and leads the way into the kitchen. First, he entrusts the hessian bag to the girl, knowing her curiosity will overcome her manners and that her hand will slide quietly into the depths, only to feel, not to take. That would be a step too far. She knows she is her father's darling but nonetheless he expects good behaviour and can be severe when her enthusiasm takes hold.

Ann Addy is still seated at the table, her hands fidgeting with a napkin. She smiles a welcome and he discerns no rancour in her look. His lateness for dinner would have been an irritation, nothing more. He disappears into the scullery to swill his hands.

'Sorry, Mother.' Joseph returns to the kitchen and drops into his usual chair, the rush-bottomed carver with the high ladder-back and curved arms. As young Dinah ladles beef stew over boiled potatoes and green beans fresh from the garden, with his forefinger, he idly traces the pattern of the green oilcloth.

'My morning was successful and I'm right pleased with what the jeweller has made for us.' He deliberately embraces each of them in ownership of the new brooch. It belongs to them all, just as Elizabeth had belonged to them all. His dearest wish is that Mary-Ann will one day wear the brooch with pride and respect. But she will only be a temporary guardian and perhaps she will share it with Frannie and then pass it down to her own daughter. Thoughts to be discussed later, when his girls are older.

'Don't keep us dangling, Joseph, show it to us, won't you?' His mother is eager to see the brooch but Joseph shakes his head as the tasty dish of stew and vegetables is placed before him.

'Later, after I've eaten and we can see it at its best. So, what have you been up to Miss? Helping your Grandma and Aunt Mary?' He knew that during the long school holiday his daughter would easily get up to mischief without the daily routine of learning.

Mary-Ann's response is stalled by the appearance of her Aunt Mary who has been busy up in the room, once Joseph and Elizabeth's sitting room, now the nursery. She has just settled the little one for an afternoon sleep, affording the household an hour or so of peace and quiet. Mary-Ann could scarcely tolerate her crying sister even while her mother lived, but since Elizabeth's death, she harbours an under-lying resentment that Frannie's arrival led to their mother's early departure from this world.

'Oh, pardon me, Brother,' Mary hesitates on the threshold. 'I didn't hear you return so I shall leave you be while you eat. There's plenty to do upstairs.'

Joseph regrets her discomfort. Mary Hall is constantly at the house, helping his mother with the children. She returns alone to her cottage each evening after Frannie is put down in her cradle and Mary-Ann has grumbled her way to the small bed adjacent to her sister. Mary is a valuable part of the family but is not a member of his family and, as such, respectability demands a distance between him and his sister-in-law.

Therein lies his dilemma.

CHAPTER 5

1849 Summer

Joseph reaches for the package containing the mourning brooch.

'Wait Mary, I have something to show you all. First give me a few minutes to finish my dinner. How was Frannie today?' he ends lamely, desperate to include his sister-in-law in what was to come and acknowledge her care for his baby daughter.

Mary feels the gaze of the family upon her as she joins them at table, Ann Addy appraising her, though not unkindly. The old lady is weary with trying to manage the handful of mischief which is Mary-Ann and the demands of a babe who too quickly has been weaned off her mother's milk. Mary knows Mrs Addy needs her help but is still wary of the old lady. Mary-Ann's expression is hard to discern. She neither dislikes her Aunt Mary but nor does she particularly like her. She resents that Aunt Mary lives and her mother does not. She is jealous that Aunt Mary devotes so much time to her little sister. Frannie cries a lot and needs attention, but even so …

Mary averts her gaze from Joseph as he devours his meal with enthusiasm. Instead, she addresses his mother.

'Frannie has been a handful this morning. I suppose that's what you expect at this age. She crawls all over the nursery and tries to stand up by hanging onto the chairs.' Mary isn't sure if that represents good or bad progress for a one-year-old and laughs nervously. 'Her latest game is to throw her wooden bricks about the place then chuckle when they clatter to the floor.' It all sounds very insignificant, but she has enjoyed playing with her little niece and can ignore the silly face pulled by the older one. She notes with relief that Joseph has cleaned his plate and that his hand now hovers over the small package.

'So, Joseph, you collected the brooch from the jewellers.' Her introduction pleases him and he smiles acknowledgement. As he unwraps the brown paper, a dark green leather-clad box is revealed. He moves down the table to where the light is brighter and places the box on a clean cloth.

'Who would like to open it?' he asks, expecting Mary-Ann to leap at the offer. Nobody reacts, which surprises and disappoints him equally. Recognising the significance of the moment, he nods solemnly and speaks: 'Not seven months ago we lost a wife, mother, daughter and sister, someone who will remain in our hearts for eternity. This brooch is only a representation of a treasured jewel gone from us for ever.'

Mary is surprised that her normally reticent brother-in-law could find such emotion-laden words and is slightly embarrassed by his expression of feeling. She regards him with new eyes. Joseph removes the lid and everyone leans forward for a closer look. Ann Addy nods with satisfaction. It was her foresight in clipping that tress of Elizabeth's hair that enabled this tribute. Mary looks sadly at the sight of her dear sister's brown locks woven in a lattice with Joseph's prematurely silver hair. Mary-Ann just stares. The brooch is big, the oval gold frame decorated in a scrolled design of black lacquer. She hates it and what it represents.

*

1843 May

Perhaps sensing the trauma of her birth, Mary-Ann had not been a good baby. Not in the sense that she would feed and sleep and grow strong. Elizabeth was weak after the protracted birth and the need to provide her new baby with sustenance drew even more energy from her. Elizabeth Vazin spoke anxiously with Ann Addy.

'The lass has no strength; she cannot give the child the milk it needs. Will you let me find a wet nurse who can help?' Ann Addy recognised her grand-daughter's constant crying stemmed from her mother's lack of milk but hesitated to call in an outsider.

'Surely we can manage without. I've heard tell that some wet nurses secretly feed syrup of poppy to the child to ensure it sleeps through the night. Imagine that. And how easy would it be to find someone decent to come to live in? Would she bring her own babe with her and, if not, how would we know that it wouldn't starve to death? One hears such dreadful tales.'

'Let me ask around the village. We would only take someone respectable and clean and we both know that such women often have desperate need of money. I hear that our dear Queen has not given the breast to any of her children and I am pretty sure that the wet nurse for her latest little princess was not of aristocratic standing.' She chuckled at the thought of a titled wet nurse.

Elizabeth would have none of it. She felt deep shame that it had taken her over three years to conceive and now it was suggested she could not satisfy her baby. In private she wept angry tears but outwardly she was positive.

'Thank you for your concern but she is my child and I will gain strength and nurse her myself. Come, Mother, let's start to feed me up.' Ann Addy nodded with resignation and rose heavily from her chair.

'Ay, lass. I understand but your child must be nourished else she will not thrive. Elizabeth Vazin assures me she can find someone clean who can come in and provide the extra milk the little one needs. Perhaps just in the evening so that the babe is satisfied and goes through the night?' she added in hope of a good night's sleep for them all. Joseph was looking drawn.

Elizabeth persevered, however, and over the weeks Mary-Ann slowly gained weight though she was to remain a skinny, demanding child for years to come.

1849 Summer

The muted reception of the mourning brooch leaves Joseph somewhat dismayed. Has he chosen the wrong setting? Is the brooch too soon? Surely not. He looks to his mother for her opinion and notes not for the first time that she looks weary. His concern is mixed with frustration that this tiredness is no doubt due to the disturbed nights now created by young Frannie. He needs to speak to her soon, alone.

'Joseph, you have chosen handsomely. Anyone would be proud to wear this brooch and honour the memory of Elizabeth.' Not quite the warm words he hoped for from his mother. He smiles at Mary, hoping for greater enthusiasm.

'Indeed, it is a fine piece, and when your maids are grown, I am sure they will wear it with pride.' Her words make him look again at the brooch. True, it does look heavy, but that is the fashion. Perhaps his mother will wear it in the meantime? No, save for her wedding ring, she wears no adornment since the death of his father. Perhaps Mary then? She loved her sister and could be trusted to pass it to Mary-Ann when the girl is old enough for such jewellery. Yet something more to discuss with his sister-in-law, but first his concern must be with his mother and the care of his children.

1843-1847

Following the difficult birth of their first child, Elizabeth regained her strength albeit slowly. Those were good times but as each month passed and Mary-Ann emerged from babyhood and began her staggering steps around the sofa, Elizabeth and Joseph waited for signs that they would be blessed a second time. Without doubt a son was in their prayers.

Elizabeth was active in the running of the farm, happily taking responsibility for writing up the old ledger covered in marbled paper, the record of calving, stock sales, grain contracts and quarter rents going back to Joseph's grandfather. She managed the hens and selling their eggs and was always ready to share in the long days of harvest. She and other women of the village followed the men as they scythed their path through the ripened corn, each woman bending to gather a sheaf and nimbly string it ready for the stooks.

The seasons passed, as did the years. Mary-Ann became a lively if somewhat spoilt child. Her father thought the world of her and her mother sought to temper his indulgence with a strict regime. Mary-Ann knew better than to rebel against her mother. Instead, she learnt to work around her. Deviousness was too strong a trait to attribute to a child, nonetheless …

Forbidden from nearing the flashing blades wielded by the men, Mary-Ann loved to dart in amongst the women. She would wear boots and long socks to protect her skinny ankles from the sharp stubble. She gazed after the rabbits running for cover as the harvesters drew ever nearer to the centre of the cornfield. She was mesmerised as the dogs ran after the rabbits and watched, fascinated, should one succeed in pinning down its prey. She sought sanctuary in one of the stooks, a little wigwam of six sheaves propped against each other to dry before the carting-in. Within weeks the first grain would be trundling the short distance down Millgate to the Bentley mill.

As the farm bore fruit, Elizabeth and Joseph waited patiently for a second child. Generously they welcomed the arrival of sons to Joseph's brother, Godfrey, and to Elizabeth's brother, Henry. Widow Hall felt for her daughter as she cradled her latest grandchild.

'God give you patience, Elizabeth. I cannot imagine how hard it is to see these babies coming into the world, while you wait for a son.'

Elizabeth smiled and stroked the fluffy head of her new nephew.

'Patience is not something I have in abundance but railing against fortune solves nothing. Joseph and I are blessed with a healthy child in Mary-Ann. Just think of those in our family who have lost their little ones in early childhood. That is true despair. I pray that we shall see another child and, God willing, a son, but I must be content with what we are given. So many others have far less than I.'

1847 Autumn

When she fell pregnant for the second time, Elizabeth again hesitated to speak of it beyond Joseph. Only once her body swelled did she reveal to the family the good news. She was distressed when her mother showed only muted pleasure.

Widow Hall was sitting alone in the cottage she had rented since giving up the farm tenancy after the sudden death of her youngest son, John. Elizabeth despaired at the translucent paleness of her mother's skin and the attacks of coughing which overtook the poor woman.

'Good news, my girl. You have waited long enough and may it be a lad, a lad as strong and as good a man as his father.'

1849 Summer

After Mary-Ann is put to bed without too much protest, Joseph offers to walk his sister-in-law the short distance home. The August evening is kind and the dried grass fragrance of the parched land lingers as they stroll the dusty lane. The corn is ripening well and pray God there will be no storms to beat down the crops before harvest.

Joseph halts at the tiny cottage where Mary now lives alone following Widow Hall's death in January, just twenty days after her daughter, Elizabeth. Both Addy and Hall families struggle with their grief but it is the demands of everyday life that rise to the fore and dictate what is to follow. There are two little girls in need of care.

Joseph does not find conversation with Mary as easy as with her sister. Elizabeth had views on everything and never shirked from sharing them. Mary is more reticent, whether from shyness or perhaps because she does not possess Elizabeth's depth. However, within her hands lies the solution to his problems.

CHAPTER 6

1849

Joseph recognises that the world is changing around the Addys and his wider family. From visits to Doncaster, he witnesses industry, with all its voracious clamour and dirt, taking over the cities of Britain. Many of the younger lads in the village now find work in manufacturing to be better paid than on the land. Railways stretch out to link towns across the country. The railway station down the road at Stockbridge was opened a year ago but, thus far, Joseph has not seen the need to try this newfangled form of transport. For many, the fear of these iron-clad war-horses, shrieking and steaming at great pace along their tracks, is mitigated by the desire to reach nearby towns in a fraction of the time required by the mail coach, perhaps to travel inexpensively away to the coast or up to London. Joseph is content to bide his time.

Even Mary showed unexpected enterprise when, soon after her sister's marriage ten years back, she announced her intention to seek a position away from the village. Her mother's farm would not sustain a member of the family who could not contribute significantly. Money needed to be earned elsewhere. A diligent scholar, she had learnt sufficient to apply for the post of companion. An advertisement placed by a Sheffield widower, a retired druggist, sought genteel companionship for his daughter, at eighteen a similar age to herself. Mary breathed deeply for courage and moved away from her home.

At the time, Widow Hall was accepting of Mary's decision. She struggled to keep the farm viable. Her son, John, then fourteen, was a hard and willing worker but she still had to pay her two labourers. Until her lad was old enough to take over the tenancy, she relied on the guidance of Joseph to work the land.

Would Betsy Hall have persevered so long, to the detriment of her health, had she known that young John would be taken from her just as he reached eighteen? While she bounced Elizabeth's precious first-born on her lap, she watched helplessly as her son fought bad health before God claimed him soon afterwards. She reflected bitterly on the Lord's circle of life that brings a child such as Mary-Ann into this world only to take another before he reached his prime. And John had been such a dear, loving boy. Elizabeth would find her mother seated alone in the kitchen, apron thrown up over her head to hide the weeping.

1849 Summer

Having seen Mary safely inside her cottage, Joseph returns home in the dusk to find his mother seated in the parlour, her eyes closed. Joseph hesitates to disturb her but lights first one oil lamp then a second to illuminate the plain room, furnished with mahogany dresser, horsehair-stuffed easy-chairs and irritating occasional tables clothed in plum-coloured chenille.

'Sorry to wake you mother, can I fetch owt?'

She smiles and shakes her head. 'Mary safely home?' She knows full well that Mary walks home alone most evenings, perfectly at ease in doing so. 'She does well, looking after your two girls.'

Joseph lets the comment hang unanswered in the gentle lamp-light. He wants to discuss Mary with his mother but is unsure how to begin. His mother, lying back in the chair, her eyes now only half-closed, helps him along.

'So very different from her sister, don't you think?' She leaves him no chance to reply and ploughs on. This is the opportunity she has sought and she is not going to let it go to waste. 'When you first wed your Elizabeth, I wasn't much taken by young Mary. She was timid, but maybe that was just with me. I never thought she had much about her. Certainly not as bright a thing as her sister. But I have to give it to Mary, when her mother took ill last year, without a second thought she gave up her position in Sheffield and returned home to care for her.'

1848 Summer

Last year, as Widow Hall became increasingly weak, Elizabeth, weary as she was from a second exhausting birth, struggled to care for her mother. Frannie was only days old when her Grandma Hall was found by a neighbour, collapsed in the scullery. Word was sent to Sheffield and Mary arrived home, horrified to see the change in her mother: much thinner and her breathing laboured. It was her pallor that was most shocking.

Mary had run Mr Webster's household for some seven years now and declared that she was perfectly competent to care for her mother alone. Elizabeth was relieved. She needed all her energy to look after a lively Mary-Ann and her robust, demanding baby. Seeking further support, Joseph's mother suggested they call upon Elizabeth Vazin, who again had attended her daughter-in-law through the recent confinement.

'She is your friend, knows your mother and will be happy to help your Mary. Elizabeth, it is inadvisable for you to care for your mother while you are nursing the little one. What if …?'

She left unspoken her fears, fears built upon local gossip. Ann Addy had not visited Elizabeth's mother for quite a while. There was talk in the village of the poor woman coughing up blood. Consumption, the scourge that took so many young people, had claimed Elizabeth's brother, John, some years back. Now it seemed it had returned to take her mother. With Elizabeth at such a low ebb after giving birth, Ann Addy feared she could also fall to the disease.

In a low voice, she added: 'You have two children to think of now, Elizabeth. We must protect them.' Her daughter-in-law nodded her weary acquiescence. That fear had already taken hold in her mind.

The christening of Joseph and Elizabeth's second daughter, Frances Addy, henceforth known as Frannie, took place at Arksey church on the last Sunday of July 1848. Widow Hall was too weak to attend the ceremony which followed morning service at All Saints. A good neighbour sat with her so that both Mary Hall and Elizabeth Vazin could be present at the baptism, with Mary as godmother to little Frances, just as she had been some five years earlier to Mary-Ann.

1849 Summer

It was Elizabeth's choice then for her sister, Mary, to be godmother to both girls that now gives Joseph confidence as he faces his mother across the parlour. He leans back in the armchair and gazes over his mother's silver-grey head, through the window and beyond to the soft late twilight.

'We cannot carry on as we are, can we Mother?' He tries to read her thoughts as she hesitates. He needs her to acknowledge what is apparent to all the family: his children are too much for her to cope with. Soon Mary will need to leave and earn her living again. First though, she has to find another position since Mr

Webster's new wife refused to hold open Mary's job in Sheffield when she returned to Bentley to nurse her dying mother.

'No Joseph, no more we can.' At rest in the soft lamp-light, she looks even more careworn and he feels guilty. If only he had taken greater care of Elizabeth following Frannie's birth. Would that he had insisted on calling the doctor when that rash first appeared …

1848 Christmas

It was the build up to Christmas that distracted everyone. That together with the continuing decline of Widow Hall.

Mary had escaped her mother's sick room for a couple of hours and over a brew of tea sat in the Addys' kitchen helping her sister clean freshly laid eggs ready for market. Ann Addy, alerted by the murmur of the two women, appeared in the doorway.

'How fares your mother, Mary?' Her direct question belied a real sadness for the suffering of Betsy Hall.

'Thank you for your concern, Mrs Addy, but she scarcely eats these days. I make her tempting dishes but she only takes broth.'

The old woman shook her head sympathetically. Betsy Hall was sinking and the patent medicines offered by the apothecaries in Doncaster were a waste of precious money. The inevitable was awaited with both patience and sad frustration.

'I shall pray for her, Mary. Please give her my good wishes.' She turned and left the room.

Elizabeth bent over the basket of eggs, variously coated with straw or chicken muck, selected a particularly dirty specimen and wiped it carefully with a wet rag. Housekeepers from the fine houses in Doncaster would pay more for clean eggs and they were the customers she wished to attract at the market the next day. Many eggs would be needed for the baking in the coming weeks up to Christmas.

'She means well. She just doesn't have the words.' She looked up from her task and smiled at her sister. Mary shrugged her shoulders with resignation.

'I'm not bothered by what she does or doesn't say. I'm past all that. I just want it over.' As Elizabeth raised her eyebrows with alarm, she added, 'For her sake, not mine. I cannot bear to see her suffer.' Her eyes filled with tears – of sorrow, of exhaustion.

Elizabeth laid aside her cloth, wiped her hands on her pinafore and held her sister close. She kissed the top of Mary's head, careful not to disturb the fine bun of auburn hair at the nape of her neck. No words were exchanged. The gesture expressed their shared grief for what was to come.

In the circumstances, Christmas would only be a quiet celebration. Frannie was still suckling and Elizabeth's energy was at a low ebb. Perhaps it was that which made her careless as she and Mary-Ann explored the frosty lanes for holly trees.

'That bough there, Mother. It's bursting with berries,' cried Mary-Ann who was in charge of the small hand-cart fast filling with stems of holly. Her mother stretched but couldn't quite reach. Recalling her youth when she and Mary would clamber up trees along with their brothers, Elizabeth took up the challenge and found some roots to give her extra height as she grasped at the branch with one hand and hacked with her knife at the berry-laden stems. Suddenly her footing slipped and she fell heavily, the knife nicking her hand as it slithered from her grasp.

'Botheration,' was her laughing reaction, not wishing to further distress Mary-Ann who cried out at the sight of the berry red blood which oozed from her mother's left hand. The slight wound was swiftly wrapped in a kerchief and Elizabeth, shivering with cold or delayed shock, led the way home through the lanes.

Within a couple of days, a rash progressed up Elizabeth's left arm, slightly raised with the appearance of orange peel.

'I don't like the look of Elizabeth's arm.' Ann Addy spoke to her son as he entered the kitchen for his hot breakfast, returning from a cold morning's milking. 'She should see the doctor. It's nasty and spreading.'

''Appen you're right.' Joseph was equally concerned and had already spoken with his wife to encourage her to consult the doctor. In vain. 'She says she will go directly after Christmas as there's too much work on until then. You know there's no shifting her when her mind's made up.'

And so it was. Elizabeth hid the rash under her long-sleeved gowns but she couldn't hide the increasing tiredness and feverishness which overtook her. On Christmas Eve she sat at the kitchen table with her mother-in-law, intent on wrapping the small gifts, mainly for Mary-Ann.

'Get off to bed, lass,' urged Ann Addy. 'Dinah has all prepared for dinner tomorrow, so no need to fuss yourself about that.'

Elizabeth nodded and stood up wearily. 'Would you mind if I didn't accompany you all to church tomorrow morning? I feel so tired but I must try to visit my mother on Christmas Day.'

'Of course, lass. She will be cheered to see you again. But don't take Frannie with you into a sick room.' She continued wrapping a beribboned muslin bag packed with lavender, destined as a gift for Godfrey's wife. 'How is that rash on your arm, Elizabeth? Is it improving?'

'Oh, don't you mind about that. It will go in a day or two, you see.' Ann Addy looked at her daughter-in-law's flushed face and doubted it. She bade her goodnight.

Elizabeth's meeting with her mother was painful for both women. It was a week or two since she had ventured into Widow Hall's tiny cottage, only a short walk down the lane. She arrived, exhausted even by this brief exercise, and remained downstairs talking with Elizabeth Vazin before climbing the steep staircase.

'Your sister is with her at present, so bide a while. You look wore out.'

'Thanks, I will rest. I am not myself, what with feeding Frannie taking so much out of me. You remember how I struggled with Mary-Ann? It's a little easier this time, but not much. And there is this rash …' She pulled back the sleeve of her left arm. Her friend looked shocked.

'What does the doctor say about it?'

'I shall go to see him straight after Christmas. There is so much to do at present.' Elizabeth Vazin shook her head.

'Lass you should have been to see him long sin'. Such inflammation can take hold.' Realising that there was nothing to be done about it today of all days, she rose and indicated the stairs. 'Come, why don't you go up to see your mother? You'll be the best Christmas gift she gets.'

Gathering her skirt over her infected arm and with one hand holding onto the rail, Elizabeth slowly clumped her way up the uncarpeted, narrow staircase and into the larger of the two rooms of the floor above. A scarcely warming fire burned in the grate. Her mother, swathed in shawls, lay in bed propped up on pillows to help her laboured breathing. As Mary rose from a low chair to welcome Elizabeth, she marked the contrast between the ash-white complexion of her mother and Elizabeth's florid face. She had not seen her sister for a few days and was perturbed by the change in her.

'My Lizzie. So good to see thee. How does baby Frannie?' Betsy Hall stroked her daughter's proffered hand and seemed unaware of her altered appearance.

Mary stood aside and gestured for her sister to take her place at the bedside.

'I shall go down and get on with our Christmas dinner and I have some treats in store.' Her words were lost on her mother who had no appetite for food, no matter how tempting or lovingly prepared. The sisters exchanged resigned glances and Elizabeth sank gratefully into the nursing chair where many years past she and her five siblings had been given the breast and sung to sleep by this once fine-looking wife, mother, farmer, now a shadow of a woman.

'Mother, I'm so sorry not to have come before …' Betsy Hall held up a finger to silence her.

'The lasses. How are they? Young Mary-Ann? Is little Frannie grown since last I saw her?'

Her daughter could hardly speak through the emotion and smiled and nodded. *Don't let the tears come now.* More awake now, her mother looked at her intently and put a hand to her daughter's forehead.

'Lizzie, thee're burning up. What ails thee? Is it a fever?'

'Tis nothing, Mother. I scratched myself a few days gone and I have a rash. I'll see the doctor in a couple of days. Promise.' Her mother frowned but was overcome by a fit of coughing which shook her shrunken body. Elizabeth brought a cup of water to her lips; the old woman sipped and fell back exhausted.

This was their last meeting.

1849 Summer

Joseph rises from his armchair and stands with his back to the empty hearth. It is surrounded by a fine mahogany mantelpiece, crowned by a large mirror which reflects his full head of grey hair.

'It's the lasses, they are just over much for you, Mother. I, too, find them wearying even though I love them dearly. When I get in of an evening, I'm so tired that I cannot give them the love that Elizabeth would have done. You care for them, I know that, but they need the love of a mother.'

Ann Addy steels herself for what is to come. She knows her son. He is hard-working and home-loving. Where will he find a new mother for his girls? A second wife. There is only one candidate and the thought makes her shiver with apprehension.

CHAPTER 7

1849 Summer

Joseph turns from his mother towards the fireplace. He rests both hands on the high wooden mantelshelf. He looks into the mirror and sees beyond her collection of Staffordshire china horses, beyond the reflected figurines and their shameless undecorated flat-backs. He looks himself in the eye.

'It is my intention to ask Mary to marry me.'

The silence that greets his declaration tells him everything. He knows the law. For the last fourteen years it has been illegal to marry your dead wife's sister. Yet, such is the ambivalence towards this harsh bill that when it was enacted in 1835, all those who had married thus in previous years were exempt from prosecution. Since then, the only legitimate way to circumvent the law has been to marry abroad, impossible for someone of Joseph's means. He can never understand why the Church pushed so hard for this Marriage Act, which to him and many others seems so contrary to common sense. What could be more reasonable than for children, deprived of their mother, to be reared by an aunt who they have known since birth? And if their father wishes to marry her, whether out of love or expediency, why should he be prevented by this law and society's misguided sense of propriety? Such marriages have taken place satisfactorily for years and to imply that it is the slippery slope to incest is preposterous. In reality there is no blood link between a man and his sister-in-law despite the Church regarding a married couple as being of one flesh.

His mother breaks the silence with a sigh. She looks at the broad back of her son and his grey head, now bowed as he stares down into the soulless summer hearth.

'How do you imagine that such a thing could be achieved?' She also knows the law and is equally aware that support for the law divides society, divides families. Ann Addy is nothing if not practical and she can see the logic in her son marrying Mary. But.

'Everyone knows it can be done if you go to a distant church where you aren't known.' As he speaks, Joseph hates admitting that such a marriage would be based on deception. 'And in Parliament they are constantly striving to overturn the law and make such a marriage legal again. That wouldn't be the case if many worthy men did not recognise the unfairness of the situation.'

'Aye, lad, but thus far they haven't succeeded. And just as in society there are those who would change the law, so there are many equally worthy who regard such marriages as a sin and scorn those who ignore what they see is God's will.' Clearly, Joseph's suggestion of marrying Mary has already occurred to Ann Addy and she has weighed the arguments.

'Have you spoken to the lass?'

'No, of course not. Asking her could bring down the whole house of cards if she rejects me, rejects the very idea. I need her, we need her to continue looking after the girls. Who else is there?'

'Do you love her?'

'I am very fond of Mary. Who wouldn't be? She is gentle, kind and has grown into a competent home-maker. She loves her nieces and would do anything in Elizabeth's memory, I'm sure.'

'Anything?'

'True, I don't know how she regards me other than as a brother. But we are not brother and sister in blood, only in law. How can that be incest?'

Ann Addy flinches at the word.

'Even were you to find a church to marry you, how do you think people would regard you here in the village when you return as man and wife? You are respected in this community, Joseph, and people will understand your circumstances. Nonetheless you will be judged. Both of you. Your shoulders might be broad, but Mary's?'

His mother expresses all that churns over in his mind. Would Mary want to share the rest of her life with him? Have his children? Maybe a son? Would she be prepared to face family and villagers who disapproved of what he proposes?

'What is the alternative, Mother? Do I pay someone to live in? Do we really want a stranger living amongst us? Marry someone else? Who for Heaven's sake?' His voice rises with agitation, desperation.

His mother shakes her head silently. She has no answers.

'Very soon Mary will move away. She cannot afford the rent on that cottage without earning some money. We could pay her as carer for the children and that would work to some extent, while you live, Mother, but …' Ann Addy nods. She is not immortal and in the last year has aged considerably. So much illness, so much death.

'Aye, you're right. It would not be seemly for the girl to live in after I'm gone and even for her to come in each day would lead to gossip. Either way, at twenty-eight years of age, she wouldn't find a man prepared to take her on in those circumstances.'

1848 Christmas

That last Christmas night saw the collapse of Elizabeth. The exertion and emotional stress of visiting her mother had exhausted her. She had dragged herself through the rest of the day, trying in vain to respond to Mary-Ann's calls to join in with her games of fantasy.

A new doll came for the little girl. Her eyes shone with excitement as she unwrapped the box. It revealed an elegantly dressed young lady with abundant blond locks and startling blue glass eyes set in a porcelain face painted with an expression of self-satisfaction.

'I shall call her Henrietta.' She carefully straightened the rose-pink velvet gown of her new best friend and surreptitiously peeked under the full skirt to check the white linen drawers and silk-stockings. 'See Mother, see how she can dance.' The girl held Henrietta at arms' length and swung around the room as though to music. Ann Addy gazed in stupefaction at the doll, which she saw for the first time, questioning how much Joseph must have spent on such a creation.

Elizabeth felt she was burning up and could no longer bear the chatter of her daughter. She climbed slowly upstairs to the nursery to feed Frannie and settle her down to sleep. The pull on her breast as the baby suckled seemed to drag the last ounce of strength from her. She changed the child and laid her down in her cot then stumbled to her bedroom and undressed in a daze. When Joseph retired to bed some time later, he found her clothes discarded on a chair. Elizabeth lay in the bed, eyes closed and bathed in sweat. He checked the fireplace and saw the embers dying in the hearth.

'Do you sleep, Lizzie?' he whispered in case she did. Her eyes snapped open and implored him soundlessly. 'Tomorrow I shall fetch the doctor. This has gone on long enough. You need something for the fever. I shall see if Mary can spare Elizabeth Vazin to come to tend to you and look after the children. Mary can cope alone with her mother for a couple of days until you are over this.' Elizabeth nodded and closed her eyes.

Next day the doctor spent half an hour with her before descending the stairs to speak to Joseph and his mother.

'I shall send a tincture within the hour. It will reduce the fever and help her recovery from the infection. I believe that she has developed erisypelas and, sadly, that is highly resistant to treatment. She cannot nurse her baby as she needs to retain all her force. Get in a wet nurse or wean the child quickly.' Already, Frannie's angry cries of hunger could be heard from above.

'What is it that she suffers from? What did you call it?'

'Erisypelas,' enunciated the doctor. 'It's commonly known as Saint Anthony's Fire, an infection caused by a cut or bite.' Ann Addy recalled the cut Elizabeth received while gathering holly.

'Is there nowt more you can do, doctor?' Joseph was beside himself with fear and anger that the physician before him offered so little. 'Forgive me, but should we seek a second opinion?'

'You are welcome to do so,' replied the doctor, unfazed by the outburst. 'But none of my colleagues in Doncaster will suggest an alternative treatment. Get her to take my medication, keep her cool and,' he looked at Ann Addy, 'pray for her recovery.'

In the coming days Elizabeth lay in her bed, her mother-in-law and Elizabeth Vazin sharing the nursing. The tincture was fed to her without any apparent effect. Ice-cold water was taken from the rainwater butt to soak cloths to cool her burning forehead.

One afternoon, Mary-Ann disobeyed strict instructions not to disturb her mother and pushed open the door into her parents' bedroom. She stared at the flushed face of her mother, stark against the white pillows. She stared in horrified fascination at the arm which lay on top of the turned-back sheet. The skin was scarlet red.

Elizabeth Vazin looked up from her knitting. She put her finger to her lips and tiptoed across the rug-strewn boards to meet the child.

'Mother won't die, will she?'

She was ushered out onto the landing where Elizabeth Vazin stooped to face her. It was quite likely that the girl's mother would not survive. Many famous people with far more money and resources than the Addys had succumbed to Saint Anthony's Fire. She could not lie to the child but nor did she wish to fill her heart with despair.

'Your mother struggles with this infection but the doctor has done the best he can to help her. Now we must pray to God to aid her recovery.'

'This infection. Did it come from having Frannie?' Behind the simple question lay thoughts so deep they would surface again in years to come.

'Nay lass. What makes you think such a dreadful thought? Your mother cut herself. Your grandma told me. That was the cause of the inflammation. Now come along downstairs. Your father will be in soon and wanting his dinner. Go and see if you can help Dinah in the kitchen.'

The woman returned to the side of her dying friend.

1849 Summer

Joseph crosses the parlour, hesitates, then sits beside his mother on the sofa. He rests his hand on her shoulder.

'Do you think Mary would have me?' A rebuff would create such embarrassment that the girl would surely want to escape their household as soon as she decently could. Ann Addy aches at her son's uncertainty.

'She has always looked kindly on you and spoken with respect, without fear. Whether she had a beau while living in Sheffield, who knows? Did she ever tell Elizabeth of meeting anyone special?'

'Not that I am aware. She has a modest loveliness that would engage many a decent suitor. I cannot think that some unattached young man would not wish to know her better.'

'Well, Joseph, let's put the emotions of the heart to one side and be practical; she needs a position that will give her a roof over her head. You can offer that. Maybe she wishes to be wed one day and have children. If there is no young man in her life, why not it be you? She knows you, warts and all. She has seen you as a good husband to her sister, a good father to Mary-Ann. Since Elizabeth died, she has seen your despair, seen you weary when you have sought to bury your grief in long hours in the fields.

'The question you should ask yourself is whether she would be prepared for the harsh tongues of some people in the village. Many? I cannot tell. You would have my blessing for sure and, I hope, that of your brother and sister.'

'Perhaps.' Joseph reflects on the likely response from Godfrey's wife.

'Would you go to London to be wed?'

'I think not. However, I've heard tell that not all clergy are that supportive of this law. Even more turn a blind eye and are glad of their fees.' He leans back with his hands clasped behind his head. 'Maybe Sheffield is a place to start. It is far enough away for nobody to know me and if anyone recognises Mary's name, her reputation there is beyond reproach. Maybe she would know some folk there who would look kindly on our position.'

'Aye, no doubt, but first you must speak with Mary. Otherwise, there is little point to the rest.' As an after-thought she adds: 'What would Mary-Ann make of her Aunt Mary becoming her mother?'

Joseph nods. His mother, like him, is aware of his daughter's high spirits and sometimes rebellious response to her aunt.

'I am sure in time both my daughters would love her. As for Mary-Ann, perhaps not in the way she loved her mother, but enough.'

The stage is set. The actors have their roles. It needs only the words to be written, then Curtain Up.

CHAPTER 8

1849 Summer

The heat of the previous day ended in a thunderstorm lasting through the night. At dawn, Joseph is out walking his fields to see if the heavy rain has harmed the corn. He is dismayed to see that harvesting will be delayed. The barley needs to dry before it can be cut. He looks up at the sky where heavy clouds stretch to the low horizon.

He trudges back to the mistle where the lads have herded in the cows for milking. It smells of the animals and their fresh dung. A couple of local girls sit moulded into the warm flanks of the beasts. Their fingers deftly pull on the freshly-washed teats and draw the warm milk into the pails. He nods good morning to them and walks on back to the house. As he rounds the corner of the orchard, he observes Mary arriving at a fast pace, ready to feed Frannie and get Mary-Ann up and dressed, no easy feat as Miss Lazybones is still on holiday from school.

'Good morning, Mary,' he calls out to her. He wants to break the ice early. Today is the day to speak to her. 'Were you troubled by the thunder and lightning last night?' He recalls how Elizabeth never showed any fear in such storms. Would her sister be the same?

'Good morning to you Joseph. Yes, the thunderclaps and flashes woke me, but our father taught us not to be afeared.' She smiles and waits for him to approach her. 'Will the rain delay the harvest?'

'Sadly yes, but we can put the day to good use ensuring our tools are in best condition for when we start, hopefully in a few days' time if the rain holds off, the wind blows and the sun shines.'

They walk side-by-side towards the kitchen door and on the threshold Joseph pauses.

'Mary, when the children are up and fed, would you do me a kindness and spare me some of your time. There is something I need to discuss with you.' He observes the look of concern on her face. 'Oh no, there's nowt wrong. I need your help with something.' It all sounds so trivial and he is ashamed to speak so lightly of what would be a matter of great import when she hears of it.

Mary smiles and nods. 'I'll come and find you as soon as we're straight.' They enter the kitchen, he to eat the breakfast Dinah has prepared for him, she to carry a large ewer of hot water upstairs to wash the girls. For Joseph there is no turning back. He rehearses in his head the words he prepared in bed last night. Would it all be in vain?

1849 January

As the old year changed into the new, the doctor returned twice more to see Elizabeth but all he could do was to prescribe more of his quackery and watch as the fever continued. No amount of cold compresses could reduce the burning which racked the poor woman's body. Even opening the window to the cold winter air had no effect. She tossed in her delirium and Joseph watched over her day and night as his dear girl struggled her way out of this life.

By the morning of the third day of the new year, she became less restless but did not open her eyes. Elizabeth Vazin had tended to her through the previous night, insisting that she would call Joseph if there were changes. He had sat with his wife until ten o'clock, his frame shrunken back into the chair, exhausted from the vigil, dreading the inevitable. Reluctantly he had taken to his bed.

Before dawn, Elizabeth Vazin could hear the household stirring and from outside came the voices of the lads and dairy maids busy in the lantern-lit mistle washing the milk-laden udders. Joseph quietly stepped into the dimly lit bedroom. He looked upon his wife, now sleeping peacefully. He was reassured and raised an enquiring eyebrow.

'She is calmer now, Joseph. Why don't you sit with her? Hold her good hand and speak with her. I'm sure she can hear us.' The woman pulled her shawl about her and descended to the warmth of the kitchen where Dinah prepared her a welcome brew. Joseph sat beside his wife, held her uninfected hand but didn't know what to say. Was this calmness a sign that she had turned the corner or was this the prelude to the end? He stroked her tousled hair which lay about her shoulders, just as it did at night.

'You're quiet now, lass. That's good. You rest and get stronger. The worst is over …' His words drifted to nothing. He did not believe what he told her. He was losing her and his heart could not stand the pain. Her eyes flickered open, met his with a beseeching look he would carry to his grave, then closed again. Her voice, silent for some days, came on her breath, scarcely audible.

'The girls. Keep them close. Marry someone who will love them as we do.'

Joseph held back a sob. What to say?

Within the hour, without opening her eyes again, Elizabeth Addy died at the age of thirty-nine on Wednesday, the third of January 1849.

1849 Summer

Ann Addy ushers her lively grand-daughter into the garden under the pretext of collecting wild flowers. They are to be pressed between blotting paper held down by a pile of books surmounted by the brass-clasped family bible. Mary-Ann is not so interested in such things but knows better than to argue with Grandma Addy, who has a stinging right hand when vexed.

Joseph watches the two drift down the garden and into the orchard. He stands at the bottom of the stairs and calls: 'Mary, are you free for a while now?' She answers with the clatter of her neatly buttoned boots on the stairs and with a broad smile.

'Yes, Frannie is playing happily with her bricks and will be safe in her pen for half an hour. No doubt we shall hear when she becomes bored.'

Her cheeriness gives him heart. He leads the way into the parlour and closes the door. She takes the indicated chair with a look of puzzlement.

'So, Joseph. What can this be? You look serious. Is it something to do with my care of the children?'

She looks at him standing before her. Joseph is not tall, but tall enough and he always stands well, as a man who knows himself and is content in the knowing. Mary admires his full lips and generous mouth, not hidden behind a beard like so many men in the village. She cannot abide men with whiskers of any sort. What do they seek to hide?

'Good heavens, no. Well, yes,' he fumbles for the words. What did he prepare? It has flown from his mind. Joseph chews on his lower lip in hesitation at what he has to reveal. He runs a hand through the thick greying hair which falls forward in loose curls from his high forehead.

'Indeed, it is about your care of the children. Your excellent care. All of us, I, my mother, Mary-Ann, even little Frannie though she doesn't know it yet, we all owe you so much for your care and love of Elizabeth's girls.' He puts up a hand to silence her protests.

'You, of all of us, have suffered doubly in these last months. To lose your mother not long after the passing of your only sister is something nobody should bear. But bear it you did. During those dreadful days after Elizabeth passed you drove yourself to the edge of exhaustion caring for your mother during the night and your nieces during the day. My mother could not have coped without you during those weeks, and you were selfless in your love for your family. Duty alone would not have driven you through those long days.'

Mary smiles her acknowledgement of his generous words but inside she wonders what this is leading to. Sweet words before he announces the engagement of a nursemaid to replace her? It is time she took stock of her position. Seven months on from her mother's death, she is using up her savings to pay the rent on the cottage she has 'inherited'. Maybe back to Sheffield to find another position? She likes the town. Prefers it to Doncaster even though it is soot-black with its manufactories and forges. The people are friendly.

'I have to think of my daughters' future,' Joseph continues somewhat pompously.

I'm right. He is thinking to engage a nursemaid.

'Frannie is still but a babe, not yet a year old, which is probably fortunate in that she cannot grieve for the loss of her mother …' he falters, 'but no doubt she will grieve in years to come for the mother she never knew.' Mary nods. 'Mary-Ann, on the other hand, is a spirited young lady with a mind of her own and is in need of guidance as she grows up; guidance which I am not in a position to give her. And, as you are well aware, my own mother is not in good health and finds her grandmotherly duties somewhat taxing.'

'You're right Joseph. I love them as if they were my own, but I know that as both grow through girlhood and become young women, they will need a firmer hand' She decides to take the initiative. 'Is it your intention to appoint a nursemaid or governess for your daughters?'

Joseph looks at her horrified. This is not the direction he seeks. True, the whole reason for his soon to be revealed proposal is based upon the needs of his daughters, but he wishes to bring a degree of tenderness and affection into what is quickly becoming a transaction.

'By my word, no. It has never crossed my mind. I don't want strangers bringing up my daughters. Elizabeth would never forgive me. No, what I am minded to ask is whether you would be prepared to devote your life to that task, to care for and love your sister's children, and it would honour me greatly if you would do so as my wife.' There. Out. He drops his gaze, fearful of her reaction. Horror, mirth, rejection?

Mary rises from her seat and stands before him. She looks up into his face lined with tiredness and desperation. This is not what she expected. Suddenly the full implication of what he suggests hits her and takes her breath away. She gasps, blushes and hurries from the crowded room, stumbling against furniture in her way.

Joseph sinks into the chair she has vacated and drops his head in his hands. Where now?

1849 January

That winter's morning, it was Dinah's sob that alerted Mary-Ann to her mother's death. She was playing with Henrietta in the parlour, still chilly as the fire was only just lit. The passage of several pairs of boots up and down the staircase caught her attention, then Elizabeth Vazin's low voice in the kitchen followed by the outburst from the housemaid, quickly stifled. The child carefully laid her doll into her satin-lined box and considered what to do. Her instinct was to run upstairs as she guessed her mother had gone to Jesus but she had not seen a dead person before, so hesitated. Her father's heavy step could be heard in the room above and the occasional voice of her grandmother. Would he want to be alone with her dead mother? Better to enter the warmth of the kitchen on the pretence of seeking hot milk.

Elizabeth Vazin and Dinah turned as the child unlatched the kitchen door and pushed her way into that safe space that smelled of comfort, no matter what time of day or whatever was cooking. The tears streaming down the face of the housemaid said all.

'Mother?' In an instant the girl was surrounded by the arms of the good woman who had delivered her into this world. If Elizabeth Vazin could have taken the pain and loss from this much wanted child, she would have done so gladly. Instead, she held Mary-Ann close, her own tears now flowing down her thin cheeks, and whispered: 'Your mother is with the angels now. All her suffering is over. Jesus will love and care for her.'

Mary-Ann pushed herself out of the embrace, a frown of annoyance distorting her pretty features.

'I don't want the angels to have her. Why can't Jesus wait? I need her here. Now.'

Dinah sought to soothe the girl with milk and biscuits but her perplexed look remained.

'Should I go up and say goodbye?' Clearly the girl was unsure what to do.

'I would wait here with us until your father and grandmother come down. Then Dinah and I will go up and …' It wasn't the moment to describe the laying out process to the child. 'Your father will take you to see your mother all in good time.'

Ann Addy's steady steps resounded on the stairs. Mary-Ann ran towards her but stopped short as she witnessed the old lady's red eyes. She had never seen her grandmother cry.

'Mother?' she whimpered this time.

Ann Addy sank into a wheel-backed chair and opened her arms to her grand-daughter.

'Come child. This is a sad day for us all but for you, Mary-Ann, and your father it comes hardest. You have lost the dearest mother, one who loved you so deeply. We all weep to lose Elizabeth.'

'She is with Jesus?' Mary-Ann's voice emerged from the depths of her grandmother's enveloping shawl. Out of her sight, her grandmother's eyes rolled heavenwards, her faith severely challenged by an Almighty who only a few years since had taken her eldest son, George, suddenly and before his time. She cuddled the child in answer.

The room went quiet as they heard Joseph's heavy tread across the bedroom and landing then down into the hallway. As he opened the kitchen door, his eyes went straight to Mary-Ann. She stood timidly, startled by the grief carved into his face. She wanted to go to him, to rage at the unfairness of Jesus taking her mother from her. But he looked broken and she feared she might hurt him further.

The silence was shattered by wailing from above. Frannie was awake and hungry. The practicalities of life took over. Elizabeth Vazin was despatched to look to the baby. Dinah pulled out a chair for her master and offered him a brew. She took his non-response as a 'yes' and set about mashing the tea.

Suddenly Joseph rose from his seat and hastened out into the yard to despatch one of the lads to fetch the doctor, this time to certify the death. The rest of his workers shook their heads in sympathy and slunk off to do whatever people do to cope with degrees of mourning.

Back in the kitchen he reached for Mary-Ann and drew her to his knee. He smoothed her golden waves of hair. He sighed deeply and tried to find the words.

'Your mother was so poorly. There was nowt that we or the doctor could do. She has fallen asleep for the last time and we shall hold her in our hearts for ever. She is with Jesus and out of pain now.'

'I don't want her to be with Jesus,' she whispered. 'I want her here with me.'

'So do I, my sweet girl, so do I, but we have to be brave, as Mother would have wished.' He found it remarkable that his daughter did not cry.

CHAPTER 9

1849 January

Mary-Ann had seen dead rabbits carried home for the pot. One of the yard dogs had been killed in a fight. Neither upset her. This was different. She was apprehensive but needed to say goodbye. After her grandmother and Elizabeth Vazin had prepared the body of her mother, dressing it in a simple nightgown, her father led her to the bedside. She stepped forward with curiosity and shivered as the cold draft blew in through the open window.

The girl gazed at the closed face before her. Had she ever seen her mother asleep? Sometimes, when she was little, Elizabeth would tease her and pretend sleep. The child would squeal, fearing that she might fall from her mother's lap. Each time her mother would open her large smiling eyes and hug her. But not this time.

The infected arm was hidden beneath the single white sheet which covered her right up to her chin. The long brown hair was freshly sponged and lay on the pillow in a still damp cascade. Her mother's face was no longer pinched and drawn.

She wanted to climb onto the bed and cuddle close just as she did last year when Mother was heavy with the coming baby, with Frannie, and lay longer abed on Sunday mornings. Now there was no softness, no welcoming arms. She turned away, avoiding her father, and left the chilled room without a word.

Joseph looked after her, wondering yet again that she did not weep, as he did now.

Elizabeth's own mother was too ill to be told of her daughter's death. Villagers in Bentley and Arksey spoke sadly of the news. The Addys were a respected family and Elizabeth was known for her kindness to those fallen on hard times. She had been a good wife to Joseph and they felt sorrow that now he was left with two young daughters to raise alone. Unspoken, but nonetheless thought, was the need for him to marry again, soon.

The day after her death, Joseph called on Reverend Sorsby at the Arksey parsonage to arrange his wife's funeral. After expressing his condolences, John Sorsby explained that on the coming Sabbath he was already conducting two burials after morning service. There was no help for it, Elizabeth's funeral would have to be delayed until the following Sunday. Joseph, already drained of emotion, nodded blankly, rose and left. The short January day was grey and the sky threatened snow. As he rode back to Bentley, he considered with dread the prospect of his wife's body lying in the house for the next ten days. At the farmhouse, curtains were drawn and black crepe was draped over the mirrors. The family moved around silently by lamplight. Elizabeth's body was now laid out in her favourite light-blue gown and the swiftly arranged coffin was placed open on the table in the little-used dining room. For the next ten days, a single lamp burned in the ice-cold darkened room.

Under mourning skies that still did not deliver snow, Joseph, together with Elizabeth's eldest brother, Mark, led the pall-bearers to the church door. Many of the congregation who had attended the earlier Sunday morning service lined the pathway out of respect for the Addy family.

Joseph stood in the bitterly cold church scarcely hearing the words of the parson. Was it this cold on that January day when he and Elizabeth had exchanged vows before this very same altar? In three days' time they were to have celebrated their tenth wedding anniversary. Ten years of companionship. Ten good years, on the whole.

As the service drew to a close, he felt light-headed, whether from lack of sleep or food, he knew not. He stumbled after the cortege as it passed over the bedraggled winter grass between the graves of those who had gone before. Close to the north door of the church a new grave lay dug deep. The burial place where Elizabeth would rest until he joined her. The parson's final words were lost to him as he shivered in the biting wind and sleet that sliced across the flat lands from the North Sea. He looked down at the blankness of the coffin lid. How could that be his Lizzie down there?

1849 Summer

Returning from the orchard with her grand-daughter, Ann Addy needs no questions to divine the outcome of her son's conversation with Mary. Joseph passes without a word as he strides out of the kitchen door. He does not meet his mother's eye and she sighs.

'Father, will you see my flowers?' Mary-Ann turns and holds out her trug laden with wilting specimens. He raises a hand of dismissal and walks on without a word.

'Have I made him cross, Grandmother?' The girl is perplexed. Since her mother's death, her father has never dismissed her so brusquely.

'Nay, lass. Your father has to see to the cows. 'Appen one of them is ailing. That always gives him cause for worry.' The old lady gently propels the girl through the kitchen door and sets about sorting the limp flowers so that they could be arranged on the blotting paper ready for the press. She can hear movement above from the nursery. Better to keep the lass occupied and leave Mary alone with Frannie to reflect upon Joseph's proposal.

Young Frannie is still crawling around on a rug in the play-pen stood in the light of the window. The infant has scattered her wooden bricks, pushed some through the bars. Mary watches silently from the doorway as the child stretches in vain to retrieve them but they have rolled beyond reach. On hearing her aunt, Frannie offers up her arms, signalling a wish to be picked up. Mary scoops up the child and holds her close, burying her face in the girl's soft brown hair.

As Mary plays with her niece, bouncing her astride her knee and singing *Ride a Cock Horse*, her thoughts return to the astounding proposal of her brother-in-law. What in Heaven's name is he thinking? It could not be. The Law, the Church, both forbid it. What would people say? They would be shunned by all. She carries the child over to the window and looks out over the fields, today bathed in warm, drying sunshine. Considering the proposition more calmly, she understands the sense of it all. The girls need care, need a new mother, need a kindly body who would love them as Elizabeth had; someone they know and already trust. She is that person.

Marriage is what she desires, needs, otherwise how will she live now that there is no income from her family's farm, long gone even before her mother's death? In Bentley and Arksey there are no eligible men, single or widowed, who take her fancy or indeed fancy her. When she worked in Sheffield there was one young man who she met at church. He was well-mannered enough but there was scant opportunity to get to know him, to discover whether he would be the man to spend her life with. Initially she feared that her employer held aspirations of marriage. He was very attentive when she first arrived as companion to his daughter, but he was old enough to be her father. Thankfully, his eyes roved elsewhere to other better-heeled ladies.

A family of her own is her greatest wish but soon she will be too old to bear children. Time does not favour Mary and she fears losing her looks and ending up an old maid living in the almshouses in Arksey.

She holds Frannie close, nuzzling the brown mop of hair, and gently lowers the infant into her play-pen. What does she feel for Joseph? Up until today she has not really considered any sentiment other than sisterly affection. Why should she? She has known him since she was a little girl. Their fathers would meet at market. Then he came courting Elizabeth and she was curious to observe their growing attachment and speculated what it would be to have a lover and husband. From then Joseph has always been Elizabeth's and she regards him now just as she would a brother. He was a good husband to her sister - kind, sober, hard-working. Since Elizabeth's death perhaps somewhat strict with Mary-Ann. Nonetheless, he loves the girl and Mary is in no doubt that Frannie will also share that love as she grows older.

Could she consider Joseph other than as a brother? If the law were to be followed, the answer was a resounding no. Putting that aside, could she feel warmth for him, even passion one day? Warmth perhaps, passion probably not. She has known a fluttering heart but only once. The young man at church in Sheffield. He had only to glance at her and she felt pleasure mixed with panic. Was that the beginning of passion? She never knew. Perhaps she never will. So, what now? Her head aches with so much thinking.

She dreads facing Ann Addy who must have known what Joseph planned. She blushes at the thought. Does his mother condone what he is proposing? Surely not.

Her thoughts are arrested by the clatter of Mary-Ann's boots on the stairs. The latch is lifted and the door bursts open. Frannie cries out with surprise, her lower lip trembling at the loud noise. Her sister runs over to the play-pen, bends over and tousles the child's hair, a little too roughly for her aunt's liking. Mary holds her tongue. She is glad of the distraction.

'So, Miss, tell me how many flowers did you press and how many of them are new to your collection?'

Mary-Ann continues to tease Frannie, now with a knitted animal of unknown species, and answers without turning towards her aunt. Were disrespect intended, Mary cannot tell and prefers to think not.

'Only one of them was new, a tufted vetch with blue flowers, but I have pressed seven others to see whether they will be better than the specimens I have already collected.' She turns at this point, purses her lips and raises her eyebrows in an expression of, who knows what? Perhaps it is what young girls do, thinks Mary.

For the next half hour until dinner time, Mary-Ann sits reading at the light of the window, occasionally asking her aunt to explain pronunciation or the meaning of difficult words. Mary tidies the nursery, folds freshly laundered linen and tries to calm herself. She must go down to the kitchen to prepare food for her nieces and so face Joseph's mother.

CHAPTER 10

1849 Summer

Ann Addy is alerted by measured footsteps descending the staircase. She will not broach the matter. It would be hard enough for Mary to absorb Joseph's proposal and its consequences without having to discuss it with his mother. Not yet, at least.

Mary appears at the open doorway, her face tense and slightly flushed. Ann Addy looks up from where she sits shelling peas freshly gathered from her kitchen garden. She has pride in the vegetable patch tucked away near the hens and a ready source of fertiliser. Even after Elizabeth became mistress of the house, she continued to manage the plot, although delegating much of the work to her daughter-in-law and young Dinah.

'Are the children getting hungry?' She smiles up at Mary who nods and busies herself with food for Mary-Ann and Frannie. Ann Addy continues with her task, slipping the occasional pea into her mouth. The silence becomes oppressive and she searches her mind for something inconsequential to say. In vain. Her thoughts are overwhelmed by the enormity of what Joseph is minded to do.

Mary breaks the silence. 'I shall feed Frannie now and put her down for her afternoon sleep. Would you be happy to give Mary-Ann her dinner? I need to return home just now and will find something to eat there. I'll be back later.' Her excuse to avoid sitting at table with Joseph sounds hollow but her imagination deserts her. She has no appetite to eat dinner in his company.

'Of course. You get on, lass. You have much to do of your own.' The old woman is relieved that Mary will not eat with them today. The stress would be too great and she fears that Mary-Ann would sense something ill. Maybe by tomorrow Mary will have come to a decision or at least be kindly disposed towards Joseph. The trouble is, Ann Addy is not convinced that Joseph's plan is advisable, even if desirable. Were things otherwise, she would be happy to have the young woman for her daughter-in-law. She would make a pleasant addition to the household.

Dinah bustles into the kitchen bearing a jug of buttermilk. She has been at work from early morning, intent on churning butter while the dairy remained cool.

'I shall cut the butter into blocks this afternoon, if that's alright Missus?' The housemaid is still pink from the exertion of cranking the barrel. 'I'll put the buttermilk in the larder and I can make some soda bread later.' The Missus always looks forward to her soda bread.

Ann Addy nods. 'Perhaps this afternoon Mary-Ann and I can help you wrap the butter ready for market. But for now, will you get potatoes on and lay up for dinner? I've shelled peas for you and the stew smells right well.'

At that moment Mary-Ann bursts into the room, not wishing to miss what is happening downstairs. Frannie is poor company and she is bored.

'Can I shell the peas, Grandmother?' With disappointment she spots the empty pea-pods. She sighs and waves her arms, causing her pinafore to beat like wings. If only Frannie were old enough to play with. She flounces around the room, flapping and showing off.

'Enough,' snaps Mary, by now ready to return to the nursery and feed Frannie. 'You're old enough to know how to behave. Dinner won't be long and, in the meantime, make yourself useful. You can cut up the muslin for the butter. This afternoon Dinah will be getting ready for market tomorrow.'

Mary-Ann turns away to hide a scowl from her grandmother and aunt. Mary's sharpness surprises Ann Addy. Dinah beckons the girl to follow her into the scullery. If she cuts the first piece to size, Mary-Ann is old enough to copy.

By the time Joseph returns from the fields, Mary has fed Frannie and set off for home. As he stands in the scullery scrubbing his hands, he watches his daughter carefully cutting squares of muslin and is pleased to see her put to useful occupation. Too much book reading cannot be good for her. Not that he is against girls' learning. No, they have as much right as boys to be educated. He sits at the table and notes the places laid. He meets his mother's eyes and raises his eyebrows.

'Just the three of us?'

'Aye. Mary has had to slip back home. She fed Frannie before she went.' The minimal response tells him much. He shrugs and thanks Dinah as a steaming plate is put before him. He eats in silence, deep in thought. What now?

*

Mary sits alone in her silent kitchen. She has coaxed a fire sufficient to boil a kettle to make a brew. Half a loaf of bread lies on the table together with a lump of hard cheese liberated from the larder where she hoped it would remain cool in the heat of the summer. It is beaded with sweat but smells right enough to eat. She keeps little in the cottage these days since she takes most meals with the Addys.

The silence within the room reminds her that she has forgotten to wind up the clock high on the shelf, the shelf which bears what remains of her heritage. It displays the paraphernalia collected by her mother: colourful china plates that caught Betsy Hall's eye at Doncaster market; a Staffordshire china dog with madly staring eyes that follow you around the room; Mary's pencil drawing of her mother in a simple wooden frame.

What would her mother have thought of Joseph's proposal? And Elizabeth? Would she have given her blessing for the sake of her daughters? She dares not speak of it to her brothers, especially her older brother, Mark, busy running his alehouse, and she has no wish to disclose her private thoughts to his wife, Ann. A nice enough woman but with her London ways, quick to criticise the northerners she has yet to accept.

Who would listen and give a measured judgement?

She cuts two slices of bread and sandwiches slivers of cheese. The dryness of the bread is countered by the large cup of tea which she sips between bites. She looks about her. Apart from her mother's scant furnishings, there is nothing to bind her to this cottage. Nor to Bentley.

A sense of duty ties her to Elizabeth's girls, though her more tender thoughts dwell on young Frannie, just a year old and motherless. Mary-Ann is, well, Mary-Ann. For five years she was the centre of attention and the arrival of her sister definitely upset her. That is the root of her contrariness, considers her aunt. Other than for the girls, why remain? Her brothers, Mark and Henry, are bound up in their own families and neither's wife would welcome her into their home. Back to Sheffield to find a position? For how long? What if she doesn't marry, who would look after her when she is old? Again, she thinks of Arksey's almshouses and shivers.

Over and over, her thoughts tumble the options. The prospect of a roof over her head becomes more appealing. But marrying your dead sister's husband is against the law. Laws are made to be broken, says her older brother, known as a risk-taker.

But that she is not. How many couples have defied this law? As yet, she has not read of any actions taken against such people. Surely the newspapers would have picked up on that sort of court case? Would people turn a blind eye? Reverend Sorsby certainly would not; a parson to follow the letter of the law, if ever there was.

Her mind turns to Elizabeth Vazin, the wise woman of the village. Even though only some ten years Mary's senior, London-born Elizabeth has experience of life beyond Bentley and Arksey. She resolves to meet with her and seek her advice. She is trusted by the Addys and showed practical compassion in nursing Mary's sister and mother until their deaths.

For now, there are two little girls to be cared for and that means facing up to Joseph. Slowly she tidies the kitchen then pulls on her bonnet.

Ann Addy sits under the shade of the pear tree close to the kitchen door. On her lap lies her knitting but her hands are at rest. Beside her, Frannie sits on a rug, her ability to roam firmly restricted by reins around her chest which are tethered to the leg of her grandmother's chair. Mary-Ann defies her grandmother's instruction to keep out of the burning sunlight and is batting a ball against the wall of the house. The monotonous sound of the ball hitting the wall, the ground, the bat, the wall, the ground, the bat, gets on Ann Addy's nerves but she struggles to keep her eyes open and soon the noise lulls her into a doze.

She wakes to squeals of delight from Frannie who has spotted her aunt approaching through the orchard. She is pleased to see Mary and welcomes her with a smile. Now she can take herself inside to the cool of the parlour, put up her feet and drift off for a while.

'So, what shall we do this afternoon?' Mary summons her flagging energy. She is determined to direct Mary-Ann's liveliness sufficiently to tire her and thereby be less troublesome at bedtime. If she can get the children to sleep early, she can escape back home and avoid further contact with Joseph today.

Mary-Ann stops her ball game and swings the bat as though swatting flies. She does not answer her aunt. She waits to hear her suggestions. Then she will decide. She savours the power to choose. Her grandmother thinks otherwise.

'Come now, lass. Answer your Aunt Mary. What will you get up to this afternoon? God has no time for children idling away the hours. Dinah needs help cutting up butter for market or you could take some eggs down to Mrs Watts. She was not at church this Sunday gone and I hear she's ailing.'

Neither suggestion finds favour with Mary-Ann and the girl proposes an alternative.

'We could take Frannie down to the mill to see the ducks. Maybe there's some stale bread to feed them?' She adds this without much hope as she knows her grandmother hates waste and any stale bread would end up in bread-and-butter pudding for tomorrow's dinner.

'I am sure we can ask Dinah to find us a few crumbs.' Mary intervenes before Ann Addy can respond, anxious to get both girls off and away. She frees Frannie from her anchorage and sweeps her up into her arms, echoing the infant's squeals of delight. Mary-Ann observes this mutual display of affection and hits the ball hard against the house wall.

'Enough of that, young lady,' admonishes her grandmother. 'Off with your pinafore and brush your hair if you're going to be seen in the village. Those stockings need straightening too.'

Mary-Ann hates to wear stockings in this heat but, unlike her mother when she was alive, her grandmother does not allow her to run about bare-legged. Life was more enjoyable last summer she reflects mournfully, but she disappears into the house in search of a hair brush.

As they near the mill, they can hear the roar of the millrace. The power of the water as it drives the massive paddle-wheel always unsettles Mary. The constant movement mesmerises her and she feels dangerously drawn towards the edge. Holding Mary-Ann firmly by the hand, she supports Frannie in a sling about her body. They pick their way through the pungent droppings left by the Shire horses which plod back and forth, bringing carts laden with grain and taking sacks of flour to the bakeries of Doncaster.

They head for the calm of the pond which feeds the wheel. That is where they will find the ducks. Indeed, as they approach, the birds spot them and paddle determinedly towards the bank, setting up a clamour.

Frannie cries out to get down but her aunt prefers to hold her safely away from the water. Her sister is well aware of the dangers of the deep. Two years ago, a little school friend had slipped into the pond and as nobody there could swim, they watched the poor little soul founder as petticoats floated around her before her screams were doused by the waters closing over. Mary-Ann will carry that memory to her grave. She stands well back from the edge. Her intention is for the ducks to come to her.

She lays a trail of crumbs which leads away from the pond. Frannie is beside herself with excitement. As the glistening ducks scramble out of the water and waddle along the line of crumbs, heads pecking as they go, she shouts at them in her baby-talk. Soon the small bag of bread is exhausted. The ducks lumber off, quacking dissatisfaction, in search of under-water delights. Frannie's face puckers as they disappear so Mary points the party homeward and they wander back down the dusty lane. She tries to initiate a sing-song with Mary-Ann but without success. Her niece has found a stick and is busy slashing the drying grasses along the road-side, releasing their seeds and dusty scents into the still warm afternoon.

As they take tea in the kitchen with their grandmother, Frannie struggles to stay awake while Mary spoons food into her mouth. After the heat of the day and the afternoon walk, Mary-Ann is also tired and only finishes the food on her plate after her grandmother has reminded her of all the hungry little children in the workhouses. She happily follows Mary upstairs as her sister is taken to be washed ready for bed.

It is as Mary hoped. Both girls bedded down early. Their father is working late in the fields, taking advantage of the dry weather. He will come in to kiss them goodnight some hours later when they are deep in slumber. She will be long gone.

CHAPTER 11

1849 Summer

In the freshness of early morning, Joseph works in the mistle alongside his men, the smell of the cows and their steady breathing all part of his every-day. He clings to that every-day. With so much changing, he needs its reassurance. Perhaps after a good night's sleep Mary will be able to face him.

He looks up and is surprised to see Mary slip through the orchard, across the dew-wet grass. The dry path would have brought her nearer to where he is working. She avoids him as she heads towards the house, where her first task will be to wash and dress the girls for breakfast.

By the time the early morning jobs are done and he has scrubbed up in the scullery, his mother is already seated at the kitchen table laid for breakfast. Dinah brings him a dish piled with ham and eggs. He is hungry and tucks in with relish, mopping the runny yolk with this morning's bread. His mother is pouring him a large cup of tea as Mary appears with Frannie in her arms and a sullen Mary-Ann in tow.

Joseph welcomes all with a cheery 'Good morning' and uses Mary-Ann's pout as a means to divert conversation away from the subject which is in the minds of the three adults.

'Did you not sleep well, child?' He addresses his elder daughter not unkindly.

The girl sits looking at her hands in her lap. No, she hasn't slept well, mainly because Frannie was restless and crying out. Dinah sleeps in the nursery as Mary returns home each evening, and Dinah snores. Mary-Ann is out of sorts. And her mother is dead. But that is not what her father wants to hear. Even at her tender years she is canny enough to know that.

She looks up and gives a weak smile. 'Frannie cried out then I couldn't fall asleep again. I kept thinking of Mother.' She knows this will pain her father but wants to share her misery. Joseph frowns and continues eating, his thoughts bounding on to how his daughter would react to a new mother.

'You weren't woke that long, Missy. I sat with you for a while and stroked your hair until you dropped off,' says Dinah who has returned with a fresh brew of tea and caught the end of the girl's explanation.

Mary takes charge of the situation and proposes a morning of lessons. Her niece is not averse to learning and she needs to counter the boredom of the school holidays.

'This morning, let us look at the geography of the Indian subcontinent. I have a book given to me when I worked in Sheffield and we can use that for our lesson. What do you say?'

Mary-Ann has already peeked into that book and is intrigued. She replies languidly, 'I suppose so.' Her aunt smiles a tight smile and carries on spooning food into the niece squirming on her lap, who derives as much pleasure from fingering the mush as from swallowing it.

Joseph feels bound to communicate with Mary.

'That will be greatly of interest, Mary,' he enthuses. She doubts it. 'Do they grow tea there, or is that only in China?' She shakes her head indicating that she has no idea.

His frustration mounts. *Speak to me.*

Mary-Ann may only be a child but she is sensitive to the atmosphere and keeps her eyes lowered onto her thick slice of bread smeared with tasty dripping from Sunday's roast. If she listens, she might glean a clue to the cause of this taut conversation. She waits in vain.

Joseph speaks with enthusiasm about the coming day's work on the harvest and agrees with his mother when dinner would be brought to the workers in the fields. Similar sustenance would be transported later in the day to allow the men to work through until dusk. Long days, tiring days, but there was no option at this time of year with the vagaries of Yorkshire weather.

*

Aunt and niece spend a productive morning in the nursery. Mary-Ann flicks through the illustrations of the clothbound book, then sits fascinated as Mary recounts the variation in landscape and climate of India north to south, the different castes and religions that populate the land. Her imagination takes her up and away from the village of Bentley, from Yorkshire, from England. How wonderful one day to travel the world.

Dinah's call from downstairs alerts them to the progress of the morning. The food will soon be ready for the harvesters and everyone will be needed to bear the baskets through the lanes to the field. With Frannie once more strapped in a sling across her bosom, Mary picks up two baskets packed with bread, meats and cheeses, each wrapped in freshly laundered cloths. She joins the rest of the household, each laden with packages to restore energy to the farm workers. Even Mary-Ann carries a bundle in each hand as the party leaves Millgate.

The straw hats worn by the women may protect their faces from the sun's rays, now overhead, but cannot stave off the intense heat which beats down as they trudge in silence along the lane to the seven-acre field. The men spot them from afar and cheer at the sight of their dinner. They look to Joseph who nods and the men down scythes and move towards the small clump of trees which will afford them shade while they eat. The women break into chatter as they divest themselves of their burden and find relief in the relative cool under the leaves of the ash trees.

Joseph checks that everyone is served and that the stoneware jars of beer have been retrieved from the stream where they have lain cooling all morning. The women-folk have laid out a cloth and unpacked the thick sandwiches of bread and sliced cold ham served with pickles. He takes a deep draught of the ale poured by Dinah and sits on the ground, glad of the food and respite from cutting. He watches Frannie as she crawls towards him and smiles as Mary attempts to stop her eating the grass. Mary looks up, catches his grin and self-consciously smiles back. That moment of shared sympathy strikes Joseph to his heart. Not all is lost then? He looks away. Slowly does it. This will not be resolved in days.

*

It proves a satisfactory harvest and even though it is not a year since Elizabeth's death and the family still observes mourning for her and her mother, Joseph feels it would be churlish for the farm not to thank its workers for their hard work in safely bringing his corn to the rick-yard. A harvest home supper is announced for the following Saturday, with workers and their families invited. An opportunity to draw Mary closer into the life of the farm, thinks Ann Addy. She waits until Frannie is settled for her afternoon nap and Mary-Ann is engrossed in her colouring book.

'Sit with me, would you, Mary? I must gather my thoughts about the harvest supper? I don't believe you have joined with our celebrations before …'

'No, Mrs Addy. Last harvest I was tending my mother in her illness, but Elizabeth told me that it was appreciated greatly by all who attended. It is a generous gesture by the family.'

'No more than we ought,' nods Ann Addy, acknowledging Mary's warm words. 'Now lass, would you be my helper this year?' She almost adds 'now that Elizabeth is no longer here' but checks herself in time. That would undermine the subtlety of her scheme.

They sit at the parlour table and Ann bends over a sheet of paper. She dips a pen in a small pot of ink and dabs it cautiously on a blotter before carefully writing the heading: *Harvest Supper 1849*. Mary views the lowered head, padded with generous white curls. Could she call this woman Mother? She admonishes herself for the thought. For the last two weeks she has pushed Joseph's proposal to the back of her mind, all too difficult to resolve.

'Now, Mary, we only have to think about the food. The menfolk will prepare the barn for the supper and set up trestle tables. With wives and children, together with the sweethearts of the younger ones, we should be around thirty.'

Cooking for thirty? Mary is daunted at the prospect, but keeps quiet.

'What are you minded to cook for such a large number?' Would she be expected to become involved with the preparation? Looking after the two girls left her little enough time for herself, but she did not wish to appear unwilling.

'I see no reason to change what we have done in the past,' responds Ann Addy with a firmness that brooks no challenge. 'Elizabeth was happy to continue our tradition.' So that's that.

'What exactly would you want me to do? Tell me, then I can work it around looking after Mary-Ann and Frannie.' She quietly makes her point. The older woman nods and notes that Mary has an unexpected spirit, not unlike her late sister.

'If I list the dishes to be prepared, I would like you to calculate the quantities of ingredients we need to set aside. It is beyond Dinah and in any case her mind isn't totally on her work.

I suspect there is a young man turning her head. Not before time though, she has worked with us for eleven years and at twenty-four she needs to be settled.' It is out before she can think. Mary is twenty-eight and unwed. The unspoken proposition looms over both women.

To dispel the tension Mary leans forward with a smile. 'So, what is the first dish? If you name it and list the ingredients for a normal family meal, I can gross it up so that Dinah can bring together whatever vegetables and meat we need.'

Ann Addy dips the pen again and starts to list the dishes as column headings and underneath she steadily adds in the quantities of the ingredients needed for her Harvest Vegetable Soup, Harvest Pie and Apple Cake. Also, Dinah would make bread including two large loaves shaped into sheaves of corn.

'Joseph wondered if we should roast a couple of geese but I told him that would be buttering the bacon. This is quite enough for everyone.'

By the time she has finished, Dinah is bustling around in the kitchen, brewing up for tea. Ann Addy hands the pen and paper to Mary who takes a small sheet of paper for her workings-out and slowly marks up the large quantities of onions, carrots, potatoes, apples, bacon, flour and butter. Big pots will be needed for the soup and large dishes to bake the pies and the cakes. She resolves to write out a plan of who does what. She debates whether this is the right moment to suggest doing so but holds her tongue. First let Mrs Addy reach the conclusion that more help is needed, then she can put forward her solution. Mary is under no illusion as to what is going on in the mind of Joseph's mother.

CHAPTER 12

1849 Late Summer

The barn is cleared and the floor swept. Joseph watches his men assemble the long trestle table that will carry this evening's feast. The dairymaids decorate its length with jars crammed with wild flowers, and gossip excitedly about who will bring their young man to the supper. He is heartened that harvest home will be celebrated again as in years gone. Maybe it is superstitious, but if showing thanks for a good harvest will appease the gods and guarantee a repeat next year, so be it. Mindful of the loss of his wife since last year's supper, he has not engaged the usual fiddle player. People understand that this time singing and dancing would not be respectful.

Mary-Ann skitters in through the barn door and stops to look about. She has not yet seen her father and quietly he observes her. Such a skinny little thing, silhouetted against the sunshine. Is she not eating enough or is it just part of growing? He calls to her.

'Father, where do I put this?' She runs to him, holding aloft the corn-dolly made under Mary's guidance. He turns it in his hand. Finely done.

'That's grand, lass. Well made.' She beams at the praise. 'You should bring it with you to the supper and, before we eat, there will be a contest with your grandmother judging the best corn-dolly of the day.'

Mary-Ann dashes off to show her efforts to the men and girls, knowing that they will make a fuss of Master's daughter. Joseph turns towards the house. There will be mayhem in the kitchen but he wants to show his support and gratitude.

'So young Miss, did you make your corn-dolly all by yourself?' Will Barraclough has known Mary-Ann since she was born. Unmarried, he lives in the farmworkers' cottage beside the barn, which he shares with two younger farm lads. He has watched her grow and knows only too well how the lass wishes being the centre of attention. Like the rest of Joseph's workers, he wonders who will look after the two girls now. The Missus is getting on in years and Elizabeth's younger sister seems to have her feet firmly under the table. Nice enough woman, he ponders, but as the dairymaids have already pointed out, the law will not permit Joseph to marry her.

'Aunt Mary showed me how to do it, but really I made it myself without any help.' He doubts that but lets it go.

'A bright lady, your aunt, they say.' He is intrigued to know how the land lies. 'Your grandmother must be glad of her help.'

'Mm, perhaps, but once Frannie is a bit older, we won't need her and I can help Grandmother with everything.' Her self-assurance is a trait Will has come to recognise. He pushes further.

'She must be company for your father too. Does she stay on of an evening?' He knows that she does not sleep at the house and that Dinah does nursery watch each night. He is curious to know whether there is an understanding growing between brother-in-law and sister-in-law. Forgivable if there were. But difficult.

'Oh no,' dismisses the girl. 'We don't have her at night. Dinah sleeps in the nursery in case Frannie wakes. Aunt Mary goes back to her cottage and returns to get us up next morning.' The man knows that there are bedrooms enough at the farmhouse and supposes that for decorum's sake the aunt returns home.

*

The tension is as high as the heat in the kitchen and Joseph hovers on the threshold. He is assailed by delicious cooking aromas: bread, apples, cinnamon. Dinah's red face is due partly to the ovens which are baking the apple cakes, and partly to her frustration with the dairymaids who have proved more hindrance than use. Mary stands by the scullery door, directing the girls to place the baked cakes on racks to cool. They will be served with fresh cream poured over. Huge lidded pots of vegetable soup sit on the side waiting to be re-heated once the company is assembled. Rows of large baking tins are lined up and a girl spoons into them the cooled contents of the Harvest Pie, ensuring a good distribution of cooked bacon amidst the potato and apple. Dinah bends over the table, sleeves pushed up to reveal her plump arms. She chops a portion from the slabs of raw pastry then attacks it with her wooden pin, in moments rolling it out to cover the first of the many pies. They will lodge in the scullery and an hour before supper is served, she will supervise the baking of the pies, batch by batch. She has done this before. She did not need Miss Mary to suggest how best to manage. If only those lasses weren't so slow.

Joseph approaches his mother, seated by the window, out of the way of the workers. She frowns anxiously.

'Is everything going well in the barn, lad?' She does not wait for a reply. She is too preoccupied with her own responsibilities. 'Every year I worry, but every time it turns out alright, in the end,' she reassures herself.

'It will be grand, don't fret yourself, Mother. It looks as though all is coming together just fine. And Mary is helping too?' He knows of his mother's plan to draw Mary into the farm but worries that such an overwhelming event might dissuade her from becoming a farmer's wife, even without that other far greater obstacle.

'Aye, she has been a great support and has tried to organise matters, though not without resistance from Dinah,' she adds in a lower tone. Joseph smiles. He can appreciate the sensitivity of another woman making suggestions in Dinah's kitchen. He catches Mary's eye across the room and nods with an encouraging smile. Fleetingly she smiles back then turns again to supervise the cakes.

*

Mary-Ann is disappointed. She did not win the corn-dolly contest. Her grandmother chose that made by the youngest dairymaid. She consoles herself that of course her corn-dolly could not win. It would have been favouritism. Now she is full of food and very sleepy. Everyone seems to have a smile on their face and the time has come for the mothers to round up the children and herd them home to bed. The menfolk will stay on, drinking ale, smoking a pipe, recounting tales of past harvest-homes.

'Right Mary-Ann. Let's off to bed with you. Have you enjoyed yourself?' Mary stands next to the girl and aims to have her to bed as quietly as possible, so not to disturb Frannie who has been under the care of a neighbour's daughter. Then she can slip away home. She is exhausted after the day of cooking.

Mary-Ann considers resisting but in truth she can hardly keep her eyes open. Together they walk away from the lamp-lit barn into the darkness. Joseph has positioned hurricane lamps along the path and aunt and niece walk hand-in-hand towards the back door. Tonight Mary-Ann can make do with a lick and a promise and within half an hour Mary should be able to escape home. Clearing up is deferred to the next morning and thankfully she has not been asked to participate in that chore.

Her niece scrambles into bed and is soon away in slumber. Mary nods to the neighbour's daughter tucked up in Dinah's bed, and tiptoes down the stairs. As she passes through the kitchen, she scoops up a spare lantern and lights it for her walk home. She is not feared of the dark but she has no wish to tumble and dirty a good dress, let alone hurt herself. By fortune, there is a full moon and this will supplement the lantern's limited beam.

'Mary.' She stops with a gasp only a few paces out of the back door. Joseph's figure looms large, silhouetted by the hurricane lamps behind him. 'You are leaving already?'

'Forgive me, Joseph, it has been a long and busy day. Mary-Ann is safely to bed and now I need to return to mine.' She immediately regrets reference to her bed.

'Then I will accompany you, my dear. I would not rest knowing you were stepping through the lanes at this time of night with nothing but a lamp to guide your way.'

'No, Joseph, no need. I am accustomed to walking alone at night. It is not far and there are no navvies billeted around here. They are all encamped close to the railway track and their ale house. Why would they roam this far?' She allows him no opportunity to override her. 'You have your company to think of. What would they say if Master slopes away at this hour?'

'I will return to them afterwards, Mary. Will can keep an eye on things. I insist on walking with you, especially after such an arduous day when you have contributed so much to our farm's celebration.' She sighs her acceptance, he relieves her of the lamp and they fall in step. He offers his arm and it is expedient to take it. Without doubt, Joseph surrounds her with a feeling of security.

Not far up the lane they spy the wife of Jim Fields swaying slightly as she shepherds her three children home. Joseph considers the delicacy of their situation. At the current pace they will soon catch them up. Walking together through the night, arm in arm, will start the tongues wagging. He considers holding back as much for Mary's reputation as his own. But one of the children has spotted their lamplight and the woman stops and turns round. After supping much ale and blinded by the lantern, she cannot work out who follows them but would welcome to share their lamplight. She awaits their approach. The decision is made for him so Joseph speeds up and Mary gains pace.

'Well met, Mrs Fields. Will you share our lantern?' Joseph appears delighted to be able to help the family of one of his workers to reach home safely. 'Miss Hall has just put my elder daughter to bed and I could not permit her to walk back to her cottage alone.' With sinking heart, he realises that Fields' cottage lies beyond Mary's and he will be obliged to leave her at her door and continue further. He hoped that this newly found intimacy could be the stepping-stone to gain Mary's confidence.

The three adults exchange polite enthusiasm for the happenings of the evening and then subside into their thoughts. Sarah Fields wonders if she has intruded upon a lovers' tryst. Wait 'til she speaks to Jim in the morning. Mary is mortified that people will paint her in a bad light. Why did she accept Joseph's offer, his arm? Joseph despairs as to how he will find another opportunity to speak with Mary without seeming to confront her.

At her door they wait until she has entered and lit her own lamp. Joseph does not step over the threshold and only holds the lantern high to light her way. He bows and thanks her for all she has done to make the evening such a success.

'Now Mrs Fields, onwards to your home. You will be glad to be abed soon, aye, children?'

Mary stands alone in her cottage, listening to the banter and the footsteps disappearing down the lane. Is she relieved? Would she have allowed him in while she lit her lamp? Something stirs inside her but she is dog-tired. She wonders: how long before I have to make my decision?

CHAPTER 13

1849 Autumn

Tongues do wag, as Mary feared. Some weeks after the harvest home, she enters the village shop and the chit-chat comes to a halt. As she waits her turn, villagers enquire after the Addy girls and their 'poor father'. Her cheeks burn with resentment as she tries to ignore the insinuations and responds coolly.

'Frannie is still too young to realise her loss. She is but eighteen months old and this life is really all she has known. In years to come, as we talk often of my dear sister, she will come to discover what a treasure we have lost. As for Mary-Ann …'

'Quite a handful that young lady, so I hear,' butts in the blacksmith's wife. 'Only what I've heard from my sister-in-law's daughter who works at Mr Godfrey Addy's farm. Miss Mary-Ann goes over to ride out with her cousins. She must be lonely kicking around at home with nobody to play with. And no mother to keep an eye on her.'

'Indeed. For Mary-Ann the loss is great and the rest of her family is doing its best to help her bear it.' With relief Mary reaches the counter and reads from her list of commissions so she can continue on her way as swiftly as possible. She cannot bear this inquisition. But must.

During the lengthening autumn nights, Mary thinks of little else but her situation and an alternative solution to that offered by Joseph. She could return to Sheffield and find a position but it would be with strangers. London has also been a consideration but as an avid follower of the writings of Mr Charles Dickens, she fears that whilst there may be greater opportunities, within that ever more sprawling metropolis of smoke and noise there lie traps for single women without independent means and with little experience of the world. What is more, for some months now, thousands in the capital and many other cities have been dying of the cholera. Staying out in the countryside with its clean air and fresh food may be her only option.

For comfort, each evening she settles with a lamp and the latest instalment of Mr Dickens' new story about a boy called David Copperfield. How her heart goes out to that little child whose father has gone to a better place, leaving him to the cruelty of his new step-father. Mary condemns David's mother for her weakness, yet part of her recognises the helpless position the young widow found herself in. Being alone in the world without money is not a rosy prospect.

Joseph also has money worries. Following the Repeal of the Corn Laws, this February saw its full implementation. After three years of transition, British farmers no longer enjoy protection of their grain prices and this autumn the returns are not good, despite a passable harvest. He did have some sympathy with the aims of the Repealers. Keeping the price of grain high ensured that landowners prospered, but for the poor folk it was a different story when they could not afford flour for their daily bread. In Ireland the situation is now even more desperate after the blight destroyed the potato crops. But the sale of Joseph's grain represents the major part of the farm's income and for the third year running the price has dropped.

If only Elizabeth were here to share the burden. She had a good head for arithmetic and he misses her weekly update of the farm books. Young Mary has a sensible head on her shoulders. She reads a great deal, he seems to remember. Would she be willing to take it on? He could pay her for the work. He flushes at the thought of offering money to his sister-in-law. True, they pay her a small remuneration for her care of the children, but it probably does not even cover the rent of her cottage.

The fundamental problem will not go away. He needs to find a new wife. With the drop in income, he cannot afford a full-time nursery maid. He despises himself in thinking of money above the safety and care of his daughters. In any case, the thought of having a stranger living within the house fills him with dread. Mary would be the solution, not only practically, but he acknowledges he is growing increasingly fond of the lass.

*

Ann Addy is ailing. Her back aches dreadfully and the poor woman cannot get comfortable. She can no longer climb in and out of the hip bath which once a week is set up in her bedroom before the fire, even in summer. Dinah humps upstairs pails of water, heated in the copper out in the wash-house, and gradually fills the tub. Elizabeth Vazin is here to help Mrs Addy with her ablutions. She is the only person that Ann Addy trusts to help her stand in the tub and wash her clean. Were Joseph's wife still living, she might have accepted her help, but she is proud and prefers the capable but dispassionate hands of the villager who sees babies into this world and nurses the elderly out of it. Not that Ann Addy is ready to go. Not yet. She needs to see Joseph settled first. Pray God to give her strength to keep going and not be a burden on top of all else.

'How is Joseph coping?' Elizabeth Vazin soaps Ann Addy's back.

'He keeps his feelings to himself, like most of us, but I know he misses Elizabeth greatly.'

'Fortunate to have Mary to help you all with the care of the little ones.'

Ann Addy wonders if Mary has already confided in Elizabeth Vazin. Could this be a moment to test the waters?

'She is a grand lass and there is no doubt she loves her nieces. We are lucky to have her, don't you think?'

'Indeed. She is very different from her poor sister but has much to recommend her.'

'We are all very fond of her.' How to introduce the possibility of marriage?

Elizabeth Vazin is ahead of her.

'Unfair that the law changed for a widower to marry his dead wife's sister. In so many instances such a union would be the ideal solution.'

'I hear tell that there are ways around it …' Ann Addy waits for an opinion from the woman now drying her back with a rough cloth. None comes. 'I cannot see the Reverend Sorsby turning a blind eye, let alone our neighbours.'

Elizabeth Vazin grunts agreement and Ann Addy regrets broaching the matter. She is disappointed not to discover how the villagers might regard an illegal marriage and has to trust the good woman not to gossip about their conversation. She dresses and Dinah arrives to bail out the lukewarm water, a bucketful at a time. Elizabeth Vazin takes her money and leaves the farmhouse, deep in thought.

*

Late autumn sunshine greets the congregation as it shuffles its way past the judgmental eye of the parson who stands at the south door and keeps a mental note of those attending and those not. He asks solicitously after missing parishioners. Indisposed? There could be no other admissible excuse in his eyes. Mary stands apart as Joseph and his mother greet neighbours. Frannie is in Joseph's arms and Mary-Ann hops from one foot to another, longing to skip off among the gravestones but mindful of her grandmother's displeasure in so doing.

'Good day, Mary.' She turns with a smile on hearing the voice of Elizabeth Vazin. She is ever grateful to this woman who cared for her mother and her sister, and who today is accompanied by her shepherd husband and their children, two girls and two boys, the elder at fifteen apprenticed to a butcher.

'Elizabeth, my dear. So good to see you here.' Mary takes her by the arm and steers her away from the family. 'I would very much like to talk with you but you must be busy with your farm, your family and your good work with so many others.'

Elizabeth Vazin shows no surprise at the request and nods her acquiescence. 'Tell me when would be a convenient time and I am happy to meet. It is always a pleasure to talk with you, especially about your time in Sheffield. I find life somewhat narrow compared with my younger days in the south. But maybe that is circumstances rather than geography,' she considers ruefully.

Within the Addy group, the matriarch of the family has spoken with her children, present at church with their spouses and her grandchildren, and now she is ready for her Sunday dinner. She ushers Joseph towards the gate but not without observing the close-knit bonnets of Mary Hall and Elizabeth Vazin. She smiles. Another step forward.

*

Mary pours a glass of raspberry cordial and hands it to Elizabeth Vazin. She has lit two lamps to brighten the room and the range burns up to lend warmth. Mary does not wish to delay her friend unnecessarily.

'I need your advice, Elizabeth. I am faced with a choice which will determine the rest of my life and were it a simple decision, I should not be troubling you. I know one thing though, whichever path I take, my life will be hard. The question is, which road will be the least difficult to follow?'

Elizabeth Vazin shows no emotion. Ann Addy's remarks have prepared her and since Mary's request for a meeting, she has given thought to the likely conundrum.

'As you know, since my mother lost the farm, there has been little or no money coming in. Before that I had already moved away to seek a position and an income of my own. When Mother took ill, it was only right that I should give up that position and return to nurse her. Now, with our Elizabeth gone, I have been glad enough to care for her little ones, until …' Here she falters. 'But the time is come for me to consider my future. The Addys need someone who can look after the children with a greater commitment than I can offer, given the situation. So, I should look for another position elsewhere.'

'Have the Addys asked you to look for a new post?'

'Oh, good heavens, no. That, you see, is my dilemma. Joseph has asked me to be his wife.' There is no point in beating about the bush. She awaits a look of dawning comprehension on the older woman's face, but instead sees a gentle smile.

'And what would be your decision, Mary dear? Joseph is an honourable man and would not have made such a proposition without deep consideration. No doubt he has also discussed it with his mother. Ann Addy would have strong views for and against.' She does not enquire whether Mary loves Joseph. Such an emotional element is frankly inconsequential in the circumstances. Much bigger issues are to be resolved than whether or not they share affection.

Mary drops her head into her hands and shakes it slowly. How can she articulate her thoughts?

'I know that at my age this is probably the best opportunity I shall be offered: a good roof over my head; financially more secure than I could ever be alone; a kind and honourable man for husband; two little girls I already love and with God's grace maybe babes of my own one day.' She sits up, tears in her eyes and twists a handkerchief in her hands.

'I believe that I would be accepted by his mother and the girls. Frannie knows me longer than she ever could her poor mother. But tell me, Elizabeth, what would people say? The law now forbids what Joseph suggests. Even if we were to go elsewhere to be wed, afterwards we would have to return to the farm but as man and wife, man and wife beyond the law. Would we go to prison for it? And if not that extreme, we would not be welcomed back at the church in Arksey nor would we be accepted by our neighbours. Even Joseph's wider family may not support his decision.' She sits back in the upholstered armchair, exhausted by her disclosure.

Elizabeth Vazin remains silent in the lamplight. She sees only one road to take but wants Mary to discover that route for herself. Giving advice without building the foundations to the solution rarely leads to its acceptance.

'You have laid down the challenges which face you if you move on.' She indicates the pile of periodicals on the table beside Mary. 'You do not need to read the stories of your Mr Dickens to know what can befall a single woman without money. But this decision should not be taken based on what is the least testing solution. Rather more, you should consider which would bring you greater happiness. In that case, the prospect of a kind, dependable husband who would care for you and your children, God be willing, outweighs the likelihood of opprobrium from others.

'Joseph is respected. Many people reject the fairness of the law and even in Parliament I hear they seek to repeal it. Your neighbours will understand that for the good of his children,

Joseph should re-marry. Far better to marry someone who is known by his children, someone who is held in high regard for being a dutiful daughter and sister in times of difficulty. You should accept his proposal, my dear Mary.'

CHAPTER 14

1849 Christmas

With memories of the previous Christmas, Joseph has no heart for festivity. His mother struggles to move about the house. She dreads the stairs. At his behest, she remains abed until mid-morning and wonders silently if this will be her last Christmas. Down in the kitchen, Dinah rejoices that it is her last Christmas with the Addys. Soon she will marry her sweetheart and move on. Mary, busy in the nursery, knows she must reach a decision. After Christmas she will give her answer to Joseph. Only Mary-Ann is excited.

Since late summer when Joseph laid his proposal before Mary, nothing further has been discussed. She is conscious of his eyes upon her as she goes about her care of the girls and she is grateful that he does not urge his suit. So many months on, the tension between them has relaxed.

Ann Addy is impatient. She no longer has time to waste and is anxious to expedite matters. Joseph brings to her bedroom a cup of tea and a bowl of porridge.

'Have you eaten your own breakfast, lad?'

'Yes, and about to go back out again. We're clearing ditches today. We must be sure they can run clear into the dikes before the winter storms set in. This low-lying land floods soon enough without blockages making things a darn sight worse.'

His mother is not listening and raises her worries about the coming Christmas.

'Your sister, Nancy, has invited us to eat with them after church on Christmas Day, but I don't think I could manage to climb into the trap, do you?'

'In my view, Mother, I do not think it advisable for you even to go to church on Christmas Day, let alone afterwards to our Nancy's for dinner. You've not been up to going to church these last few weeks and it would be madness to force yourself to do so, just because it's Christmas. We can make it a happy day here just the four of us. Well, five if Mary does not intend to go to one of her brothers. It would certainly be a blessing if she were to spend the day with us. Dinah will be up to her eyes in cooking and that lass's heart is elsewhere now that she has settled the day to be wed. She won't have time to look after the girls. And it would be too much for you, Mother.'

'Will you speak to Mary, then? Will you ask her to talk with Dinah to work out what needs preparing? We don't need overmuch. There is always too much cooked and not eaten at Christmas time. And apart from anything, Mary would be very welcome here on Christmas Day. She is family after all.'

Joseph considers how best to approach Mary. The last thing he wants is for her to think that the invitation is one only of necessity. He knows that Dinah would not wish to spend Christmas night looking after his daughters. Would Mary be prepared to sleep that night in the nursery?

Before heading off into the grey December morning, Joseph seeks out his sister-in-law. He finds her down in the kitchen encouraging Frannie to walk without holding onto the furniture.

His daughter has passed the stage of staggering a few steps before plumping down onto her well-upholstered backside which always elicited a surprised squeak then giggles. How blessed they are to have a happy child. Frannie spies her father and lets go of the tablecloth and walks determinedly towards him, arms outstretched. He crouches down, reaching towards her, and lets her amble right up to him, all the while greeting him with incoherent baby talk which clearly has great meaning to her.

Mary-Ann observes from the kitchen table where she is practising her letters. Her fingers are chalky but she is proud of the cursive Fs which fill her slate.

'Mary, we must talk of Christmas.' Mary straightens up and Mary-Ann sits with ears pricked.

'Yes, indeed, it is but a few weeks off.' Mary offers her brother-in-law no indication of her feelings for the coming season. In truth, she dreads the prospect. As the unwed sister, she must wait for her two younger brothers to toss a coin to see who will invite her to their table on Christmas Day. She is fond of both but hardly sees either of them these days - Mark busy all hours in the ale house, Henry working as a clerk in Doncaster where he and his wife now live.

Joseph is aware that Mary-Ann's hand is poised over her slate but does not move. He is glad of the girl's presence to deflect any suspicion of hidden intent in what he is about to say.

'My mother and I, and Mary-Ann,' he gestures towards his daughter, 'would be most happy if you were to spend Christmas Day with us.' He hastens on before she can respond. 'If, however, you feel duty bound to go to one of your brothers, we would understand and respect that wish. It is just that my mother cannot easily leave the house to visit my sister and your company would brighten this little family no end.' Mary-Ann has never heard her father make such a pretty speech and waits intrigued to hear her aunt's response.

'Well Joseph, that's very kind of you. Very kind of you all. Until now, I have not heard from either of my brothers, so I am very happy to accept your generous invitation.' She too is glad of Mary-Ann's presence. 'We shall have to plan some parlour games to amuse us all after dinner, won't we Mary-Ann?' The girl nods thoughtfully.

On Christmas morning, Mary stays behind to look after Frannie and keep Ann Addy company, while Joseph takes Mary-Ann to church. Apart from the practicality of this arrangement, she cannot bear the looks of villagers seeing her in church beside Joseph less than a year after his wife's death.

Joseph arrives early at All Saints and, hand-in-hand with his daughter, walks to Elizabeth's grave to place a holly wreath on the memorial stone. They stand in silence, he with his thoughts, Mary-Ann wondering if she is permitted to speak to her mother, aloud, not just in her head. She decides perhaps not. After the service, they linger to answer neighbours' enquiries about his mother's health then cross over to The Plough, pay the stable lad, and trot home.

Bundled up in rugs and shawls to stave off the cold, Mary-Ann thinks ahead to the Christmas dinner which Dinah is preparing, then the exchange of gifts. She has been busy in recent weeks making the presents that she will give to her family: a blue felt pen-wiper for her father; a stuffed red felt ball for Frannie; a cardboard pill-box covered in coloured stars for her grandmother and for Dinah a box of spills made from rolled-up newspaper. All had been fashioned in secret with considerable help from Mary. When she realised that Mary would also be with them on Christmas Day, she turned to her grandmother for inspiration.

'She reads many books so why not make her a book-marker? We can find a piece of card and you can either paint it or embellish it with cut-outs from my ladies' magazines.' Together they squirrelled time when Mary was occupied with Frannie and created a very fine book marker.

Soon after their return, the family sits down to eat in the dining room, heated for the occasion by a roaring fire which today thankfully does not smoke, as the wind blows in the right direction. Joseph turns to the family and asks them to join him in saying grace and then to remain silent for a minute while they remember their darling Elizabeth, wife, daughter, mother and sister. For all in the room the moment is alive with emotions.

Dinah has done them proud with a large roast capon accompanied by piles of roasted potatoes and vegetables. The plum pudding is flamed with brandy and everyone agrees it is the best meal of the year.

They discuss who was at church, what the parson preached, who sent good wishes and promised to visit. Tomorrow, Ann Addy's son, Godfrey, and daughter, Nancy, will come over with her grandchildren. At the end of the meal, Joseph thanks Dinah who scurries off to clear away and escape into the arms of her family or maybe her sweetheart.

They retire to the comfort of the parlour with its over-stuffed armchairs. Ann Addy lies back in her usual chair, her silver head resting on the newly crocheted antimacassar which defines her as a lady not too old to lend style to her country home. She closes her eyes.

'Grandmother, you cannot sleep. We are opening our gifts now.' Mary-Ann pleads.

'Worry not, Mary-Ann, I am merely resting my poor old eyes. Fetch down the bag next to my bed, would you, lass?' The girl dashes from the cosy room, up the cold staircase into the chill of her grandmother's bedroom. As ever, she is struck by the smell of age. Old curtains, old rugs, old clothes. In the gloom of the December afternoon, she discerns a tapestry bag full of little packages and carefully carries it back down the steep stairs, holding on to the banister for fear of slipping.

She is greeted by the sight of her father sitting on the floor with a big box covered in brown paper tied with string. Is that for her? She passes the bag to her grandmother and cannot contain her excitement. Will she have to wait for everyone else to open their own presents? She cannot bear it.

Joseph does not believe in teasing. He beckons the girl to sit beside him.

'This, Mary-Ann, is for you. You have been such a good girl over the last year and have helped us look after your little sister since we lost your mother.' She bubbles with glee inside, delighted by the praise but not sure she has really done much to help with Frannie. Her fingers twitch to help with the string.

'Shall I undo the knots?'

She knows she must not tear at the wrapping and that it must be carefully folded and conserved for another time. But she wants to rip the paper, all the quicker to get into the box. Printed on the outside in large letters: *Pollock's Toy Theatre.* Her eyes widen. She allows her father to open the box and he gently removes an ornately coloured proscenium arch attached to a box-like construction, representing the stage and back-drop to her very own toy theatre. She crouches down to see more closely.

'Let us stand it on the table, shall we?' Joseph lifts it up onto the table. Mary-Ann claps her hands and hugs him.

'Thank you so much, Father.' She turns to Mary because she recognises immediately that she will need an ally in this new venture. 'Will you help me with my first play, Aunt Mary?'

The request fills Joseph with hope, hope that from now his daughter will grow closer to the woman he wishes to become her new mother. Mary, too, is surprised but gratified.

'Indeed, Mary-Ann, and my gift to you is the story of *Cinderella.*' She hands her niece a package containing backdrops and characters to cut out and colour. When Mary-Ann spies the state coach in which sits Cinderella, her joy is unbounded. With sparkling eyes, she kisses her aunt and beams at her family.

Frannie is aware that things are happening and wishes to join in but toy theatres are not for little fingers and she is diverted with various stuffed animals and the felt ball made by her sister which contains a little bell which tinkles as she tosses it about.

Ann Addy views the scene and is satisfied. Just as it should be, she thinks. She no longer cares what the world says?

During the afternoon the girls play contentedly, Ann Addy nods in her chair, Joseph falls asleep and Mary watches. Watches and reflects.

At the first sign of tiredness, Mary whisks Frannie and Mary-Ann into the kitchen, leaving mother and son to doze on undisturbed in the firelight. Soon both girls are fed and are taken upstairs. Mary adds more coal to the nursery fire and slips into Mrs Addy's room to light the ready-laid coals for when she retires later. Mary-Ann talks to Henrietta, recounting the excitement of the day, while her aunt changes Frannie and lays her down in her cot.

'Your turn now, Miss.' Tonight there is no quibble from Mary-Ann who places her best doll in her box and quickly undresses in front of the flaming fire. Mary positions the guard in front of the grate to avoid sparks leaping out onto the child's nightdress, and moves the felt-covered hot water flask further down the bed.

'In you go, and why don't you try to dream up a story for your new theatre? We can show your cousins tomorrow what you have planned.' Mary-Ann nods, closes her eyes and drifts away with thoughts of Cinderella, the Prince and Dandini.

Mary turns away. Now downstairs to spend her evening with her own Prince Charming?

CHAPTER 15

1849 Christmas

Ann Addy wakes to the soothing tick of the grandfather clock and the settling of logs burning low in the hearth. Joseph dozes in his chair. Seven o'clock chimes.

'This won't do,' exclaims his mother and he jolts awake. 'We need more wood on the fire, Joseph.' She suspects the girls are long gone to bed and that Mary will be doing something useful in the kitchen.

Joseph finds his sister-in-law at the kitchen table, laying out a selection of bread and cheese with his mother's special pickle. She smiles up at him as he enters. 'I thought we might feel peckish a little later, despite our big dinner.' He crosses towards the back door and grins at her sheepishly.

'Well, I'm ashamed to say that I do feel somewhat hungry, but not for overmuch. That will do very well. I'll just stoke the fires and let Mother know.'

Mary is happy not to be walking up the lane tonight, back to her lonely cottage, no light or fire to welcome her. This has been a happy day, so far.

The three of them sit at the kitchen table and cut into the Stilton cheese that Ann Addy ordered from the market. A large raised game pie is retrieved from the larder.

'I had Dinah make this for when the family comes tomorrow. They'll be arriving at different times throughout the day and always welcome a bite to eat. No harm if we take a slice for now, just to check it's up to her usual standard,' the old lady excuses with a chuckle.

Joseph's knife cuts into the glazed golden crust and through the chunks of rabbit and venison. The jelly glistens on the dark meat and Mary cannot remember when she last enjoyed such a delicacy.

A game of cards is proposed and the three sit at the baize-covered table placed comfortably closer to the fire and play a few hands of whist. A bottle of Madeira wine is open on a side table and Joseph tops up their glasses as the evening progresses. Mary is happy to be playing cards. It avoids the need for conversation other than pleasantries.

The clock strikes nine o'clock. Ann Addy straightens in her chair.

'Forgive me, both. I can no longer continue. My back aches too much and I feel the need for my bed.' Joseph stands to help move her chair and to support her on the painful journey up the stairs.

'Thank you, my dear Mary, for all you have done for us today. What could have been a sad time for us all has turned out to be a gentle happy occasion. I hope you won't be too cramped up in the nursery tonight and that Frannie sleeps through without disturbing you.'

Mary blushes at the kind words. 'Oh Mrs Addy, it has been my pleasure. It was so kind of you to invite me to join you all. I cannot remember such a happy Christmas Day in many years.'

'Come, Mother, let's be doing.' Joseph lends his arm and the two figures fill the doorway as they head up the chilly stairs.

Left alone in the parlour, Mary feels a tremor of panic. It is too early for her to go up to bed but the prospect of another hour alone with Joseph fills her with a mixture of emotions. The Madeira wine and the warmth of the room have relaxed her in a way she has not experienced before. She feels comfortable and safe but fears that Joseph will use this opportunity to press her for an answer to his proposal. She reaches for her bag, removes a small book and chooses a chair beside a lamp. By the time Joseph is returned, she appears absorbed in the pages of her novel.

He returns the card table and chairs to their usual positions around the room. He takes the poker and pushes the charcoaled wood to the back of the fire. He selects a log from the basket, one that will burn up and brighten the next hour or so of the evening. If he can sustain the cosy atmosphere a little longer, maybe it will work in his favour. He places the log onto the hot embers and straightens up, the while watching flames welcome the newcomer. Soon the dry wood starts to crackle and flame up in its turn. Satisfied at his handiwork, Joseph takes his place in an easy chair opposite Mary. She feels obliged to look up.

'Your mother safely to bed?'

'That she is, God bless her. Though I am not sure she has many Christmases left in her. It grieves me to see how she has aged in the last year.'

Mary nods but refrains from speaking. She fears being trapped in questions about the future.

Intuitively, Joseph turns the subject away from his family and to hers, asking solicitously about her two brothers, their wives, children, their work. Mary is glad to tell him about the progress of the two men, both having chosen to move into Doncaster to make a living. She worries about them living in such smoky, unhealthy conditions, but acknowledges that there is more money for them there than out here on the land.

'I suppose it's a question of chicken or egg, which comes first? The men move into the towns to seek more money, leaving a shortage of hands to work the land, therefore more machinery is needed. Or do farmers prefer to invest in one implement that will do the job of five men who then have to look for work elsewhere.' He scratches his head at the conundrum.

'There has always been change, Joseph, and there always will be. We just need to keep up with it otherwise we won't survive.' He likes her use of the word 'we'.

'I just want to do what's best for the farm, Mary. The harvests of the last few years have been poor and the price we receive for grain continues to fall. We may be tenant farmers but Addys have tended the land hereabouts for generations. My brother, Godfrey, already has sons to follow him, but I don't want to be the last one in my line and see the farm fail under my management.' He stops short, disturbed at where the conversation has drifted, despite his good intentions.

Mary blushes as she recognises his embarrassment. She studies the book in her hand, its inexpensive cloth cover, the title printed in black across the front and the spine. Her finger slowly traces a wandering path across its surface. Where will it all lead? Her heart aches for this kind man, but what he asked of her is too much. She seeks to ease his sadness.

'Joseph, please believe me when I say that I fully understand your situation. It was wrong of me to walk away from you without a word when you spoke to me in the summer. The enormity of what you proposed simply took my breath away.'

He covers his eyes with a hand. This is precisely not what he wanted tonight. He wanted to pretend, just for one evening, that they were comfortable in each other's company, that this is what it might be one day.

'Please Mary, let's say no more.' He drops his hand and looks over to her. 'I regret having spoken to you as I did. It was wrong and I should never have put you in that position. Please say you forgive me.'

'Of course, but there is nothing to forgive. I repeat, I understand that you must find a wife to be mother to your girls, perhaps one day to bring you sons who will farm at your side. And with your mother ailing, you must hasten to do so.' The passion in her voice surprises him. She puts her book to one side and stands. 'The woman you choose to be your wife will know her good fortune in finding a truly fine man in you, Joseph Addy. She will be proud to be at your side in raising your children and to give support as you farm your land. Everyone around here knows you as a fair master of your men and that you work as hard if not harder than the best of them. No, let me continue.' She raises a hand as he seeks to interrupt. 'With Elizabeth it was a true love match on both sides. The woman you take for your next wife will live in her shadow and will know that such love can never be repeated. But take heart, Joseph, respect for each other, affection even, will grow into a companionship which will bring reward in time. I pray you find such a good woman soon.'

Joseph groans in despair and looks away. Mary walks over and places a hand on his shoulder.

'Nay, Joseph. Do you not believe what I say?'

He lifts his hand and covers hers. He cannot speak. Mary fears the closeness and gently extricates her hand. He stands and looks down at her, his face contorted with anguish.

'Mary, can you not see, the woman I wish to be my wife is you.'

Distressed at his words yet excited by his closeness, she sighs and turns away. Seated once more, she reaches for her book and returns it to her bag. After a long silence which Joseph dares not break, in case she walks away again, Mary looks up at him bleakly.

'How could it be, Joseph? How could it be done?'

Hope leaps within him. She has not refused him. He digs deep into the thoughts and plans of recent months and takes time to respond. This is the chance to allay her fears, though his solution is not without peril. He longs to sit beside her and take her hand in reassurance but instead resumes his seat opposite her.

'The law forbids a man from marrying his deceased wife's sister. Whether we agree with the rectitude of such a law matters not. It is a fact. But we know that some people have found ways around it. Not legal, to be sure, but maybe enough. The way chosen by such people is devious and that goes against everything I have ever been taught. Honesty is my way but in this case the law will force me to be devious too.

'Everyone knows I need help with my girls and soon. There are two options open to me, either to engage a nursemaid or to marry. Do I want a stranger come to live in my home? Frankly, no.

'The second option is to marry again. Yes, but whom? Where do I go to meet a suitable lady? Other than going to market and to church, I hardly ever leave the farm. There is nobody suitable for me to marry. I've no illusions of romance at this age. What I wish for is the affection of a good woman who would bring companionship into my life and care and love into the lives of my daughters. Yes, I would want a son, if God permitted, but my first priority above all else is the care of Mary-Ann and Frannie.' He clears his throat and sips from the glass of Madeira at his side.

'So, how might this be achieved? From what I understand, those couples who have gone through with such a marriage have done so at a distance from their home. It is well recognised that not all clergy are supportive of this law and in any case, there are many parsons who will marry anyone without asking questions too closely.

'So, let us assume that such a marriage service can be arranged. What next? How would my new wife be received by those I hold dear and by the community in which I live? Most important to me will be the views of my daughters. That problem is halved as Frannie is too young to have an opinion and will accept whomsoever I choose. The problem is totally removed with regard to Mary-Ann as I would not have chosen the lady in the first place did she not have my daughter's acceptance. As for my mother, law-abiding as she is, nonetheless she has no qualms and supports me fully.

'My wider family?' Josephs shrugs his shoulders. 'I would hope for their love and forbearance and I believe my sister would be relieved to see any solution to my predicament. With regard to my brother, I don't imagine he would give it a second thought, although maybe his wife would be less accepting. As we don't see much of them, I think that my new wife and I could live with the occasional cold shoulder.

'Sadly, I cannot see that we would be accepted at All Saints. That thought grieves me as I would hope that the loving God would look kindly upon my situation and would welcome into his church a good woman as mother to my girls and wife at my side. Pray God that our friends, neighbours and the folk who work for me will not shun me. Some will but most will not, especially if the woman at my side is already admired and respected as a loving and dutiful daughter and,' he hesitates finally, 'sister.'

Mary clasps her hands in her lap and does not look up. So many of her unspoken questions answered, so many fears expressed. Could she take a step of such magnitude?

'Joseph, I have the highest admiration for you as a man, as a father. I thank you for your honesty. It would be wrong for me to accept your offer …' His heart plummets. 'But so would it be wrong to reject it. Please let me sleep on it. Let me awake tomorrow with my mind clear and I shall tell you tomorrow whether or not I could be your wife. Until then, I wish you good night.' She rises and swiftly departs the room.

In the nursery by the light of a single candle, Mary slips out of her best dress and into her nightgown. The bed which awaits her does not offer the same comfort as her own but as she lies on the lumpy mattress, she knows that sleep would evade her even on the softest goose down.

Despite the enormity of the decision she must take, she feels strangely at peace. To hear spoken aloud the challenges that have crowded in on her over recent months, to hear Joseph's measured tones articulate the likely outcome of his plan, all bring clarity to her mind. Her life as it stands cannot continue. To follow Joseph's path would be difficult but she would have his support along the way. The alternative path is obscure and full of difficulty, if not danger. She takes comfort that Ann Addy is aware of the dilemma and has chosen reason, not convention. Her support as a mother-in-law would counter the wagging tongues of the village shop. The people of the parish? She would regret not being able to worship at the church she has attended since childhood.

What would her mother have said? She was a God-fearing woman but one who had lived through hard times and would not wish them on her younger daughter. She cares little for what her brothers might say and even less for the opinion of her sisters-in-law. Indeed, they would be relieved of the obligation to house her in later years. But what of her sister? What would Elizabeth have said? Her sister's death came too swiftly for any discussion about Joseph and a future marriage, though Elizabeth was a practical soul and would expect him to re-marry. But marry her sister? With a ten years' age gap, the sisters were never close but nor did they squabble. They were of different natures: Elizabeth headstrong and assured; Mary more thoughtful, but less confident.

Finally, there are the nieces. Mary adores young Frannie and has no concerns about bringing her up as her own. She has no illusions about Mary-Ann. She can never replace the girl's mother and nor would she wish to. Raising Joseph's elder daughter will not be without difficulty and the girl will challenge her all along the way. Could she cope with constant confrontation from a child who will need a mother's love and guidance as she grows into a young woman? Indeed, she must, for the sake of her dead sister.

Mary turns onto her side and from the glow of the dying embers in the grate she makes out the silhouette of Mary-Ann, curled up in her small bed. Frannie is hidden from view but the sound of her dream-induced snuffles reaches out across the room. Mary is content with her decision.

CHAPTER 16

1849 Christmas

Dinah is back at her post early the next morning though the rings under her eyes tell tales of a late night. She carries hot water up to the nursery for Mary to wash herself and the children.

'A good evening, then?'

Mary chooses to ignore the impertinent question and counters: 'Did you manage to meet your young man yesterday? How lovely that next Christmas Day you will be together.' Dinah is easily diverted by talk of her forthcoming marriage and does not pursue her prying. Her family knows that Mary slept the night at the farm and today the story will be broadcast more widely. Conjecture is rife in the village.

Ann Addy is absent from the breakfast table and Mary is conscious that she sits with the girls and Joseph, the model of a happy family. He is not long returned from overseeing the milking as they are one man down this morning. His face looks strained, his eyes heavy from lack of sleep. Her final words had been hopeful, but what if he was deluded and now she is of another mind?

Mary-Ann chatters on, excited that today there would be visits from family, each bearing a small gift for her. She is anxious to set up her toy theatre but is mindful that some cousins are clumsy clods.

'Father, shall I build my theatre on the table in the dining room? I would like to show it to some of my cousins but it must be out of reach of the little ones. Their fingers would be less respectful.' He offers to help her set out the theatre and raises a questioning eyebrow in Mary's direction.

Mary starts to clear the table: 'I too would be glad to assist, Mary-Ann, but I must return to my home this morning. You have many of your family visiting and I do not wish to be in the way.'

Joseph is distressed at the thought of her leaving them today and touches the shoulder of his daughter.

'Mary-Ann, before I help with your theatre, please would you be so kind as to go up to your Grandmother. Dinah is aiding her with dressing and I know would be glad of your assistance.'

The girl is puzzled at the request but knows better than to argue. As the door latches behind her, Joseph leans across the table to where Mary is wiping porridge from Frannie's face.

'Please don't leave us today, Mary. In any case, we need time together. Last night …

His sister-in-law smiles and leans towards him, her hands clasped before her on the table.

'My answer, Joseph, is yes, I should be honoured to become your wife.' As his eyes light up she puts a finger to her lips. 'But we must tread gently and slowly. For me to be at your side today would not be advisable. I can see from your face that a weight has been removed from your shoulders but we are still a few weeks away from the twelve months since Elizabeth was buried. Were I to remain when the family call today, you would not be able to hide your feelings and your sister and sister-in-law would soon deduce what you plan. Better I slip away and return later to put the girls to bed.'

'My dear Mary. I am without words. Thank you, thank you from my heart.' He wants to hold her hand but knows this is not the moment. 'Though I regret it, I understand and respect your decision to return home. We shall speak further this evening, my dear.' His face is aglow with pleasure and he leaves the kitchen, calling Mary-Ann to descend and set up her theatre. Mary sits back in her chair. It is done. Well, not done exactly; this is but the beginning.

*

Joseph is glad to hear the arrival of his sister Nancy, accompanied by her husband William Stacey and two of their children, Charles and Eliza. He likes William and looks forward to hearing about his brother-in-law's farm, half as big again as Joseph's, located across the Don in Armthorpe, not far from Wheatley Hall. Mary-Ann runs out to greet her older cousins who she hopes will make a fuss of her and admire her new toy theatre. Nancy descends stiffly from the trap and her brother observes that at fifty and after seven children she is even stouter. He welcomes them all and Nancy draws him to one side.

'Tell me Brother, how is it with our Mother? Is there anything you need me to say or do? I know how stubborn she can become.' They walk slowly towards the back door and he shrugs, longing to say that she need worry no more as a solution is found. Instead, he shakes his head.

'Her back troubles her greatly and the stairs are the bane of her life. She comes downstairs mid-morning, struggles to get comfortable during the day, eats her dinner then spends the afternoon lying down on the sofa, sleeping as best she can. Come the evening, she takes to her bed earlier and earlier. The doctor recommends laudanum for the pain but as it makes her so sleepy, she puts off taking it until really necessary. It saddens me to see her so. But come, look for yourself.'

During the visit, Nancy quizzes her mother about her health, the running of the household, the farm and, of course, the care of Joseph's girls.

'What of that Mary? I see she is not with you today. Is she sick? How long will she stay? Do you pay her? How much? You cannot carry on like this. Do you want me to find a nursemaid or a governess? Young Mary-Ann is a confident young thing.' The last comment is not a compliment.

The Staceys are about to take their leave after a meal of cheese, cold cuts, pickles and Dinah's game pie, acclaimed by all. The sound of an approaching horse and trap heralds the arrival of their brother, Godfrey and family. Nancy delays her departure.

'Good day, Brother. It was too cold at church yesterday to do more than exchange wishes and gifts.' Godfrey herds in his four eldest children, three lads and ten-year-old Frances, and apologises for the absence of his wife and the three youngest.

'How fares your Susannah and new baby, John?' Ann Addy is fond of her daughter-in-law and proud that the Addy name will continue through Godfrey's five sons.

Joseph directs the children where to take coats and bids Dinah to make up a brew of tea for their new guests. Mary-Ann is thrilled to see more cousins and pulls Frances by the hand, determined that she will be first to admire her toy theatre.

Godfrey talks quietly with his mother who tries to disguise her constant discomfort. On his insistence, she takes to the sofa and lies sipping her tea as the younger children roister around her. She watches them and reflects: *We did well, my John and me. Not perfect, but all in all, a good family. A body could die happy with less.*

After the menfolk have exchanged views on the state of their respective farms and the upcoming weather, the Staceys take their leave but not before Nancy has wagged her finger at both her brothers: 'Mother cannot continue like this. Joseph, you must find more help with the house and with those girls. It cannot carry on like this.'

Joseph agrees and reassures them that he has a plan and will inform them very soon. He wants so badly to tell them, but is mindful of Mary's request to refrain until the year of mourning for Elizabeth has elapsed.

Godfrey does not linger. He is anxious to return in daylight through the lanes to his farm in nearby Arksey. He feels sorrow for his brother's situation, newly widowed, two little girls and his ailing mother to care for. A new wife is the only solution but the man hardly leaves the farm so where on earth he is to find someone, Heaven only knows.

By the time that Mary pushes open the back door and shakes the rain from her cloak, the house is restored to calm, other than for Mary-Ann. She has had the most wonderful day showing off the new toy to her cousins who, like her, have never visited a real live theatre. She is still bubbling with ideas of what spectaculars she wants to create and perform to her family.

'It has been a grand day, thank you Mary. Mother is still resting in the parlour and I shall sit with her. If Dinah can put tea on the table, we can have the lasses fed and up to bed.' She takes from his strained politeness that he is anxious to spend time alone with his mother and she can guess the reason.

Joseph leaves the bustle of the kitchen and enters the parlour, cosy in lamp and firelight. His mother, stretched out on the sofa, opens her eyes as he enters. He notes the empty glass at her side. Another dose of laudanum.

'Mother, I have good news. Mary has agreed to be my wife.'

Her eyes open wide then close. In relief? In concern? Both?

'Joseph, the pair of you have made a very difficult choice, but you have my blessing. No matter how others may regard your situation in future, I shall stand by your side. I only wish I were stronger in health and could go out and meet any dissenters face to face.' Her vehemence touches him deeply.

'Will you speak with Mary this evening, after she has put the lasses to bed? It would strengthen her greatly to hear from your lips that we have your support.'

Later, Mary enters the warmth of the parlour. How different from last evening's game of cards. Tonight, this is no contest of chance. The die is cast. She has chosen a course and only Fate knows where it will lead.

Mary is aware of a change within her. Yesterday she felt cast adrift, unsure of where life would take her. Now, with her mind made up, she feels a surge of courage and enters the parlour, head high, hands held before her but no longer meekly.

'Ah, my dear Mary. Forgive me for not sitting up but I'm uncomfortable and feel so sleepy these days. Joseph has told me of your decision and I thought it best for us to speak of it alone, just the two of us.'

The firelight flickers and shadows prance around the room. Mary admires the old lady's snow-white hair held in check by a black lace cap, closely tied under her chin. She takes a straight-backed chair and brings it into the line of sight.

'Thank you, Mrs Addy, I am glad of the opportunity to talk to someone about it.' She will not admit that she has sought advice already from Elizabeth Vazin.

'These have been hard times for us all, this last twelve months. You lost your sister and your mother so close together but you did your duty by both of them and now you continue to do so by us.' She holds Mary's gaze. 'I think we are agreed that our first responsibility is to care for Elizabeth's daughters. No need to discuss 'owt else. Joseph has chosen the path he thinks best for him and I cannot find a better solution, even though what he proposes is outside the law. However, as far as I'm concerned, it is a bad law and one which can only harm loving Christian families.'

Mary lowers her eyes. Mention of the law and Christianity pains her deeply. She takes a deep breath. 'Would that the law were otherwise, but it is not and the gossip and opprobrium which will follow our marriage cannot be worse than if I were to live here unwed. That I have your understanding and support fortifies me in what is to come.'

'Well said, lass. Come, give me your kiss. You deserve happiness and I hope that with my son you will find contentment at least.' As Mary leans over her, she offers up her cheek. 'Please call Joseph to join us. We must discuss matters in more depth.'

Mary finds Joseph in the kitchen. He stands talking to Dinah, now resting her feet by the fireside and wondering what the Missus has been doing with Mary in the parlour and Himself prowling around, keeping out of the way. Mary is usually off up the road by now.

'Joseph, your mother would like a word please.' Dinah raises her eyebrows as the pair disappear together. What's afoot?

Mrs Addy has swung her feet around to the floor and sits with her right hand resting on an ebony-topped cane.

'So, Joseph, what now?'

Mary takes a seat in an armchair and Joseph stands facing both women, his back to the hearth. His silhouette against the fire is broad, steady.

'Within a few weeks we shall reach the anniversary of Elizabeth's passing. I had thought that shortly afterwards it would be suitable to tell close family and friends of our intentions. On reflection, that would be the wrong decision. It would permit those dissenters to raise their voices against us at a time when we shall need conviction to go forward with our plan. Instead, I shall use the coming months to find a church that will marry us.

'My first thought was London but we do not have any connections there and to travel so far in order to achieve anonymity seems unnecessary when there are many towns and cities within easier reach where we could find sympathetic folk to aid us without censure.' He walks about the room, the better to marshal his thoughts.

'I am minded to go down to Sheffield. Mary, you know the town better than I and your guidance would be welcome. Do you know people there who might be sympathetic to our cause? You would need to stay in the town for the three weeks while the banns are read in church.'

Mary is startled that he has thought so far ahead already. She only said 'yes' this morning. This has been a plan in his mind for some time. She raises a quizzical eyebrow and Joseph continues swiftly: 'Do you have someone in mind, Mary? I had not thought that the Websters would look kindly on such subterfuge.' Her frown makes him regret use of the word 'subterfuge'. She smiles back at him. She cannot afford to be thin-skinned about words at this stage. They will only become more hurtful in the months to come.

'Let me think about it, Joseph, but that sounds like a good place to start. Now, I must away, it is late. May I suggest I leave you both here? I fear that young Dinah suspects that something is up and we are not ready to disclose our plans just yet.' She nods to them both and although Joseph feels he should take her hand, show some degree of warmth towards this woman who today agreed to be his wife, he stands apart and nods farewell.

CHAPTER 17

1850 January

A new decade begins. For Joseph it is just another working day. As usual, he wakes to the clatter of steaming milk pails carried across the yard to the dairy. But wait, for him this is the beginning of the year which will lead either to disaster or success.

Mary wakes to the New Year and lies in the darkness praying silently that God will forgive her coming sins. Whether the Lord heeds her, she knows not, and if he chooses not to forgive, so be it. The freezing cold greets her as she slides from the covers and pushes her toes into her slippers. The more quickly she is dressed and out of the house, the sooner she will be on her way to the farm, the warm kitchen and the pot of tea that awaits her.

Mary-Ann hears Dinah rise and dress but snuggles down. Last night her grandmother instructed her to make a wish the moment she woke on New Year's morning. Then, as she lay down and Mary tucked blankets around her, she considered what that wish might be. Now, as Dinah coaxes a fire in the nursery hearth and Mary lifts Frannie from her cot, she remembers. She screws up her still closed eyes. *Please bring back mother.*

Ann Addy's 1850 will not start for an hour or so, when the weak January daylight suggests its way through the chinks of the bedroom curtains. Not only will this be her last decade, it will also be her last New Year's Day. She suspects as much and is not dismayed.

*

The winter is unrelenting. Each day is a struggle for the farmers to feed their stock, milk their cows, bring their produce to market, whatever the weather. Each morning, Mary walks her niece to the crossroads where they meet other scholars heading for the school in Arksey. The straggle of children of varying ages is shepherded each day by a different mother. She hates when it is her turn to walk them along the lanes, through the mud, the frozen ruts, sometimes deep snow. The older ones give cheek, the youngest ones dutifully hold hands. Mary-Ann keeps herself apart. Her special school friend, Susan lives in Arksey and they will meet in the classroom, barely warm despite the coal fire in the corner. At this time of year there is less excuse for the older lads to miss their schooling, but come the spring and summer, when there is much to do on the land, the parents of able-bodied sons need their hands to lighten the burden and the boys willingly skip their classes.

As she trudges back from Arksey, Mary pulls her cloak tightly under her chin and has time to reflect upon her position. Ostensibly nothing is different but in reality, everything is. She is conscious of the implicit change in her status within the house. The way that Joseph and Ann Addy address her has altered, albeit subtly. They speak more warmly and include her in exchanges of opinion and even decision making. Dinah might have noticed but she is off and away come February. A new girl has been found, Harriet; at twenty-one, a similar age to her predecessor but more experienced and hopefully with her mind more on the job in hand.

It is rare for Mary to be alone with Joseph and when so, she still feels a reticence. Not exactly shyness, more uncertainty. Neither has any illusions about the transaction that they embark upon, but she welcomes the softening in his manner towards her.

It encourages her and she is glad that some months remain before the deed, to allow her to cultivate a greater degree of tenderness towards Joseph. Hitherto it has never crossed her mind to think of her deceased sister's husband as other than a brother. Which draws her back yet again to the law which hangs over them like the sword of Damocles.

*

It is this fear of the law which nags away at Joseph. He needs to understand the implications of what he has in mind but fears to reveal his plan to any other. Soon after he and Elizabeth wed, he drove into Doncaster to visit the chambers of Baxter and Somerville, the solicitors who had drawn up the testaments of his father and elder brothers. When setting up his own will, he had become friendly with one of the clerks, Henry King, whom he had known at school in Arksey. Maybe a conversation would clarify the situation.

They meet in a tavern over a mutton pie and a glass of ale. Joseph comes quickly to the matter.

'I need to re-marry for my daughters' sake. My mother is old and infirm. Frankly, the cost of a governess is beyond me with farming as it is.' The clerk nods. His chambers are handling a number of bankruptcies of farmers in the region, particularly tenant farmers who cannot borrow against the value of the land they work.

'But I wouldn't want you to think that my consideration is financially grounded, my first wish is for the wellbeing of the girls. Henry, I need your total discretion although I accept you cannot promise such until you hear my question.' The clerk shuffles uneasily in his chair and looks about the room to check who might over-hear them.

'My dear Elizabeth had a sister, Mary, much younger than her. It is she who comes each day to care for the girls and in my view, and that of my mother, she would make an ideal mother for

Mary-Ann and Frannie. I wish to marry her.' He sits back in his chair and watches his old school-friend take in the full import of Joseph's declaration. Both men drink deep in the ensuing silence. Joseph continues: 'I am fully aware of what the law states in this regard but what I need to understand is what is likely to be the outcome if we are successful in marrying in a church where we are unknown?'

'The discretion you ask is fully promised, old friend.' Henry smiles sympathetically and runs the back of his hand across his forehead. 'However, I have not come across such a case within our chambers so would need to investigate further. I imagine you have considered the repercussions in terms of your position within your community and are more concerned about likely penalties in legal terms.'

'How would the law regard any children born to such a marriage?' Joseph is thinking ahead. There is no need to discuss with Henry how he and Mary would weather the possible reaction of family, friends and neighbours.

'My immediate recollection is that such a marriage would be regarded as void by both the ecclesiastical courts and by the law of the land. The implications of that would be that your children would be regarded as illegitimate and therefore ineligible to inherit as of right.' Joseph frowns and Henry hastens to add: 'However, there would be nothing to stop you making a will which stipulates to whom you bequeath whatsoever you wish. This would solve your problem.'

Joseph sits in silence. Iniquitous law to render his future children bastards. Henry remembers more.

'You should take heart, though. For some years Parliament has been debating a bill for the reversal of the 1835 Marriage Act, even more so since a Royal Commission investigated the situation. Many influential politicians wish to see it scrapped. It is only a matter of time and surely such a division of support would indicate that a marriage as you propose would be acceptable to many and that the majority of others would turn a blind eye.'

This intelligence is indeed helpful and as Joseph rides homewards, he ponders on what his friend has revealed. Yes, a marriage to Mary would be against the law, strictly speaking, but the actual ramifications would not be as severe as he had feared.

*

Mary rehearses her words. Mark has always treated her kindly and his chosen trade has moulded his outlook on life. Live and let live. But will this be a step too far even for her older brother? Certainly, her younger brother, Henry, would disown her if he knew of her plan. It is a bright morning early in March when Joseph drives Mary into Doncaster. Mary-Ann believes her aunt is visiting the dress-maker. Ann Addy knows there is another destination in mind.

As they pass the last cottages on leaving the village, they are greeted by elderly men, now too old to work on the farms but still drawn to the soil. With the sleeves of their collar-less shirts rolled to the elbows, waistcoats still buttoned up against the fresh breeze, each cottager tills his tiny patch of land, planting vegetables to sustain them through the year. Joseph waves at each in turn and they speed on through the thin sunshine. Making their way through a town thronged with market-goers, they stop in Corn Market where Mary alights and walks through the crowd into New Street where the George vies for trade with numerous other hostelries.

Avoiding the tap room, Mary enters the inn through the kitchen door to be greeted stiffly by her sister-in-law, none too pleased that Mary arrives unexpectedly. Mary senses the irritation and, after fussing over the latest baby, suggests she might take a walk with her brother. Mark's wife struggles between relief for her to be gone and curiosity for the purpose of her visit.

'Well Mary, now that the year of mourning for our sister and mother is past, what do you intend to do with your life?' It is a Hall family trait to come straight to the point. Mary takes her brother's arm and smiles to herself.

'That is why I am here to talk to you, Mark.' She is glad to be at his side and not speaking to his face.

'Will you return to Sheffield and find a position there? You must find life very narrow stuck at the Addy's farm with the old woman breathing down your neck.' Mary frowns. Is that how people see her life now?

'I think not, Brother. To be a companion is fraught with problems. An older lady will eventually die; a younger one will, one supposes, eventually marry. Either way, no post is assured for long and there will come a time when I am too old to seek such work.' She hesitates. 'And I do not wish to become a burden to my remaining family.'

'So, what is your plan, Mary? Have you found a beau lurking in the pews of Arksey church who will take you in marriage?' He chuckles at his wit and she stops in her tracks, stony-faced.

'Do you imagine that nobody would wish to do so? Am I that plain that a man would not desire me for his wife?'

'Lord, no.' Mark is genuinely crestfallen that his words have injured her. It is just that she has never walked out with anyone, as far as he knows.

'What I am about to say will no doubt disappoint you, maybe even anger you. It is, however, the path I have chosen and I wish you to swear solemnly that you will tell nobody of it, not even your wife. Will you do that, Mark, on our mother's name?'

Surprised by her tone, he nods and raises his hand as though taking an oath. 'I swear.'

'And promise you won't tell our brother, Henry. He was always a bright lad and has set his own course. He will do well, no doubt, and I don't want him mithered with my problems.'

Slowly and allowing no interruption, Mary lays before him Joseph Addy's proposal, her concerns, her decision and the declared support of Mrs Addy. They have wandered off the main thoroughfare and now stand in the more secluded Bower's Fold. Mark leans against a wall and pushes back his cap. This news he never would have predicted. Mary regards her brother, noting with sadness his flushed face and the odour of beer on his breath so early in the day.

Mary takes advantage of his shocked silence and continues: 'Mark, we need your help but I am anxious for the sake of your reputation and your livelihood to distance you from the deed. You have spoken in the past of an old schoolfriend who now lives in Sheffield. That's where Joseph and I believe we can be wed. We cannot do it anonymously, but if we go to a town where our circumstances are unknown, our small deceit will go unremarked. Would you write an introduction for Joseph and myself to meet your friend in Sheffield to discuss our situation?'

Mark removes his cap and runs a hand through his hair. He stares about the alley, unable to meet his sister's eye.

'Dear God, Mary. What are you at? Have you taken leave of your senses? You will deliberately flout the law? What penalty do you risk?'

'Please Mark, don't take on so. We know it will not be easy but you must read in the papers that there are many in Parliament who wish to see this cruel law withdrawn. Yes, there will be those who decry what we do, but others, more merciful in their judgement, will look the other way and be kind to us, or at the very least ignore what has happened.'

'But your children, Mary, surely you will have children? What of them?' Mary turns from him in embarrassment and looks the length of the lane back to where the main road bustles with carts and people about their business.

She speaks into nowhere with a flat voice: 'Indeed, in the eyes of the law, any children will not be legitimate, but Joseph is a good man and will ensure that they and I are looked after in the event of misadventure.'

'So, if he dies leaving you with little ones, there will be a roof over your head? A tenant farmer cannot assure that, my lass.' Mary's face reveals her anxiety as he questions her prospects. But what other are her options? The decision is made.

Before escorting his sister back to the ale-house, Mark Hall promises to write to his friend, Samuel Binns, requesting that he receive Joseph at his house in Sheffield to hear out his request. As they turn the corner, the couple see a waiting trap ahead of them, Joseph seated leaning forward with elbows on his knees, the reins loose in his hands. He is deep in thought and unaware of their approach. Mark pauses. *So, Joseph sent Mary alone to ask for help. Hiding behind her petticoats.*

'Sister, I shall leave you now. Go to Joseph and with my blessing, but right now I have no words for him. It is too soon.' He bends forward and kisses her forehead beneath the brim of her black felt bonnet. She shrinks from his beery breath but is immediately ashamed. Her brother will not let her down.

Joseph smiles down at Mary as she approaches. He descends to help her into the trap and sees the back of his brother-in-law moving swiftly away, not stopping to bid him the time of day. A sign of how it will be? He has never had much time for Mark. Word has it that he drinks the profits as soon as he makes them. Some husband, some father.

CHAPTER 18

1850 Early Spring

It is Joseph's first time. He wishes to appear at ease but is not. Apart from his mother and Mary, people think he is at market. Instead, he is travelling by railway to Sheffield. At the temporary station in Doncaster, soon to be replaced by a smart new building in time for the September races, he hesitates, fearful of taking the wrong train.

He is curious to examine his fellow passengers but they are so closely packed in the small carriage that a glance is construed as a stare. That consideration does not hinder the lass opposite, perhaps twelve years of age, her blond curls reminiscent of his Mary-Ann. Good Heavens, how long before he loses his little girl and has to deal with a pretty creature with a mind of her own, just like this young miss. She stares at him, examining his clothes, his shoes and his hat held awkwardly on his knee. The luggage rack above is stuffed with parcels and packages, leaving no room for his Sunday hat of brown felt with its low crown and wide brim.

The young girl's companion, her mother or perhaps governess, sits uncomfortably bolt upright in the corner of the carriage, overwhelmed by her crushed crinoline. Joseph is reminded of one of his hens in a nesting box. Thank heavens his Elizabeth never resorted to such nonsense. Her gowns were quietly fashionable, or so he supposed. He has chosen a carriage as far from the locomotive as possible. Experienced travellers recommend it as expedient in order to avoid the risk of burning embers and smuts flying in through the windows.

As he looks out of the carriage, somewhat perturbed by the speed at which they are travelling, his mind wanders to what might be Mary's tastes. Her choice of simple clothes is no doubt dictated by a lack of money. He would like to see her set up well, particularly for their wedding day. It may be the second time for him, but for her it will probably be her one special day. Perhaps his mother would give her a gift of money to enable her to choose something suitable.

*

'I've settled the Missus in the parlour.' Elizabeth Vazin swings the heavy kettle onto the hob. The family are grateful for her capable nursing of Ann Addy, now increasingly infirm. She takes no nonsense and insists that the old lady comes downstairs every day, no matter how great a struggle.

Mary puts her sewing to one side, out of reach of Frannie, an inquisitive little soul. She takes cups and saucers from the dresser and opens the crock wherein lies a fresh seedcake. Harriet has settled in well as house-maid and is a better baker than Dinah.

The two sit with their tea and enjoy a slice of cake. Mary is relieved that Harriet is in the dairy making butter, Mary-Ann at school and Mrs Addy resting in the next room. She needs to ask Elizabeth Vazin a great favour and to hold tight a big secret. Her voice is low even though it matters not were Mrs Addy to overhear.

'Joseph is gone to Sheffield today. He is not at the market in Doncaster. That was but a pretence.' Elizabeth Vazin leans back in her chair and nurses her cup. She raises an eyebrow, encouraging more.

'The decision is made. We are to be wed. Yes, I know.' Mary leans across the table to the older woman. 'You, yourself, said I should accept his proposal and indeed I have done so. Our plan is to marry at a church in Sheffield and Joseph is this day meeting with a friend of my brother to ask for his help. If he will allow us to use his home as our address for the reading of the banns, then we are permitted to use the same one for both parties. That way we avoid involving the church at Arksey.'

The older woman toys with the crumbs on her plate and nods as she absorbs the plan. 'So, you would need to live in Sheffield for three weeks to be a resident of the parish. What of Joseph? He could not spare time to be away from the farm that long.'

'No, indeed. It is his intention to travel down three Saturday afternoons running, stay the night in a local hotel and after the reading of the banns at the Sunday morning service, he would return home. With the railway it is possible for him to travel such distances in good time. It is a marvel that he can journey to and from Sheffield in one day, though it disturbs me that these engines travel at such great speed.

'My request to you, Elizabeth, is that you would take my place here for those three weeks of my absence. We need someone we can trust to be discreet in looking after the girls for that time.'

'Mrs Addy is content with your plan?' Mary nods. 'When will you tell Mary-Ann?'

Mary rises from her chair, ostensibly clearing the tea things but in reality to gain time for her answer which she knows will displease.

'Her father will explain that I am her new mother when we return from Sheffield, after we are wed.' She does not permit her friend to question. 'He cannot trust her not to talk about it at school or to the farm hands while I am away. We cannot risk someone, for whatever reason, alerting the authorities to what we have in mind and preventing our union.'

'And the rest of the family?' Elizabeth Vazin can guess at the reaction from Joseph's sister and sister-in-law.

'Mrs Addy will stand by Joseph when he tells them. We know it is likely to be difficult but we must weather the storm for the sake of the children.'

Standing across the table from Elizabeth, she leans forward on her hands.

'I know we shall be shunned by many, maybe within both our families, but we shall be strong.' Her voice drops and her former fervour dissolves into bleak acceptance of her lot. 'What else is there?'

*

The door of the neat semi-detached villa is opened by a housemaid and Joseph is shown into the front parlour. A somewhat portly Samuel Binns walks forward from the fireplace and greets him with a warm hand-shake. He introduces Joseph to his wife, Sophia, a slightly-built woman seated in an upright chair. Tea is brought into the room by the maid and Mrs Binns pours.

The couple are fully aware of the reason for this visit. Mary's brother has written to them, with wording provided by Joseph, explaining the situation and the request. Joseph senses their unease but cannot let that deter him.

'It is a great service that you do to allow me to present my case. I have no doubt that what we are asking will conflict with your understandable unwillingness to go against the law in any way whatsoever.' He has rehearsed these opening lines during the railway journey.

Husband and wife exchange glances, she with a stony face, he with anxiety. Their visitor surmises that Mr Binns is for them, Mrs Binns is agin. Joseph proceeds to paint the picture of their circumstances: a happy marriage cut short, two very young girls in need of a mother who will love them as her own. He alludes to the possible dangers of uncaring step-mothers but veers off that path when he recalls that the couple have not been blessed with children but have a fostered son. He addresses the wife.

'Mrs Binns, Mary has known my daughters since birth and loves them dearly. Frannie has no recollection of her mother, sadly, and has been cared for only by Mary. My older daughter misses her mother, of course, but she is comfortable with her aunt and who knows how she would react to a stranger coming into our home as a new mother?'

Mrs Binns nods briefly and with sympathy. Her mouth relaxes. She asks various questions about the practicalities of what is foreseen and, on an unspoken signal, hands the matter to her husband.

'You will understand that we have thought at length about your situation, Mr Addy, and although we have concerns about contravening the law of the land, we have real reservations about the ethics of this particular law. We do not subscribe to the hypothesis that a sister-in-law is a blood relation, consequently,' Mr Binns smiles broadly at Joseph, 'the law is an ass and we are only too pleased to oblige.'

This hoped for outcome is unexpected, given Mrs Binns' earlier formidable expression, but now she too is smiling gently and Joseph beams his gratitude.

On the return journey, by the time he descends from the railway carriage at Stockbridge station, Joseph has worked out the next stage of the process. Holy Trinity is the church recommended by the Binns and he needs to decide on the preferred timing and work backwards from that point. He cannot wait to reach home with the good news.

*

On the last day of March, as the Reverend Sorsby proclaims the joy of the risen Lord, Joseph sits in his familiar pew and regards the congregation about him. He views the farmers, their weathered faces scrubbed shiny, like himself dressed for Easter in their best or nearly best clothes, each man uncharacteristically at rest. These are men who usually find it hard to sit still for any length of time, unless, in the case of some, with a full tankard of ale in hand. Today each sits alongside his wife and children, children drilled into silence and good behaviour in the House of the Lord. He reproaches himself for the envy he feels for those flanked by so many strapping lads. He counts the children and wonders at the strength of the wives who have given birth to eight, even ten children, to say nothing of those babes who were lost or survived but a short time.

How many of these seemingly upright Christians will turn against him when he returns from Sheffield with his new bride? Joseph knows which neighbours have troubled homes. In this community it is hard to hide the fact when a bully beats his wife and children; when a drunkard relies on his pony to deliver him home from the alehouse; when a philanderer dallies with other women. Yet, as Joseph knows well, not all women are angels. He has seen rugged labourers skulk into the rick-yard sporting a vixen-inflicted black eye. How lucky he was with Elizabeth. A strong-minded woman though never one to scold.

Mary-Ann sits in the pew between her father and aunt. Mary has left a goodly distance between her and the girl. It is noted by the women of the congregation and they suspect that Miss Hall is trying too hard to demonstrate a respectful distance. She cannot win. The same tongues would have criticised had Mary sat closer to her niece. Joseph knows that on such occasions there is no right way to behave. Some people will find fault whatever. Such is the smallness of their world. What would they think if they knew what lay behind their forthcoming journey to Sheffield?

Samuel had made the necessary introductions and Joseph wrote to the parson at Holy Trinity requesting that he and Mary be wed early in June. He gave Samuel's Sheffield address as Mary's place of residence and explained that, out of expedience, he wished to use the same address for reading the banns. Joseph and the Binns held their breath and, just before Easter, were relieved to read that the parson would comply with this unusual, but not illegal, request for a joint address for the betrothed couple.

Joseph regrets that Mary will never enjoy the happiness of a bride-to-be when friends and family congratulate her on her coming marriage. For someone who has always been in service to others, whether working for the Webster family or caring for her sister and mother, Mary deserves to be fussed over. At least his mother recognises the need to bolster Mary and she has offered a gift, a secret betrothal gift, to the girl who will marry her son.

'Please Mary, I wish you to accept this small sum. Your own mother and father are not here to provide you with a trousseau and it would give me great pleasure knowing that you will find some pretty things to wear for your wedding day.'

*

Mary does not try to hide her fear as she awaits the train at Stockbridge station. Even with Joseph at her side, he now a veteran traveller with one return journey already under his belt, she feels light-headed as they stand, slightly distant from each other. Should they be seen by acquaintances either at this little station on the outskirts of Arksey or later in Doncaster where they will board the onward train, they would say that Mary was visiting the family in Sheffield where she had worked previously and Joseph had offered his company on this, her first experience of the railway. It was rather contrived but seemed to satisfy one

Arksey farmer's wife who greeted them with slightly raised eyebrows. The woman would recall the meeting several weeks later when news broke of the illicit marriage.

The pungent smell of smoke, the angry hiss of steam, the grinding clank of metal terrifies Mary as they move across the platform to change trains at Doncaster. For the first time, she wishes to take Joseph's arm but both agree that it would not be appropriate. Her terror continues throughout the journey, compounded by the tightly packed carriage where every word spoken is overheard by fellow passengers. Joseph sits equally uncomfortably at her side so there is no way to exchange messages through eye contact as they hurtle with unconscionable racket through the countryside. Joseph has managed to secure a window seat for her, thinking it will amuse her to view the landscape from a new perspective. He sees now his mistake and her lowered head indicates that she is avoiding sight of fields and woods rushing past at a frightening speed. Should he exchange places? To do so while the vehicle rocks along could be foolhardy and one or both of them could be thrown to the floor.

Sophia Binns stands anxiously at the main entrance to the station in Sheffield. She has yet to experience travel on the railway and is admiring of those who have.

'Miss Hall,' she holds out a gloved hand. 'You are most welcome. And Mr Addy, so good to see you once more.'

She leads them out into the street and sends a boy to secure a cab to take them the short distance to her home. There the couple will rest and refresh themselves with a light luncheon before walking over to Holy Trinity for the arranged meeting with the parson. As it is a weekday, her husband, Samuel is at work.

Over lunch, the two women exchange pleasantries mainly about Mary's previous employment with the Websters. No, Mrs Binns does not know the family. She, like her husband, is not

Sheffield born and bred and they reside in the town only because of Mr Binns' work as a chemist in the dyeing trade.

The meeting with the clergyman does not last above half an hour. His perfunctory questioning is soon satisfied and they agree a date for the marriage ceremony for early in June. The couple confirm they will attend the church for the three previous Sundays, Joseph hands over the required fees and they walk out of the rectory surprised but relieved the matter was settled so easily. They return to the church where Mrs Binns sits quietly in the rear pew, alone with her thoughts of the challenges that await this very nice couple.

Back in Bentley, Joseph drives Mary back to her cottage and helps her down from the trap. Having said all that was needed during the drive from Stockbridge station and with the eyes of neighbouring cottagers upon them, he touches his hat and bids her goodnight. Nobody is fooled.

CHAPTER 19

1850 Early Summer

Mary sits on the edge of the bed and surveys the neat room. It overlooks the tiny garden which fronts the Binns' villa. Joseph has delivered her, on this second occasion only slightly less terrified by the shrieking metal monster that drew them along the iron rails. He has withdrawn to his hotel and tomorrow they will attend the first church service at which the banns will be read. She tries to calm herself but is tense with apprehension. She comforts herself that what they are doing is required for the sake of Elizabeth's daughters; that now her own future is more secure. And yet ... In just over two weeks' time she will be married, of a fashion, to Joseph Addy, her deceased sister's husband. Today, his physical presence beside her on the train brought home the reality that this man is soon to share her bed.

It is evening and the setting sun's rays are reflected in the net-curtained windows of the terraced houses opposite. Her room is in shade and she quietly moves an upright chair closer to the light of the window in order to read. After an early supper with Samuel and Sophia – they insist on first names – she bade them good night and retired to her room to allow them their privacy. She wonders how she will pass the coming weeks so closely confined with strangers, albeit kindly strangers. She picks up another instalment of David Copperfield. Three new chapters.

She is mildly irritated by Mr Dickens' story of his hero's ardour for the empty-headed beauty, Dora. As someone who has known not exactly poverty, but who has had to work for her living and manage on little, Mary is exasperated by Dora's attack of the vapours when her future husband reveals that he has not much money and she will need to cook and manage the household on a shoestring. Can a man really be so besotted that he cannot see that disaster lies ahead? She gazes out at the waning light and thinks of her own future husband.

How does Joseph view her? He has chosen her to be his wife, but that is a practical decision. Does he find her pretty? Does he consider her manner agreeable? He has no idea of what she thinks about matters of the day. They have never spoken at any length about anything, be it how the girls should be raised, how the farm progresses, how she will be accepted by his wider family. She assumes he wants more children. A son, without doubt. Such is the basis of the marriage contract which she will sign within weeks. This is not how she imagined marriage would be though she is wise enough to recognise that the romance in the novels she devours is not real life. She has seen friends marry for many reasons with varying degrees of success and happiness. And yet … It would be so good to feel a flicker of love, let alone passion for Joseph. Her experience of such is only through the pages of literature and she suspects that the allusions to passion are diluted for the eyes of lady readers.

Mary gives up on thoughts of reading and slowly undresses, overtaken by tiredness from the day's travel. As she slips beneath the sheets and closes her eyes, she smells lavender and comforts herself with the memory that her dear sister once loved Joseph with her full heart.

*

The next morning Joseph arrives and the four of them walk to the parish church to hear the reading of the first banns. Mary wears her Sunday-best gown and a green straw bonnet tied beneath the chin. In the circumstances and given their anonymity within Sheffield, Joseph offers his arm and they head towards Church Street and Holy Trinity, topped by its imposing tower and spire. Within the church, the Binns lead them to their regular pew and make space beside them for the couple. As the service progresses towards the reading of the banns, Joseph seeks to allay his trepidation that their plan may be discovered. He looks about the ancient building and up to the very fine hammer-beam roof. On the south wall lies the Shrewsbury chapel which Sophia showed to them during their first visit, and he wonders why the Earls of Shrewsbury have links to a church so far away from Shropshire. He reproaches himself for such stray thoughts and awaits the reading of their names. It comes, is not challenged and, for this week, it is over.

Declining the invitation to luncheon with them, Joseph bids farewell to the Binns and turns to take his leave of Mary. Both feel awkward. The Binns turn away and greet others from the congregation.

'Well Mary, we have taken the first step.'

'Indeed Joseph, and we are fortunate to have the help of such kind people.'

He nods and hesitates, unsure what to do next. He needs to leave or he will miss his train. He cannot shake her hand. He has never shaken her hand. But nor can he just turn on his heel and walk away. She senses his unease and speeds to resolve matters. She reaches out with both hands and clasps his between them. Why is she surprised at the roughness of the skin? He is a farmer after all.

'I wish you a good journey home Joseph, and give my love to your mother and the girls.'

*

The housemaid clears away the breakfast dishes. The Binns' three-year-old son, Henry, is brought to the table by his nursemaid. Sophia takes the lad onto her knee and points to Mary.

'Say good morning to Miss Hall, Henry.' The boy looks with solemn eyes at the woman across the table. He mumbles something indistinct.

'He does not know me so he will be shy for a time.' Mary smiles brightly at the child but does not attempt to engage further with him.

'Did you know that Henry is fostered?' Sophia believes that such matters should be aired. Mary nods. 'So, with your own experience of looking after your sister's girls you will understand some of the sensitivities of such a situation as ours.' Mary listens with interest to Sophia's words as she recounts the story of Henry's arrival.

After four years of marriage the couple despaired of having a baby and, being good Christians, agreed to foster. Nobody could live in a town like Sheffield, where industry mushrooms year on year, without seeing the pitiful sight of young children begging in the streets or else starve. The Church was Samuel's chosen route and two years ago they were led to an establishment on the outskirts of Rotherham where children from supposedly 'good' homes found haven. The proffered boy had been given up by its mother, a lady of breeding, they were told. They learnt that the child had been conceived in sin and the mother's parents had sent her to the north of England in secrecy for her confinement. The boy was re-named Henry and brought to his new home in Sheffield with much love and hope.

Poor mother but what good fortune for that child, thinks Mary. Easier too, when you gain a child as a baby, not as a growing girl, she ponders ruefully.

'Now, my dear, enough of that. Today we have a very important rendezvous. I shall introduce you to my dressmaker as

I understand from Joseph that you wish to have a new gown made for your wedding day. I am most excited at the prospect,' says Sophia.

The next two weeks pass steadily, punctuated by fittings at the dressmaker's, shopping in the emporia of Sheffield for a wedding bonnet, gloves and shoes, and by Joseph's arrival for the second reading of the banns.

On this occasion the pair are able to take a walk alone. He offers his arm and Mary leads him through the sweeter smelling parts of the smoke-blackened town.

'You must miss the fresh air of home' suggests Joseph as he sniffs and surveys the haze that cloaks the buildings. Mary laughs. She is used to Sheffield after her time with the Websters but they lived in the outskirts, on the hills west of the polluting air.

'The Binns have chosen to live closer to Samuel's place of work and so the dirt is harder to avoid. But more than the fresh air, I miss Mary-Ann and Frannie. Do they ask after me?'

Joseph is heartened by her words but is careful in his response. After telling Mary-Ann that Mary is nursing a friend in Sheffield for a couple of weeks, his daughter shrugged and since then has not asked about her at all.

The week before the wedding, the gown is delivered and, at Sophia's behest, Mary tries it on with the bonnet, shoes and gloves. She has chosen a pale-blue cotton, printed with curling tendrils separated by undulating lines. The full skirt is supported by numerous petticoats as she has rejected the notion of a horse-hair crinoline. The bodice is pleated over the bust into a V-shaped point at the waist. The bell-shaped sleeves reveal lace trim to a plain undersleeve. These and a white muslin shawl collar bring a touch of modesty to the dress which subsequently will become Mary's best gown.

'Perfect,' cries Sophia, adjusting the matching bonnet to reveal a little more of Mary's face.

Mary stares at the figure reflected in the cheval mirror. She cannot believe that she is this elegant person. She has never worn anything so lovely and fears that there will be few occasions on which she could wear it again after her wedding. It is unlikely that they will be invited to polite society again. But it makes her look quite pretty. She smiles back at her reflection.

*

It is the morning of their wedding. Joseph travelled down on Saturday to hear the third reading of the banns at the Sunday morning service. Yet again uncontested. He takes comfort from that but will not relax until the marriage ceremony is over and the register signed. Outside the hotel, the street bustles with people about their Monday morning business. Carts and horses add to the clamour. He has been awake since dawn, as befits a farmer, and now prowls his room, already dressed in his new dark-brown suit with a cream silk stock tied at the neck. He wishes the clock would run faster. He does not want time to think. A knock at his door, perhaps Samuel to bring encouragement.

His brother, Godfrey, stands before him. Joseph steps back in consternation.

'May I come in?'

Joseph steps aside, at a loss for what to say. He guesses his mother has revealed the subterfuge. How can he warn Mary? Clearly Godfrey is here to block the marriage, to prevent the Addy family being dragged into disgrace by his actions. In three-quarters of an hour Samuel and Sophia will arrive at Holy Trinity with that dear innocent girl believing she is about to be married. Anger rises in his throat. He will not permit her humiliation. He will marry her no matter what his older brother wishes.

'Godfrey, as the head of our family, you no doubt consider what I plan to be abhorrent, but, even though this marriage may split our family asunder, trust me, it will take place. I shall give my two daughters the mother they deserve. If you take action to prevent it, you will no longer be welcome in my home.'

His brother stands before him, hat in hand, appearing as shocked as Joseph. He shakes his head and reaches out a hand of protest.

'Joseph, that was never my intention. Look lad, our mother has explained all and sworn me to secrecy in order to protect your plan. I am here to support you, to stand by you today and in the future. What the rest of the world says and does is another matter. The law is a cruel one and we have to think of your young lasses and their future lives. I'm here to accompany you to the church and carry the ring, if you wish it.'

Joseph sits down and puts his head in his hands. For a man not given to expression of emotion, he is deeply moved by his brother's words. He looks up and smiles.

He stands, shaking his head.

'Come, Brother, give me your hand. I thank you from my heart that you are here.'

Now they will set forth towards the church and his bride.

CHAPTER 20

1850 3rd June

Samuel Binns leads Mary arm-in-arm as they walk to the church, Sophia following close behind. To passers-by they appear a smartly dressed party and only the small bouquet of white roses in Mary's hand proclaims her to be a bride. As they leave the sunshine and enter the porch, the ecclesiastical cold envelops Mary and she shivers. Her eyes adjust to the darker interior and she observes a few parishioners occupying the rear pews, out of curiosity, out of love of a wedding, who knows? All are strangers.

In the front pew, as expected, stands Joseph. He is not alone. As the three newcomers walk down the aisle, the sound of their footsteps causes the stranger to turn towards them. She catches her breath. Godfrey. The steady procession continues and halts before the waiting minister who greets them with a solemn smile. She dares not look at Joseph, who steps out into the aisle. Her eyes remain cast down.

Throughout the service, bare of hymns or joyful music, Joseph stands rigid beside Mary. They are so close to achieving his intended plan but there remains one hurdle. He trusts that Godfrey is true to his word and that nothing will intervene at this late stage.

The clergyman reads the crucial part of the liturgy, the hem of his white surplice reflecting purity into their eyes lowered by guilt.

'I require and charge you both, as ye will answer at the dreadful day of judgment when the secrets of all hearts shall be disclosed, that if either of you know any impediment why ye may not lawfully be joined together in matrimony, ye do now confess it. For be ye well assured, that so many as are coupled together otherwise than God's Word doth allow, are not joined together by God, neither is their matrimony lawful.'

He pauses, as custom demands. Everyone in the bridal party holds breath. Oblivious to the tension around him, the clergyman proceeds.

'Wilt thou have this woman for thy wedded wife?' Throughout their responses, neither Joseph nor Mary exchange looks, both tense with fear for what they do. But soon it is over, the register is witnessed by Samuel and Sophia, and the small group repairs to the Binns' home for tea and a cold collation. Godfrey is introduced to the benefactors and as there is little more that links them, conversation turns to arrangements to return to Bentley.

'There is a train early this afternoon and I am minded for us to take that one.' Joseph wishes to be home as soon as possible to move forward to the next stage. 'Will you travel back with us, Brother?' He does not consult his new wife and realises immediately his discourtesy. 'Mary, that would be acceptable to you also, my dear?'

Mary flushes out of irritation that her opinion was initially overlooked. She feels flustered then vexed at her lack of composure. She smiles brightly at the two brothers.

'Indeed, it would be good to have your company on our journey, Godfrey. I look forward to hearing about your children. It is some while since I saw them all.' In truth, talking to Godfrey within the confines of a full railway carriage will be preferable to stilted conversation with her new husband.

The farewells are sincerely meant. Mary cannot thank Sophia sufficiently for her generosity over the last weeks and knows that, despite the distance, they will remain friends.

Years hence, that friendship will indeed be needed.

'Please come and visit us soon,' she whispers down from the cab, unsure whether she is in a position to extend invitations to her new home.

*

At Stockbridge station, the newly-weds take their farewell of Godfrey. He will collect his horse from the nearby stables and ride home to break the news to his likely unforgiving wife. Joseph sends for the trap. As they wait under the canopy, he regards his wife anxiously. It is their first time alone all day.

'Nearly home, my dear. I trust you are not too fatigued.'

'No, Joseph. Although I am weary, there remains sufficient spirit to carry me through the coming hours.' Mary knows there will be a warm welcome from Mrs Addy and her friend, Elizabeth Vazin. She looks forward to being back at the farm, but ahead lies her first night in Joseph's bed.

The trap arrives, driven by young John Downing, who stares unblinking at the sight of his master in a smart new suit, arm-in-arm with Mary Hall, dressed in a pretty gown and matching bonnet, a small bouquet in her hand.

As he starts to load the trunks into the back of the trap, Joseph speaks out:

'Take care of Mrs Addy's trunk, John. Ensure it is safely stowed.'

With eyes out on stalks, the lad clambers up alongside the boxes. Joseph hands up Mary into the front seat, leaps up beside her and urges Molly forward. That is one sure way for the news to travel round the village, thinks Joseph.

It is early evening as the trap turns into the yard. Before stepping down, Mary looks up at the nursery window and is relieved to see the curtains shut against the summer evening light. Elizabeth Vazin has put both girls to bed and the explanation to Mary-Ann will wait until the morrow, as planned.

It is Elizabeth Vazin who opens the kitchen door and walks towards them, arms akimbo, while the lad runs ahead of the bridal pair, anxious to drop off their luggage then stable Molly before tearing home with his burning news.

'My, don't you both look fine,' she exclaims as she takes Mary's hands in hers and kisses her cheek. The lukewarm smile from Mary is put down to fatigue from the day. Joseph thanks her heartily and takes Mary's arm to lead her into the house. He feels he should mark the occasion.

'Welcome to your new home, Mary.' Elizabeth Vazin takes Joseph's hat and Mary's bonnet. She hands them to an astonished Harriet whose mouth droops open with unspoken questions.

'Take these upstairs Harriet, would you? Into the Master's bedroom. Then we might need something light to eat.' The girl nods and flies upstairs, her mind racing at the speed of her feet.

'Your mother is in the parlour and anxious to see you both but soon she will need to get to her bed.'

Ann Addy beams up at them from the sofa where she has been dozing. Albeit a summer evening, there is a small fire in the hearth as the old lady feels the cold. The evening sun dips in the sky but still casts a shaft of light across the room.

'Come Daughter, tell me how it went. You look a positive picture in your gown. You chose well with the fabric and the style of it.' Joseph withdraws from the room to allow the two women to talk and seeks out Elizabeth Vazin.

'How was Mary-Ann over these past three days? Did she question why I was away longer this time?' She draws him into the dining room, away from the kitchen where Harriet now prepares a tray of sandwiches and a pot of tea.

'Today she became somewhat restless. This was the third time in as many weeks that you've been gone. I told her that tomorrow morning she would find you returned safe and well and she seemed satisfied at that. Joseph, after I've helped your mother to bed, I shall be off home. Mary told me that she wished to be the one to attend to the girls on the first morning after her return.' Joseph nods.

'Dear Elizabeth, we cannot thank you enough. Will you continue to come in to help care for my mother? I fear that it would be too much for Mary to manage on top of all else.'

She reassures him and slips away, leaving him to return to the parlour where his mother and wife await.

Joseph talks and his mother listens, asking Mary the occasional question which she answers quietly and briefly. She is so tired but her body is coiled like a spring. She has no idea what she should do next nor when. She would give anything to change out of her wedding gown and lie on her bed but does not know how to suggest such a thing. Ann Addy comes to her rescue.

'Mary, please call Elizabeth Vazin to get me to bed. Joseph, you can help us mount the stairs. And you, Mary, you should change out of your lovely gown into something more comfortable. Your trunk is already upstairs, I expect, and you can unpack while I am being prepared for the night. Joseph will show you where things can be put.'

So it is that Mary walks into the room where some eighteen months back she saw her sister die. She hesitates on the threshold, viewing the bedroom, its yellow floral wallpaper softened in the twilight; the two mahogany presses with a matching chest-of-drawers; a wash-stand with blue and white porcelain bowl and ewer decorated with a Chinese scene; a low nursing chair with olive green leather seat. The double-bed. She hears a step behind her and her body tenses.

Elizabeth Vazin stands beside her.

'Come, Mary, let me show you what's what. Joseph is still answering his mother's questions about today.' She gently draws Mary into the room where nothing remains of her lost sister. Throwing open one of the presses, she reveals its readiness to accept that which is Mary's. She leaves her to unpack the clothes brought back from Sheffield. It all looks so meagre hanging within the cupboard. The remainder will be collected from her cottage in the coming days.

By the time that Mary has changed, Elizabeth Vazin has helped Ann Addy to bed and is ready to take her leave.

'The girls are fast asleep and tomorrow they will be happy to wake and meet their new Mamma.' Mary doubts that would be the sentiment of Mary-Ann but nods with a smile.

Together they descend the stairs and find Joseph seated in the parlour with lamps lit. He stands to shake Elizabeth Vazin by the hand and Mary walks her to the kitchen door. Harriet is gone to her room in the attic, wondering how she can convey the news to the village next morning. No doubt the lad has already told the farm hands who share rooms above the stables. What a thing.

'Don't be afeared, Mary, Joseph is a kindly man. Your sister never suggested otherwise. All will be well.' Mary wonders whether she alludes to her future marriage or the coming night.

She returns to the parlour bathed in soft lamplight. Should she have brought her sewing, a book? She sits on the sofa. Joseph smiles across at her. Both are ill at ease. He stands and walks across to the window. Outside is darkness, the moon obscured by clouds. He turns to face her, his hands clasped before him.

'Mary, I thank you from the bottom of my heart. I promise that I shall do all in my power to give you a safe and happy life. None of this will be easy for you, I know. Just because my brother and mother have accepted our marriage does not mean we shall escape the disapproval of most. Woman-kind can be especially cruel and I shall do what I can to protect you from malicious tongues. But there will be hard times for you.' He throws wide his arms to emphasise the point. This is not what Mary wishes to hear on her wedding night. Joseph ploughs on further.

'When it comes to my daughters, I hand to you the decisions on how they are brought up and disciplined. I know that I can swing from being indulgent towards Mary-Ann and being harsh out of fear for her becoming wayward. You, I am sure, will find the middle ground.' It is as she hoped but she knows that the middle ground will be rocky.

'Joseph, I can only do my best and I thank you for the confidence that you show me, but all I ask is that if you disagree with how I manage your daughters and your home, please be good enough to tell me in private. I will need your support from the first hour of tomorrow.'

She gains courage and stands.

'As for now, my dear, I fear I must go to bed. The day was long and so much has happened that I feel quite weary. Please forgive me if I retire so early.' It is half past nine.

'Aye lass, off to bed and I shall try not to waken you when I come up, maybe in about an hour. Sleep well, Mary.'

Both have signalled the rules of engagement for this night at least and the tension ebbs from Mary's shoulders as she stands shielded by a folding screen decorated to match the walls. She slips out of her day dress and into her new nightgown, already laid out on the counterpane. Which side of the bed is hers? Elizabeth Vazin has left a clue in a small crystal vase with a rose placed on the low cupboard to the right side of the bed. She climbs between the linen sheets. Her hand feels under the pillow and discovers a sprig of dried lavender. She curls up onto her left side and feels herself sink as her muscles relax and her mind is lost in the fragrance of the lavender. She sleeps.

An hour later, Joseph has locked up the house, damped down the fire and treads lightly up the stairs. He enters the nursery. His daughters have shifted into dream sleep, little sighs and mumbles occasionally escaping their lips. He watches their silhouettes revealed by the lamp left on the landing and is overwhelmed by a sensation of great sadness. He has not felt this deeply for them since the day of their mother's funeral. Why again now? Is it guilt that he has brought a new mother in Elizabeth's place? He rubs his eyes. What was the alternative? He turns to go. This won't do. He is tired yet knows he has done right.

Stepping gently into the bedroom, he quietly undresses behind the screen and is undecided between opening the door of the press to hang up his clothes or laying them quietly over the back of the chair. He chooses the latter and quickly dons his nightshirt. He tries to avoid the creaking floorboards which he has never noticed until this night, and lowers himself onto the mattress, pulling the bedclothes over his shoulders. They lie back-to back, she now awake and feigning sleep. Joseph's breath is soundless as he accustoms himself to the body at his side but as his tiredness overwhelms him, he breathes deeply and evenly and is asleep. For tonight both ignore what the morrow will bring.

CHAPTER 21

1850 June

Mary-Ann recognises footsteps in the nursery. Not the heavy tread of Elizabeth Vazin but the lighter foot of her aunt. It is as expected. Her grandmother informed her of Mary's impending return. The girl keeps her eyes closed. It is three weeks since Aunt Mary left her and Frannie to be looked after by the midwife. Three weeks of washing in lukewarm water, rough towelling down after a bath, no chance to get down from meals until every scrap was eaten. Because Aunt Mary went away. Gone to Sheffield. Why Sheffield? She neither knows nor cares. But she does.

Where is her father? She hears the clatter of farm-hands out in the yard and knows that he will be out to see them before coming to his daughters. Overcome by curiosity, she half opens her eyes. Aunt Mary is bent over the chest of drawers, quietly arranging the day's clothes. Next, she will waken Frannie. A ewer of hot water stands ready beside the bowl. The girl closes her eyes as her aunt turns towards the cot where her sister now stirs. Mary-Ann has no wish to speak and will only do so when spoken to.

'Hello my sweetheart.' Mary greets the infant who rewards her with a broad smile and a babble of enthusiasm. She looks over to Mary-Ann's bed to see whether the girl's sleep has been disturbed. Eyes are closed but Mary suspects they are purposely so. *So be it, Missy.*

By the time Frannie is washed and dressed, Mary-Ann has overcome her pout and has scrambled from her bed in search of the chamber-pot.

'Good morning, Mary-Ann. How good to see your smiling face again.' The girl grimaces from her squatting position and remains silent. Under Mary's direction she washes and dresses herself and in silence the three descend the staircase for breakfast in the kitchen. Mrs Addy is still abed, Joseph is not yet returned from the milking and Harriet scurries from pantry to kitchen to scullery, silent with eyes downcast other than the odd furtive glance at the new Mrs Addy.

Without the grandmother at the table to contribute to conversation, Mary's attempts to talk with Mary-Ann falter. The girl replies in monosyllables to queries about school and her grandmother's health and brighten up only when her aunt informs her that her father wishes her to miss school today. Her pleasure is quickly tempered by unease. Why? He has never suggested such a thing before.

She hears his step and the door swings open. She wants to rise from the table and run to hug him but holds herself in check.

'Good morning all,' Joseph beams his greeting as he drops his hat onto the window seat. To her astonishment he walks first to Aunt Mary and kisses her lightly on the cheek then does the same to Frannie and lastly, to her. She has never seen him kiss Aunt Mary. She sits before her unfinished breakfast, motionless, watching. Harriet has started to clear the dishes, her eyes still lowered, her ears flapping to pick up any scrap of conversation.

'Harriet, leave the dishes for now. Would you get working on the laundry, please? One of the men has filled the copper for you and stoked the fire.' He sits down at the head of the table as the house-girl flusters off to the wash-house across the yard.

'So, Mary-Ann, have you been good for your grandmother while I've been away?' The girl nods and continues to stare at him. He discerns fear and uncertainty in her eyes. 'Good lass. Now, I have some news for you. Good news. You have a new mother.' As he speaks, he takes Mary's hand in his and indicates the gold band on her finger. The colour drains from his daughter's face and fear overtakes the uncertainty.

She whispers: 'But I have a mother. It's just that she isn't here anymore.'

'Aye, lass, I know that well and we all miss her and honour her memory, but two little girls need a mother. Someone to care for them and guide them as they grow from childhood into young women, someone who will love them dearly. You have known your Aunt Mary since you were born, as has Frannie, and she loves you both with all her heart.' He clears his throat. 'I married her yesterday and she is now your mother.'

Mary observes the scene. She sees the bewilderment in the child's eyes and recognises the ache of loss and fear of the new. She reaches both hands across the table towards Mary-Ann and speaks gently.

'I shall never replace your mother in your heart. Before my dear sister died, I promised her that I would care for you and Frannie and this is the only way I can do so. Mary-Ann, when you are older you will understand. For now, we can continue as we have since your mother died, the only difference is that I have married your father and now live with you all.'

A thought occurs to Mary-Ann. 'Have you told Grandmother yet?'

Joseph exchanges a look with his wife. 'Indeed, Mary-Ann. Indeed. She has given us her blessing and is happy you girls again have a mother who will cherish you as did the mother who gave you life.' He smiles around the table and feels that this is quite enough for now. 'So, Miss. You have a day off school to spend with your family, so would you come with me this morning as I walk the fields?'

She nods, though the skies are cloudy and promise rain. She looks down at her plate with its half-eaten slice of bread and butter. It would choke her to eat it now. Mary intervenes.

'I'm sure you've eaten enough for now, my dear, so why don't you run up to your room to fetch your walking boots and perhaps a shawl in case it's cool out there.' Permission granted, the girl gets down from the table and without a word leaves the room. Mary picks up Frannie and takes her onto her knee to continue feeding the toddler. She glances enquiringly at Joseph.

'Well, now the lass knows. It's a lot for her to take in.' He had not expected a rapturous reception of the news but the non-committal response has disappointed him. This is the first opportunity to speak to Mary since he bade her goodnight last evening.

'I expect half the village also now knows we are wed, if young John Downing has broadcast the news.' He is unsure how to proceed next. He fears that tongues will be wagging and wants to protect Mary from cruel looks and words. He will speak to Harriet and the farm-hands. His mother's blessing is a valuable endorsement and he will use it freely. The Missus is respected. He intends to take Mary on his arm to church on Sunday but in the intervening five days he cannot expect her to hide away at the farm.

'Why don't you take the girls to the shop this afternoon? I could walk up with you if you wish.' He does not want for Mary to bear unkindness alone. He has no idea how the news of their marriage will be received. Mary wipes Frannie's face and stands to take the child back to the nursery. She doesn't want to face the women of the village alone and this is probably the best solution.

'Of course, Joseph, that would be a grand idea. Now I need to get this young lady settled then take your mother her breakfast if she is awake.'

That afternoon the little family walks along the lane, relieved that the rain holds off. Frannie is held in her father's arms, though wriggles impatiently as she wants to walk. Mary-Ann dawdles behind the couple, a switch in her hand to slash at the high-growing nettles bordering the road. Along the way they pass villagers' cottages, some with elderly men quietly tending their vegetable plot, some with tiny children, too young for school, racing around amidst lines of washing floating in the soft breeze. Joseph is gratified when the old men tip their cap to him, as customary. Have they not yet heard or are they indifferent, accepting the ways of the world?

Closer to the shop, they come across a small group of wives, heads bent close. Glimpsing the Addys, the women fall silent. One was at school with Mary. They stare at the family and nobody speaks.

'Good day to you,' calls Joseph with a smile of confidence he does not feel. Mary smiles hesitantly at the blank faces. Mary-Ann watches. They hurry on towards the shop, somewhat subdued. As they approach, the door opens and the housemaid from a neighbouring farm emerges, her basket laden with provisions. She is startled by the sight of the Addys bearing down on her and nods briefly at Joseph before scurrying off.

Mary-Ann presses forward and leads the way through the open door. She knows how to charm Mrs Watts, who manages the shop, and hopes to leave with a dab of sherbet as a treat. But there are others already waiting to be served. Two local women, Ann Fisher and Eliza Broughton, break off from their conversation with Mrs Watts and turn to examine the newcomers. Ann Fisher, first in the queue, turns back without a word to reel off her list of groceries. For a moment, Eliza Broughton fumbles in her copious bag and suddenly dashes for the door.

'Oh dear, I have forgotten something, Mrs Watts. I shall be back later.' The door closes on an uncomfortable silence as groceries are lined up on the counter, the cost totted up and coins are handed over. As Ann Fisher hastens to pack the items into her basket, she drops a packet of tea. Joseph stoops to pick it up.

'There you are, Ann. Good day to you.'

The woman flushes with confusion, grunts a sort of thanks, darts a look at Mary then shoots out of the door. The shopkeeper stands behind the counter, her hands at the ready to serve, but clearly embarrassed.

'Good afternoon Mr Addy, Miss …' Her voice falters. Joseph takes Mary's hand and smiles at the shop-keeper.

'Have you not heard, Mrs Watts? Miss Hall has done me the honour of becoming my wife and the caring mother to my two daughters. Am I not fortunate?' He defies her to think otherwise.

'Good heavens, I had no idea,' she lies. 'Well, I am sure you will be very happy. Now, what is it I can get you?' Joseph stands aside for Mary to approach the counter. The few items were soon fetched and the transaction completed politely but coolly. Mary cannot wait to leave.

CHAPTER 22

1850 Summer

It is mid-morning when the letter arrives, hand-delivered by the parsonage housemaid. Joseph is out in the fields and his wife takes the envelope. She hesitates then places it on top of the roll-top bureau which contains all the documents and records of the farm. She runs a hand over the smooth polished oak. Mary knows that it will be her task to manage the books, just as her sister once did. She is slightly daunted then chastises herself for lack of confidence. She excelled at school in both mathematics and the written word and is more than competent for the role ahead.

Soon Joseph will be in for his eleven o'clock mug of tea and a buttered scone. Mary-Ann is at school and Harriet in the scullery, hot and bothered as she heats the flat iron to smooth yesterday's laundry. Her mother-in-law lies dozing on the sofa in the parlour. Mary keeps one eye on Frannie who babbles away as she practises walking around the kitchen table and chairs. She hears Joseph push open the kitchen door and lowers the kettle onto the trivet over the fire.

'It's a grand day and the wheat is coming on well,' he announces as he sits down and takes Frannie onto his lap, intent on feeding her crumbs from his scone. Mary scalds the tea and leaves it to brew.

'A letter has come from the parsonage. Shall I fetch it for you now?' Joseph looks up from his daughter and nods with a puzzled frown. His wife returns with the envelope and pours his tea. There is silence in the room broken only by the sound of her slowly stirring in two spoonsful of sugar and his breaking the seal of the envelope. Even Frannie remains silent as if aware of its import. Joseph's frown deepens as he reads the neatly penned lines.

'Reverend requests I call upon him this afternoon.' They sup their tea in silence, neither doubting the reason for the summons.

'Do you wish me to accompany you, Joseph?'

'Nay lass. Better I see him alone. And perhaps no word of this to my mother. No need for her to be mithered just yet.'

Joseph approaches Arksey's handsome parsonage, newly built by Sir William Cooke in the Gothic style with pointed arch windows. The same housemaid who delivered the envelope opens the door. She drops a scant bob when she sees Joseph on the lower step and ushers him in whilst avoiding eye contact.

'Do come in Mr Addy,' welcomes the Reverend Sorsby ushering the farmer into his well-appointed study and offering a chair. 'What good weather for our crops, don't you think? Would you care for a cup of tea?' Joseph declines politely and the housemaid withdraws relieved.

'Forgive me if I come directly to the point but I have heard a disturbing rumour which I am sure you can set to rest.' He hesitates and Joseph is determined not to help the man but to force him to pick his words carefully. 'Word has it that you have married Mary Hall, your sister-in-law. Mr Addy, your deceased wife's sister. Is this the case?'

'That is so, Reverend.' He awaits the onslaught.

'My dear man, what were you thinking?' The parson rises from his chair and paces the room back and forth. 'You cannot be ignorant of the law which forbids such a union, let alone be unaware of the teaching in the Bible. What you have done is wrong not only in the view of society but in the eyes of God. You must know that any children of this illegal union will be ...' he seeks to put this delicately, 'unrecognised legally and by your community. What do you say for yourself, Mr Addy?'

'Sir, last year you buried my dear wife, Elizabeth. She left me with two small girls, one no more than a babe. My situation is not uncommon and you will have known many a widower in need of a new mother for their children. My dilemma was to seek a new wife, preferably from my own community and swiftly, too, as you well know that my mother is failing. That new wife would become mother to my children so should be acceptable to them. Frankly, in this neighbourhood I knew of no such person except for one, Mary Hall, the lady who has cared for my girls since their mother's death. She loves them and they love her. Indeed, Frannie probably has no memory at all of her mother.' Joseph is in full spate and surprises himself at his temerity in holding up a silencing hand when the parson seeks to intervene. In frustration, he pushes a hand through his full head of hair.

'I am well aware of the law but I am equally aware that there are many in the land, some in high places, who would repeal this cruel law if they could. My actions and intentions towards Mary are honourable and I shall protect her fully to the best of my ability. Equally, should God bless us with children, I shall extend my protection to them, whatever the law may say. I hope that you, as God's representative in this parish, will show the same compassion that our Lord gave to those deemed to be sinners in his own times.' Joseph rises to his feet and hat in hand stands respectfully before the clergyman, 'If you cannot find it in your heart to do so, may that rest on your conscience. The devotion of my family is important to me and I intend to bring my family to church each Sunday as before. We shall take our places in the family pew as have Addys for generations. I pray that you will not ban us from attending your church, Sir, but for now I have a farm to run and I wish you good day.'

There is a gasp of astonishment from the parson as Joseph nods briefly, turns and leaves. The glazed front door rattles as he closes it firmly behind him. The clergyman sits back in his chair. What to tell the bishop?

Mary greets Joseph with an anxious look. Mary-Ann is back from school and is itching to tell her father that she needs to write a poem about a cow and is distressed that she knows insufficient about cows to conjure up a four-line verse. Clearly Joseph wishes neither to discuss her poetry nor the subject of his conversation at the parsonage. Mary intervenes.

'Your grandmother knows all about cows, Mary-Ann. She was a farmer's daughter long before she became a farmer's wife. Take your slate and sit with her in the parlour. She will be happy to help you and together you can match words about cows and make them rhyme.'

The girl likes the idea and speeds off towards the parlour, slate and chalk in hand.

'Now, my dear?' Joseph warms to her gentle tone and recognises that it is the first time she has used a term of endearment, albeit modest.

'He is against us. As simple as that.' He sits opposite her at the kitchen table, his face defiant, his hands clasped before his outstretched arms. She reaches across and takes his hands in hers. She knows what this will mean for them, for any future children. People will cut them in the street. When they go to church they will be shunned. Will their children even be baptised? It is all as she feared.

The following days test Mary's courage and Joseph's patience. The farm hands are too embarrassed to refer to his marriage. Nobody offers congratulations or good wishes. Mary sends Harriet for all shopping errands and she stays on the farm, not venturing out into the village.

'It is all preposterous,' explodes Ann Addy, outraged by the narrow-mindedness of her neighbours. Secretly she is worried by the words of the parson and is concerned that the church service next Sunday may go badly for the newly-weds.

'I am minded to go to church this Sunday. It is too long since last I went.' Joseph is surprised by his mother's words. Walking is painful for her and sitting for any length of time equally so.

'Are you sure Mother? How will you get up into the trap? The pain would be too much for you.' He knows why she wishes to attend the service and honours her for it but seeks to dissuade her.

'My mind is made up, Joseph, and I shall go.'

Two days later, heads turn as Ann Addy processes painfully down the aisle flanked by her son and new daughter-in-law. Mary-Ann follows, a step behind. They take their usual pew on the north side of the aisle. The generous among the congregation admire the fortitude of the old lady in defying any criticism of her family. The majority, however, stare with emotions ranging from curiosity to disdain to downright hostility.

The Reverend Sorsby glares as his eyes sweep his flock and he spies the Addys. The sermon is hastily edited during the reading of the first lesson as he sits on the stone sedilia at the back of the chancel. Joseph watches with discomfort as the parson climbs the steps to the heavily carved wooden pulpit, the pulpit from which the parishioners of Arksey have been addressed since 1634 in the reign of Charles I. The Reverend Sorsby enters the pulpit, grips the wooden rim with hands wide apart and pauses for dramatic effect. When he speaks, his words are amplified by the carved canopy above, decorated with flamboyant vanes which, in Mary-Ann's eyes, resemble a large threatening spider.

The three Addys sit rigidly as they listen to the words, ostensibly declaimed to all present, but, in reality, directed at them; the sanctity of the family, obedience to God's laws, all obliquely referring to their sin. Mary's cheeks burn and Joseph and his mother seethe; while Mary-Ann tries to work out the meaning of the geometric designs of the carving.

At the end of the service a few friends shake their hands as they pass through the south door but the parson deliberately remains engrossed in conversation, his back turned to them as they leave his church. Joseph is furious, not so much for himself but for the slight to Mary and, above all, to his mother, a devout churchgoer who has attended All Saints since she learnt to walk, many, many parsons before this one.

Elizabeth Vazin and her husband approach them. The shepherd tips his hat to Mrs Addy and Mary then greets Joseph with a warm handshake. It does not go unnoticed among parishioners streaming out into the sunshine. Mary-Ann wants to take her posy to her mother's grave but hesitates to remind her father. The sermon has floated over her head but she is aware of an unease, the same tension she felt in the shop. She doesn't understand why her grandmother has struggled to church this morning.

Joseph's attention is drawn to his daughter's flowers but he is torn between aiding his mother back to the trap and respecting his dead wife. He whispers to Mary who takes the girl's hand and leads her around to the other side of the church. This part of the graveyard is almost deserted, save for an elderly couple bent over a worn tombstone, brushing away leaves to reveal the names of family members who died in the last century. At her sister's grave, Mary stands aside as her stepdaughter lays the flowers gathered from the garden. By the time they return to the gate, Mrs

Addy is safely stowed in the trap and most of the congregation has dispersed. Of the parson there is no sign.

In the following days, Ann Addy fumes and reaches a decision. She will never darken the door of that church again as long as she lives. Only in her coffin will she return. A timely premonition.

The following Sunday, Joseph attends church again with his new wife but his mother remains at home. Indeed, she remains abed and stays there also the next day. And thereafter. She is tired. Her back aches. She eats little. As the days pass, Joseph becomes increasingly concerned. Mary tries to tempt her with tidbits but even broth is refused. She turns to her mentor, Elizabeth Vazin.

'I despair. What can we do? It is as though she has given up the struggle. Life has not been easy for her but nor has it been so hard in comparison with many other people. I fear it is the disgrace that we have brought on her family.'

'Don't say such things,' whispers Elizabeth Vazin as they sit over a cup of tea in the kitchen. 'The Missus was always happy with Joseph's decision to take you to be his wife and mother of her grandchildren. She knows you are a good person and it would be her wish, I am sure, to see Joseph increase his family, maybe one day to have a son who could take his place.'

Mary blushes at the suggestion. Thus far Joseph has only kissed her chastely on the cheek. At night they lie together but apart, each aware of the other's body beside them, both embarrassed to find themselves in the same bed. The thought of any child, let alone a son, is long off. Perhaps it is for her to take the first steps.

CHAPTER 23

1850 Summer

Midsummer Day and Joseph drives his new wife to Wheatley Hall, for generations the seat of the Cooke family, an imposing three-storey classical mansion set close, too close, to the old course of the meandering River Don. It is the day for tenants to meet the estate manager and pay their dues for the coming quarter. Other local farmers arrive, some riding in traps beside their spouse, many alone on horseback. Most linger for the mid-day meal traditionally provided by Sir William Cooke for his loyal farm tenants. Joseph has always enjoyed this opportunity to sit with his neighbours over the plates piled generously with boiled hams, cold game pies and pickles, served with welcome pints of ale, but this time his aim is to introduce Mary to the agent as it is she who will manage the books in future.

The agent is either unaware of their real status or indifferent to it. He invites them into the estate office, sparsely furnished with a desk and chairs, the surrounding shelves piled with ledgers. Mary stares at the large map on the wall and recognises the number of fields now farmed by her husband. She glows with pride of his position within this community. To be an Addy, albeit illegitimately, must stand for something.

Mary is aware that none of the other wives accompany their husband into the manager's office to settle the quarter's accounts. Instead, the women hover together, happy to meet their neighbours, share gossip and bemoan the long hours their menfolk work in the fields. She knows many of these women but none looks her way or beckons her to join them. She lowers her eyes and keeps to Joseph's side. Her passive demeanour does not reflect the simmering anger she now feels. Since the public castigation by the parson, Mary has thought long and hard about her situation and is now resolute. She will hold her head high and brazen it out.

Already Mary has faced and won over Joseph's wider family. His sister, Nancy, is fond of her much younger brother and is relieved that he has found a way out of his dilemma. Nancy seeks to reassure Susannah, wife of her brother, Godfrey, who was shocked that he secretly attended the illegal marriage and is embarrassed that, somehow, he is complicit in the crime.

Today is another milestone in the Addy campaign to gain acceptance in the community. All Cooke's tenant farmers are gathered in the stable barn redolent with the scent of hay and today set up with lines of tables and chairs ready for the luncheon to come. The wives witter in groups and in low voices conjecture whether this year Sir William himself will grace them with his presence. He has done so in past years but today the word is that he is ailing so an appearance is unlikely.

'Excuse me, Joseph, I would just like to share a few words with Martha.' Joseph watches with surprise as his wife slips away from him and walks steadily towards the gossiping wives, her shoulders back, a smile on her face. The band of women hold ground for a moment but on hearing her name called, Martha turns with a smile, a smile that freezes as she recognises Mary and knows that her response will be judged by her peers. But the circle is now broken and Mary enters in and embraces her old school-friend. They exchange niceties and Martha responds to questions about her children's health and progress and feels obliged to ask after the Addy girls.

'Both are fine, thank you. Mary-Ann does well enough at school and Frannie grows stronger by the day. My dear sister, Elizabeth, would be proud of them.' She smiles brightly at the gathering, daring them to speak against her. Some return the smile, sympathetic to her situation; most purse their lips and turn to continue earlier conversations. Mary takes her leave with dignity and returns to her husband's side. Another bridge crossed.

The ride homewards takes them alongside the River Don and as they cross the bridge towards Bentley, Joseph reaches to grasp her hand.

'That was well done, Mary. Slowly we shall show our neighbours that we Addys live honourably despite that wretched law.'

Their sense of well-being dissolves soon after their return. Harriet discovered the Missus half out of bed and in distress. Elizabeth Vazin was called to help and, immediately Joseph steps over the threshold, the wise woman instructs him to send for the doctor.

That evening a sombre mood descends on the house. The doctor's words were non-committal but decidedly discouraging. He has prescribed a little physic and explained that other than keeping her out of pain with the help of laudanum, there is little he can do for a lady of such an age.

In the following days there is no time to dwell on whether or not the family and wider community will accept their marriage. Each evening Joseph returns from the fields, exhausted since harvesting has started early, and is distressed to mark the decline of his mother, a decline that seems to gain ground each wearisome day. He washes then climbs the stairs to her bedside. The room is cool, despite the warm weather, and flowers, gathered by Mary-Anne from the wayside, brighten her grandmother's sick-room. Mary has sprinkled essence of lavender on the old lady's pillow to calm her laboured breathing. He draws up a chair to sit by the bed and takes his mother's thin bony hand in his own. He wants to stroke it but fears his coarse fingers might damage the paper-thin skin which barely contains the veins that snake beneath the speckled surface. The opiate has consigned her to a drowsy state and although he longs to speak to her, hear her voice once again, he is reluctant to waken her to renewed pain and discomfort. He knows she wishes this would end soon and he closes his eyes in prayer that God will comply for mercy's sake.

'Will it be a good harvest, lad?' He opens his eyes, startled that she has woken.

'God be willing and as long as we have no storms, all should be well.' He lies. The crops have not fared well this year.

'I have been dreaming of George.' Joseph readies himself for what is to come.

'Of happier times, I hope.'

'Yes, of happier times when you, Godfrey and George were all young lads together. What mischief you got up to. Drove your father to distraction.' A smile lights her face then she frowns. 'But life didn't go right for George, did it? I thought he was all set up when he married Hannah. Good family, bit of money behind her. Shame they only had the one boy but maybe things started going wrong between the two of them soon after he was born.' Joseph makes no comment as he reflects on the stories of violent rows between the couple and his shock on seeing Hannah with unexplained bruises on her arms and face. His remonstrations were dismissed by George and although the physical manifestation of anger reduced, the discord continued until eventually Hannah moved out with their son, Will, to live in a small cottage on land owned by her farming brothers. The Addy family closed ranks. His father refused to discuss it. Ann Addy was ashamed and heart-broken.

'The one good thing was that your father never lived to see George's end.' Her voice quivers. 'Why did it happen, Joseph? Why did he die like that?'

Joseph will never forget the day George's body was found that spring some six years back. He had been helping with a difficult calving when one of the farm hands ran into the mistle, his face white with shock. The sight which met them in the barn is engraved on his memory. His brother was dead, no doubt of it, but there was not a mark on him. They called out the doctor, even though there was no use for him. He in turn summoned the coroner and George's body was taken directly to the mortuary in Doncaster. Joseph's next thought was that young Will must not hear of his father's death from villagers. Joseph chose to break the dreadful news to Ann Addy and remain with her at the farm. Elizabeth went straight way to see Hannah Addy, still their sister-in-law and mother to George's son, who listened with a stony face then asked how did he kill himself? No word of suicide was ever raised by the family nor by the coroner, who could not explain how a strong man of forty-one just dropped down dead and simply wrote on the death certificate: '*Died by the Visitation of God.*' People in the village talked, of course, but George Addy was buried and mourned. Again, the family closed in on itself.

'It happens, Mother. Sometimes a strapping figure of a man has a seizure and that's it. Gone.'

Ann Addy slips back into sleep while life continues about her, each dusty long day. Mary expected that in this, her first harvest at Joseph's side, she would be out in the fields with all their farm hands, working until dusk to bring in the wheat, but instead she directs the provisioning of the workers and sits in turn with Elizabeth Vazin as they minister to the needs of the old lady in her final days.

On Thursday, the fifteenth day of August, in her seventy-third year, Ann Addy breathes her last and drifts away to meet her Maker. Mary is seated sewing beside the bed, recognises the slowing breaths and awaits the silence.

Joseph is sent for and arrives, his face dusty and streaked with sweat. Tears track down his face as he kneels and clasps his mother's hands. Mary hesitates only a moment then falls to her knees beside him. She rests an arm over his bent shoulders and weeps with him and for him. This is her closest physical contact with her husband and she is ashamed to be conscious of such.

That night she and Joseph lie in their bed, both awake. The day has been full with people. People distressed, people with questions, people awaiting instructions. He rode with the sad tidings first to Nancy then to Godfrey. Elizabeth Vazin and Mary laid out the body and the two brothers gently carried their mother down to the dining room where she was placed in an open casket.

'Joseph, you need to sleep. You must be exhausted.'

'So much in my head, I cannot still my thoughts. I expected this day but now I am ill prepared for it.'

She sits up. 'I have lavender oil. Would you let me rub it into your temples? It is soothing and might bring you peace.' Without waiting for his response, she slips from the bed and in the darkness feels her way through her bedside drawer.

'Lie still and let me do this for you.' Ideally, she would stand behind him seated in a chair and would massage the oil into both temples simultaneously. Tonight, she has to kneel beside him on the bed and lean over with both arms to smooth in the drops of oil with her finger tips. She is conscious of his nearness. Her hair, loose about her shoulders, cascades down and brushes his face. His eyes remain closed while she strokes his temples with a gentle rhythm. As she continues, she is aware of a change in Joseph's breathing. It grows deeper, not shallower, as she anticipated. Her own body experiences disturbing sensations.

Joseph's eyes fly open and she gasps as his hands reach up to touch her bare arms. She fears he wishes her to stop and she withdraws her hands from his face. But that is not her husband's intention. His hands slide from her arms to grasp her by the waist and to gently pull her on top of him. The closeness frightens but excites her at the same time and through the thin cotton of their night clothes she feels the hardness of his desire for her. She understands instinctively what is expected of her and relaxes her body against his as he rolls her onto her back and pulls up her nightgown. He kisses her for the first time full on her mouth, softly, though she feels the pent-up tension trembling his body. The kissing becomes more insistent and she finds herself responding with unexpected ardour. She needs him now as much as he needs her.

Later, as they fall apart from their coupling, their bodies cool in the night air drifting through the open window. Mary lies wide awake. Her body aches from Joseph's ardour but overwhelmingly she feels complete. She is now a woman. Her urge is to roll towards him and to run her hand over his body, because now she may. She hesitates, unsure how he would react to such an immodest act.

He lies half awake, his physical exhaustion compounded by the strong emotions he has just expended: desire tempered with tenderness. The physical pleasure is mixed with deep guilt. Guilt for betraying his Elizabeth and guilt for enjoying pleasures of the flesh on today of all days. He quietly weeps.

In the darkness Mary hears his sadness. She already knows why he sheds tears. Her own eyes fill and she rolls away to her side of the bed. How hard is this mountain to climb? Gaining acceptance among their neighbours is a challenge she accepts. Winning the trust of Mary-Anne will come in time, she is sure. But rivalling her dead sister each night in the bed-chamber? How long before Joseph will accept her for herself?

CHAPTER 24

1850 August – 1851 March

Sunshine through the small pains of the window paints a path of light across the gloomy study. The Reverend Sorsby shuffles papers on his leather-topped desk, avoiding eye contact with Joseph.

'She was a good age, your mother.' Joseph stares at the dust dancing in the sunbeam. 'And a devout member of this congregation. We missed her attendance in recent months.' He hastily adds: 'Due to her ill health, of course.'

'Reverend, I am here to arrange the funeral of my mother and her burial beside my father. But before we get down to details, I think you should know something of my mother, something that may dissuade you from conducting the service.'

The parson leans back in his brown leather chair, prepared for a challenging exchange after the plain-spoken words of their last conversation. He clears his throat and nods for Joseph to continue.

'Mother attended All Saints on the Sunday following my marriage to Mary, full knowing what had passed between you and me at our last meeting. It required great personal effort to do so, but it was her way to demonstrate her support in a difficult situation. She was rewarded for her pains by your sermon which was a lightly veiled castigation of my wife and myself, by association, also of the Addy family. That day she vowed never to return to your church other than in her coffin.' By now Joseph's cheeks are flushed with agitation and in the August afternoon heat he feels suffocated by his second-best suit. 'In the circumstances, Sir, you may prefer to invite a colleague to conduct the service.'

He rests his hands on his knees and observes the clergyman's mouth tighten. There is a pause as Sorsby stands and turns towards the window, his hands clasped behind his back. He speaks:

'Your mother is not the party at fault in this sad matter, Mr Addy, and should be accorded the full respect she deserves. I shall do my duty by her and conduct the funeral and burial rites, as required of me by the Church of England, and it only remains for us to agree the day and time.'

The day is set. Word is put out that all are welcome to join the family for refreshments at the farm following the burial. The day before the funeral, Joseph has a request.

'Mary, would you do me a kindness please? Mary-Ann is far too young to wear it but I would be glad for you to wear Elizabeth's mourning brooch tomorrow.'

His wife is startled by the suggestion. She has never envisaged that she would be expected to wear this item of jewellery which so sharply underlines her own position.

'Do you think that would be appropriate, Joseph?' She worries what the wider family might say when they see the brooch for the first time.

'Nothing could be more appropriate, Mary. Elizabeth loved my mother dearly and it will symbolise her presence in honour of my mother.' Nothing more to be said.

The next day, Ann Addy is laid to rest beside her husband at a service led by her two sons. At the church where the Addys have worshipped for generations, the male members of the family raise their voices in thanksgiving for her life, alongside the men from the farm, scrubbed up for the occasion. They are accompanied by neighbouring farmers and villagers, all with high regard for this woman who supported her husband, bore him children and showed kindness to those less blessed.

Waiting at the farmhouse, Mary is entertaining Nancy and Godfrey's wife, Susannah. Garbed in mourning black, her sisters-in-law sit quietly in the parlour, attending the arrival of the menfolk together with the wives of local farmers and neighbours, who out of custom have not attended the funeral. In the ponderous silence, Susannah steals a glance at the brooch at Mary's breast. At first, she wonders if it is a Hall family heirloom but she soon reaches the conclusion that such an expensive piece of gold jewellery would be beyond the means of Mary following the death of her widowed mother. She longs to examine it more closely but dares not. And then the thought comes to her mind: could this contain the hair of her brother-in-law and Elizabeth? Surely not. Surely, today of all days, Mary would not flaunt so brazenly her illegitimate status.

The sound of traps and horses relieves the tension and Mary springs to her feet to welcome the visitors. Harriet, supported by Godfrey's housemaid, flusters in and out, anxious to serve the cold collation to the assembly. But the anticipated numbers do not materialise. Apart from the family and Elizabeth Vazin, nobody else has accepted the invitation to join Joseph and his wife for the high tea. Mary looks beyond the familiar faces and is dismayed to see how few have come with Joseph. Is it a sign of continued disapproval of their marriage? She fears that she will be criticised for having provided far too much food. After the family settles, she slips out to the kitchen and instructs Harriet to take the unwanted food to the barn where the farm hands and dairy maids are celebrating the life of Ann Addy in their own way with a few flagons of beer.

Joseph's nephew, Will Addy, is affected more than most by the loss of his grandmother. She had always held him close after the unexplained death of her son, George, Will's father, at the age of forty-one. His grandmother never expressed any disappointment in George and the failed marriage, unlike other members of the family. Will avoids his Uncle Godfrey and Aunt Susannah. Despite respectful words exchanged after his father's modest funeral six years ago, he and his widowed mother heard little from that branch of the family. Will's sympathy lies with Aunt Mary, another outcast in the eyes of the good people of the neighbourhood. Heaven knows, his Uncle Joseph had little option and Mary will make a good mother to his children and, pray God, bring him more in years to come. The young man approaches her.

'I trust you are well, Aunt.' Mary smiles warmly at the civility of this young man, now nineteen and standing tall. She knows that his mother, Hannah, now re-married to the local miller and with a new young family, never forgets her roots and regards herself at a station above all the Addys. Joseph's forbidden marriage must have been the final straw.

'Saddened, Will, but I am happy that your grandmother's distress is now at an end. I shall miss her. She was my friend.' The young man admits to himself that his own mother has been none such a friend to Mary.

'May the rest of the Addy family remain so, dear Aunt.' He lowers his voice. 'I wish you and Uncle Joseph the happiness you deserve.' He bows and joins his cousins who have congregated around the buffet table.

The Will is read a few days later and Ann Addy's few personal belongings are distributed among her children without question. Her jewellery goes to her surviving daughter, Nancy, who sweetly passes on to Mary a small brooch of Wedgwood's blue jasper.

'She was fond of you, Mary, and I know she would prefer to see you wearing something pretty at your throat rather than …' Nancy's voice trails away. How can she criticise the cumbersome brooch which her brother had made to commemorate his first wife? But it is as heavy in sentiment as in weight. Mary is relieved that once mourning dress is laid aside, she will be able to deck her gown with a symbol of respect for her mother-in-law that represents happier thoughts.

That summer, the Addys are not alone in suffering the loss of a loved one. The village is shocked to learn of the sudden, unexplained death of Elizabeth Vazin's husband, Thomas, at only thirty-four, five years younger than his wife now heavy with child.

Even this strongest of women buckles with the loss of her soulmate and the prospect of giving birth to a fatherless child with four other mouths to feed. Joseph wonders how she will manage to maintain the family's smallholding, even with the help of her sixteen-year-old son, John, now apprenticed to a local butcher.

In the heat of the following weeks Mary wishes to support her friend but feels drained of energy. The gathering-in nears completion and the harvest home must be planned. The thought of food makes her nauseous. She already suspects she is with child. Since their first coupling, Joseph has turned to her increasingly and she has marked a change in her own feelings. His initial tentative lovemaking has become more urgent and her own response surprises her. From acquiescence she has progressed to anticipation and, of late, initiation. In consequence, pregnancy is not a surprise. She hesitates to tell him until she is sure but Joseph is above all a farmer and understands the rhythms of nature. He notices no gentle rebuff of his advances in what would be her bleeding week. Dare he hope that Mary could already have fallen pregnant? Once again, he feels the quickening of his heart countered by a pang of regret that Elizabeth did not live to bear him a third child, perhaps a son.

When after two months there is no bleed, not only is Mary certain, but so is Harriet as the laundry has disclosed no bloodstained linen for many weeks. The housemaid knows better than to question her mistress and holds her tongue.

The crops have not been the best but the thanksgiving celebrations play out. The harvest home supper is yet again overshadowed by a death in the family and Joseph, in thanking the workers, invites tankards to be raised to toast the memory of the Missus. In reply, Will Barraclough, his leading hand, leaps onto a bench and taps his tankard with a spoon.

'Let us all together thank Master Joseph for our good fortune in knowing Mrs John Addy, God rest her soul.'

Tankards are raised and a shrill female voice calls out. It is Harriet.

'And a toast to the new Missus, Missus Joseph!' There is a pause of only a second and the dairymaids stand with their tankards high: 'The new Missus!' The men quickly follow suit and Mary blushes with the attention and warmth of their wishes. Joseph beams his gratitude.

This summer night soft breezes steal through the open window to cool the bedroom where they lie, each taking comfort from the kind-hearted sentiments expressed that evening. Not everyone has taken against them. Mary seizes the moment. She stares up into the darkness.

'Joseph, I believe I am with child.' There is no immediate response and she thinks he has fallen asleep. She rolls slowly onto her side, away from him. Another time, then.

'God has been good to us after all, Mary, and chosen to bless our union. Let the naysayers mark that.'

This is not the response she hoped for but she accepts it as a truth. She feels him turn towards her and he lays a hand on her shoulder. 'Thank you, lass. This is indeed joyous news.' With that he turns back and is quickly asleep. Mary lies with her eyes closed. This is now her function in life, to bring him children and care for the family. He is a good man. It could be so much worse. Reading Mr Dickens' novels has taught her that.

Almost as though a character in one of Mary's stories, Elizabeth Vazin faces an impecunious future when in October she gives birth to a boy child. In deep sorrow that her son will never know his father, she names him Thomas. Her daughters, now eleven and eight, become his nursemaids so that their mother can resume work on their farm and for much-needed payment as a nurse of others.

In gratitude for what Elizabeth Vazin has done for his family, Joseph presents her with a gift of money, ostensibly for the boy's future but, in reality, to tide them over until she can earn again.

It is at Christmas that Mary-Ann and Frannie are informed that in the New Year they will have a new baby in the house. At two and a half years of age, Frannie seems to grasp that Mamma will have a new doll, just as she has received in her Christmas box. She is thrilled with her own dolly as she is forbidden to touch Henrietta, the fashionable doll that is still prized by seven-year-old Mary-Ann, even though she professes to have outgrown such things. The ban on Henrietta is soon validated by her little sister's custom of dragging her new doll by the hair as she tears around the nursery.

Mary-Ann's feelings about the forthcoming sibling are harder to measure. It irritates Joseph that anything concerning Mary is greeted by blank equanimity. Mary is relieved that there is no open rebellion. A warmer relationship would be preferable but she settles for the expressionless response to the news. The girl has many school-friends who each year see the arrival of yet another sibling. Her small family is far from the norm. In reality, Mary-Ann quite envies the rough and tumble of local farming families. Being the eldest is lonely at times.

The winter is hard and Mary struggles with the baby she carries within her. She is desperately tired and depends increasingly on Harriet to care for Frannie who is proving a handful as her energy and new-found naughtiness drive her into constant mischief.

To Mary's distress, the baby demands an early entry into the world and with only the support of Elizabeth Vazin, Sophia Elizabeth Addy makes her entrance on a blustery day in late March 1851. The infant complains bitterly at her lot as she lies in her mother's arms. Her father looks down on his tiny, freshly washed daughter, and counters his regret that it is not a boy child with concern that the poor thing is far from robust. He has seen animals born thus that did not thrive.

CHAPTER 25

1851 - 1852

Joseph leaves the brisk autumn sunshine and plunges into the cool dark of the church. In his arms he bears a small wooden coffin. It harbours the body of his youngest daughter. Aware that many are surprised that the girl is to receive a Christian burial, her mother keeps close to her husband's side, eyes downcast with grief and fatigue from six months of nursing her sick child.

That morning she could hardly endure the pain as Sophia's body was lifted from her arms and laid in the tiny, satin-lined casket. Dressed in a white cotton shift, the infant resembled one of Mary-Ann's wax dolls. Standing now on the cold flagstones and holding onto the pew to steady herself, Mary is barely aware of what is said as the service proceeds. She hears not the words spoken by the parson, only the sound of his voice. A single thought floods her mind: what Joseph once saw as God's blessing on their union is revealed now to the world as His curse for defying the law.

From the day of her birth, Sophia Elizabeth struggled. Brought too soon into this world, she lacked strength to thrive, despite abundant milk offered by her mother. Joseph reflected ruefully on the contrast between the two sisters he had married.

Elizabeth, who struggled to get with child, brought forth two healthy babes yet strove in vain to feed the first one. Mary fell pregnant immediately but this daughter …

Frannie had cooed over her baby sister, unaware of the frailty of the poor soul. That Sophia is no more will soon be forgotten by a little girl who at every turn finds life an adventure. For her older sister, the last six months have been disturbing. Mary-Ann observed the pregnancy and birth as dispassionately as any farmer's daughter seeing a cat's belly swell then the birth of a litter of kittens. It was the helplessness of the baby that struck her most. Her memories of Frannie's arrival were vague and, if anything in those early days, she felt mainly jealous of the attention diverted to her new sister. This time, older and more aware of family tensions, she noted her father's unease following the birth. Her stepmother appeared desperate from the outset and struggled to pay any attention to her or Frannie. That suited Mary-Ann and the new-found freedom was welcomed.

The sun shines down onto the small grave dug beside that of her sister, Elizabeth. Mary is mesmerised by the light dancing on the tumbling leaves which carpet the graveyard. Her brother Mark rouses her from reverie. His face is strained. In the summer he buried his own daughter who lived but two months.

'Come sister, let us share our sadness.' He holds her close.

Mary stands back and whispers bitterly: 'What God is ours who takes two innocent little girls? You have not sinned in the eyes of the Church, yet you also suffer such a loss.'

Joseph witnesses their exchange and swiftly takes leave of the small group of relatives who attended the burial. He urges Mary to depart and helps her up into the trap. There is to be no celebration of a life that struggled for half a year before succumbing to some fever which any healthy baby would have survived. The death weighs heavily on the couple and there are no words to share.

The sense of isolation continues for days. Mary goes about her tasks like a mechanical automaton. Her stepdaughters' lives continue as normal and, while Mary-Ann is at school, she sits with Frannie to teach her numbers and letters. She finds the little girl's innocent ways a diversion as long as she stifles the thought that her Sophia would never need schooling.

The weather turns for the worse, nonetheless Joseph throws himself into preparing the land for next year's crops. Each evening he returns weary. Meals are eaten in silence and a feeling of desolation permeates the home. Harriet fears that the family she serves is cursed, just as her mother predicted when told of the marriage.

Elizabeth Vazin understands loss but she is made of sterner stuff. She calls in on the way to the village shop and encourages Mary to join her, bidding her wrap up against the wind which gusts the tardy bronzed leaves from the oak trees. Together they walk along Millgate, rutted from generations of farm carts bearing corn to the mill, roots to market, beasts to slaughter. The wise woman makes no allowance for sensitivities and speaks straight.

'Have you started relations again, Mary?' Her friend is shocked at the directness. She does not reply. What is there to say? During Sophia's short life there was little opportunity for 'relations'. The nurse employed by Joseph to help her after the birth, was a larger-than-life middle-aged woman brought over from Pontefract. Nurse Mountford had cared for Godfrey and Susannah's children and now took charge of this nursery, Frannie and Mary-Ann included. Once Mary was healed from the birth and Nurse moved on to the next baby, her energy was sapped by caring for her sickly child. Frannie, missing the attentions of Nurse Mountford, became ever more clinging. At the end of the school day, Mary-Ann would disappear, who knew where. Her stepmother felt only relief. Joseph made tentative attempts to make love but when Mary lay unresponsive, like a rag doll, he turned away embarrassed and frustrated.

'It has been difficult,' falters Mary. What more is there to say?

'I have no doubt, my dear, but there is no time to be lost. You must be thirty-two by my reckoning and your Joseph is a good ten years ahead of you. He's a farmer. He needs a lad. That's all there is to it.'

Mary has no response. It is true. She must bear him a son even though the prospect of another pregnancy daunts her and she dreads the possibility of losing another child.

'But what if I cannot make strong babies like my sister could?' She pulls her shawl closer and holds onto her bonnet as the wind tugs more fiercely.

'Sophia came early. Had she stayed put another month, likely she would have survived and proved a fine little lass. Just because it has happened once, it does not mean such misfortune will be repeated. Your own brother has known such a loss only recently but other of his children thrive. You owe it to yourself and especially to Joseph to provide him with another babe.'

They continue along the road in silence; silence broken only by the prattle of villagers in the shop. Elizabeth Vazin takes the lead and draws Mary into conversation. Whether her neighbours have accepted her position or whether they have sympathy for her loss, Mary discerns less hostility towards her. If the latter is the cause, what a price to pay.

As they leave the shop, Elizabeth Vazin stops and turns to Mary.

'There is something that you and Joseph need to know. It is a whole year since my Thomas died and it's been a hard year. I'm grateful for the kindness you both have shown me but I've had to make some difficult decisions, rather as Joseph did when he lost your sister. For the sake of my children, I needs must re-marry.'

Mary is surprised but quickly understands her friend's position only too well.

'Of course, that has to be a solution, but who …?' She is unaware of any alliance.

'Will Barraclough has been paying court these last six months,' says Elizabeth Vazin evenly. 'Yes, a good eleven years younger than me, but a kind man, not seeking children of his own and willing to take on mine.'

Unable to prevent herself, Mary raises her eyebrows in astonishment then immediately collects herself and smiles warmly. She takes her friend's hand.

'Then Joseph and I wish you both well. Do you plan to marry soon?'

'Next month, quietly. In Sheffield,' she adds with an ironic smile, 'with no fuss.'

*

And so, in the following weeks, Joseph observes a change in Mary, a softening in her demeanour both with the children and with him. He makes overtures and their love-making resumes, albeit without the enthusiasm they had once known.

Soon, Mary is once again pregnant. As before, she holds the knowledge close and, as last time, Joseph senses her condition. He is cautiously pleased. Could this be the son he hopes for?

By Christmas, Mary's belly starts to swell and her husband feigns surprise when she breaks the news to him. He is clearly happy and even ventures an attempt at humour.

'I wonder if one day we can time things more fortuitously and this Mary and Joseph can bring forth a baby of our own on

Christmas Day.' At once he regrets the facetious comment and Mary turns an incredulous face to him. Her belief in a great, all-loving God has been severely tested and such an allusion to the Holy Family appals her.

As the new year advances, Joseph tends his wife with great care. Together with Elizabeth Vazin, now Barraclough, he strives to ease her burden. He speaks sternly to Mary-Ann when her sullenness towards her stepmother becomes apparent even to him.

'Your mother needs your help, Mary-Ann. In the summer you will be blessed with a new brother or sister.' He awaits a positive response and when none comes, he adds: 'We shall all rejoice, shall we not? In the meantime, I ask that you behave as your own dear mother would have wished. Do you understand?'

The girl looks up from the toy theatre where her thoughts have been lost in the story of *Cinderella*. Her small hands twist the wire side-sticks and the cut-out card figures of the Prince and Dandini dance on the cardboard stage. True, her stepmother is far from wicked but who is to say that her coming half-sister or brother will not prove to be a rival to the affections of her father?

'But Father, what if the new baby should die,' she looks back at the miniature theatre, 'like Sophia Elizabeth?'

Her father is shocked that the fears that dominate his own thoughts should also be those of his seven-year-old daughter.

'We are all in the hands of God, my lass, and although last year He chose to take little Sophia as well as Uncle Mark's baby girl, we must pray that He chooses to let our next child live, as he did you and Frannie.'

Joseph is not a man to soften truth, even to a child. Life is hard, cruel and unfair. To shield his daughter from the reality would be a disservice. Growing up on a farm, the girl has seen the cycle of life and death with all the hardship in between. Mary-Ann must grow her own defences.

The early days of summer are gently warm and Mary ripens along with the fruit in the orchard. Since she has been sicklier during this pregnancy, Elizabeth Barraclough predicts the birth of a boy. Joseph prays that this baby lives and strives hard not to hope for a son.

As the days heat up, the Addy family is reminded again of the fragility of life. News reaches the farm that Godfrey's eldest boy, his fifteen-year-old son, has drowned in the River Don. Along with other lads of the village, he had ended a long day in the fields. In the still warm air of the July evening, the temptation to cast off their clothes and plunge into the river was irresistible. A couple of the boys found themselves in difficulty as the currents pulled them into deeper waters. The stronger lad reached safety but Joseph's godson and namesake was not an experienced swimmer and struggled in vain. The whole of Arksey turned out with dogs and flares and his naked body was found in the early hours, caught against the posts of a landing-stage further downstream.

Joseph is grief-stricken. He loved his godson for his good nature and enthusiasm for the land. Mary is deeply shocked and, with her imminent confinement, begs Joseph to permit her to stay away from the wake. She cannot bear to face Godfrey and Susannah at their time of loss when she was so close to giving birth. Have she and Joseph brought down a curse onto the whole Addy family?

In late July, Joseph is working with his men in a far meadow. They spy one of the dairy maids running across the field, waving her bonnet from a distance. He guesses the reason and reaches for his shirt. This time the birth is harder. Elizabeth Barraclough is in attendance and after some hours calls for the doctor. Joseph prowls the ground floor of the farmhouse, searching from room to room to find a distraction from the sounds of distress from above. Harriet has been despatched to take the girls to Godfrey's farm where they can sleep the night, fast approaching. By early evening the word is out around the village. The doctor has been called to the Addys. The curse prevails.

Thanks to the skill of the doctor and the years of Elizabeth Barraclough's experience, by late evening a boy is delivered. He tried hard to enter this world back-side first until eventually he was turned. But at what a cost to Mary. She was badly torn and lost not a little blood. The doctor does what he can and impresses upon the midwife that she is to stay by Mary's side through the night and the next days. He has delivered a boy but nearly lost the mother. The coming days will be crucial for her survival and he prescribes various physics to ward off the birth sickness. Joseph is joyful to have a son but is fearful for the life of Mary. Please God, don't let him lose a second wife.

The village knows only that the Addys have a boy. Pray this is the end of the curse. In memory of his grandfather, John will be his chosen name. A baby neither bonny nor slight, he demands to be fed and, after only scarce consultation with Joseph, Elizabeth Barraclough arranges the services of a wet-nurse; Mary is in no state to breastfeed the child. The daughters stay away a further night. Frannie demands of her sister why they may not return home to welcome their baby brother? Mary-Ann does not reply. She suspects all is not well and is not sure how she feels or should feel.

Joseph quietly enters the room where Mary lies half asleep. Elizabeth Barraclough rises and leaves them together. He leans over and kisses his wife's damp forehead. She opens her eyes and they fill with tears.

'Hush my dear, all will be well,' he hopes. 'He is a grand lad and you have done fine.' She turns her head away and the tears roll onto the white cotton pillow. Whether her baby lives or not, she cannot tell, but she fears she is dying.

CHAPTER 26

1852 – 1853

He holds his son in his arms, counts his fingers and toes and looks down into those angry, screwed-up eyes which demand everything from him: food, protection, love. Pride suffuses his being and he determines to start preparations for harvest with renewed zeal now that his farm has a future. Husbanding the land has never had greater meaning.

Slowly, so painfully slowly, Mary recovers her strength but it is some weeks before she is able to bring John to her breast and the wet-nurse is dismissed. Joseph does not know what to say to her. She has given birth to the son he desired but he knows that she is damaged in the process. What can he say other than words of encouragement and kindness? He feels guilty and helpless.

During the first six months of her son's life, Mary wakes each morning with the fear that God has taken him in the night. She slips from bed, pulls a wrap about her shoulders and tiptoes to the nursery doorway. From the threshold, she sees that Nurse Mountford, newly returned from Pontefract to care for their son, is already about her tasks. Frannie now shares the nursery with her baby brother and she sleeps through the morning ritual, waking only when John stirs, crying out to be fed.

John's siblings regard him with curiosity. Frannie welcomes him as another doll for the family and has only a vague recollection of how his sister once lived and then vanished. Mary-Ann, at eight years old, is unsure whether it is preferable to have a brother rather than another sister, so reserves judgement. In any case, she revels in having her own bedroom, for now. If more babies arrive in the nursery, she suspects she will have to make room for Frannie.

The question of John's baptism looms large in their minds. Little Sophia was baptised only in the days before she succumbed and then only after Joseph begged the parson to be merciful and accept a dying child's soul into God's love. This time, Joseph is determined that his boy will be received at the font of All Saints where Addys have always been baptised.

Whether the precedent was set with Sophia's death, whether time has softened the stigma of the Addys' illicit marriage, the parson agrees. Furthermore, there has been another similar marriage within Arksey and it could not be closer to All Saints. The landlord of The Plough, opposite the church, lost his second wife, Charlotte, like his first, soon after the birth of yet another child. As a result, Will Trout was left to care for eight children and, in need of help, he turned to Jane, Charlotte's widowed younger sister. She willingly moved in as his housekeeper accompanied by her own four children. Not unexpectedly, tongues wagged at the arrangement and within the year the couple took themselves off to Hull to marry incognito, just like the Addys. Joseph speaks to Will soon afterwards on his next visit to the smithy, also run by the Trouts for generations.

'May your fortunes improve now, Will. You have seen much sorrow and Mary and I wish you and Jane well.' The two men stand outside in the sunshine, away from the heat and smoke of the blacksmith's furnace.

'Thank you, Joe, your words are welcome. 'Tis strange how our lives have followed similar paths. Jane and I owe much to you and Mary for showing the way. It cannot have been an easy decision to cock snooks at the law. Many of us were angered that Parson laid into you from the pulpit. When Charlotte died last year, I was in just the same position, except with many more children than you. When, over the months, I saw how the village eased towards you both, I took heart and decided to seek the same solution. It was only fair to Jane, what with her living under my roof and people whispering, especially after my mother died.'

'Aye, it was my mother's poor health that brought things to a head for me too. Nonetheless, we feared the interference of our families and kept our plans secret. I hear that you had no such worries?'

Will Trout laughs. 'Indeed so. The parson in Hull may have suspected summat was up, but never questioned when all these folk from Doncaster way descended on his church. We all went over by train. Right excitement for everyone.'

The railways are opening up new horizons and not only for illicit marriages in distant parishes. The year of John's birth, a direct line opens between London and Doncaster. Joseph welcomes the opportunities this will bring for his young family in future years and, in the meantime, hears at market how beasts could be shipped straight to Smithfield Market for sale to butchers feeding the ever-growing population of the capital.

As John defies all fears and thrives beyond six months, Joseph takes time to observe his daughters. Frannie, now a lively and kindly three-year-old, is always willing to aid her stepmother, though frequently is more of a hindrance than help. Mary-Ann, at eight, grows ever more distant. He no longer tries to build bridges between her and Mary. It is as it is.

His main concern is for his wife and the toll that childbirth has exacted. He dares not ask for more intimate information, in case she misconstrues it for pressure to resume marital relations.

He fears to be rebuffed and confines his affection to a gentle touch to her shoulder.

Slowly, Mary's health improves. At last, she can enjoy motherhood and Joseph sees light return to her eyes. He is fond of her. She is a good mother to their son and his daughters but he knows, as does she, that she can never replace Elizabeth in his heart. So much he longs to discuss with his own dear girl. What would Elizabeth have said about Mary-Ann's schooling, the plans to build further railway lines through the area? Sir William Cooke has sold off more land which will take the line northwest out of Doncaster cutting far too close into the village of Bentley. Those living on the western side of Arksey, already blighted by the line to the North-East complain about the terrifying noise and soot emitting from the trains which pass close to their homes. Yet more farms will be divided by the track, making it harder to work the land and move stock from field to field.

Joseph's greater fear is for the disruption to the neighbourhood while the line is under construction. He has heard from neighbours that the Cookes have allocated a site to the north west of Bentley for an encampment to house the men who will build the railroad. Villagers have memories of the last line built through the area and although the nearest township for the navvies lay some distance away, tales abounded of stock being stolen, houses broken into and young women being accosted by the uncouth and often drunken men who toiled in all weathers to prepare the permanent way and lay the track. Furthermore, the presence of hundreds of men brought no money into Bentley or Arksey as the company provided workers with accommodation, a shop and drinking establishment. Joseph feared for his dairy maids and spoke to them severely about the need for caution. His warning was greeted with giggles but the menfolk supported Joseph with unfounded stories of girls missing from their beds and discovered weeks later with throats cut after unspeakable atrocities.

Now the navvies are back and Mary-Ann eyes the men as they swagger through the village. She notes disapprovingly their coarse clothes and even coarser language. Harriet hurries the girls on towards the bakers, chattering loudly to drown out the calls of the lustier workmen.

'Where do they come from?' Mary-Ann, from a sheltered upbringing, has never seen such types before. The men labouring on her father's farm may wear worn clothing, but none dare behave in such an uncouth way, at least not around the farm.

'All over,' responds Harriet, shuddering as a couple of the navvies pass far too close to her and the girls. 'They move around the country, picking up a few new men along the way, but many of them have come over seeking work from Ireland. Poor souls have desperate lives over the water. The potato harvest has failed year after year and whole families have starved to death.'

She checks herself, knowing too well that Joseph would not approve of her discussing the plight of the Irish in such graphic detail to his young daughters. Many people in the village are less sympathetic towards these unaccompanied men who, as everyone knows, are of the Roman persuasion and therefore not like the rest of us.

Mary-Ann puzzles why the families should die from hunger just because they could not eat potatoes. Why not fill up on bread in that case? Miss Smith, who teaches the girls at the local school, is keen for her pupils to take a charitable view of the less fortunate in this world. She uses a large map to show those nations where little girls live in circumstances so different from their own and now benefit from the protection afforded by their allegiance to Great Britain and our dear Queen.

Mary-Ann gazes at that wall map, even during classes where it has no relevance, and day-dreams. To journey to distant lands. Even to visit London would be an adventure. Nobody from

Bentley or Arksey has travelled so far, she is sure. Maybe the parson?

Her teacher marks her restlessness and speaks to Mary as they meet one day in the village. After pleasantries she comes straight to the point. Miss Smith is stern of appearance but after many years of teaching, recognises talent in children.

'Mary-Ann is somewhat restless in class these last few months and I am concerned that we do not satisfy her potential as a scholar.' She pauses with raised eyebrows in anticipation of a response.

Mary hesitates before answering. She does not feel in a position to comment.

'It has been a difficult time for her following the birth of her brother but I cannot say that I have remarked any change in her behaviour. What makes you suggest that she is restless?'

'On many occasions she does not pay attention. Unlike other children who struggle with the notion of bettering themselves, she does not gaze out of the window watching passing clouds. No, Mary-Ann gazes absently at the map of the world which hangs beside the black board. She is a polite child but I suspect she requires greater challenge than I can offer.' Mary opens her mouth to say that this absent look is Mary-Ann's normal appearance at home, but the schoolmistress presses on.

'Have you and Mr Addy considered sending her to an academy for young ladies, perhaps in Doncaster where there are a couple with good reputations? It would be necessary for her to board, of course, but perhaps that would be good for her. She does not have siblings of her own age at home and sometimes farm life can be solitary for a lone child.'

Mary is shocked at the idea that Mary-Ann should be sent away to school and knows immediately that any such suggestion must not come from her, the stepmother. She smiles calmly at the elderly teacher.

'You present an interesting proposition, Miss Smith. One that we have never considered before. If I may, could I suggest that we agree a time, out of school hours, which would be convenient for Mary-Ann's father to visit you to discuss your thoughts. It is he who would make the final decision on such a matter.'

And so, it is agreed. Joseph leaves the meeting at the Arksey schoolhouse with conflicting thoughts. Rather than ride straight home, he leads his horse across the road to the churchyard, hitches it to a post and strolls through the graveyard to where Elizabeth lies buried.

'What should I do?' his thoughts appeal to his dead wife. 'Would it be right to send the girl from home at eight years of age? Would it even be necessary, had you lived? Will she think that Mary lies behind the decision? Heaven knows I have attempted to form a bond between the two but neither seems willing to try.' He crouches down to tidy the grave but answer comes there none.

He spends the evening discussing with his present wife the notion of sending his daughter away from home. Mary holds her tongue until she gauges Joseph's support for the idea.

'You are correct, my dear. Mary-Ann would benefit from meeting a wider circle of girls of her own age and from good homes. She is quick to learn and needs to be challenged. I fear that our local school restricts her. Education should offer new horizons. I hear that the academy run by the two Misses Legge is not too large and offers a fine start in life for a young lady. There she would be taught French and music, none of which she would find in Arksey.'

Joseph is gratified that her view concurs with his growing conviction that a boarding school would provide an ideal solution. At the same time, he is surprised that his wife has already investigated the possibilities. They agree to visit the suggested academy and to talk to other members of the Addy family with daughters studying there. For the present, nothing is to be said to Mary-Ann.

In the meantime, the girl continues to gaze at the map of the world during lessons and at home she creates stories of travellers across continents to be enacted through her toy theatre. In her thoughts she is already thousands of miles away from Bentley.

CHAPTER 27

1853 February

The younger Miss Legge, Miss Maria Catharine, a slightly-built woman around forty, stands just over five feet high but her presence fills the study.

'Mr and Mrs Addy, you are welcome. Please take a seat.' Joseph discerns a refined Durham accent. The headmistress indicates for the housemaid to bring in the teapot which will match the four china cups and saucers already placed on a tray to one side of her small desk. Mary wonders how she found space for it as every other square inch of the surface is hidden from view by piles of papers, books and a large inkwell which appears to be fashioned from the foot of some hoofed animal, perhaps a deer. A cylindrical ceramic pot, sitting in the north-east corner of a blotting pad, contains an array of pens, the pristine nibs reflecting the light which intrudes timidly through the heavily curtained sash window. Outside, the bare branches of a sycamore tree gesture towards this small assembly gathered in Miss Legge's Academy for Girls.

School was never a favourite of Joseph and the smell of dusty books and ink generates unease. However, he reminds himself that he is the customer and that it is for him to question Miss Legge. It does not proceed as expected.

'So, Mrs Addy, your sister was Mary-Anne's mother.' The couple, seated in high-backed chairs on the other side of the desk, freeze at this bald statement of fact. Mary blushes, waiting for Joseph to take the lead.

'Indeed so, Miss Legge. My two daughters were left without a mother some years ago and I was honoured that the present Mrs Addy agreed to take care of them with such devotion. But we are here to learn more about your establishment and methods of teaching. First, would you please explain how many scholars you teach at one time?' He is indignant that the schoolmistress has enquired into their circumstances and would happily terminate the interview at once were it not a fact that the school is rated the best in Doncaster and that other members of the Addy family have given encouraging references.

As Miss Legge is about to respond, the elder Miss Legge, Miss Mary Caroline, bursts into the room like a cannonball, followed sedately by the housemaid and the teapot. Similar to her sister in height and coiffed with the same style of hair severely swept into a tight bun at the nape of her neck, she is as fat as her sister is slender, almost as wide as she is tall, if you take her billowing skirts into account. Joseph rises and bows to the schoolteacher who lets out a laugh of delight.

'Mr Addy, this is a great pleasure. As you know we already have the honour of teaching some young ladies from your wider family and we look forward to hearing more about Miss Mary-Ann.' This Miss Legge takes the teapot and pours a cup for each of them. She babbles on explaining the confusion caused by her parents' unimaginative naming of her and her sister.

'Many was the squabble over who owned which handkerchief when the initials MCL belong to both of us,' she chuckles. Mary warms to the older woman. Her younger sister frowns at the frivolity.

'To answer your question Mr Addy, we currently have fourteen young ladies, of whom twelve are boarders.' She removes a pair of horn-rimmed spectacles and lays them in parallel with the northern border of the blotting pad before her. 'We find that to achieve the best results, it is imperative for our students to live under our roof so that we can ensure diligence and monitor behaviour at all times. Sadly,' she returns her spectacles to her nose, 'it occasions that those who return home at the end of each day can be led astray by extraneous influences.'

Joseph wonders what influences could be that harmful, but allows the comment to pass.

'My daughter would return home at the weekend as part of the arrangement, I understand?' His query is answered by the elder Miss Legge before her sister can open her mouth.

'Indeed Sir. We believe it is important that those who are able to reach home between Saturday morning and Sunday evening, should do so, in order to maintain the bonds of a loving family.'

Joseph cannot quite reconcile this with the earlier warnings of extraneous influences and surmises that this arrangement allows the staff to have a quieter weekend with only long-distance boarders remaining at the school.

After the tea is drunk, the headmistress leads the Addys on a tour of the academy. The ground-floor includes the dining room at the front of the house, where two oblong tables, covered in homespun cotton cloths, are matched by a dark oak dresser at one end. This is where the girls stand in line to be served. Mary wonders which of the two sisters best reflects the quality and quantity of food on offer. The vestiges of the girls' dinner hover in an odour of cooking which is neither appealing nor repellent, just unpleasant.

Next lies the schoolroom. The girls, seated in the rows of forms and desks, stand to attention as they enter. The young woman who is instructing them in the intricacies of irregular French verbs, stands unsmiling as the headmistress ignores her and waves a hand over the assembled pupils.

'Our young ladies come mainly from the North-East of England at ages from seven years onwards. At sixteen they are deemed prepared for life and return to their families ready for what the future will bring. This class comprises the older girls who by now should be able to converse in French within polite society.' The teaching assistant lowers her eyes, hoping that this is not put to the test.

The party sweeps out of the classroom and up a curving staircase to the smaller schoolroom where younger girls are sitting at embroidery. Mary recognises that this was once a very fine house and wonders how the sisters came to own it.

'How long have you been established here in Doncaster, Miss Legge?' She floats the question, interested to see which sister responds.

'There has been an academy here for many years and we had the good fortune to acquire it four years ago, since when we have made improvements and carved an enviable reputation,' responds the younger Miss Legge.

The other rooms on the first floor are marked Private, no doubt the sisters' quarters. The entourage climbs a more prosaic back staircase to reach the dormitory floor. Off a small landing, a number of rooms have been opened out into a large space and rows of bedsteads line the walls. Each is neatly made up with pillow and blankets. At both ends of the room are positioned fires which at this time of day remain unlit. The skylights, which scarcely illuminate the room, frame the grey, February sky and Mary shivers in the cold. A smaller room is provided for the ablutions of the young ladies and Joseph notes that this does not include a fireplace. He comforts himself that his daughter will return home at weekends and will be able to have a hot bath in front of the nursery fire at least once a week.

Back in the headmistress's study, the younger Miss Legge passes a paper towards Joseph. It lists the fees and what parents should provide in terms of clothing and linen. The Addys bid farewell to the Misses Legge with the promise of a response in the very near future.

The couple walk briskly towards the inn and their pony and trap, Joseph silent in thought. Mary has reservations but needs to know her husband's views before voicing her own.

'Miss Legge's establishment is highly regarded in the area and, from what we hear, it seems that families from further afield have heard of its reputation and send their daughters for a good education.' Her voice falters. She cannot rid her mind of the bleakness of the dormitory. Joseph nods but does not reply. They continue in silence and soon they are trotting at a smart pace along the muddy roads back to Bentley before the winter evening draws in. Mary huddles deeper into her cape, pulled tight against the cold wind. One gloved hand grips the hood close to her head while the other steadies herself as the trap sways and jolts over the rutted way.

The lamplight and warmth of the kitchen greet them as they arrive back at the farm. On the rug, Frannie plays with her little brother who is learning to crawl. Their older sister, tired from her day at the village school, sits at the table with a colouring book which lies untouched. The cries of delight from Frannie alert the household to their arrival and Joseph stoops to sweep John into his arms.

'Have you been shopping in town?' Frannie hopes for sweeties. Mary-Ann looks up, waiting to hear the reason for the visit to Doncaster in such inclement weather. With a flourish, Joseph produces the anticipated butterscotch from his coat pocket and leaves the room to change out of his smart clothes.

Harriet is busy preparing food for the children and is equally curious.

'Seen any nice new dresses for spring, Missus?'

'No, I had no time for such things. We had people to see, here and there.' Mary also departs the kitchen to exchange her afternoon dress for something more homely. She pauses in the doorway.

'Have you lit the fires in the nursery and in Mary-Ann's room? It's a rare cold night tonight. Maybe snow tomorrow.' She sees again the simple iron bedsteads at the top of the house in South Parade. Would a new girl be given the bed furthest from the two fireplaces?

Mary pulls her crocheted shawl around her as she watches Joseph add logs to the parlour fire. A plaid rug covers her legs and feet which rest on a low embroidered stool, raising them above the draughts which plague the old farmhouse. She is impatient to reach a decision and is irritated by her husband's continued silence on the matter in hand.

'What is your decision, Joseph? Will you send Mary-Ann to this school, or not?'

He straightens up and rests a hand on the mantel-shelf. It is a ploy she recognises as his means of assembling his thoughts. He rearranges the china figurines that he has known since childhood. She waits. He clears his throat but does not look at her. Whatever decision he has reached, he is not at ease.

'You are correct in that the school has a reputation beyond question and I have heard nothing ill from other members of my family who have educated their daughters there.' He pauses and the silence declares his doubt.

'But you have concerns, my dear? Is it the teaching staff, the accommodation?'

'You know that I do not believe in mollycoddling my children. Life is not easy and they have been born not to great wealth but to a family which is loving and comfortably off. A somewhat Spartan establishment will make her appreciate what she has at home and realise that not all young ladies enjoy her good fortune.' Mary concurs wholeheartedly but feels her views on Mary-Ann's selfishness would not be welcome at this moment.

'So, yes, on balance I believe it would be good for her to be educated by the Misses Legge and we should suggest that she starts at the beginning of the summer term, after Easter.' Mary murmurs her agreement. It will be less cold than to start during the winter term. Marginally less.

The next day, on her return from school, Mary-Ann is chivvied by Harriet to the parlour, already brightly lit against the early darkness. Her father, freshly washed and changed after the short winter's working day, sits near the fire. He pats the sofa inviting her to join him. She does so willingly. Other parts of the room are notoriously chilly. She looks up as her stepmother walks through the door, smiling anxiously. Her father clears his throat. She is attentive.

'Your teacher has told us that she believes you have great promise, Mary-Ann.' While he pauses, the child wonders if this is a positive or negative comment on her scholastic prowess. She sits expressionless, looking up at her father.

'She believes that her school does not provide you with sufficient opportunity and has recommended you move to another establishment which can prepare you better for your future as a young lady.' Mary-Ann is intrigued at the prospect of becoming a young lady, something she has not considered before.

'As you know, a number of your more distant cousins have had the good fortune to attend the academy in Doncaster run by Miss Legge and her sister, and your mother and I consider that you also would benefit from such schooling.' Her father pauses for her opinion but notes her eyes stare up at him in bewilderment. He presses on. 'It is too late for you to join the classes during this term so we propose that you start after Easter. You will of course be a boarder during the week so that the travelling does not disrupt your studies.' There, it is out. He looks over to Mary for her approval. Was he too blunt?

Mary-Ann continues looking up at her father then drops her gaze. Her face remains impassive. Her stepmother tries to imagine what is coursing through the girl's mind. She knows that change is disturbing at any age and does not wish her stepdaughter to think that she is the instigator of this move.

'I hear that the young ladies leaving the seminary are known for their talents in watercolour painting, music and dancing. None of these would be available to you at your present school and you have such an artistic side, my dear.' She falters as Mary-Ann's blank eyes momentarily hold her gaze.

The girl turns to her father.

'Thank you, Father. May I go now?'

Joseph frowns and puts an arm around her shoulders.

'Do you have nothing to say, Mary-Ann?' He avoids asking her directly if she is happy with the proposition. 'Surely you can see this will be a grand opportunity for you to meet a wider circle of young ladies who could be your friends in the future?' That has not occurred to her. That could be useful. She nods and smiles weakly at him.

'Indeed Father. Thank you. May I go to my room?' He pats her on the back in acquiescence and she walks swiftly from the parlour. Mary joins Joseph on the sofa and they wait in silence until they hear the girl reach the upper floor. Joseph scratches his head.

'Have we done the right thing by her, Mary?' He wanted to ask: would Elizabeth have sent the girl away?

'Of course, we have. It could be the making of Mary-Ann. Who knows what opportunities this will bring, whom she will meet? It could change her life.'

CHAPTER 28

1853 February

Her silence is not sullenness. Mary-Ann has nothing to say. She is considering her father's announcement. When faced with uncertainty she has learned to hold her tongue. This will hold her in good stead in years to come. Far better to watch, weigh and then decide.

Next morning, as usual, Joseph is out of the house early so it is Mary who observes the girl's demeanour. Breakfast is followed by the usual scurry to dress warmly for the walk to school with the string of village children. When she turns at the bottom of the yard to close the gate, Mary-Ann does not return her stepmother's cheery wave.

As the children straggle along the by-ways, Mary-Ann keeps herself apart, choosing not to walk beside the other girls who giggle over boys and pull each other's ribbons. Instead, she considers last night's conversation. Miss Smith told her father that she has outgrown the village school. Perhaps that is right. Her mind wanders constantly in class and she knows that her restlessness disrupts her fellow pupils and annoys her teacher. She steps carefully along the road. It snowed lightly last night and the white coating has turned to brown slush under the boots of the reluctant children ahead of her. She does not know anyone who has attended Miss Legge's Academy for Girls. The words of her stepmother come to mind: *You have such an artistic side*. Has she? She is not aware of such gifts. Artistic? The description appeals to her. The alternative, staying on at the village school, would not feed such talents and it would be a pity not to allow them to thrive. Painting, music, dancing. She looks at the surrounding girls. *None of you will have these opportunities. You will remain in this village all your lives.*

*

The difference is noticeable from the moment Mary-Ann walks out of the early winter dusk and in through the backdoor. Other than the usual exchange of civilities, she says nothing to her stepmother but the stress of last night has evaporated. Soon she has changed from her school clothes and pulls on her pinafore ready for play with her brother and sister. This consists of helping John to walk and dictating to Frannie how to arrange her dolls in a pretend schoolroom. The younger girl moves her little people obediently since she has never seen the inside of the schoolroom and is in awe of her older sister.

When Joseph returns from the afternoon milking, the children have eaten and are about to be taken up to the nursery. Mary-Ann holds back and, after Mary has departed carrying John and with Frannie in tow, she approaches her father seated by the fire warming his hands. He looks tired and she stands for a moment, hands clasped behind her back. He looks up and in that moment he sees the light from the fire and lamps enhance her mass of golden red hair. She is going to be a beauty, no doubt about it.

'Father …' She is unsure how to continue. She should have practised her words. He sits back in his chair and smiles encouragement. 'How many weeks is it before I start my new school? Will I come home on Saturdays and Sundays? Will anyone sleep in my bed here while I am away?'

Joseph laughs. 'Why lass, we shall have to get the calendar to work out how many weeks, but it's February now and Easter falls at the end of March this year, so it won't be that long. And yes, I shall come and pick you up on Saturday mornings and take you back Sunday evenings after tea. You will have plenty of time to see John and Frannie and, of course, me and your mother.' He ruffles her hair.

'And my bed?'

'Why should there be the need for anyone else to sleep in your bed? Nay lass, it's yours alone. Now, off you get to bed, there's plenty of school days left for you in Arksey in the meantime.'

Mary listens with relief to her husband's confirmation of what she suspected. Mary-Ann has accepted the decision. Tomorrow she will start the list of what is to be prepared for the first of Mary-Ann's life adventures.

*

Doncaster is not new to Mary-Ann. Her mother would take her to Thomas Keaton, the draper in High Street, and together they would search through rolls of material to find just the right weight and the best colour for a new dress. Before Easter she returns to the same draper's, this time with her stepmother, to buy fabric for the school uniform. At first sight, Mary-Ann dislikes the indigo blue cotton unrolled before them. Plain and so dull, it seems to suck in all the daylight. She says nothing as the shop assistant plies her large shears with a regular scrunch.

They walk back towards the trap bearing a large brown-paper bundle destined for the Bentley dressmaker. Mary has an idea.

'My dear, it is a bright spring day, so why don't I drive round to South Parade and we can see your new school, from the outside at least?'

'Can we go inside too?' Mary-Ann holds the parcel while Mary climbs up, then passes it to be stowed safely away. The girl scrambles onto the seat next to Mary.

'Not without an appointment, no. But perhaps we could arrange that for another day. Shall we go?' The girl nods.

Mary heads along High Street past the grandiose Mansion House where elegant balls are held for the gentry. She picks her way slowly through streets which are busy but not so crowded as when the wool market runs. She is a competent driver but dislikes the chaos of waggons and carts criss-crossing before her. Fortunately, Molly is of solid stock and although she is scared of steam engines, other horse-drawn vehicles do not disturb her. Patiently she wends her way towards the open avenue that is South Parade and steers the horse up onto the parallel road that is Hall Cross Hill. She draws rein a few houses short of the academy and points out the house.

'See the one with three storeys, to the left of the smaller, new house? That's where your father and I went to visit. The windows on the ground floor, the ones on the left, that's the dining room where you will eat. On the other side of the front door is one of the classrooms. From memory, I think it's for the older girls. They were learning French when we went in. I think your classroom is upstairs, on the first floor. Those windows at the top ...' She hesitates at the memory and chooses her words with care. '... they are the dormitories where you and your classmates will sleep together.'

Mary-Ann looks at the building which gives no hint of what lies behind the tidy façade.

'Thank you, Mother. Can we drive past slowly please?'

The trap moves forward at a measured pace and, as it draws level with the building, they strain to see in through the windows. Not a great deal is visible but at that moment the front door flies opens and a round figure bustles out. Mary recognises the elder

Miss Legge swathed in a cloak, with a large umbrella brandished in one hand. Mary-Ann stares, fascinated by this person who turns at the bottom of the steps to walk briskly in the same direction as the trap. Mary averts her gaze, embarrassed to be found spying on the establishment, and shakes the reins to encourage Molly into a trot. As they gain speed and leave the small body that is waddling her way along the pavement, Mary-Ann turns around to look. Miss Legge waves her brolly in friendly acknowledgement, even though she has no idea who they are.

'Who was that?'

'Miss Legge. One of the Miss Legges. The older one but she is not the headmistress. That is her younger sister.'

'She looks jolly.' The girl smiles. Mary thanks heaven that it was not the grim-faced younger sister who emerged from the school.

'Yes, my dear, I think she is.'

*

The term will start two days after Easter Sunday. On the Monday afternoon Joseph straps a trunk to the back of the trap and drives Mary-Ann towards her new life. She sits between her father and stepmother and contemplates what it might be to be educated as a young lady.

As they speed through the flat countryside, now springing back to life at the end of winter, Mary tries to ease the tension. She recalls the first time she travelled to Sheffield to work as a companion.

'There was nobody to meet me off the coach when it arrived at the post house. I was frightened that my bags would be stolen by one of the shifty-looking lads milling around us passengers while our luggage was handed down from the roof. An older lady had sat next to me all the way from Doncaster and she caught hold of one boy and quizzed him until she was satisfied that he would carry my bags and lead me to the address of my new employer. I will never forget her kindness.'

'Were you given a warm welcome?' Joseph chips in, wanting to continue the distraction and give it a positive slant. Mary plays the game and refrains from describing the drab, cold little bedroom which the family allocated to their new companion.

'Mr Webster was a very correct gentleman so not given to effusive talk. His daughter, on the other hand, was delighted to have another young woman of a similar age, and we warmed to each other immediately. I was confident at once that I would pass my two months' probation.'

'Did you miss your family, your home?' Mary-Ann reveals what is uppermost in her mind.

'Of course, I did, lass. I wrote to my mother every week and she wrote me a few lines in return. She wasn't too good at her letters. Your own mother wrote to me when she had time and so each week, I would look forward to receiving post from Bentley.' Mary puts an arm around Mary-Ann's shoulders. 'There will be no need for letters for you as we shall see you in person every Saturday and Sunday. Won't that be good?'

Mary-Ann remains silent. She never receives letters. It would be good for someone to write to her.

On arrival at the academy, Joseph lifts down her trunk and she follows her stepmother into the hallway. A handful of girls in indigo blue dresses lean over the bannisters to examine the new girl. Mary-Ann looks up at them hopefully. None smiles back, the blank faces masking curiosity.

The headmistress awaits the party in her study. She moves from behind her desk and greets the parents with a hand-shake. She turns to Mary-Ann and smiles with her lips.

'Welcome Mary-Ann Addy. I trust that in years to come you will look back on your years at my academy as providing the strongest foundations for your position within society, within the world.'

Joseph hears words promising strength of character whilst Mary regrets no warmer sentiments are expressed. Mary-Ann fixes upon her position within society, within the world. Today is the beginning.

CHAPTER 29

1853 Spring

It is late afternoon and Mary-Ann has said farewell to her parents. Wearing a long holland pinafore matching her indigo day dress, she now sits on a bench at a long table. It is covered with an oilskin cloth of a colour which could be described generously as sage otherwise a drab green. Down the centre lie platters of sliced white bread, some cut more daintily than others, each piece smeared with a suggestion of yellow butter. A large pot is being passed up and down the facing rows of chattering young ladies. Each one dips the long-handled spoon and drops onto their individual plate a dark red viscous liquid. As it reaches Mary-Ann, she carefully takes a spoonful, ensuring that she does not sully the table covering. It is jam but not the thick fruit-laden conserves made by Harriet, instead a thinner, runnier version. She takes a slice of bread and butter and watches to see what happens next. Nobody has started to spread the jam. They sit in silence, waiting.

The door opens and everyone stands. The younger Miss Legge processes into the room, erect and unsmiling. Filling the doorway behind her appears the beaming elder sister whose eyes roam the assembly until they land upon Mary-Ann. She flashes a smile of welcome then sweeps after her sister to take their place at the head of the room. Without a sign, everyone puts hands together and heads are bowed. Grace is spoken in unison and Mary-Ann struggles to follow the unfamiliar prayer. Her father uses a shorter form of words to thank God for their daily bread.

Miss Legge addresses her pupils: 'Girls, you may be seated.' She waits a moment until silence is restored. 'Today we start a new term. For some it will be your last before you move on into the World at Large. This is the term when we judge your progress. The report which your parents will receive at the end of term will demonstrate your level of devotion to your studies. I am confident that you will not let them down in that regard.' She stares around the room to underline the imperative of their diligence in the coming months. 'We also welcome a newcomer today. Please stand up, Miss Mary-Ann Addy.'

The girl feels her cheeks flare pink as she stands awkwardly, the bench digging into the back of her legs. She steadies herself with hands on the table then removes them quickly, unsure if this is bad manners. On Miss Legge's nod, she sits down, conscious of the curious gaze of the girls seated opposite. The start of the meal is signalled and the girls quickly spread their bread with jam and begin to eat. Nobody talks. Mary-Ann works out that there are two slices of bread for each pupil but as she is slow to finish her first one, the piece remaining on the plate is snatched by a girl who has no compunction in taking more than her share. She notes the perpetrator and will remember this unkind deed.

The rest of the tea comprises a thin slice of seedcake and a mug of tea. Afterwards the girls disperse in chattering groups for the next half-hour of recreation. Within moments they are swallowed up by the house. Mary-Ann feels loneliness sweep over her and she makes her way upstairs towards the dormitory where earlier her stepmother helped unpack her trunk and place the small amount of clothes and personal effects in the cupboard beside her bed. Another girl is already seated on a bed next-door but one from Mary-Ann's. She looks up at the sound of the newcomer's footsteps and regards her without a smile.

'Hello Mary-Ann Addy. I'm Hannah-Mary Willey.'

Mary-Ann is taken aback by this direct approach. She smiles tentatively and wanders over towards the bespectacled girl who appears to be of a similar age to herself.

'Hello.' She looks onto a plain oval face with high cheekbones and a strong chin. 'How long have you been at the academy?' Before committing herself to friendship, she needs to gauge whether Hannah-Mary's direct approach suits her.

'This will be the end of my second year. I'm a full boarder. Are you a weekly girl?' Mary-Ann nods, pitying anyone who has to remain at this place for months on end.

'You must live nearby to do that. My family's farm is towards Bradford – that's where my father and older brothers work so they are all too busy to come and see me during term time.' Her matter-of-fact explanation is followed by a direct question of her own. 'Do you have brothers and sisters, Mary-Ann?'

'I'm the eldest, then there is Frannie who is now four. My little brother is nearly one.'

'I've nine brothers and sisters. The eldest is twenty-five and the littlest is nearly three.' Mary-Ann looks astounded. How do they all fit into one farmhouse? It must be massive.

Despite her abrupt demeanour, the girl has an energy that is infectious and Mary-Ann is quick to follow when suggested that they might explore the nooks and crannies of the house, forbidden or otherwise. This new disregard for authority appeals.

As classes do not start until tomorrow, the routine of the day is somewhat disrupted but Hannah-Mary is canny and along the way, as they slip down uncarpeted passages, through many doors, up and down staircases, she points out where to hide, the quick escape routes to avoid the monitors, and those places where people rarely come, ideal for quiet moments to read or just think.

'Why would I need to hide?' asks Mary-Ann, who cannot for the life of her imagine playing something as frivolous as hide-and-seek in this house of education.

'You'll see,' warns Hannah-Mary. 'Some of the older girls get bored and like to take it out on us younger ones. It's good to be able to disappear then they'll catch someone else.' Mary-Ann is shocked at this bleak analysis. Back at Arksey village school, she was aware that some of the girls resorted to name-calling and tugging hair, but nobody every suffered beyond that. The boys' class was different - boys enjoy fighting. But girls?

That night, after prayers are said beside the bed and candles are extinguished, Mary-Ann lies awake with her eyes closed. She is tired but her head swarms with thoughts, like bees in a hive, and she is conscious of the other girls lying around her. The steady breathing, even snoring, indicates that many are asleep, at peace with their first night back after the Easter holiday. One girl can be heard whimpering, trying to stifle her sadness. That would not be Hannah-Mary, she reassures herself. Hannah-Mary can cope with whatever life brings. Tonight, she does not feel the need to cry. It is too soon to say that she misses her family. Harriet's cooking is a different matter. Perhaps the food will be the greatest trial. She falls asleep, thinking of warm bread with pats of melting butter, slathered with real strawberry jam.

Next morning, she awakes to the clanking of scullery maids carrying buckets of steaming water into the small room adjacent to the dormitory. These young girls, scarcely older than Mary-Ann, fill the eight basins which will serve the ablutions of the twelve girls. The two dormitory monitors are first in line to wash and select six other girls to join them. Mary-Ann wonders if it is always the same six who benefit from clean hot water. She doubts that the maids will return with fresh water and by the time the second group reaches the basins, the water will be tepid and sullied. In the coming days she discovers that the favoured six changes each day but you could still be unlucky several days running.

As she waits in the queue for the second shift of washing, she spots Hannah-Mary returning to dress, her face pink and shiny from rubbing it clean. She smiles at her but Hannah-Mary does not return the greeting. Mary-Ann is puzzled then realises the girl is without her spectacles.

She is just dressed when a hand-bell is rung, calling all children to prayers. They stand in the dining room and the older Miss Legge reads out the Collect of the Day followed by a scripture reading. One of the teachers strikes up on the piano. Relieved that she knows the words to the hymn, Mary-Ann joins in timidly. After grace, the girls sit down, by this time famished and happy to eat whatever appears before them.

A big bowl of hot, unsweetened porridge stands at the end of the table. The monitor fills individual bowls which are passed down the line. Mary-Ann is glad she is mid-way along the table as she fears that the last girl could receive short rations.

A prayer ends breakfast then she faces her first class. She follows Hannah-Mary into the schoolroom for the more junior pupils and waits to be told where to sit. Her friend sits on the front row but the seat allocated to Mary-Ann is mid-way towards the back. The wooden desk has a sloping lift-up lid which she raises surreptitiously. Some dusty books, a pen-holder, assorted nibs, stubs of chalk and a slate. As the class assembles, the ink monitor circulates through the room with a long-spouted can, carefully filling the ink-wells sunk into the upper right corner of the desk. Mary-Ann sees that it is the girl who took her slice of bread last night and studiously avoids eye contact.

To Mary-Ann's delight, it is a geography lesson and Miss Jameson, a tall young woman with unruly blond hair, announces that her topic this term will be North America. Her brother has emigrated to Boston and his regular letters inspire her to research this exciting young country. During the class and throughout the term, her newest pupil is enraptured both by the enthusiasm of her teacher and by the pictures painted of the varied terrain, climate and people.

Arithmetic, never Mary-Ann's strong suit, is the subject of the second class of the morning. The silence of the schoolroom is broken only by the scratch and squeak of chalk on slate as each pupil attempts to answer the problems set out on the blackboard. Still the same teacher but even the charm of her smile cannot counter the feeling of panic surging within Mary-Ann. The numbers float before her eyes. She guesses the answers. She guesses wrong. Miss Jameson strolls among the desks, looking over shoulders, patting some on the back, pointing out errors to some. She stops at Mary-Ann and the girl looks up, her eyes betraying her fear. A quick glance tells all and her teacher nods and walks on. When names are called for answers, Mary-Ann is not included. Her humiliation is postponed.

At the end of the morning, Miss Jameson calls the girl to her desk, which stands on a low dais at the front of the room.

'Mary-Ann, it will take a while for you to settle into a new school. We all have different ways of teaching so I wonder if I may spend some time with you later today, when I can explain our particular approach to arithmetic?' The girl looks worried but nods. 'Splendid, come and find me at four o'clock.'

The afternoon is overshadowed by the prospect of wrestling with arithmetic, even with a teacher as lovely as Miss Jameson. Mary-Ann sits with a small group of girls in a sunny, well-lit room and gets down to hemming white muslin. What the purpose of this needlework could be is not explained but the girls are permitted to talk as they stitch. She is disappointed that Hannah-Mary is not among the sewing group and hopes to sit beside her at supper.

As four o'clock chimes from the grandfather clock in the hallway, Mary-Ann timidly knocks on one of the doors marked Private. Miss Jameson beams down at her nervous pupil.

'Come in, my dear. Sit yourself down and why don't you tell me a little about your family and your life at home?' Mary-Ann is taken aback. Not what she expected. She sits with her hands folded before her and explains that her mother died after Frannie was born and her father then married her aunt. She is so busy selecting what to tell and what not to tell that she does not notice the slight raised eyebrow and hardly suppressed smile which greets this last revelation. 'Then my sister Sophia was born but died soon after and then my brother John arrived. He's nearly one year old.'

'So, living on a farm there is plenty happening out in the fields, lots of animals?' ventures Miss Jameson.

'Yes, but it is usually wet and muddy and I prefer to be indoors where I can play with my toy theatre. I have scenery and characters for *Cinderella* and *Little Red Riding Hood*.' Impressed by the girl's enthusiasm, her teacher notes it for future reference. Slowly, a picture of Mary-Ann's interests emerges: her areas of confidence, her underlying fears, and although unaware at this point, with this knowledge, Miss Jameson will become a major influence in the girl's future life.

'Now, let's take a look at this morning's arithmetic.' Somehow it all feels less daunting now.

CHAPTER 30

1853 Spring

As she lies in the darkness of the dormitory, Mary-Ann is reminded of the animal noises that emerge from the mistle where cattle shelter from the cold on winter nights. Steady breathing, the occasional grunt, a body turning within its nest. Comforting sounds. She is tired but her mind churns. The hour spent with Miss Jameson. She adores Miss Jameson who took her through the process of arithmetic, problem by problem. She paused regularly to check that her pupil followed her logic. Put so simply, how could she not? The girl wonders if she revealed too much about her family. Her father gave instructions not to talk about the family's private affairs. Surely there was nothing said that should have been concealed?

The next morning, she is pleased to be among the six chosen to wash in hot water. Hannah-Mary stands at the adjacent bowl and Mary-Ann notices that the girl carries not an ounce of fat. *Needs a good meal inside her.* The words of her mother come to mind. Even though Hannah-Mary has a prickly side to her, Mary-Ann has taken to her already. She wonders if she might invite her to visit the farm one weekend. She might be impressed by the toy theatre and perhaps even by Henrietta, though Hannah-Mary is difficult to fathom. What really lies behind those unblinking eyes?

The remaining three days of this short week unfold with the same rituals as the first. Classes are punctuated by meals, none of which are inedible but neither are they tempting. The weekend cannot come too soon nor the pleasures of Harriet's cooking. As well as learning the subjects taught at Arksey, Mary-Ann joins the French class where she is the only beginner. She does not warm to Mademoiselle but is bright enough to know that this accomplishment is expected of an educated young lady. Another four o'clock meeting is arranged for special tuition. Somehow, she knows this will not be as pleasant as that with Miss Jameson.

The new pupil is introduced to the piano and, again, talent in this area will stand her in good stead as she enters what she understands to be polite society. Her fingers feel lumpen on the keyboard and the notes dance on the stave before her. Unlike in other lessons, if you make a mistake with a musical instrument, everyone hears. Mary-Ann thinks glumly that without a piano at home to practise on, it is unlikely that she will ever make progress.

The gardens provide space for the girls to walk, even run, and she and Hannah-Mary Willey use every opportunity to walk briskly round and round, crisscrossing paths as they chatter on. They pause to watch those girls allocated seed beds where green shoots now thrust up from the dark soil. Some grow vegetables, others prefer flowers but all diligently tend the young growth.

'I have my own little garden back at the farm.' She is embarrassed to compare these neat examples of horticulture with the weed-clogged strip of soil where once her mother encouraged her to sow seeds. Perhaps she will look at it again on Saturday. Frannie is old enough to help, surely?

'There's no point in my having a plot back at our farm,' asserts Hannah-Mary flatly. 'We're high up on the edge of the moors so it is pretty exposed to the elements. My father would consider it a waste of time. Anyway, I'm away months at a time and none of my brothers or sisters would bother to tend it for me.' Mary-Ann is surprised by such a dismissal of the Willey siblings.

'Perhaps they are all busy working on the farm that they don't have time for such things?'

'No. My older brothers are off in Bradford, working all hours for my father in his wool business. The younger ones are at school. As for my sisters...' A shrug of the shoulders dismisses the notion. She bends and irritably snaps off the golden head of a dandelion to prevent it going to seed. Her own yellow hair falls free of its navy ribbon and luxuriant waves drop down to obscure her face. Mary-Ann resists the urge to admire the thick mane for fear her compliment would be dismissed.

At breakfast on Saturday morning, the weekly boarders gobble up their food before dashing back to the dormitory to change into home clothes. Hannah-Mary sits in the hallway without expressing emotion and watches girls of all ages stream down the staircase to assemble in the front classroom, all impatient for the clock to strike ten. Then the anxious wait. First one girl spies her family, then another, and another. Mary-Ann hopes that her father won't be late. She does not wish to be the last to leave. That would be so shameful. She spots Molly trotting up the hill, bounds out into the hall, casts a swift 'Bye' in Hannah-Mary's direction and flies off. She stops in her tracks as she sees the headmistress standing station at the door.

'Mary-Ann Addy.' She walks quickly to where Miss Legge points.

'I do hope that in the few short days you have spent at our academy, you have learned that decorum is expected of young ladies. Is that not so?'

'Yes Ma'am.'

'Indeed. In which case, shall we walk down to greet your father? No doubt it was seeing him which caused this outburst of energy?' She opens wide the door and together they descend the steps to where Joseph is now standing beside the trap. He raises his hat to Miss Legge and is amused to see that his daughter stands close to the head teacher, her eyes modestly downcast.

'Mr Addy, how good to see you again. I am sure that for you the last few days have flown as swiftly as they have for Mary-Ann.' She puts a hand on the girl's shoulder and propels her towards her father. 'We have found her a hardworking young lady and a pleasure to have among us.' She addresses her pupil: 'I trust that you will have much of interest to recount to your family, Mary-Ann, and we look forward to seeing you again tomorrow evening by six o'clock at the latest.'

Joseph smiles and helps his daughter to climb aboard. He takes the reins, held the while by a gutter urchin, slips the lad a coin then joins Mary-Ann for the journey home. He turns to wave goodbye to Miss Legge but she is already gone and other parents are arriving.

'So, lass, how are you? You've been sorely missed by everyone, especially by Frannie.' He puts an arm around the girl and Molly trots homewards.

Frannie has dragged a milking stool to the farm gate and sits quietly waiting for her big sister to return, a rag-doll as companion. Already she is in awe of anyone who goes to school in Arksey, but an academy in Doncaster. How fine is that?

Her squeals of delight attract the attention of Will Barraclough and he sweeps her up under one arm, rag-doll, stool and all, and opens the farm gate in a wide arc. Molly trots through towards the cart shed, Frannie wriggles free and chases after.

Mary observes the change immediately. Her stepdaughter never stops talking and is spurred onwards by questions from all sides. Even Harriet wants to know about the food.

'What's for dinner today?' Mary-Ann tries to guess from the cooking smells emerging from the oven.

'A nice bit of hot pot, just as you like it, with some neck of lamb to make it tasty.'

Harriet disappears into the scullery with the girl's bag of washing and is glad that there is a spare set ready for her to take back tomorrow.

Frannie stands beside Mary-Ann who is being treated to a cup of tea and a biscuit. She tugs at her sister's sleeve.

'Will you come? I've had nobody to play with.' The plaintive voice touches Mary-Ann. She has missed the little mite after all. They disappear up into Mary-Ann's bedroom where the toy theatre is set up on a table. First, she greets Henrietta who remains where left, propped up on a lace-edged white pillow at the head of her bed, glass eyes focused on the ceiling. She wants to whisper her news to her elegant friend but hesitates in front of Frannie. For the first time she considers that it might be a little babyish to still talk to her favourite doll. Nobody at the academy has a doll with them, not even in bed. She will confine her conversations with Henrietta to more private moments. After all, she will be nine years old next month.

Downstairs Mary kneels on the rug in the parlour where young John is mastering the art of locomotion, progressing from a determined bottom shuffle to a wobbling crawl. Her husband is in the yard paying his workers their weekly wage. She knows the exact sum as yesterday she called at the bank to withdraw the money. The budget needs to be managed prudently at this time of year when there are so many outgoings and little to sell to balance the books. Mary now plays an important role in the running of the farm and recognises the need to plan ahead and lay money aside for leaner times. The school fees for Mary-Ann are an additional expenditure but nobody questions the value of a good education for the girl. Mary, more than many others, recognises the need for women to have as many opportunities as possible, given their dependence on the goodwill of men from childhood through to marriage. Every day she thanks God for blessing her marriage to Joseph Addy.

The following day after church, Mary-Ann is surrounded by former school-friends, eager to quiz on every aspect of her new life. Selective in what she recounts, she chooses to concentrate on the more exotic elements of the seminary: the French, the piano lessons, Miss Jameson's geography class. She exaggerates slightly the number of new friends she has made but talks glowingly of her special friend, Hannah-Mary Willey, who is also a farmer's daughter.

This Sunday, the dinner is extra special to celebrate Mary-Ann's first weekend home and the smell of roasting lamb greets the family on their return from church. She savours every mouthful and tries to block from her mind the coming six nights away. This will be her first full week and she fears it will be harder.

Indeed, as Molly trots down Millgate later that afternoon, Mary-Ann turns briefly to wave her kerchief to the receding little group at the farm gate, then snuggles up against the bulk of her father. She comforts herself with the knowledge that in her bag, hidden amidst her linen, lies a tin box full of Harriet's unctuous fruit cake. She will find the right moment and share it with her friend.

And so, another week begins, then another, and another. Gradually Mary-Ann becomes accustomed to the annoyances of academy life – washing in second-hand lukewarm water; indifferent food; girls with mean spirits to be avoided at all costs. To her surprise she begins to feel more confident in her French classes. Mademoiselle has complimented her on her accent. And although she will never shine with her piano playing, already she can deliver a simple melody. It is in geography that the girl excels. Miss Jameson continues to enthral her as she describes the rocky terrain of many parts of North America and explains how Great Britain is dependent on the southern states of America, where the cotton is grown to feed the hungry mills of Lancashire. Her star pupil asks question after question about the indigenous people, the cities, its agriculture, industry and landscape. It is a young nation, a growing nation, an exciting nation. Mary-Ann dreams.

CHAPTER 31

1853 Late Spring

During one visit home, Mary-Ann asks her father whether she may invite Hannah-Mary to stay at their farm.

'She returns home only at the end of term, so sees none of her family for months. She's always hungry and I know she would love one of Harriet's pies.'

As Mary-Ann's tenth birthday on the eleventh of May will fall midweek, Joseph suggests that she invites her young friend to come to the farm the following weekend, when they could celebrate together.

All is set and at the beginning of the week, Mary-Ann's excitement mounts. She returned to the seminary on Sunday evening clasping a little bundle with the express instruction not to open it until Wednesday. Each night, before slipping between the bedsheets, she takes the muslin-wrapped package from her locker and her fingers examine the lumps and bumps. What treats lie within?

Wednesday morning, she is shaken briskly awake by Hannah-Mary. She sits up startled. A small package is offered.

'This is just something I made in needlework. Happy birthday.' Mary-Ann thanks her friend and would like to peck a kiss but is discouraged as Hannah-Mary draws back sharply. Instead, she unpicks the yellow ribbon to release the pale blue square of cotton, trimmed by pinking shears, which wraps the gift. It is a pen-nib wiper of navy blue felt. Hannah-Mary has neatly decorated the four edges with scarlet blanket stitch and embroidered in stem stitch *M-A Addy*.

Mary-Ann is touched that her new friend has taken such trouble over her birthday and is pleased that the following weekend they will be celebrating together at home. She turns to her locker and fishes out the bundle from home. She knows that her main present will await her at the farm but is equally excited by these little things. The contents are tipped out onto the bed and other girls in the dormitory crowd around to see what the new girl has received. Mary-Ann knows that she and her family will be judged by what lies there.

A small paper bag contains succulent lumps of butterscotch. A twist of tissue paper conceals a small cake of rose-scented soap. A slim book with a soft cover is entitled *The Two Sisters*. Mary-Ann is pleased to note the nods of approval from the heads craned over her bed. The delicious moment is dispelled by the abrupt cry of the dormitory monitor and girls rush back to their beds to be selected for first wash. Mary-Ann is hopeful that as birthday-girl, she will be chosen. She is. Her delight is complete.

The following Saturday morning, Joseph is surprised as Hannah-Mary nods briefly in greeting. What a serious face for one so young, he muses.

'Squeeze in girls,' he cries as the three fit onto the seat, 'I thought we would have a jaunt around the town before we head home.' Molly trots off along the avenues and roads of Doncaster, past fine houses with high walls shielding elegant gardens, past austere municipal buildings testimony to their puffed-up sense of importance, past the sad blackened ruins of the fine mediaeval church of St George's which burnt down earlier in the year. From their elevated vantage point, the girls can view the shoppers, intent on finding bargains to eke out their earnings. Soon the trap is spinning over the bridge across the River Don and Bentley is quickly in sight. Mary-Ann points out places of interest, none, truth be told, of great import, and Hannah-Mary offers no comment.

Frannie, the look-out for the farm, alerts the household to their arrival, and Mary walks forward, young John on her hip, to greet the party. She kisses the top of Mary-Ann's head and offers her hand to the quiet girl beside her.

'You are most welcome, Hannah-Mary, and please convey our thanks to your parents for allowing you to stay with us and celebrate Mary-Ann's birthday.'

Before dinner, Mary-Ann shows her guest around the farmhouse. As the girls flit from room to room, Frannie trots on behind them, an eager smile on her face, hoping that they will include her, notice her even. She is in luck; Hannah-Mary is part of a large family and seeing to the little ones is a duty of everyday life and one has to make the best of it.

'May I show you my room too, Hannah-Mary?' Frannie is anxious to share her precious things. They have reached the nursery, where the room is divided between the large cot in which John still sleeps, and the neat little bed which is Frannie's. Lying on top of the pillow is a rag doll with yellow wool strands for hair and her facial features picked out in embroidery with buttons for eyes. Mary-Ann is somewhat embarrassed as it has become grubby over time, but Hannah-Mary recognises it as a much-loved friend and comforter.

'What is her name?'

'Lizzie.' The little girl anticipates a further question. 'It was my mother's name.'

'Ah yes.' Hannah-Mary recalls that Frannie will have no memory of her mother. Such things happen.

'My room now,' blurts Mary-Ann and the two girls disappear from the nursery leaving Frannie to cradle Lizzie and re-arrange her woollen locks. In Mary-Ann's room, her father has set up a truckle bed for the guest. There is little time before dinner, but enough for Hannah-Mary to see the famous toy theatre which has been in their thoughts during recent weeks. It is exactly as she imagined and she looks forward with restrained anticipation of what is to come.

Before they eat, Joseph presents the birthday girl with her gift. It is large, flat and quite heavy. Mary-Ann lays it on the rug. Kneeling, she works apart the knotted string and peels back the wrapping paper. It is a looking-glass in an oval frame to stand on the chest of drawers in her bedroom. She is delighted and kisses all of the family in turn. What a grown-up present. Hannah-Mary wonders at the vanity of the gift. Not something she would ever receive from her father.

Over the dinner-table, Joseph enquires about Hannah-Mary's family farm: what stock they keep, which crops they grow, how many men do they employ? He is impressed by her knowledge.

'Would you care to take a walk around our farm this afternoon? Or do you have other plans?'

Without a glance at her friend, Hannah-Mary nods politely.

'Thank you, Mr Addy, I would find that most interesting.'

Mary concludes that their visitor is a girl who knows her own mind.

The tour of the farm is not prolonged, especially as Mary-Ann trails behind. She urges them on when they linger at the smelly pigsty or lean on a gate to view the fields of growing wheat.

On their return, they devour milk and a scone then disappear into Mary-Ann's room. Frannie turns away tearfully when the door is closed against her, despite assurances that it will be a surprise for Sunday.

It is directly after Sunday dinner that the secret is revealed. Over recent weeks, during precious spare time at school, the two girls have devised a play for the model theatre: *Cinderella*. By Sunday afternoon they feel sufficiently confident to perform their little story before Mary-Ann's family. Joseph has carried the theatre down into the parlour, set it up on a table and the family sits before it, Frannie on Joseph's knee, John on Mary's lap. Harriet hovers in the background and the performance begins.

Seated either side of the theatre, Hannah-Mary and Mary-Ann take their parts and give voice to the characters who they shunt on long wires across the cardboard stage: Cinderella, the wicked stepmother and the two ugly sisters.

Everyone (other than wriggling John) laughs, sighs and oohs in the right places. It is clear that the girls have not only worked hard to stage the play, but have enjoyed every minute of it.

That evening, on his return from the academy, both girls safely handed over to the teachers, Joseph settles in his armchair before a small fire against the chill of the late spring evening.

'Who'd have thought our Mary-Ann had it in her? She was always bright but what we saw this afternoon demonstrated a side of her that I haven't seen before. The lass has imagination and not a little confidence.'

Mary looks up from her book. 'Indeed, Mary-Ann will go far, if I'm not mistaken.'

'And young Hannah-Mary, she appears to be from a good family. Brought up with discipline, I'd say.'

'Indeed, Joseph. Just the sort of person we would hope to become part of Mary-Ann's world. Perhaps we shall see more of her. And she has several brothers too, I understand.'

Her husband gives her an old-fashioned look. Surely at ten one does not need to consider such things?

Back at the academy, the two girls share the events of the weekend with those schoolfriends closest to them. There is great admiration for the pantomime performed in the toy theatre and some of the more creative pupils suggest doing something similar within the academy. Perhaps the elder Miss Legge could be inveigled into helping them. She is such a good sort and as the teacher of English, she is bound to be interested in the theatre.

In fact, only last year Miss Mary Caroline Legge visited Pollock's new toy-theatre print shop in Hoxton whilst staying with friends in London, and indeed embraces the idea wholeheartedly. She orders larger scale sheets for *Cinderella*, deemed a juvenile drama suitable for her young ladies. She cajoles the academy's handy-man to construct a bigger, more robust version of Mary-Ann's cardboard structure, then delegates to the more artistic pupils the task of cutting out and assembling the scenery, characters and costumes printed on paperboard. She has opted for the 'Penny Plain' as opposed to the 'Tuppence Coloured' printed sheets and now instructs the girls how to embellish the costumes with paints and scraps of cloth and tinsel. Those more dramatically inclined are given speaking parts to memorise and the more dexterous learn how to manoeuvre the tiny figures across the stage as the drama unfolds, based on the production originally devised by Hannah-Mary and Mary-Ann.

Because of the theatre's size, the audience is limited but a series of performances is established for the last week of term. After the first show, the word is out and enthusiasm for the academy's very own *Cinderella* is unbounded. After the final performance, where the two Miss Legges are seated in prime position in the front row, the senior mistress stands and faces those present, including the two friends who have guided their fellow students throughout.

'May I congratulate all who have been involved in this splendid affair, from my sister, who has master-minded the whole, to those of you whose nimble fingers have created the scenery and characters so admirably, to those of you who have performed at each show. It has been a triumph of working as an ensemble, greatly to your credit. And especially our thanks to Miss Addy and Miss Willey whose idea this was originally. I applaud you all.'

The audience has been joined by other pupils and the applause sweeps around the room to the great joy of the two friends. As they help dismantle the theatre and pack away scenery and characters, the euphoria ebbs away. Tomorrow the academy closes for the summer holidays. Hannah-Mary is surprised to admit that in fact she will miss her friend, but during the long journey home, a solution presents itself.

CHAPTER 32

1853 Summer

Their carrier pulls on the reins. The horse snorts and drops his head seeking grass.

'Yonder lies Moor House Farm. We'll be there soon.'

Joseph and Mary-Ann follow his directing finger to a distant stone homestead, located up from the main road. The house and farm buildings crown the hilltop and well-maintained stone walls enclose the surrounding pastures where cows graze.

Father and daughter are weary from the long journey travelling up by railway, changing to the final line in Wakefield. Now, this last stage is in the carrier's cart towards the village of East Bierley.

They follow the lane which leads up to the Willeys' farm. As the trap approaches the house, their arrival is announced by a couple of brindle-coloured yard-dogs who chivvy at the legs of the irritated horse. Joseph gazes at the low-lying, L-shaped building with its narrow stone-mullioned windows and stone roof-tiles. A couple of hundred years old, he muses.

Hannah-Mary appears leading a small group of children and is joined by an older lady, clearly Mrs Willey. Hannah-Mary formally presents her mother to Joseph who bows in return.

'Mr Addy, we are very happy to have Mary-Ann to stay with us and I am most grateful that you should accompany her on the journey.' He thanks her warmly and, as he is taken indoors for refreshments, he notices a date inscribed above the door lintel – 1632 – and smiles that his estimate was close. The carrier is shown to the kitchen where he will be fed, ready later to transport Joseph back to the railway station.

The visitors are seated in the low-ceilinged dining room and over meat and potato pie, Joseph talks at length with Mrs Willey and learns that her husband is away from home today. It appears that their main living comes from his wool business in Bradford where their two older boys also work.

So, thinks Joseph, that's how they can feed and clothe this size of family. The Willeys' farm is a quarter the size of his own and the income from it must be slight.

Elizabeth and Louisa, the Willeys' eldest daughters, nineteen and twenty-one years of age, busy themselves with serving the meal and are clearly used to performing domestic tasks around the home. Hannah-Mary is not the only child away at school at present and her middle brothers, John-Henry and Francis board at the Fulneck School in Pudsey. They answer Joseph's questions confidently and politely. At fourteen, John-Henry is about to follow his two older brothers into the wool business, as, will twelve-year old Francis who, in time, will prove to be the most successful of them all. Three younger siblings sit quietly at the table listening to the conversation of their elders.

Joseph leans back in his chair, replete from the excellent pie prepared by one of the older daughters, but aware he must soon take his leave.

'I am most grateful, Mrs Willey, that you should welcome my daughter into your home for these last two weeks of the school holidays. I know that she will be happy to help in any way that you see fit.' He turns to his daughter and ruffles her hair, to her chagrin and the amusement of the two older boys seated opposite. Mary-Ann's face flames red and she glares at her father. He ignores the reproof.

'It is also a matter of great reassurance that your husband will escort both girls back to the academy for the start of the new term. If in the meantime that proves to be a problem for him, I will happily return to accompany them.'

Farewells are exchanged and Mary-Ann stands with her friend at the top of the lane watching the cart swing right onto the road and disappear over the brow of the hill. She is excited to be so far from her family but also a little nervous. Hannah-Mary wishes to settle her in tidily so suggests with a slight frown: 'Come, we shall take your box upstairs and you may unpack.'

They pass by a dark staircase to the upper floor and into a room with two large beds, dominated by massive roof beams.

'Louisa and Elizabeth share that one.' She indicates a bed with a patchwork coverlet of floral fabrics in pinks and greens. 'This bed I usually share with Betsy-Emma and it's where we shall sleep. It is very comfortable.' She notes Mary-Ann's look of concern. 'Don't worry, I've told Betsy-Emma she will sleep along with Richard and Benjamin. She doesn't mind at all for a couple of weeks. Do you?' The younger sister has followed the two girls up to the bedroom and stands at the door. She shrugs. Mary-Ann resolves to make friends with Betsy-Emma over the coming days.

The two weeks pass quickly and for Mary-Ann, so used to the quiet of a smaller household, each day is a bewildering whirl and every room is full of people. Each has a role to play in the running of the home and when Mr Willey returns from business, everything falls into place. The mad chatter of earlier is replaced by respectful silence and Mrs Willey watches each child to forestall any misdemeanour.

The greatest challenge for Mary-Ann is the presence of the brothers. The eldest two, Charles and Godfrey, leave for Bradford early each morning with their father. She feels shy and uncomfortable in their presence. Charles, at twenty-five, seems quite remote, albeit kindly. Godfrey, on the other hand, is a very different character. He is disrespectful to all the females in the house, except his mother, and Mary-Ann is wary of him. All three men return home early evening, tired and hungry and with little to say. But it is the two middle brothers, John-Henry and Francis, who discomfort her more. She has not been brought up with brothers and, out of sight of their father, these lads are quick-witted, tease their older sisters and rag the younger siblings unmercifully.

Although on holiday from school, the boys work each day on the farm and sometimes spend a day with their father in Bradford. With no full-time house-servant, the older girls' time is spent collecting eggs, picking vegetables for the day's meals and helping with the sewing and mending for this extensive family. The two eldest sisters take the youngest children down into Birkenshaw village and Hannah-Mary and Mary-Ann follow in their wake, meandering from shop to shop.

As the evenings are still light and the weather quite warm, after supper several chairs are carried into the garden which looks out over three counties – Yorkshire, Derbyshire and Lancashire. Other than Mr Willey who remains inside to read his newspaper, the family sits in the evening sunlight discussing the doings of the day. The younger boys cannot remain still and their passion is playing cricket. They persuade the girls to join in and soon Mary-Ann has to learn how to run and catch a ball and not mind if she tumbles in the process. Grass stains that would horrify her stepmother are shrugged off by this family and she learns to wear a pinafore over her frock.

'Come now, Mary-Ann. Your turn to bat.'

She shrinks at John-Henry's suggestion and shakes her head wailing: 'I don't know how to play. I'll do it all wrong and our side will lose.'

At the end of the game, the lad grabs a bat and walks over to where she sits.

'You will have to learn, Mary-Ann. Come on, let me show you.' He takes her hand and pulls her up from her chair. She throws an imploring look at Hannah-Mary, who simply shrugs. What else should one expect from brothers?

'You can't be a Yorkshire lass who doesn't know how to handle a cricket bat,' Betsy-Emma giggles. 'John-Henry plays for his school so you've a grand teacher there.'

Mary-Ann feels awkward as the boy places her hands around the handle and, together, they thrust the bat forward. Everyone is watching, amused, but she hates to be the centre of attention. She longs to throw down the bat and run into the house, probably to cry, but knows that this is not acceptable in this family. On instruction, she stands upright, rolls her shoulders then bends into a drive. The onlookers soon find another subject of interest and she and John-Henry are left to their lesson. Encouraged, she begins to hit the leather ball with enthusiasm if not proficiency. They stop when five-year old Richard, the conscripted bowler and fielder, complains he has had enough. Over the two weeks, Mary-Ann makes progress and discovers that she can run quite fast if she gathers up her skirts and sprints towards the far wicket. She also learns, the hard way, to hold the bat firmly protecting her legs when Godfrey bowls. His delivery is fast and hard and makes no allowance for her inexperience. A bruise she can tolerate, but not a broken leg.

All too soon, the holiday draws to a close and they retrieve their boxes for the return to Doncaster. Mrs Willey packs warm clothes for her daughter's autumn term at the academy. They are to depart on the Saturday morning and Mary-Ann is sad to leave the clamour and disorder of the Willey household. The two older sisters have become her role models, both kindly of nature and confident in themselves. The middle boys have softened their teasing and she will miss them. Only Betsy-Emma is the least sorry to see her go but only so that she may regain her bed.

'Please present our respects to your parents, Mary-Ann.' Mrs Willey presses a cloth-wrapped bundle into her hands, a fruit-cake. There is one for each girl returning to the academy and its unsatisfactory cooking. She kisses both on the cheek and steps back to wave them off, surrounded by her unruly offspring, like a mother hen amidst her poults. The girl wipes a tear, sniffs and waves in return.

'Come back again, Mary-Ann,' shouts John-Henry.

Mary-Ann views the return to school with mixed feelings. She looks forward to visiting her family again on the following Saturday and it will be good to see Miss Jameson and hear news of the brother's travels but this term she regards the restraints and routines of the academy in a different light. While Mr Willey stalks up and down the platform at Wakefield railway station, irritated by the wait before the connection to Doncaster, in the privacy of the Ladies Waiting Room she speaks in a low voice.

'Do you not find it a trial to return to the academy after weeks of freedom with your family? Especially as you cannot go home at weekends.'

'Absolutely not. You have only two siblings, therefore you cannot appreciate how difficult it is to live within a large family. There is a rhythm to my life which I can tolerate and I know that this is my stepping-stone to a more rewarding time to come.'

Mary-Ann absorbs this fatalistic approach but cannot quite accept such a philosophy. It would be better were she so to do, but she is more impatient than her friend. To her, the restrictions of academy life seem oppressive after only one term but perhaps something else may have caused this unrest?

'Well, at least we can arrange for you to stay with us at the farm many times this term,' she smiles, bucked by the thought that Christmas falls only three months away.

The first week back at school speeds past and it is soon Saturday. Mary-Ann receives the warmest of welcomes when she returns to her family. Even John, stumbling along in his smock, gurgles at her, his first attempt at speaking.

'Hello little man.' She picks him up and whirls him round. Frannie tugs at her arm.

'Come and see what I have made.' She leads her big sister out into the garden and down a narrow path through the shrubbery. They turn off under a large laurel and there, sheltering under the wide evergreen leaves, stand two large chunks of wood, hewn from a recently felled tree, now seats for Frannie and her chosen guest. An old rug lies before the logs and the space is decorated with pretty stones and twigs in artistic arrangements.

'It's my secret place but you can come here whenever you like,' she proclaims proudly.

After two weeks at Moor House, Mary-Ann has become more aware of the kindness of families. Whereas some months ago she would have given this habitation a mere glance, now she appreciates the dreams and endeavours of her little sister, playing alone for hours on end.

'Come, my dearest Frannie.' She pulls the child towards her and hugs her gently, stroking the brown straight hair, tied loosely into bunches. 'This is magnificent, and I feel honoured to be allowed to enter your special place.'

It is good to be home, albeit for only one night, and to see that little has changed in the last few weeks. Now she regards her family, her home and the farm with the eyes of someone who only now may compare because they have travelled and seen elsewhere. She likes that thought: to travel and see elsewhere.

CHAPTER 33

1853/1854 Winter – 1856 New Year's Day

Back in Bentley, Mary frets. She worries how Mary-Ann is coping in that ill-heated dormitory now that the autumn nights have drawn in and chilly air suggests the onset of winter. She has packed the girl's box with extra warm socks to supplement her uniform stockings and is busy crocheting her a shawl.

The approach of Christmas generates mixed emotions. She looks forward to the excitement of the children, especially as John, now nearly eighteen months old, is more aware of life around him. By contrast, every January brings the anniversary of the deaths of her sister and mother, to say nothing of the prospect of months of bleak weather. She hates winter.

Greater fears she harbours within her heart. There are no signs of another child despite Joseph's frequent attempts to make her pregnant. Should she call it lovemaking? She has nothing to measure against. She has no sister or close friend with whom to discuss such matters. After three years of marriage, should a wife expect to feel loved during coupling? There is no unkindness in the process, but she hoped for more tenderness. Perhaps that is something Joseph reserved only for Elizabeth. Perhaps she should applaud his faithfulness to his first love. One thing remains, however: she has not fallen pregnant again.

The seasons change, Christmas is celebrated, January and February are survived. Come the spring and the birth of lambs and calves, her own barrenness is not discussed. Instead, Joseph is intent on working the farm, providing for the family he has. At the end of each day, he walks the farm carrying his son seated astride his broad shoulders, the lad holding tightly to his father's mane of hair. Frannie often tags along, full of questions about the farm, the animals, the crops.

'Well lass, you would make a good farmer's wife with all the knowledge you're storing up inside your pretty little head.' Frannie beams with pleasure. She looks into Mary-Ann's mirror and does not see prettiness reflected. A serious, anxious face gazes back. She enjoys these times alone with her father. Yes, John is there too but his baby talk doesn't count. When Mary-Anne is home, she dominates the conversation. Understandably, her life is so full. Frannie has seen what education brings and cannot wait until September when she will start at the village school.

Mary-Ann has now attained that reassuring rhythm of life advocated by Hannah-Mary: term-time weeks of studying, weekends at home, some accompanied by her best friend, then two weeks of the summer holidays at the Willeys' farm. This year her visit is even more enjoyable as she knows what to expect. Much is as before but this time the elder sisters, Louisa and Elizabeth, take the two girls into Bradford to explore the town. Intriguingly, Louisa, more than ten years Mary-Ann's senior, has recently made the acquaintance of her cousin, Will Addy, who has moved up to the area to work for a local farmer he met at Doncaster's wool market.

Truth be told, Mary-Ann hardly knows Will who became estranged from the Addy family after his parents separated and even more so following the early and unexplained death of his father, her Uncle George. Over luncheon, Mary-Ann quizzes Louisa who is clearly happy to talk of the blossoming friendship.

'Will became restless working for his uncle and I think he wanted to strike out and make his own fortune, especially after his mother remarried and started a new family. He enjoys farming life but I can see that his heart is now set on distant horizons.' Mary-Ann raises her eyebrows to encourage more. 'There are so many opportunities over in America where it is easier to find a farm of your own. As a tenant, of course.'

'You would have to be brave to venture there just now, though. It all sounds to me rather lawless,' counters Mary-Ann.

'Nonsense,' retorts Hannah-Mary sharply. 'All you need is back-bone and to be prepared for hard work.' Her companions are taken aback by her judgement.

'Well, if that is what it requires, Will has such strengths and more,' adds Louisa warmly. 'I have no doubt that were he to decide to emigrate, he would make a success of it.' The two friends will remember her words in years to come.

After their shopping, the sisters proudly show Mary-Ann the newly-built St George's Hall, an imposing classical building resplendent with Corinthian columns, where concerts are attended by the great and the good of Bradford. Then they all return to Moor House in the company of Mr Willey and the brothers. John-Henry at fifteen now also works within the business as a wool sorter, separating the long staple wool destined to be spun for worsted. Despite a long day at work, each summer evening the brothers still find energy to play a couple of overs of cricket before heading to bed.

Mixing with the lads is all part of Mary-Ann's growing up, whereas Hannah-Mary is quite oblivious of the effect on her friend. Boys have been one of the irritating parts of her life seemingly for ever, something simply to be endured. For Mary-Ann, as for many other pupils at their all-girls academy, the behaviour and habits of young men are a closed book. Her experience has been shaped by the rough and tumble of boys at the village school, whereas the Willey brothers represent a breadth of personality from the upright civility of Charles to the polite kindness of John-Henry. Godfrey is a thing apart and Mary-Anne suspects he has gained his surly nature from his father whose strictness brooks no bad behaviour in his presence.

*

Farm life in Bentley is dictated by the seasons and, as the year 1854 closes, Joseph looks back on a moderately successful harvest. The farm ledger, carefully administered by Mary, shows a satisfactory return. He considers the folk he employs and wonders how long he will be able to keep the younger men and women. More villagers are rejecting the hard agricultural life endured by generations of their parents. Instead, they seek employment in the burgeoning industries of Doncaster, especially if protected from the weather at the Plant, the new works where carriages and trucks for the railways are repaired. Over a thousand men, many incomers to the region, are now employed by the Great Northern Railway. How ironic that this railway, whose track has taken valuable farming land from the village, now takes its farm hands. Lasses, too, are attracted to life in town where among the increasing number of prosperous families, they can find domestic work including board and lodging. He wonders for how much longer Dick Guest can carry out the heavier jobs around the farm now he has reached seventy. He has been a loyal servant to the Addys over the years and Joseph will not discard him and instead gives him lighter work. He acknowledges that, with the advent of machinery, fewer farm hands will be needed in future, but such machinery has to be afforded and Joseph has decisions to make.

During the following year, his children continue to thrive. Frannie enjoys her schooling even though she struggles at times. However, she is a typical Addy, a hard worker determined to keep up with the rest of the class. All are fond of the girl, that happy soul that her mother never knew.

Now eleven, Mary-Ann gives no cause for worry. With each term she develops further into a confident young lady. Her unruly hair, now darkening towards titian and neatly controlled in twin braids during the school week, cascades free at weekends. She has a zest for life and to Joseph's eyes resembles a young colt straining to escape the stable for pastures new. She still shows childish enthusiasm for all she does but the petulance, which often overshadowed her disposition in earlier years, has disappeared, hopefully for good, muses her stepmother.

Her eyes shine with glee when she recounts to her family tales of her latest and now third annual visit to Moor House.

'We went into Bradford again.' Mary-Ann holds court at the dinner table. 'Hannah-Mary knows her way around and this time we were allowed to go alone without her elder sisters.' Her stepmother frowns at this news.

'They say many foreigners live there now,' ventures Joseph, who reads the local press from cover to cover and is aware of a large influx of Irish and Germans over many years.

'Oh yes, in the market we came across lots of strange accents and stalls selling food I've never seen before. It was exciting. It seems that all these foreigners came to Yorkshire to work with the wool. Hannah-Mary says the Irish started coming some ten years ago during the Great Famine, and the Germans have been here for years, trading wool with the Continent. Did you know, Father, Bradford's worsted cloth is recognised as the best in the world?' she concludes triumphantly.

Joseph smiles indulgently across the table to Mary and muses where will this lass end up?

'Oh yes, and the ice-cream sellers, they come from Italy. Well originally, of course, not every day.' His daughter chuckles at her own joke. 'One of them has a live monkey who sits on his shoulder. We could feed him nuts.'

Frannie squeals with delight mingled with terror at the thought of being that close to a real live monkey. John looks up from his place at the table, diverted from prodding stew around his plate as he makes the sound of a steam train puffing along a circular track. He laughs with the rest of the family, even though he does not understand why. Mary melts inside to see his happy smile.

Joseph takes pleasure that John is turning out to be an adventurous three-year-old who runs rings around everyone. Mary has proved to be a good mother, not only to her own child, but also to his daughters. It is easier with Frannie, who has known no other, but with Mary-Ann his wife still treads gently. The girl's spirited nature can be testing but he makes sure that her stepmother is to be respected and obeyed. What either really feels about the other, Joseph cannot tell. He is simply grateful that peace reigns during the weekends when his daughter returns from the academy.

Another winter approaches and evenings are spent around the fireside, Joseph with the local newspaper, checking on fat-stock prices and news of the region and beyond. Reading continues as one of Mary's past-times and although her husband does not begrudge her this pleasure, he muses that she would not have time to sit thus for an hour each afternoon were there a house full of children to care for. He envies his brother Godfrey for his gift of sons and reflects on Hannah-Mary's large family. Children are an expense, certainly, but his own farm could sustain more. He dares not raise the question with Mary. He does his duty every Saturday night and sometimes during the week if he is not too tired. Most likely a problem with the Hall women, he thinks. After all, it took ages for Elizabeth to fall pregnant with Mary-Ann, then years before Frannie. He must be thankful for what he still has. So many in the area have lost sons fighting for Queen and Country in the Crimea, though for what, he is unsure. Pray God let peace fall soon.

As Joseph walks the land on the first day of January 1856, he has every reason for cautious optimism. The last year's crops and sales of beasts returned a slightly increased income for the farm. As he watches young John running ahead with the dogs, he looks forward to another turn of the seasons and, God willing, all will be well. Maybe another child? Mary is not yet too old. Perhaps Frannie would benefit from the additional tuition at Miss Legge's academy? Mary-Ann continues to blossom there and his younger daughter probably needs more help. He will discuss it with his wife, share his thoughts for the future. After all, his brother, Godfrey's daughter, Mary, was sent as a boarder to a school in Pontefract when she was just six years old. And she has turned out a lovely young woman.

As they reach the wooden bridge over the Ing, John turns back to his father with a smile that echoes his father's optimism. In a year's time Joseph will stand in this very spot and remember this moment and will never trust his faith again.

CHAPTER 34

1855 December – 1856 Summer

Mary does not share her husband's optimism. She is strangely uneasy as another year begins. Amidst their Christmas festivities, Joseph and the children were oblivious to her fears.

Early in December, during a shopping excursion to Doncaster, she had arranged to meet her brother Mark, choosing early in the day, before The George became busy. She was greeted by his wife, Ann, who bustled around the private parlour above the public rooms, her mouth tight with anger or frustration, Mary could not tell. She noted a steely determination in her sister-in-law's eyes and to lighten the air, asked after the children and Ann's family up in London. They were interrupted by the appearance of Mark hovering in the doorway, as if unsure whether to enter this scene of polite gentility.

Mary was taken aback by his appearance. Unlike his wife who was conservatively but smartly turned-out to welcome customers, he was dressed like a common labourer. But it was his face that shocked her. Red-rimmed eyes indicated a lack of sleep and in the poor light of a winter's morning his skin was puffy and florid. He moved forwards into the room, his own parlour, yet as an interloper.

'Brother, how are you my dear?' Mary stepped forward to kiss his cheek but flinched at the smell of alcohol on his breath. Ann missed nothing, sniffed and excused herself.

'I'll be off downstairs, if you don't mind. We cannot leave the taproom unattended for any length of time. Who knows what people get up to?' She threw an accusing look at her husband and sallied forth.

Brother and sister sat together and Mary prattled on about family life at the farm.

'Have you seen anything of our brother? Henry rides over from time to time and we shall see him at church on Christmas Day, no doubt.' He nodded without conveying meaning. She continued: 'I don't expect Martha will be joining him, though. Her confinement will start any time now and she will be especially careful as it's her first.'

Conversation was one-sided and, as she struggled to find matters to engage Mark, she noticed his hands as he clasped and unclasped them, then thrust them between his knees. Nothing, though, could disguise the tell-tale tremors. Should she speak of it? She hesitated but the moment was lost. He rose with an attempt of a smile.

'I am sorry Mary that I don't come out to see you and Joseph. The inn demands our full attention and we dare not leave it in the hands of others while we take a day's leave. Same reason I don't have chance to visit my brother either. I rely on him, like you, to call by when he can. I know that he does not approve of my chosen way of life but he must know that farming was never my destiny.'

Mary ignored the implication that she could not be proud of the brother before her and leant forward, catching the trembling hands in hers.

'Mark, promise me that you will seek help. It is clear to me that you are working too hard and that your health is suffering. Please go and see a doctor and find out what's to be done. It distresses me to see you unwell.' Her brother smiled at the euphemisms and nodded his agreement. Her weak smile in return indicated tacit understanding that he would do no such thing.

This memory haunts Mary as the third of January occasions a small ceremony at her sister's grave. Mary-Ann is back at the academy but Joseph and Frannie take a wreath of fir cones to commemorate the seventh anniversary of Elizabeth's death. Is Mark destined for an early grave too?

Next day she visits her brother, Henry, ostensibly to offer support to Martha, due to be delivered any day now. Elizabeth Barraclough is already in the house, ready to render her skills to preserve the life of mother and child. Mary speaks privately with her brother.

'When did you last see our Mark?' Her question is laden with concern. He shrugs, fully aware of his brother's condition.

'Just before Christmas, but only briefly. I cannot abide the smell of the alehouse and it distresses me to see how my older brother has taken such a path. What a family we are.'

Mary is stung by the implied criticism of her illegal marriage.

'So, what's to do, Henry? Do we just stand by and let him drink himself to death? Whatever we think of him, he has a wife and children to support. And he is our kith and kin. There must be something.'

'Look Mary. Only he can stop this onward descent into damnation. The Lord will forgive him if he changes his ways, but Mark must decide to take the path that He decrees: the straight and narrow path of righteousness. God save his soul because there is nowt that you or I can do.'

Mary is not surprised by Henry's fervour. From a small child, he was the most God-fearing in the family. None of them felt they were ever going to be good enough to attain his pious standards. She wonders whether Martha shares her husband's strict views. She suspects not. Two days later, her sister-in-law is delivered of a son and the Hall family rejoices while Joseph sighs that still there is no sign of a further child for him and Mary.

*

As he watches the slightly-built figure of Frannie slipping and sliding her way to meet the line of children heading for Arksey school, Joseph is minded of his plan. He intends to offer her the same education as her sister. His suggestion was not received enthusiastically by Mary but he is undeterred. That evening, newly returned from the second milking of the day and with winter darkness returning the labourers to their homes, he sits with the family around the supper table. He gauges that this is the moment.

'Frannie, would you like to join Mary-Ann and continue your schooling at the academy?'

Mary is startled by the bluntness of his proposition. Frannie drops her knife with a clatter and sinks back in her chair. The reaction surprises Joseph. Surely, she would be happy to join her older sister with all the opportunities that Miss Legge's academy offer. But Frannie is only seven years old and her father does not understand that, although she misses Mary-Ann, she loves her home and especially mothering young John.

She sits opposite her father. At the other end of the kitchen table, her little brother is oblivious to the drama. He is bent on driving his mother to pleasurable distraction with his questions. The girl has said not a word and is paralysed by the prospect of having to leave all this behind to live among strangers, in a class of younger girls far removed from Mary-Ann.

Joseph pulls his chair closer to her and she jumps as the wooden legs shriek across the stone flags. John pauses to look up briefly then resumes his pursuit of knowledge with his doting mother.

'You know how much Mary-Ann enjoys her life at the school and you would come home every Saturday to be with the family.' His daughter sits staring up at him and he sees her eyes welling with tears. She has her mother's eyes. Frannie bites her lip and nods, not daring to speak, hoping that the tears will stay inside her eyes and not betray her by overflowing down her cheeks. She isn't a baby anymore.

Mary becomes conscious of the girl's distress. She is opposed to the idea of the academy for Frannie and believes it is far too early for her stepdaughter to be launched into a world which may not always be kind to her.

'What your father means to say is that we would be happy to give you the same opportunity as Mary-Ann to learn new things and meet lovely friends like Hannah-Mary Willey.' The girl nods, still fearing to speak. 'But remember one thing, my dear, we would not force you to go, should your heart be set against it.' Mary finishes with a smile at Frannie and a pointed look at her husband. 'That's right, isn't it?'

The girl relaxes back into her chair and, with a serious face, responds with a tremor in her voice: 'One … one day I would be happy to attend the academy, Father, but I have not been long at the village school and I have so much to learn first. I would not wish to let you down because I could not keep up with the other girls. And John is too young to be on his own. I remember that when I was his age it was Mary-Ann who took care of me. It's my turn to look after him.'

For Mary it is like a knife to her heart to hear this. Her gaze drops to her hands lying motionless in her lap. Has she been so wrapped up in her own child that she has neglected this poor lass, a wee thing who never knew her own mother? She dares not meet Joseph's eye. He would be thinking the same.

The subject is dropped and Frannie happily continues her daily battles with writing, reading and arithmetic surrounded by the village children with their varied abilities and backgrounds. Certainly, the village school knocks off the corners and prepares you for life in a very different way to the academy, contemplates Mary.

*

Spring brings the welcome news that hostilities in the Crimea have ceased and that a peace treaty will be signed in Paris. The towns and villages across the land look forward to the return of their sons who have been away fighting in foreign lands. For the Addys, life is more prosaic and Joseph hopes that the low rainfall of recent years does not continue as the yield on his crops has reduced commensurately.

By May, the Addy family is again in mourning. Joseph's sweet niece, Mary has finally succumbed to the consumption which brought her low since Christmas when the coughing started. Yet again, Joseph tries to console his brother, Godfrey, in yet another loss. The sadness overwhelms his own wife as another month passes and still no sign of a baby.

'What is the point to bring a child into the world, nurture and protect it; see a son grow strong then drown; see a daughter blossom into a lovely woman then sicken and die?' Her faith falters further.

Come spring, there is talk of a blazing row between the Hall brothers. Henry has challenged Mark on the amount of alcohol he drinks. Mary knows that he no longer tries to hide his condition and she is horrified to see how his children avoid him at all cost. His wife, Ann, is proud and reluctant to discuss their situation.

'Please tell me Ann, does he strike the children, does he strike you when he is inebriated?'

Her sister-in-law will not wash her dirty linen in public and resents his family descending on The George to question how they live.

'Of course, not,' she snaps. 'I was brought up in London and I know how to handle a man when he is in his cups.' Mary winces to think of Ann's past life that has prepared her with such skills. She probes further and soon realises that her concern is not welcome and that the Hall family should mind its own business and leave Mark and Ann to manage their own problems.

*

On any farm, summer means hard work, and this year is no exception. Joseph is grateful when John Willey offers to send one of his sons to collect Mary-Ann for the annual visit to his farm. John-Henry is delegated to this task and arrives one afternoon in August with his sister Hannah-Mary. They will stay the night and tomorrow all three will catch the train at Stockbridge to travel north.

Mary is intrigued to meet more of the Willey family. She finds Hannah-Mary a sensible if slightly prickly girl and the brief acquaintance with the father last year assured her that they are God-fearing folk. She eyes John-Henry who greets her husband with a respectful hand-shake. Joseph notes that the lad, now nearing eighteen years old, is a good-looking, sturdy young man. Mary-Ann appears at the farmhouse door and welcomes the brother and sister with a wide smile. John-Henry grins back and waves.

Over supper that evening they learn more about the wool trade and it is clear that John Willey has a thriving business up in Bradford.

'We buy in the wool from all over the region and then sell it on to the spinners and then the weavers.' John-Henry displays enthusiasm for his family's company.

'I hear tell that many of the home weavers are losing work due to the introduction of mechanised looms,' probes Joseph. Mary-Ann sits quietly, listening intently.

'Aye Sir, that is true and sadly for it, but Bradford's worsted is the best and sold throughout the world and we have to remain competitive, especially against the French. The powered looms produce cloth at a phenomenal rate and more cheaply than the weavers in their own houses.'

Joseph nods. He too must make decisions which will affect the number of men he employs in future.

The journey north to Bradford is blessed with fine weather and the three travellers enjoy the breeze on their faces as they cover the last stretch from Birkenshaw station up to Moor House. Throughout the journey, Mary-Ann was quieter than usual but only Hannah-Mary noticed. John-Henry concentrated on the view from the railway carriage, talking from time to time about his work and the family. For the first time, Mary-Ann struggled to find something to say to him. He is no longer just one of Hannah-Mary's brothers, he has become a man, and at thirteen, she is unsure what to talk about, without sounding like a silly goose.

Her awkwardness is dispelled as soon as they arrive at the farmhouse and she is greeted warmly by Mrs Willey. She thanks John-Henry for his kindness and once more she is back amidst a family full of contrasts but one where she feels at home.

CHAPTER 35

1856 Autumn

It is Henry who brings the news to Mary. Intent on sweeping autumn leaves from the farmhouse door, his sister does not hear his arrival. A hand on her shoulder makes her start but her quick smile of welcome disappears as she notes her brother's frown. She bids him follow her into the kitchen and sends Harriet to collect eggs.

'It's Mark. There's been trouble at The George and the magistrates are threatening to revoke his licence. Ann goes before the bench next week to try to have it transferred into her name. Sister, the man is beyond help. We should look to have him put away, for his own sake, let alone that of his family.'

Mary is stricken. 'No, Henry, not that. On my mother's grave, we must do all we can to prevent such a thing. What does Ann say?'

'She's at her wits' end. Her sister, Eliza, has been working for them as barmaid for some while and is a trusty pair of hands, but you need to be firm to keep control of the types that frequent ale houses.'

'And the doctor? Can he not help him? Surely there is another way. I cannot bear to think of him shut up somewhere. Truly, he would go out of his mind.'

'He already is out of his mind on occasions. It's not just the tremors now. He starts raving, seeing things. Ann is paying someone to keep him out of harm's way. She doesn't want her clientele, as she calls them, to witness the family's shame.'

'So, what are you saying, Henry? Do you wish him taken away so he can get better?'

'Aye, mebbe that's the only hope. Is Joseph about? I'd like to discuss it with him too.'

Mary is affronted that her brother does not consider her opinion of value but calls out into the yard for one of the lads to fetch her husband.

Together the men discuss Mark's predicament and conclude that the family should help Ann pay for him to be taken to the institution in Doncaster where genteel families send relatives with 'problems'. No doubt only for a short while, they reassure Mary. She agrees. What other solution is there?

None of this is discussed in front of the children. The fewer people who know, the better, and Mary does not wish to burden the girls with the shame of her family.

At the academy, Mary-Ann is becoming more proficient at French and dreams of one day travelling across the Channel to visit Paris. In the meantime, she and Hannah-Mary pore over the ladies' magazines which illustrate the latest fashions emanating from that capital of style.

At the village school, Frannie is happy to plod along, mindful that she must study diligently as one day, hopefully not yet, she will be sent to Miss Legge's academy for young ladies. If she receives good reports in the meantime, possibly her father will allow her to remain at the local school.

*

By the middle of November over in Doncaster the news from The George is more encouraging. After a month's convalescence, as they call it, Mark has returned from the institution to his family. He is subdued, probably as a result of the doses of laudanum administered to calm him, and his children greet his return, hopeful that their father is now cured. His wife is less convinced and instructs all the staff to prevent him from drinking any alcohol whatsoever.

Sadly, the craving is too great. As December approaches, a busy time for all innkeepers, Ann Hall is distracted, and the deviousness of the dedicated drinker wins through. Secretly he stashes away bottles and his alcohol-induced torpor is misdiagnosed for the continued treatment of sedation.

At the Addy farm there are other more pressing anxieties. In autumn there is an outbreak of scarlatina among schoolchildren in Doncaster and there are real fears that it might spread to the children of Arksey and Bentley. Mary hears talk among villagers in the local shops that cousins living in Doncaster are infected. Still, no sign of any illness here. She wonders whether she should keep Frannie home from school until after Christmas. She is less concerned about Mary-Ann, even though she is amidst it all in Doncaster. The academy is on a slight hill, above the noxious air of the poorer parts of the town and the young ladies do not come into contact with other children.

She is loth to travel into the town herself and feels guilty that she has not yet seen Mark since his return from the cure. Joseph suggests that he might take her into Doncaster and together they could seek Christmas presents for the three children. While there, he would be happy to accompany her to The George and see her brother.

Within the stable-yard of the tavern, Mark's ostler takes the reins from Joseph and accepts the coin which will ensure the safekeeping of the brown-paper parcels stowed under the seat. The Addys make their way through the public rooms and up the staircase past the guest rooms and up again to the family's private quarters. Joseph sent word ahead that they would be calling and Ann Hall rises to meet them as they enter the parlour. Her demeanour indicates that their visit is inconvenient and Mary immediately apologises.

'Please forgive us if we are disturbing your day but we are anxious to know how fares Mark, now that he is returned home?' She gives an encouraging smile. *Please tell me all is well.*

'I told your Henry that there is no point in paying out good money for my husband to remain in that place. If it were simply a case of feeding him the poppy, we could have done that well enough here at a fraction of the cost.' She does not invite them to sit and indicates they should follow her to one of the bedrooms. Joseph pauses on the threshold and Mary takes a sharp intake of breath. Mark lies on a single iron bedstead and at his side sits a middle-aged man smoking a pipe. The room is sparsely furnished, without carpeting. A meagre fire burns in the grate. The floor either side of the bed is spread with newspaper.

'He vomits.' Ann does not wish them to think they cannot afford carpeting.

Mark is restless in the bed, his arms and legs struggling against the blankets which aim to keep him confined. His eyes sweep over them and beyond but, to Mary's horror, she realises that he does not see her. His mouth is working and he mumbles softly to himself. Occasionally he laughs. It is a chilling sound.

'This is William Scales.' Ann makes a one-sided introduction.

'Good-day Mr Scales, I am Mr Hall's sister, and this is my husband, Mr Joseph Addy.' Mary is desperate to bring civility into this blighted room. 'It is good of you to sit with my brother while he is resting.' Scales shrugs.

‘It costs less for me to pay Scales to watch over him than to take one of the inn servants away from the work they need to do.’ Ann does not allow for niceties. She is past that now. She just needs to survive.

‘I understand that the magistrates have transferred the licence to your name, Ann. That must be a relief.’ Joseph trails off, not knowing what else to say. He sees that Mary is devastated by the state of her brother and wishes to remove her from this place as quickly as possible.

‘Indeed,’ is Ann’s non-committal response. She turns towards the door. ‘I shall be down in the parlour when you are done.’

Mary approaches her brother and steels herself against the sour smell which rises from this body lying in clammy sweat and heaven knows what else.

‘Dear Brother,’ she whispers. ‘May God love you and care for you.’ She cannot bring herself to kiss his forehead and despises herself for it. Joseph takes her hand and they leave. Her brother continues to murmur incoherently.

The news of her brother’s death is brought on Saturday afternoon by one of the inn-servants. Mark died that morning attended by William Scales who had struggled much of the night to calm the poor man’s raving. His body gave out just after daylight. At forty-two years of age, it could take no more. Scales signs the death certificate with his cross.

Mary-Ann is already home and together with Frannie is told that Uncle Mark has gone to Heaven. Tomorrow they will pray in church for his soul and for his family, Aunt Ann and their four cousins. Mary shudders to think how they will cope now. Joseph privately ponders that someone as tough as Ann Hall may well do better for her family than ever her husband did.

The following Tuesday, the Reverend Stoddart officiates at All Saints. Ann has closed The George for the morning and travelled to Arksey with her older children and the inn-servants. At the graveside, they stand in the bitter cold and the widow declines the arm of her brother-in-law Henry, preferring the support of her sister, Eliza. This day has to be endured and then she will gather herself together and face a future which will be hard but, dear Lord, so much easier without Mark.

Once home in her bedroom, Mary removes her black cloak and bonnet and longs to lie down, to remove all memory of the last few weeks. Behind her, the door opens and in the gloomy light of a December day stands young Frannie, leaning shivering against the door jamb.

'Mother, may I go to bed now, I really do not feel well. My throat is really sore.' Mary is at her side in a moment and feels the girl's burning forehead. Even in this light she can see the flushed red cheeks which frame the whiteness of the skin surrounding the mouth. She rolls up Frannie's sleeve and to her despair sees the tell-tale wine-red rash along her arm. Scarlet fever. But how? Where did she catch it?

The girl is propelled into the nursery but then Mary stops. No, she cannot be in the same room as John. She leads Frannie into Mary-Ann's room. The girl resists.

'No, Mother. Mary-Ann will be fair vexed if I sleep in her bed.' Her protestations are overruled and she is so weak that she allows herself to be undressed and tucked up in bed. In moments, she is asleep. Mary turns to see young John at the door.

'Out,' she says sharply, so much so that tears spring into her son's eyes. That is not her way, to speak harshly. He wonders what he has done. She longs to hold him but dares not in case she is also contaminated. Instead, she laughs and says that he is to go down into the kitchen and ask Harriet to give him some hot milk and a biscuit on Mamma's say so. He trots off contentedly. All is right again in his little world.

The household is soon alerted and Frannie's bedlinen is removed and taken into the yard to be burnt. Mary scrubs the bedstead and all the toys that Frannie and John have touched. She does not know what to do with the cloth dolls beloved of both children, so she wraps them in brown paper and takes them down into the cellar for now.

Since John is frightened to sleep alone without his sister, that night Mary moves into the nursery. Frannie lies in the adjacent room and throughout the night Mary shares her time between the two rooms, wiping her stepdaughter's body with cooling wet cloths. By lamplight she refers to her sister Elizabeth's 1840 edition of Buchan's *Domestic Medicine*, scanning the pages to find the best treatment.

Sleep evades Joseph also. He lies awake, planning his actions for the morrow. First thing, send a lad to Doncaster to fetch the doctor. Then, a message to the academy. On no account should Mary-Ann be permitted to return home this weekend. Pray God his little lass will have turned the corner by the next week. He is reminded that on the following Saturday all the young ladies return to their families for Christmas. He cannot think that far ahead.

As the doctor takes his leave the following morning, he confirms that there are now two cases of scarlet fever in Bentley and four in Arksey, all children from the village school. He has left remedies for them to administer to Frannie and stresses that the outcome will depend on whether the fever breaks or not.

Mary wishes to send John away to her brother, but Joseph dissuades her as he surmises correctly that Henry would not want a child from a contaminated family to mix with his own. No, they have to keep John close but away from his sister.

Another night and yet another passes. The girl is restless and her body burns with heat. Her parents look on helpless with little confidence in the laudanum-based concoction they feed her. Mary has little contact with John, just in case, and it is down to Harriet to amuse him during the day. By Friday though he has little appetite, either for food or play.

'Missus.' Harriet stands quietly at the doorway to the sickroom. Mary turns to see the servant holding John by the hand. At once Mary is beside him, on her knees, viewing with horror the same flushed face displayed by his sister.

'Oh, dear God,' she whispers. She scoops him up in her arms and carries him back into the nursery. Deftly she undresses the little lad to reveal the pink mottling. She shakes her head in disbelief.

'No, no, no,' she moans. 'Not this, please God, not him too.'

CHAPTER 36

1856 December

The doctor removes his coat to examine the boy. Joseph stands at the window and looks out over his fields, seeking solace from nature. The barren winter landscape offers no consolation. Mary kneels beside the bed, ready to answer the doctor's bidding. John lies with eyes half closed and responds to the request to open his mouth. His throat is coated white. Just as the doctor anticipated. He covers the boy's scarlet-stained body, straightens up and reaches for his coat. Joseph hastens to help him.

'It is of course scarlet fever.' The doctor hesitates. He has attended many of the Addy family over the years and has grown to like Joseph. This is a severe blow for the farmer. His voice softens as he delivers his warning. 'Sadly, this little lad does not have the robust constitution of his sister.' Mary's face pales. 'In addition to the syrup of poppies each evening, I prescribe emollient clystors and will send the medication and syringe this afternoon. Will you be able to administer this?' She nods agreement but quite dreads the notion. No matter how efficacious the remedy might be, the child will resist the insertion of the metal syringe into the rectum. She shudders.

The house is silent as each goes about their business without fuss. John's parents exchange no words. What is there to say? They are lost in their own thoughts. Harriet brings to the nursery a pail of pump water freshly drawn and icy cold. Mary repeatedly rinses a linen cloth, wrings it out and bathes the burning face and neck of her son. Joseph carries Frannie back into her own bed in the nursery. There is now no need to separate brother and sister.

Frannie's fever continues but she is calmer. Mary bathes her skinny body to ease the itching of the scaly skin, now starting to peel. The doctor has warned that she could remain thus for two to three weeks before the disease has run its course. The girl takes a little broth.

'My throat hurts when I swallow,' she protests.

'I am sorry my pet, but you must take nourishment. How else will you grow strong again?'

'Does John also take some broth?' Her bed has been positioned so that she cannot see her little brother, who lies quiet now. During the night her sleep was disturbed by the sound of the boy having a fit, both parents at his side, bathing his legs and feet, as instructed. Only the syrup of poppies calms him back into a stupor rather than a sleep.

'Not just yet, Frannie. He is at an earlier stage than you and we cannot give him to drink while he is sleeping, else he might choke.'

Christmas looms and Joseph makes a decision. Messages are despatched to Moor House. Would they accept Mary-Ann over Christmas? He could not bear the thought of her staying on at the academy with only the Misses Legge and any orphan girls for company. Within a day they receive welcoming news from Mrs Willey and a note is sent to Mary-Ann. Joseph would like to deliver it in person but knows that he risks infecting the girl and her fellow pupils.

Mary-Ann is already distraught at being separated from her sister and brother, but she recognises the peril of returning home too soon. Her distress is mitigated somewhat by the prospect of a

Christmas spent within Hannah-Mary's large family. She makes a list of extra warm clothes for Harriet to pack and send to the academy ready for the journey to East Bierley. She feels guilty to be deserting her family at a time of need but understands the wisdom of the decision. Pragmatism is instinctive for Mary-Ann.

The doctor calls a second time and sees some improvement in Frannie. Her body temperature has reduced and now she is able to take softened foods since her throat is less inflamed. His greater concern lies with her brother.

John continues to convulse unless he is fed syrup of poppies. Mary is unconvinced that the clystors are doing him any good and challenges the doctor.

'Sir, I followed your bidding and apply the clystors daily but the only result is to cause him great distress and I beg leave to desist from further applications.'

The doctor nods. He, like so many of his calling, follows the prescribed methods of the day but he also is not convinced of the healing powers of all procedures.

'Continue with the syrup of poppies and persuade him to take liquid, if you can. A body can manage without food for longer periods, but water is essential for survival.' Mary flinches at the word 'survival'. She knows that her son's life is at risk but rejects the word spoken aloud.

In the coming days both John's parents pray for his deliverance. Neither articulates the thought but foremost in their minds stands the question: is this God's punishment for their marrying against the will of the Church? As word spreads around the village that Joseph's only son and heir shows no sign of improvement, it is precisely this thought that permeates the superstitious minds of the ungenerous.

Messages of support, jars of conserves and honey, freshly baked pies arrive at the farm from Joseph's brother and sister and from Mary's sisters-in-laws. Their thoughtfulness is a fleeting consolation, but the moment is quickly gone, and John's parents are back in the present and the reality is terrifying and relentless.

A week after their son showed the first symptoms, the fitting ceases. A good sign? Sadly no. The uninterrupted stupor is now a precursor to the end. In the early hours of Saturday, the twentieth day of December, death comes for John Addy, aged four years and five months. Joseph is at his son's side, taking his turn to see the night through. He has struggled to stay awake in the low lamp-light, the only sounds the hissing of coal burning in the grate, the laboured breathing of his daughter and son. Eyes closed but still awake, he hears John gasping to fill his young lungs. Joseph is torn between staying with the boy, to lift him up and ease his breathing, or to go and wake his wife. The decision is taken from him. With two long drawn-out breaths, there are no more. Stunned with grief, Joseph stares through tears. He gently shakes his son but there comes no further breathing. He buries his head in the blankets and sobs uncontrollably. His dear boy, his son.

Frannie is awakened and calls out into the dimness. 'Father, what is it? Please Father, why do you weep so?'

In the adjacent room, Mary, only half sleeping, wakes to hear their cries and scrambles from bed with a cry of pain resembling no human voice. She stands shivering with cold and shock. Her baby. Her baby is gone. She pushes Joseph aside to kneel and kiss her child while he is still warm. Why God? Why take him? What was his sin?

Mary and Joseph weep over their son. Separately, they weep. In the cocoon of her bed, Frannie pulls the blankets tighter around her and over her head. She cannot bear to see the grief of her parents and turns away into her own tears of guilt. She brought this sickness to the house.

In Doncaster later that morning there is little conversation as Mr Willey departs the academy with the two friends for their journey north. Mary-Ann is sorrowful believing that her brother and sister lie desperately ill and, for the first time in her life, she leaves her family to spend Christmas elsewhere. News of her brother's death has not reached her. Joseph decided that she should not be told.

Mary-Ann fears that the coming days will require all her courage. She cannot inflict her misery on her friend's family so must adopt a mask of ... of what? She cannot appear merry. She does not feel such and it would be inappropriate in any case. A mournful face, albeit representing her inner self, would be unkindness to her hosts. She judges that a quietness with occasional, gentle smiles would be most fitting. Throughout the visit, Mary-Ann and the Willey family will conspire to play out the charade.

The funeral arrangements are settled by the evening of John's death. Word has spread around the village and among the family. During the afternoon his parents receive messages of condolence and Godfrey Addy and Henry Hall each ride over to express in person their deep sadness. Mary cannot receive them. She lies prostrate in bed, still in her nightclothes, unable to wash and dress. Her eyes are closed but she doesn't sleep.

Elizabeth Barraclough is brought in to support Mary. Kindly but practical, she helps the bereft mother to wash and dress then turns her attention to Frannie. The girl has lain facing the wall since hearing Mary's scream of agony. She is exhausted and can muster no energy to fight this cruel disease. Let it take her too. Had she not introduced the scarlet fever into the home then her brother would still live. Her thoughts seek out every corner of her memory. Her mother died so soon after her birth. Was she the cause that time, too?

Two days later, Elizabeth Barraclough remarks a change in the little girl. She takes it upon herself to rearrange the nursery and positions Frannie's bed nearer to the window to benefit from the thin December light. John's bed has been moved. It remains in the room but its emptiness is less strident. Mary walks listlessly into the nursery and stops short when she sees the altered furniture. She is too exhausted to object.

'Mother.' Her attention turns to Frannie. The child is reaching out her arms and tears flow down her distraught face. Mary sits beside her and holds her close. 'Mother, I am sorry, so sorry. It was all my fault.' She sits back, holding the girl's shoulders, and frowns through her own tears.

'What's that you say, lass? What fault?'

'It was me. I brought the fever to our home. John died because of me.'

Mary looks deep into Frannie's eyes. 'Oh no, lass, by no means. The scarlet fever is in the village, in the air about us. Nobody believes that it was your fault,' she lies. Enough that the girl should lose a dearly loved brother; no need for her to bear the burden of causing his death.

For the second time, Mary defies convention and follows her husband as he bears the coffin of their boy. This time it is Godfrey who helps his brother carry the pine box down the aisle of All Saints. It is placed gently on an over-large trestle at the foot of the chancel steps while Mary clings, for fear of fainting, to the acorn-shaped finial atop the pew end. She cannot wrest her eyes from the coffin's unadorned lid and stands shivering with anguish and from the bitter cold of this ancient church which has witnessed seven hundred years of such sorrow.

At the burial she can scarcely stand and her brother, Henry, supports her as John is lowered and gently laid onto the coffin of the baby sister he never knew. Her two babes. Her only babes. Oh cruel, cruel.

CHAPTER 37

1856 December – 1857

The morning of Christmas Eve, Joseph rises wearily from bed. Mary lies still, eyes closed. She wants sleep to return, for ever. What point is there in continuing? She became his wife to care for his daughters but also to produce sons. She has failed. Her body aches with the pain of loss. During his four years, John grew into a spirited, adventurous soul. Now no more his cheerful welcome as she enters the nursery; for Joseph, no willing companion for his evening round.

Joseph enters the nursery and sees a pale face emerge from tumbled bedclothes.

'Father,' Frannie smiles hopefully. He draws back the curtains onto a grey Sunday morning. Snow in the offing. He forces a smile and turns to greet his daughter.

'How is it, my lass? Do you feel a little stronger this morning?'

'Does Mary-Ann know what has passed?'

'Nay, why bring her sad news when she is far from us. Better that we tell her when she can grieve amidst her own.' He seeks to encourage his daughter. 'And by the time we go to fetch her back, we shall bring her the good tidings that her sister is on the mend.'

'Am I getting better, Father? Shall I not die just yet?' Joseph's heart aches.

'The doctor is pleased with your progress and tells us that you have a robust constitution to overcome this dreadful fever.' Apparently satisfied, she snuggles back into her nest.

Mary does not rise and her husband is glad to have the animals to tend. He finds comfort from the indifference of the pigs whose only interest is fodder. Elizabeth Barraclough and Harriet discuss what is to be done and conclude that nobody will fancy a celebratory meal tomorrow, Christmas Day. There is no point in disturbing the Missus, so Harriet wanders out to the mistle where Joseph is inspecting his cows for the second time that morning.

'Master. What shall I prepare for dinner tomorrow? There's a capon waiting in the larder and the pudding is ready for steaming.' Joseph looks at her blankly. What is the girl blathering about? 'Tomorrow, it's Christmas Day. I don't like to bother the Missus. She's still abed. What do you want to eat, roast capon or something simpler?' Joseph shrugs and shakes his head. 'Right then, it'll be capon and leek pie.' Ever the practical, Harriet turns on her heel and returns to the kitchen, her mind already marshalling the ingredients. The pudding can keep until next year.

*

Christmas Day at Moor House Farm and Mary-Ann is reluctant to leave the warmth of the bed she shares with Hannah-Mary. The small panes of the mullion windows are obscured by fanciful designs in ice, the work of Jack Frost. She has never known such bitter cold and in the small hours could hear the wind howling around the eaves, bringing snow direct from all the Russias. Following the overnight snowfall, the day is bright and Mr Willey insists that the family trudge through the drifts to the morning service down at Birkenshaw church. After joining in the seasonal hymns sung lustily by villagers, they return shivering to a roast goose dinner. Unusually, there is wine on the table and Mrs Willey persuades her reluctant husband to allow the two school-friends a small glass with their meal. Hannah-Mary is glad that Mary-Ann is with them, hopeful that the presence of an outsider will dissuade her father from his usual testiness at mealtimes. The taste of the red wine is not unpleasant, but Mary-Ann has no wish for more. She feels it warming her body. As her neck becomes red, John-Henry teases her so she blushes all the more and prays that Mr Willey does not notice.

After dinner, the presents are exchanged, and Mary-Ann is relieved by the absence of extravagant gifts among the family. She gives Hannah-Mary a copy of Charles Dickens' latest tale and is thrilled to receive in return a book of adventure stories set in the American Rockies. How imaginative of her friend. Mrs Willey presents her with a bright red woollen scarf, comforting in many ways, and explains the absence of gifts from Bentley.

'Your parents will have something for you when you are back in Doncaster. The last weeks have been difficult for them ...' Her voice trails away and Mary-Ann nods vigorously.

'Oh yes, of course. I do understand and it is so kind of you all to invite me to share Christmas with you.'

At this point, Mr Willey withdraws, insisting that his wife accompany him in reading quietly. The rest of the family fall into a game of charades. Mary-Ann joins in and soon the laughter succeeds in suppressing thoughts of home. She observes this large disparate family, particularly Louisa, the bride-to-be who is cherishing this, her last Christmas before her spring wedding. What adventures lie ahead with her marriage to Mary-Ann's cousin, Will Addy and, most exciting of all, the voyage out to their new life in America. Only Godfrey seems not to fit in and fortunately, as soon as the meal ended, he disappeared.

Despite the worry she bears, everyone treats Mary-Ann as before, but John-Henry is particularly protective. He notes her watching Benjamin, at five still the 'baby' of the family, and realises that he is of a similar age to Mary-Ann's brother lying perilously ill in Bentley.

'Please show me your gift, Mary-Ann.' She looks gratefully at the young man who has emerged from the gangling youth she met on her first visit to Moor House. She slips away to find the precious book and is pleased when he follows her. They sit at the dining table, now cleared of dishes, enjoying the warmth of the waning fire and, above all, the quiet.

'Peace at last,' he murmurs in the deep tones she has grown to admire. Suddenly she feels quite awkward. How ridiculous. She has known him long enough. Now though, she is aware of him as a man not a boy. To cover her shyness, she opens the book at the preface with its map of North America. Together they seek out Illinois and the area where Louisa and William intend to farm. Mary-Ann's finger traces another route across the land.

'Miss Jameson is our geography teacher and, a while back, her brother emigrated. This is where he landed, and we have followed his progress across the country. I am sure his sister would love to join him eventually.' John-Henry is struck by the light shining in her eyes and warms to her enthusiasm.

'Aha, do I detect a small sign of envy in your voice, Miss?' he teases. 'Daresay you too would like to travel overseas one day, am I not right?' Mary-Ann pauses. The question has never been posed before, but she needs only seconds to consider. Her face reveals the answer.

'Oh yes. Can you imagine anything more exciting? But that would be only a dream. I haven't travelled beyond Doncaster and Bradford and I must discover London before I look beyond.' The young man will recall this conversation in years to come.

*

Back in Bentley, the Addy family endures Christmas Day. Before returning to spend it with her own, Elizabeth Barraclough encourages Mary to wash and dress so that Joseph will not eat alone. Harriet lays table for them in the warmth of the kitchen and what was intended as a comforting homely meal is eaten in silence other than the Master's words of thanks as the young woman serves up. Mary picks at her food and looks regretfully at Harriet as unfinished plates are cleared away. She excuses herself and steals away up to their bedroom, without energy to face Frannie and the empty bed beside her. Joseph follows her up the stairs, but his sole aim is to ensure that Frannie has eaten with Harriet's help and that she feels loved on this sad Christmastide.

Immediately after Christmas, Joseph calls the doctor to his wife who remains in bed, white as the sheets and as lifeless. Before taking the stairs, he briefly paints the picture. The doctor nods, already expecting the grief to have taken its toll. The examination of the patient takes but minutes and down in the parlour he puts a hand on Joseph's shoulder.

'This is the second child she has lost and also your only son. Her deep grief is understandable, Mr Addy, but we have to address it at once otherwise she will sink into melancholy from which she will never rise.' He hesitates before adding, 'And melancholy will not be conducive to her bearing further children, especially after the difficulties she experienced during her last confinement.'

Joseph, already desolate, stares bleakly back at the doctor. 'What can be done, then?'

'At all costs you should protect her from aught of a disagreeable nature. Grief indulged destroys the appetite and the digestion. We have to change her outlook. It is utterly impossible that anyone of a dejected mind could enjoy good health. Not just my view, Sir, but that of eminent men of medicine. You should turn her mind to new objects and when she tires of such, find something new. She must mix with people of a cheerful disposition and simple pursuits can bring diversion. I warn you though to guard against drinking alcohol, the course of many similarly overwhelmed by grief. Therein lies ruin.' This final exhortation is delivered with a warning raised finger. He turns abruptly towards the door, adding, 'My boy will bring a tonic this afternoon which will help her in the coming weeks. But hark my words, Mr Addy, stimulate her mind.'

In the next few days, Joseph watches as Elizabeth Barraclough administers the doctor's tonic to his scarcely responsive wife. He lacks energy to carry out the instruction to stimulate Mary and instead sends word to Moor House that he will come to fetch the two girls and return them to the academy for the start of the new term.

As the carrier's cart struggles up the ice-rutted lane, the verges piled high with cleared snow, the younger members of the Willey family alert their mother to the arrival of Mary-Ann's father. She braces herself for what is likely to be a difficult meeting and checks the small pile of trimmed cotton handkerchiefs discreetly placed behind a bowl of dried lavender.

Mary-Ann throws herself onto her father as he struggles out of his great coat and many scarves. Already, she is weeping with relief at seeing him. Mrs Willey ushers them both into her small parlour. The rest of the family melts away out of respect; only Hannah-Mary lingers in the freezing hallway.

Joseph sits beside Mary-Ann and takes her hands in his as he sorrowfully tells her of the death of her brother. They weep together, as does Mrs Willey, who rises, hands handkerchiefs to both and leaves them to their grief. She passes Hannah-Mary and wordlessly shakes her head, dabbing her eyes. The girl leans back against the wall, her face creased in a frown.

The journey back to Doncaster passes almost in silence. Mary-Ann is held close by her father. Hannah-Mary wills her friend to be strong. It is still too soon for them to return to the

Addy's farm, even though Frannie is making good progress. The girls wave farewell to Joseph from the door of the academy and he is relieved to see Mary-Ann enveloped in the arms of the stout, elder Miss Legge. He dreads returning to the silence of his home.

That silence continues relentlessly over the coming weeks. The greyness of the short winter days seems interminable, despite being punctuated by occasional sunshine reflecting off fresh snow. Joseph calls upon his wider family to help carry out the doctor's bidding to spark Mary's interest. To no avail. She rises late, wears the same gown day after day until Harriet hides it and leaves out an alternative. When the tonic is finished, she demands more be fetched from the apothecary. Poor Frannie is much improved but the atmosphere at home is dire and she follows her father about the house from the minute he comes in from the farm. It is far too cold for her to accompany him outside and the girl feels suffocated by the enforced confinement. She tries repeatedly to speak with her mother but Mary gazes at her, almost unseeing.

By the end of January, the Misses Legge feel that Frannie is sufficiently out of quarantine to allow her sister to return home for weekends without risk of bringing disease to her classmates. Mary-Ann is excited to return home for the first time in months and Joseph hopes that her visit will bring cheer to the family.

She is shocked by the change in Mary. Always neatly dressed and full of quiet confidence and kindness, her stepmother is now a shell. Her hair is in need of washing. The cuffs of her blouse are slightly grubby. There are a few marks on her skirt. Does Father not notice such things? She is struck mostly by the eyes. If they are the windows onto the soul, Mary's soul is long departed.

Finally, she turns to Frannie, dear Frannie, now thinner than before, and the joy in meeting again is shared equally by the sisters. They hug closely and Frannie whispers, 'Please can we play with *Cinderella* this afternoon?' The escape into the imaginary world of fairy-tales is what the little girl needs and later that day Joseph discovers them crouched over the toy theatre, re-enacting the familiar story with a solitary audience of Henrietta, the much-missed costume doll. He envies them their diversion.

Slowly, Frannie regains strength and by mid-February is strong enough to attend school, mornings only. By now though, she has her sights set elsewhere.

'Father, do you think I am now old enough to join Mary-Ann at the academy?'

Her father pauses, his heart lurching at the prospect of losing this final vestige of brightness but recognises that he must let her go. His mood sinks at the thought of life alone with Mary.

CHAPTER 38

1857 Spring

By early spring a new headstone is erected in the churchyard of All Saints, Arksey. It is carved with an angel bearing a shawl to swathe the little ones and is inscribed:

In memory of

two beloved children of

Joseph** and **Mary ADDY

of Bentley.

Sophia Eliza

died September 12th 1851,

aged 6 months,

*and **John***

died December 20th 1856,

aged 4 years.

If faithful here we soon shall leave this world for one above.

And with our children ever live in bonds of joy and love.

Heaven rejoices - Nature weeps.

*

Down the road in Doncaster, the latest recruit to Miss Legge's academy kneels in prayer at the end of her first day. Frannie screws up her eyes all the better for her prayers to reach God. Under her arm she cuddles Rabbit, the washed-out woolly animal Mother gave her when she was little. She prays first for her father, trying to forget his mournful eyes as he waved her farewell this morning. *Please let him be sad no longer.* She thanks God for her dear sister, Mary-Ann who stood protectively at her side throughout the day, reassuring her at every turn. She asks the Lord to keep safe her own sweet mother, long departed, unremembered yet not forgotten. Also, the souls of darling Sophia and John, both now held in His arms. Finally, she begs Him to cherish and comfort dear Mother who grieves so deeply at her loss twice over. Please give her strength to seize life as before, to be the dear mother who has loved and cared for her since for ever and may Mother forgive her for bringing the illness that took her sweet boy.

At the farm it is the silence that Mary dreads. She waits until Joseph has risen and headed into the yard before she opens her eyes. Harriet brings a ewer of hot water and departs the room with a gentle reminder to wash before the water cools. The bedroom fire dies down and the chill of the spring morning encourages her to remain in the shroud of her bed.

It is Harriet who now watches over her mistress's clothes and removes from the closet whatever she deems in need of washing, sponging, mending. Once Mary would have reached for the needlework basket and set about repairing a hem or a tear. Not now. She is oblivious. She looks out at the daffodils nodding in the orchard, but they do not cheer her spirits. She turns to the high shelf of the dresser where stands the bottle which will help her through the day. She pours a couple of drops into a small glass and adds a splash of water. The very act of swallowing the few mouthfuls of the diluted tincture is sufficient to bring calm to her troubled mind.

Later in the day, before the Master returns from the fields, Harriet will notice that the level in the bottle of port wine has reduced. It is not that she is actively measuring the contents, but she is nobody's fool and sees what she sees. She holds her tongue. It is for the Master to find out, not for her to add to his burden.

Mary is visited by the wives of her brother, Henry, and of Godfrey Addy. Both sisters-in-law find it difficult to talk with Mary. Conversation is limited and they are reluctant to speak about their own families. They ask after Joseph and the two daughters but Mary struggles to find much to say. She explains briefly that the girls return home each weekend, occasionally accompanied by Hannah-Mary Willey, but disappear upstairs to play in their own world. They study hard, they continue to grow and need new clothes. What else is there to say? Despite the challenge, these kindly visitors return regularly, but neither woman can forget the curse brought down upon this forbidden marriage.

During the week, with the girls away, Joseph walks on eggshells. Desperate to be kind to Mary, he is nonetheless frustrated that she appears to make no effort. He insists that she continues to do the farm's accounts, which she does automatically and efficiently. It does not require any emotional engagement to work with the books and each week enter the figures.

As for the future, he is resigned to there being no more children. They had been warned as such after John's birth, but following the lad's death, there is no question of any intimacy. If only she would allow him close to give her comfort. He cannot know that she only manages to survive each day if she lives it devoid of emotion. Care, comfort, compassion are feelings she can no longer embrace. Far safer for her sanity to bring down a shutter and view life dispassionately. She knows this hurts

Joseph, who is a good man, but also knows he would not force himself upon her. She regrets that she can no longer bear to take Frannie on her knee and cuddle her as before. The distress in the girl's eyes, as her shy approaches are rebuffed, is equally painful for Mary, but she dares not open a chink even for this slip of a lass.

In early April the Willey family travel down to Arksey to attend the wedding of their daughter, Louisa, with Will Addy, Joseph's nephew. The bride chose to marry in the beautiful Norman church where her husband was christened and his father buried. All Saints is alive with family and friends. Out of courtesy, Joseph exchanges a few words with Will's mother, once married to his late brother, George. He has never liked the woman, but she is a member of the Cockin family, well-regarded in Arksey and there are a number of her kin present at the church. At the wedding breakfast afterwards, he encounters Maria Cockin. This independent-minded spinster listens enthusiastically to Joseph's plans for the cultural improvement of his daughters and has recommendations of her own to make. Has he heard of the art exhibition recently opened in Manchester?

Some months later, Joseph is relieved when Frannie declines the kind offer from the Willey family to join Mary-Ann at Moor House for the last three weeks of the summer holidays. Until then, both daughters remain at Bentley, Mary-Ann for the most part engrossed in reading, occasionally visiting former friends from Arksey school. Frannie stays at her father's side as he works the fields. He rejoices in her natural enthusiasm and unbounded energy. The girls are the only source of conversation as they sit for supper together with Mary, and he loves their curiosity and eagerness to discover more. He recalls the conversation with Maria Cockin but presents the idea as his own.

'I read in the paper that in Manchester a fine exhibition of great art has opened to much acclaim. It has the support of the Prince Consort and people are travelling to see it from all over the country, even Mr Dickens.' This aimed at stimulating interest from his wife. 'Perhaps we should visit. What do you think?'

'Manchester. I have never been to Manchester,' cries Mary-Ann with glee. Frannie is caught up with the idea of any adventure and bounces in her chair with excitement. Joseph turns with a smile towards his wife.

'What say you, Mary? It would be good for the girls' education to see so many fine paintings under one roof. They'll not see the like around here and they say it's as good as anything in London.' Before she can respond, Joseph throws his arms wide in a gesture the girls have never seen. 'And it is too far to go there and back in a day. We shall have to stay the night in an hotel. What about that?'

Mary looks at him with fright at the prospect of leaving the farm even for a day let alone overnight. Her fear is countered by the beaming faces of their daughters and she is persuaded that she must suppress her own reservations for their sake. If Charles Dickens felt it warrants a visit …

An excursion train to the exhibition is laid on from Doncaster and the family joins crowds packed into the numerous carriages. Along the way, Joseph explains that a thousand wealthy art collectors from the North-West of England have loaned paintings, sculpture and other artworks to be displayed for all to see, from aristocracy to the working man. Some enlightened industrialists, such as Titus Salt up near Bradford, have even arranged special trains to bring their workers for the day at full pay. When eventually the Addys arrive at the railway station, newly erected at Old Trafford to serve the Art Treasures exhibition, they marvel at the enormity of the massive hall, a gargantuan edifice of brick, iron and glass. Inside, they wonder at the high glazed roof through which sunlight streams to illuminate the tide of visitors way below, surging through the vast halls and galleries.

Joseph is well-informed and has bought a catalogue to guide their visit. He is pleased that they are attending on one of the more expensive days. He cannot imagine the crush on the cheap ticket days, when working men and their families swell the crowds further. There is little structure to their tour, and they struggle to get close to the more famous exhibits. Joseph distracts the children by pointing out the many paintings which, on the upper levels, hang some seven frames high. Some works are already known to the visitors. Many a home is decorated with a print of one famous painting or another and Frannie is thrilled to spot Hans Holbein's majestic portrait of Henry VIII, looking just like he does in her schoolbooks. Mary-Ann is taken by the direct gaze of the boy dressed in blue satin painted by Thomas Gainsborough. She stands before the canvas and tries to imagine his thoughts as he posed in his finery on a wind-swept fell. Where was he travelling to with his coat tucked under his arm?

Mary finds the crowds disconcerting and tries to keep close to Joseph. She is desperately tired and longs for a cup of tea and a quiet moment to take a nip from the phial in her bag. It is forbidden to bring one's own food and drink into the exhibition and the lines at the refreshment stands are long. She calls out to Joseph that she will join the queue and that they should meet her later. The way is not clear, and she finds herself standing at the edge of a group looking with discomforted fascination at Henry Wallis's painting of the impecunious young poet, Chatterton, who has just committed suicide. Her eyes are riveted on the grey-green face of the corpse on the verge of falling from bed, the empty phial of arsenic just out of reach. The poverty of the attic recalls the deathbed of her brother, Mark, and she shudders. This image of desolation will remain long in her memory.

Later, it is a weary party that steps from the local train into the middle of Manchester. Joseph hails a cab to take them to the modest hotel recommended by their more travelled neighbour, Maria Cockin. Even though far from overpowering in its decor, the hotel dining room is nonetheless intimidating. Never before have they stayed in such an establishment. Mary-Ann has positioned herself with her back against the wall so she may watch the room, especially the comings and goings of the waiters, two elderly men dressed in black suits. Only two other tables are occupied. At one a gentleman dines alone. Two middle-aged ladies are drinking soup remarkably silently when the Addys arrive, and their eyes sweep over the family before returning to the clear brown liquid before them. Frannie does not have the same view as her sister and is reprimanded in a low voice when she cranes round to watch another single gentleman enter the room and take his seat. They eat without conversation, and the silence is oppressive.

Mary endures the meal, plain but well cooked, and longs to escape to the room she shares with the girls. Concealed in her carpet bag is a second phial with her tincture. Joseph begins to relax as the meal progresses but there is no conversation, each of them conscious that words spoken will be overheard.

Mary-Ann absorbs the whole and enjoys what she sees. The crisply starched white linen tablecloth and napkins lie smooth beneath her touch. The dark green and cream striped wallpaper lends a quiet elegance and gentility to the scene. She begins to appreciate what lies beyond the confines of Bentley and Doncaster. She likes what she sees.

CHAPTER 39

1857 Summer - 1858

The visit to Manchester Art Treasures dominates Mary-Ann's conversation as she joins Hannah-Mary at Moor House for her summer visit. During the first meal, the girl's eyes sparkle as she relates the adventure of travelling to this by-now-celebrated exhibition. The older girls listen politely to the list of famous people who have viewed works by a further list of famous artists, in turn owned by yet another list of famous connoisseurs. Little interest is shown among the male members of the family, and Mr Willey openly disparages the cultural excursion.

'Seems to me that some folk have more money than sense, to spend it buying paintings to hang on the wall. Far better use it to help them that have nowt.'

John-Henry courageously ignores the father and reveals his curiosity.

'So, Miss, what was the best thing about your visit: a particular painting, Mr Hallé's concert, staying in an hotel?'

Mary-Ann plays with the napkin on her lap, conscious of the censorious eyes of his father. How difficult to respond. She smiles at the young man and he is enchanted by the spark in her eyes.

'It is impossible to say. Everything, but everything was so exciting. To travel such a distance by train, to see all those paintings, some among the best in the world, that was glorious. I didn't even mind being jostled in the crush of the crowds. And yes, I did enjoy the hotel and eating in that dining room, served by waiters. It was all so different from anything I have known. I loved every minute.'

Hannah-Mary is startled by her friend's vehement enthusiasm but is equally taken aback by the look of fascination on the face of her brother. John-Henry returns Mary-Ann's smile, but his eyes convey a deeper meaning. His sister is somewhat uneasy but reflects on the possible reasons and implications and settles back in her chair with the satisfaction of those who think they are the only ones to know a secret. Further down the table, her mother observes the fourteen-year-old girl and recognises the beginnings of a particular friendship, and like her daughter, she is comfortable with the knowledge.

The year continues. The rhythm of the seasons dictates Joseph's life. The girls' studies move forward and individually they develop at their own pace. Frannie is diligent and tries so hard but does not shine at any academic learning. Her needlework, however, is praised by all and at the end of the year she presents her parents with a cross-stitch sampler. Along the top run four rows of the letters of the alphabet, in both capitals and small letters. Below, two peacocks in silhouette stand guard amidst vases of flowers. Together they frame the pronouncement that

There is nothing so much worth

as a mind well instructed.

Frances Addy December 1857.

Mary-Ann surprises herself with her ability to converse in French, albeit simply, and her piano playing is more than passable. She would love to have a piano at home but fears that such expenditure would be frivolous and, in any case, she cannot imagine her family singing together as they do at Moor House. Indeed, she never hears Mary sing at all these days, especially as her stepmother no longer attends church on Sundays.

Mary's absence is noted by all their neighbours but nothing is said. They suspect the reason and the kindlier souls sympathise, while the more judgmental nod knowingly with the thought that the wrath of the Lord lies behind the deaths. Mary herself has not the slightest doubt that she is cursed by God for having sinned and He has punished her cruelly by taking her beloved children. Her fulminating anger drives her into further despair and she rails silently against a God who would allow innocent children to die. If God has turned his back on her, she will do so to Him. Each Sunday she ensures the two girls are smartly turned out but never waves them off as they set out with their father to Arksey church. Instead, she turns to her latest book while Harriet prepares dinner.

This Christmas will be a subdued affair, coming so soon after the first anniversary of John's death. Mary-Ann tries not to draw comparisons with the happy time spent with Hannah-Mary's family a year since. Then she was shielded from the awful truth and permitted the chance of some pleasure. Guiltily she remembers that Frannie was so close to death at that time and could not enjoy any sort of festivity. However, she is about to be heartened by the arrival of a letter.

The day before she returns home for Christmas, the postman delivers to the farm an envelope boldly addressed to Miss Mary-Ann Addy. Her father regards the missive with uncertainty. The simple cream paper envelope bears a penny stamp and is sealed on the back with red wax imprinted with a W. He waits until his daughter settles in before taking her aside.

'A letter has arrived for you. Who could it be from, do you think?' He hands the letter to Mary-Ann and watches with interest as she blushes. She is excited to be the recipient of mail and curious to know who would write to her.

'May I use your paper-knife Father?'

Already she is halfway towards the bureau but needs the key to unlock it. He smiles and obliges, handing her the carved ivory-handled knife. She removes two sheets of neatly written script and turns quickly to the second page to identify the sender.

'Oh,' she blushes again, 'It is from John-Henry, Hannah-Mary's brother.' She becomes flustered. 'How kind of him to write.'

'Indeed,' says Joseph in measured tones, 'And I'm sure he would be happy for me to read it once you have done so.' The flush remains on the girl's cheeks. She is left in no doubt that her father regards it as a matter of propriety that he should monitor any personal address from a young man, whoever he may be. She longs to take the letter to her room but is obliged to sit and read it before her father.

The words are full of cheer and through them she hears the voice of John-Henry telling her about his work and the family's plans to celebrate Christmas together. They all have such fond memories of sharing the festivities with her last year. He remembers the book his sister gave her and enquires if her geography teacher has more to report about life in North America. He asks if he may write to her from time to time but would not presume to do so without her consent. Mary-Ann passes the letter to her father with a hopeful smile. She glows at the thought that John-Henry would wish to correspond with her regularly and hopes her father will approve. Joseph quickly scans the pages and is satisfied that the lad is courteous and genuine.

'What say you, Mary-Ann? Would you care for your friend's brother to exchange letters with you occasionally?'

'Why Father, such correspondence would be most interesting, don't you think? And young ladies need to be skilled in the art of letter-writing. Certainly there is nobody else who will write to me otherwise.'

Joseph smiles inwardly as the girl rationalises the reason for initiating such future correspondence and nods sagely. The girl skips off to create a special place where this and future letters will be treasured.

Later that evening as he and Mary sit reading in the lamp-lit parlour, he drops the weekly paper to his lap and chuckles over the matter of the letter. Mary looks up from her latest novel which has engrossed her all evening. She raises a quizzical eyebrow.

'Our lass grows into a young lady, don't you think? She is delighted that a young man wishes to correspond with her. I suppose it is to be expected. She'll turn fifteen next summer then before you know it, sixteen.'

Mary struggles to think that far forward but, mindful of the fate of wronged young ladies of good upbringing lying within the pages of the novels she devours, she raises a word of caution.

'Mind that it is clear that he may only write to her here at the farm. Such friendships can be misconstrued by others and girls can be particularly hateful to each other. It is imperative that she maintains her reputation.'

Joseph is taken aback by her earnest response but agrees with a nod.

The reply to John-Henry is written following Christmas Day. Mary-Ann sits at the table in the warm kitchen, with paper, pen, ink, blotting paper and pen-wiper at the ready. She starts to write, her arm cradling the paper to prevent curious eyes from reading over her shoulder. It won't be finished in one sitting, even though all over Christmas she has been rehearsing the words to write. Half-way down the first page she drops an ink blot and has to start again. The Addy's Christmas is edited for John-Henry's benefit. She paints a brighter picture than is the case and enthuses about the fine roast capon and sumptuous Christmas pudding, all the better for maturing over the last year. Frannie helps write a new play for her theatre. They will perform it this afternoon when

Uncle Henry brings his family to high tea. She wishes that Hannah-Mary were with her as they work so well together. Poor Frannie cannot remember her lines and is less adroit at manipulating the tiny figures.

So begins a correspondence which will endure for many years and, in time, span continents.

As the new term begins, Mary-Ann wonders whether her friend knows that John-Henry writes to her. She enquires as to how the family spent Christmas and is envious to hear that the days were spent much the same as last year, in Hannah-Mary's words, full of 'rumptuousness'. Soon she realises that John-Henry has not informed his sister of his letter-writing. Maybe he fears rebuff. Certainly, her response to John-Henry would have arrived at Moor House the day that Hannah-Mary travelled down to Doncaster. Did her letter, with its pink sealing wax imprinted with a simple A, cause as much interest as had his to her?

It is only several weeks later, during a wet weekend spent at the Addy's farm, that Hannah-Mary finds out. By this time Mary-Ann has already stowed three letters in an empty biscuit tin, its lid depicting a snow scene of a family alighting from a mail coach. It is Frannie who discloses the liaison.

'Which is your favourite brother, Hannah-Mary?' All three girls are lying on the floor by the nursery fire, creating another new play for the theatre.

'I don't have a favourite brother. It's just that some annoy me less than others.' Her concentration in colouring a new costume for the leading lady does not waver.

'Is John-Henry one of those who annoy you?' This with a sly wink at her sister. Mary-Ann elbows Frannie sharply then regrets it for drawing attention to the matter. Hannah-Mary rises into a sitting position and puts her head on one side.

'What are you both up to?'

Frannie giggles and Mary-Ann blushes scarlet. There is no point in avoiding the subject.

'My little sister,' she emphasises the 'little', 'is a mischief-maker.' She hesitates to find the most appropriate way to explain the situation. 'Before Christmas, John-Henry sent me a letter asking if he may correspond with me. That's all,' she ends lamely, turning back to the theatre to adjust the scenery unnecessarily.

Hannah-Mary laughs dryly. 'Is that all?' She reflects for a moment. 'It will be good for him. His writing is poor and I hope you will correct his spelling when you reply. Ha, so he is trying to improve himself then?'

Somewhat piqued by this harsh interpretation of John-Henry's intentions, Mary-Ann is nonetheless glad not to be teased about having a beau. Although …

The summer this year is wet and Mary longs to feel the sun on her face. On rainy days during the holidays, the girls become bored and squabble and she simply cannot find the energy to distract or amuse them. She encourages them to play upstairs in the nursery so that she can spend her afternoons with her latest book and her hidden source of solace. By the end of the day she struggles to make conversation with Joseph. Her reactions are slower and she has the sensation of floating above life, looking down on herself.

After a year of trying to understand his wife and to make allowances, Joseph has now reached a point of exasperation. He does not wish to be disloyal to the woman whom he once urged into a marriage of convenience, but he longs to share his concerns. Although his sister, Nancy, would be sympathetic, he is reluctant to reveal his predicament.

Michaelmas arrives but Mary no longer accompanies him to pay the quarterly rent. Increasingly she shuns company and prefers to remain at home with her books. As tenants gather to pay their dues, farmers exchange greetings and wives huddle to exchange gossip. Joseph tips his hat to one of the Cockin brothers, today accompanied by his sister Maria.

'Good day to you, Joseph, has this quarter served you well?' Maria Cockin has a direct manner of speaking which he knows alienates her from some people. He finds her approach refreshing and her apparent interest in his farm is welcome.

'We farmers always find fault with something whatever the season.' With a smile, Maria Cockin agrees. 'But this year the harvest was reasonably good and we have some fine beasts to take to market in the months up to Christmas.' He is curious to know how her brother's farm has fared. 'And how does your land fare?'

Maria Cockin is as smart as she is direct and parries his question without disclosing the situation of her brothers' farms. The family is one of the most well-to-do in the area, the wealth spread among them.

'As you say, farmers always want better but I have not heard more complaints than usual.' Abruptly she changes the subject. 'Your good wife is not among us today? I trust she is not unwell.'

Joseph is guarded and protective in his response.

'She does not enjoy the best of health.' He pauses as he feels obliged to expand on this and adds: 'Since the death of our lad, she has struggled somewhat. It is hard for her.' Maria Cockin frowns in sympathy.

'As someone who has not borne a child, I cannot imagine the pain she must feel.' She forebears to ask, but has an idea that an earlier child also died. 'One can only trust in the strength of the family and friends to carry her through. But time and patience are both necessary, I fear.'

'Indeed, Maria, and thank you for your kind words. Now, my turn to see the agent so I wish you good day.' With a smile and a bow, he departs. The brief conversation has heartened him. It offered no solution but to receive a considered view from someone he respects gives him encouragement. He ponders briefly why she never married. Perhaps directness is not to everyone's comfort.

As he walks towards the land agent's office, he comes across Elizabeth Barraclough.

'Elizabeth, how are you?' he greets her with a friendly touch to her shoulder.

'Well, Joseph, and how are you and the family?' Her question is accompanied by eyes searching deep into his. He knows that she will not be fobbed off by platitudes and frowns, pausing to consider his reply.

'Life is not happy in my home, I must confess. Mary still suffers following John's death, and I fear for her mind.' Abruptly he stops, looking around to see who else is near. 'Elizabeth, please may we talk privately? I, we need your help.' After agreeing to meet at her home, he tips his hat in farewell. Could this wise woman help his Mary through her despair?

CHAPTER 40

1858 Autumn

Joseph sits awkwardly in Elizabeth Barraclough's cramped parlour. He declines the offered cup of tea and has every intention of getting straight to the point. Instead, he falters and looks away.

'It will be ten years this Christmas that my Elizabeth took sick.' She remains silent, unmoved by his show of emotion. After a while, he recovers and looks her in the eye. 'That girl, she was my life.' She nods and waits.

'I am at a loss with Mary. What more can I do to help her? The doctor told us she should be out walking, breathing the fresh air. How do I draw her from this darkness? Many folk have been kind. You also have done much, yet all she desires is to sit reading. For some months now she complains of shortness of breath and walking is painful. Have you seen her legs and ankles, how swollen they are? The doctor gives her medication to little avail.' He stands and walks to the window. He looks out towards a neighbour's cottage.

'The girls return from school each Saturday but I know they look forward to leaving the next day. They don't see a happy home. What think you, Elizabeth? What should I be doing?' He returns to his chair in exasperation.

Elizabeth Barraclough has listened sympathetically, hands crossed in her lap.

'Joseph, I cannot promise any improvement in Mary's health. She was once blessed with a strong constitution but her physical well-being is being ground away by the pain of bereavement like water on a stone. We've all lost someone dear and that loss is never-ending. Each of us finds different ways to cope and some of us are more successful than others. You, Joseph, have your farm. Mary does not have such responsibilities to draw her out of the depths. She believes that your daughters no longer need her. I doubt that is the case but it is her thought. Bigger than that though is her belief that the passing of Sophia and John is God's judgement on her for taking the place of her sister against the laws of the Church.'

With a roar, Joseph rises again from his chair.

'Utter nonsense. We all know that this law is made by those who read the Word without compassion. Each year in Parliament many strive to overturn such a vindictive ruling. Today, nobody in this village or Arksey would spurn her for marrying me. We are not the only couple to wed as such and even the new parson greets me warmly. And would welcome Mary too if she did but come to church each Sunday.'

'There is one impediment to her recovery which you should remove, Joseph.' He frowns. 'The doctor doses your wife overly with medication. I fear that Mary has become too dependent on the poppy, whether she knows it or not.' The woman notes Joseph's shock. 'What do you imagine these doctors give to patients when they really know no better?' Her contempt for the medical profession is well-known locally. Furthermore, her skill with natural remedies has held her in good stead throughout the years of caring for birthing mothers and easing the sick and elderly into a better place.

He nods. It would explain Mary's lethargy and the bad dreams which cause her to call out at night as she tosses and turns. He does not recall seeing her take any such tincture but perhaps that is the slyness of the addicted. A shiver passes through him.

'What would you do to unbind her from such practices?' He knows that, uncontrolled, opium can drive people beyond their demons into madness. 'Her behaviour is never apparently strange. Are we perhaps timely to prevent things getting worse?' His companion nods and perceives that he is ill-equipped to find a solution alone.

'I need to speak with Mary, with your permission.' She hesitates awaiting his confirmation, an emphatic nod. 'She will not enjoy what she hears but I fear that gentle suggestions will be to no avail. I shall visit her on the morrow, while your daughters are away at school.'

Elizabeth Barraclough arrives unannounced at the farmhouse. She passes Harriet in the kitchen, declines a brew of tea and indicates she will join the Missus in the parlour.

Mary looks up from the sofa where she sits barefoot, her painful legs stretched out. She is surprised to see her friend framed in the doorway. Caught off-guard, she has no time to compose a polite smile and a look of dismay betrays the true feelings of this disturbed woman. She marks the place in her book and rises stiffly from the sofa, clearly in discomfort from her swollen legs. Elizabeth Barraclough cannot help but notice that as the closed book is laid on the mahogany side-table with one hand, the other slips something small into the pocket of her gown.

'Good afternoon, Elizabeth, what a pleasant surprise.'

'I have not seen you for some time and thought we would meet at Wheatley Hall on quarter day, but Joseph came alone.' Mary nods and smiles wryly. She offers her visitor a seat but Elizabeth Barraclough prefers to stand. Mary regains the sofa with a sigh. Her friend's face is stern.

'He really does not need me on such occasions and all the papers were in order. I still see to all that.' Her defensive response provides a stepping-stone.

'I have no doubt, my dear. You have always been quick with the accounts and I imagine that Joseph relies greatly on your book-keeping abilities, as he relies on you to run his household and instruct his daughters.' Mary notes a hint of criticism and flushes.

'The quarter day dinner always takes up so much time and I do not have the energy to sit gossiping with the ...' She is about to say 'wives' but recalls just in time that Elizabeth Barraclough is a wife but equally a rent-payer and her tone sounded disparaging, at the least. She avoids her friend's eye and looks out through the leaded windows. 'I am so, so tired, always. Each time I walk up the stairs, I become breathless.'

'Which is why I'm here, lass. I worry about you and want to help.' Such kind words from friends and family have the effect of drawing a curtain in Mary's mind. They are meaningless; they cannot help so she nods with an empty smile.

'Show me the medication you receive from the doctor.' The forthright demand is accompanied by Elizabeth Barraclough's stretched out hand. Mary looks fearful.

'Why? I am not sure where it lies. Somewhere in my bedroom, I'll be bound.'

'So not in that phial which you slipped into the pocket of your gown?'

Mary flushes and this time there is anger in her face. 'I beg your pardon? What do you accuse me of, Elizabeth Barraclough?'

Her accuser blanches at the implied reminder of status and softens her approach. 'Many, many times in my life I have seen the effects of the poppy. Indeed, there are times with long labours that I too have prescribed its use. And believe me when I say that I recognise over-indulgence. Too often have I seen the aftermath when a body can no longer live without it. It destroys, Mary. It destroys the person, their family. No amount of grieving for your lost children is worth ruining your life and that of Joseph, a good man who has given you a home and treated you honourably and with respect. You cannot continue as such. It has to stop.'

This last is delivered with a vehemence that shocks Mary, who lies back on the sofa, eyes closed, tears slowly meandering down her cheeks.

'I cannot live this life any longer,' she whispers. Elizabeth Barraclough bends nearer to catch the words. She offers no touch of solace. She awaits further explanation. None is forthcoming but she remains unmoved. Eventually, the silence is broken by a quiet voice.

'I am not the first woman to lose her innocent babes. Where is the God of Love who allows a woman to suffer such pain in giving birth to a child and then rewards her by taking its life? Joseph claims I am mistaken in the belief that God is punishing us for our sinful marriage, but I do not believe him.' She looks imploringly at Elizabeth Barraclough. 'I know well that his two girls need me for their mother but how can I guide their lives when I see no future for them? To marry, bear children, die or watch them die? Joseph is the dearest of men and would never force himself upon me, and he is still young. He wants a son, I know it, but I cannot give him one. I feel shrivelled up inside, years before my time.

'Yes, I do turn to my 'friend' for solace. A few drops are all I need to soften my senses, to lift me beyond this existence. Then I can lose myself in the stories of Mr Dickens, Mr Trollope, Mrs Gaskell. I enter a different world. Not a better world but not this world.'

'I cannot believe my ears, Mary. The poppy has turned you selfish and self-indulgent. You are not the kind, responsible sister that Elizabeth entrusted with her girls. I am truly sorry for the loss of your little ones but enough is enough. I wish to see your doctor. When does he call again?'

Mary shakes her head. 'He will only come when we ask.'

'Then I shall ask Joseph to instruct him to attend you, with me present.' She nods at Mary and withdraws, leaving her friend to her confused thoughts.

The consultation with the doctor is icy. He resents the implied criticism, especially from the local wise woman, that he has over-medicated his patient. However, with Elizabeth Barraclough's persistence, he agrees that Mary's tonic should be reduced and the dosage intervals strictly prescribed. If she takes more than stipulated, she will go without until the next round.

Over the coming months, Mary gradually weans herself off the poppy but the frequent purchase of sugared dragees perhaps indicates a need to disguise the smell of port wine on her breath. Harriet is reprimanded and threatened with dismissal for smuggling in the tipple. However, by Christmas, the family recognises an improvement. Mary is again interested in the girls' stories of life at the academy and, for the first time in a good few years, a happier atmosphere reigns about the home.

Frannie, ever thoughtful of others, voices her concerns to Mary-Ann while they decorate the parlour on Christmas Eve.

'Have you noticed how much Mother struggles to get about these days?' She passes a pretty glass bauble to her sister who perches on a chair to reach the higher branches of a fir tree cut from nearby woods. 'Her poor legs are so swollen that she struggles to pull on her boots.'

'Mm,' answers Mary-Ann who is concentrating on tying a ribbon to secure the shiny trinket. 'I suppose that's why she never goes to the shop in the village, let alone Doncaster.' She wonders who has chosen their Christmas gifts this year, then is ashamed of the thought.

Mary is indeed house-bound and increasingly reliant on Harriet for purchasing necessities and occasionally, with great stealth, a new bottle of port wine. The doctor calls but offers little of merit. Elizabeth Barraclough's herbal remedies come highly recommended and she takes them dutifully though without much faith in their efficacy.

As another year dawns, Joseph looks forward but with little expectation. Mary-Ann, who will be sixteen in May, looks forward to the next letter from John-Henry, busy in Bradford working for the family business. Frannie hopes her school report will improve in the coming term; she tries so hard. Mary is tired. All she sees ahead is another year of struggle. She longs to escape.

CHAPTER 41

1859 Spring

As the year progresses into spring, Mary descends once again into darkness as her body swells and her breathing becomes more laboured. Letters are exchanged with their friends in Sheffield, Samuel and Sophia Binns, now moved to their new home in Far Gate. After reading of Mary's poor health, Sophia is most concerned and writes to ask if her husband might visit when the weather improves. The prospect of seeing Samuel is welcomed by Joseph and he is keen to gain his friend's opinion. Although a chemist serving the world of manufacturing, Samuel also associates with pharmacists and might suggest alternative treatments.

By late spring, Mary has given up the daily battle with the stairs and chooses to remain in her room. Out of respect for his wife's ill health, Joseph has removed to another bedroom. During the long evenings alone, he sits with a lamp in the kitchen, reading the newspaper or mastering the farm accounts until tiredness drives him up to bed.

Samuel arrives one Saturday in early May. He is shocked to see Mary abed during the day. And so drawn. After a few minutes, Joseph withdraws, leaving Samuel to talk with Mary, and descends to the parlour to engage his daughters in a game of cards.

'Samuel, how kind of you to visit us. Do you have business in the area? How are dear Sophia and young Henry? By now he must be twelve or thereabouts.' Mary speaks slowly but without pause for a response as she has no wish to hear the real reason for his presence. Samuel sits upright on a rush-bottomed ladder-back chair and smiles gently at the woman who has aged so very much in the nine years of knowing her.

He talks quietly and Mary leans back, listening intently to the everyday of his little family. Samuel and Sophia were not blessed with children of their own but in fostering Henry they have found happiness. Inwardly she questions why, in that case, she cannot be content with the two girls, not hers by birth? Samuel probes gently, anxious to assess the extent of her illness. After a while he perceives that she has tired and rises to take his leave.

'Sophia would dearly love to see you and help with your recovery. Perhaps something might be arranged.' Mary nods her acquiescence though with little faith and, as Samuel gently draws the door behind him, she closes her eyes to escape the now.

Down in the parlour, Samuel sits back in the armchair offered by his friend.

'Your dear wife is much changed, Joseph. That I expected from what you wrote but it seems that nought prescribed by your doctor is helping to any great extent. You mentioned dropsy in your letter and possible disease of the liver. She does have a slight yellowness to her eyes. What medication is she given?'

Joseph talks through the various potions, the occasional bleeding. It distresses him to think what the poor woman endures. Samuel nods sympathetically.

'Beyond the medication, your wife requires constant attention to keep her spirits high. Is there a chance that your elder daughter could finish her schooling and return to nurse her mother back to health?'

'That cannot be, Samuel. Both my lasses must have a good education so that one day they may find good husbands of equal intellect who will honour and treat 'em well.' Joseph is wedded to the notion that girls should be instructed just as much as lads. 'There is a good woman in the village, Elizabeth Barraclough, who comes often to aid Mary, but she has other calls on her time. So, as you see, for hours on end my poor wife lies alone without vitality, with only her thoughts to divert her. 'Tis a bleak life, that's to be sure.'

Returned to Sheffield, Samuel talks at length with his compassionate wife. Sophia stands at the parlour window, gazing out over busy Far Gate, and after a few minutes' reflection, turns to her husband with an earnest frown.

'There is but one solution: Mary must be brought here to convalesce. I have the time to engage with her and I would like our own good doctor to see her and give his opinion. The journey will be challenging but not impossible. What say you?'

The Binns' proposition requires not a little consideration. Even without the practicalities of transporting someone who walks only with difficulty, Joseph fears that Mary will consider he is discarding her, out of his life, of no future use. He could not bear for her to think such. He consults Elizabeth Barraclough after Sunday service, waiting for the moment when his daughters disappear to place fresh flowers on their mother's grave. She considers the Binns' proposition, inspecting her highly polished black boots for guidance, then nods.

'Such travel will require great effort, but if her friend Sophia can tend her constantly, the lass will have a better chance than she has here. If you would like my help, I am ready to accompany you both on the journey.'

Joseph chooses his moment to tell Mary of the invitation. He reminds her that their friends have moved to a busy part of Sheffield, not far from the Cutlers' Hall and there will not be the quiet she enjoys at the farm. Although touched by their kindness, she views the prospect of the journey with disquiet and her immediate instinct is to decline the offer. As ever, Joseph will not press her but, after a few days passed largely alone in a house where the only distraction is the chatter of Harriet, Mary reconsiders her situation.

Each day, Joseph speaks with her briefly when he comes in for breakfast and dinner at mid-day. After returning from the fields of an evening, he tells her of the day's events, all related to the farm. Not once does he reveal impatience with her situation, but neither does he talk of improvement. She suspects that the Binns' invitation would suit him too. If only she could believe that convalescence with their friends would restore her to her former strength. When next she visits, Elizabeth Barraclough supports the plan.

'You need to have people about you who can care for you throughout the day. The Binns have a housemaid so your friend will have time to read to you when you are too tired to pick up your books. Mary, if you can find the strength, you should go and I would travel with you.'

Joseph informs his daughters of the suggested convalescence in Sheffield.

Mary-Ann is curious to know why the Binns can offer a greater chance of cure than the local doctors but has no comment to make. Privately she works out that Harriet will have more time for household duties, many of which now fall to herself and Frannie. Mary-Ann dares not grumble that her Saturday afternoons are now spent with needle and thread. Frannie is quite content to sit mending but Mary-Ann is less skilled and quickly becomes maungy when she marks her workmanship inferior to that of her sister.

The journey to Sheffield is more taxing than they had thought and Mary requires a week of quiet to recover. Sophia's own doctor attends and is non-committal before the patient. In the parlour he is more enlightening.

'Your friend is very poorly, Mrs Binns. Has her husband spoken of a diagnosis?'

'Dropsy and disease of the liver. That is what she has been treated for over the last year or so.'

'Hm, indeed. Her shortness of breath, her swollen legs and feet, all indicate dropsy. Furthermore, her colour prompts me to consider she does indeed suffer from disease of the liver.' Sophia nods. 'Do you think her husband is aware of the advanced stage of his wife's illness?'

'I think not, Doctor, otherwise he would not have permitted her to travel here to recuperate. Do you consider that she may not improve, not even a little?'

'Sadly no, Ma'am.' He stands to take his leave and passes her a slip of paper covered in hand-writing. 'Take this to your pharmacist. It will not cure her but alleviate the breathlessness somewhat.' He pauses and chooses his words. 'I fear that the damage to her liver is probably so extensive that imbibing whatever wine she fancies will do her no more harm and is likely to remove some of her fears day to day. I recommend she is not moved again and that you keep her comfortable and unexcited for her remaining time. No,' he responds to Sophia's enquiring face, 'I cannot predict how long that will be.'

Samuel and Sophia await Joseph's coming visit with unease. Before he mounts the stairs to see his wife, Joseph asks for the verdict of their doctor. He is bid take a seat in the parlour. Sophia explains Mary's condition and ends with a reassurance:

'Joseph, please know that Samuel and I will do all we can for dear Mary. Perhaps you now wish that she had never agreed to visit us and were safe at home in Bentley. She greatly misses you and your daughters but we promise to provide her with the constant care she will need. You know that you can visit whenever you wish and bring the girls too.'

Joseph listens but scarcely hears. How has it come to this? His wife should be in her own home among her own family, not here. But it dawns upon him that perhaps she has never considered the farm her home, his daughters her family. Her true family, baby Sophia and young John, are no more. And what of him, her husband? What is he to her? Could he have been a better husband? In remorse, he drops his head into his hands.

Each week, Joseph visits his wife, sometimes bringing tempting fruits now transported into Hull on the Dutch steam-packets and ferried up to Doncaster market. She smiles her gratitude but they remain untasted. He travels during the week since he needs to be at the farm on Saturdays for his daughters, briefly home from the academy. Furthermore, he wishes to protect them from the sadness that permeates the sickroom in Far Gate. Only Frannie suggests tentatively that she would like to visit her mother but in lieu she writes little notes of encouragement for her father to take.

And so, it continues through the summer. When the academy breaks up for the holidays, the usual letter arrives from Mrs Willey, inviting Mary-Ann to stay in August. This year, Joseph hesitates. He is reluctant to release Mary-Ann whose chatter over meals relieves the strain of a home living under the cloud of an invalid, even if not present. He feels guilty of such thoughts. He knows how much she looks forward to her time with Hannah-Mary's family. Furthermore, this year there will be another element at play, the growing friendship with John-Henry. He chastises himself for his meanness of spirit and replies that he and her mother are pleased for the visit to take place. Full of joy, Mary-Ann throws her arms around his neck, then a moment later reflects on the implications. Poor Frannie will be alone with Father and now cannot escape the visits to Sheffield.

She underestimates her sister. Frannie is not dismayed at the prospect of being alone with her father. Quite the reverse. She displays a maturity beyond her eleven years. She sees her father standing alone, full of sadness, and she intends to take care of him. She will discuss meals with Harriet, ensure that laundry and mending are up to date and oversee the marketing, taking charge of the household purse. The butter and eggs to be sold in Doncaster will be ready for the carter, regular as clockwork. Each evening she will walk the fields with her father reviewing the crops and the stock. Also, she will accompany him on his regular visits to Sheffield. It is always such an excitement to travel by train and, after a few weeks, she feels quite the modern traveller, more so than Mary-Ann at any rate.

Hannah-Mary greets her friend on her arrival at Moor House. The Willey family is aware of the seriousness of Mrs Addy's illness and initially their welcome is subdued. From year to year not a great deal changes among the Willey household other than the children grow older. The teasing continues, as does the evening cricket. Betsy-Emma, only two years younger than Hannah-Mary, is now old enough to join the shopping forays into Bradford. She has a lively disposition and they need to keep a sharp eye on her. There is always one more hat shop to explore.

One evening, John-Henry invites Mary-Ann to walk out across the fields to a high viewpoint from which they can look out across the three counties and down to the spire of St Paul's in Birkenshaw. He offers a helping hand when the going becomes difficult but she is keen to show that she can fend for herself. The helpless female is not a role she seeks for herself.

'You must be concerned for your mother,' ventures John-Henry as they lean against a stone wall.

'Stepmother,' she corrects, a little too swiftly, then adds: 'Of course, and also I worry for Father.'

'Do you have any notion of when she will return to Bentley?' This is more a gateway to his real question. She looks into his open face and sees kindly eyes that slant downwards slightly at the side. He has a charming cleft in the chin. She wants to stroke it. A newly acquired beard frames his square jaw and runs up the side of his cheeks to meet his abundant wavy brown hair. His enquiring look reminds her of the unanswered question.

'Unfortunately, no.' She gains courage and entrusts him with her private thoughts. 'I think she is going to die. I even believe that this is what she desires.' Seeing the consternation on John-Henry's face, she continues: 'She lost all she held dear: baby Sophia, then John, our darling boy.' She cannot continue and tears fill her eyes. John-Henry places a comforting hand on her shoulder. Mary-Ann wishes this moment to last for ever and their eyes meet in this moment of anxiety but acute awakening.

CHAPTER 42

1859 Autumn

For Mary Addy the end comes peacefully one October morning. The street below her closed window is lit by autumn sunshine and noisy with the clatter of carts and horses, the trudge of clogs and boots.

Joseph travels at once and is grateful to Samuel for offering to complete the registration formalities. He sits beside the bed where lies the body of his wife. He is empty of feeling. Throughout the journey he has run the full gamut of emotions: grief, relief, guilt. Now he reflects only on the practicalities, so often the salve of the bereaved. He cannot help but compare this death and its consequences with those of his first wife. Sadly, perhaps fortunately, on this occasion there are no young children in need of mothering. Had they lived, Sophia would have been eight and John seven. True, his growing daughters still need a woman's guidance, but less so than in earlier days. He feels shame at such thoughts and bends to kiss his wife for the last time. He recalls her fears of being cursed and reassures her with a whisper:

'You were a good wife and mother, Mary. May God take care of you.'

The funeral at Arksey is attended by close family and friends. Her brother, Henry, the Addy menfolk and Samuel Binns watch the lowering of the coffin. Joseph regrets that there was insufficient space to dig Mary's grave adjacent to Sophia and John; now she lies separated from them by the flat gravestone of Elizabeth. He intends to erect a headstone worthy of this gentle woman, just as he has done for their two lost children.

Neither Mary-Ann nor Frannie attend the service but are waiting back at the farm, along with female members of the families. They move among the mourners, offering plates of fruit cake and cups of tea, accepting murmured words of sympathy. Frannie finds it hard not to cry. The loss of the only mother she has ever known rekindles her unspoken fears that she was the cause of the deaths of her birth mother and her brother. Mary-Ann's composure is admired by some but viewed more critically by Elizabeth Barraclough. She has seen the child grow into a young woman and has remarked in her a level of detachment that she dislikes.

What lies behind that sang-froid would not surprise Elizabeth Barraclough. Over the last few nights, Mary-Ann has lain awake in the dormitory, now moved up in seniority to a bed closer to the fireplace. She has weighed the situation at the farm and possible options that lie ahead. Now almost sixteen and a half, by May next year she will be seventeen. That is the age when most young ladies depart the academy to enter Life. As a farmer's elder daughter, she only has to look around the room and think of local farming families to guess what that might bring. Even the elder girls of the Willey family, more enlightened than many, remain at home helping with household matters. Mary-Ann squirms at the thought.

Is her father likely to marry for a third time? At fifty-one years of age, he could still consider a younger bride in order to have a son, but she doubts it. Despite owning a small acreage, he is primarily a tenant farmer without an estate to hand down.

Perhaps out of loneliness he might seek a companion for the rest of his days, but again she sees a private man who does not go about into company as a general thing. No doubt Frannie would happily make home for him in a couple of years. Mary-Ann feels no embarrassment in assessing the situation dispassionately.

Her thoughts fly more widely to the woman she admires most in the world, Miss Jameson. Before the summer holidays, the academy said adieu to their geography teacher as she departed for the United States of America to join her brother in Boston where he is now settled in work and with an American wife. Perhaps she should follow Miss Jameson's example, become a teacher and then travel? That idea is discarded as she knows she would not have the confidence to travel alone. Good heavens, the thought of travelling even to London without a companion fills her with dread.

Joseph passes among the mourners and, as is always the case on such occasions, after a while the conversation moves beyond the politely recalled memories of the deceased and on to matters of the day. His daughters are a safe topic to explore and he is glad to talk with enthusiasm of Mary-Ann's artistic talents and of Frannie's diligence and expertise as a needlewoman.

'Will you take Mary-Ann out of school now so that she can help run the home?' His sister, Nancy, is present with her much older husband, William Stacey, and eldest son, William, Joseph's godson, now in his mid-thirties and also a farmer. She has cornered him close to the fireplace and he steers her to a cooler and more discreet part of the room before he answers. This is something that he has not discussed with his daughter and he has no wish for his thoughts to be overheard.

'Why, Nancy, it's but early days to be deciding such, but I must confess I would be reluctant for her to give up her learning just now. She is bright and I believe that her mother, Elizabeth, would agree with me that girls should be allowed to achieve whatever they can. Aye, she may well marry in time and if so, pray God she finds a good man. But you and I know that she has an independent streak and might be minded to wait until she finds the right man. I have means but not sufficient to provide her own household, should she never marry. So, with her education complete, she could set herself up as a teacher, maybe with her own school.' He notes his sister's eyes widen with disapproval and presses on. 'We are not Society, Nancy, just farming stock. The world is changing and opportunities arise at every turn. I want my daughter to embrace opportunities that her mother never had.'

'And Frannie? She is, what, eleven? She needs a woman's guidance in these coming years. She is a kindly lass and homely too, but she is too young to leave school.'

'I've no intention of taking Frannie away from the academy. In many ways she benefits from such an education even more so than Mary-Ann. She is not exactly shy but is less forward than her sister and is content to remain in the background while others watch Mary-Ann. I shall rely on Mary-Ann to guide Frannie in the coming years. She is five years older and well placed to do so.'

In the following days Joseph reflects on the conversation with Nancy and concludes that he should speak directly with Mary-Ann. The following Saturday he waits until Frannie is muffled up in a cloak to brave the autumn bluster in search of outlying hens' nests. Egg basket in hand, she disappears out of the kitchen door. His elder daughter is helping Harriet clear the table of the remains of their dinner then her plan is to spend the afternoon writing a letter to John-Henry. Joseph beckons her to follow him into the parlour where a newly-lit fire is crackling and starting to bring warmth. Joseph pats the cushion beside him on the sofa. Obediently, she sits, wondering what is to come.

'I have always looked forward to Saturdays when I pick you up from Doncaster and bring you home. Your mother and I were always interested to hear of the goings-on of your week. And

Frannie's too,' he quickly adds. 'You seem content with your studies there …' He trails off, unsure how to shape the next part of the conversation. Mary-Ann comes to his aid and places her hand over his.

'Dear Father, have no fears on our part. Both Frannie and I are very happy at the academy. Although it is nothing like as comfortable as living here with you, we manage, we manage very well. And there are so many things that I enjoy greatly: dancing, piano, painting, all of which make it easier to tolerate French and mathematics. And our friends, such good friends. Imagine, had I not been sent to the academy, I would never have met Hannah-Mary Willey.' Or John-Henry, she leaves unsaid.

Joseph puts an arm around her shoulders and hugs her gently. She wonders if he is about to impart bad news and fears to tell her.

'I am greatly reassured, Mary-Ann. It was my hope that such was the case but I needed to be certain. You will understand that I now have a different future ahead of me. I must confess, I do not relish the prospect of years alone, but I want you to know that I have no wish to take you out of school to work at home as my house-keeper. Your education, and that of Frannie, is far more important. Harriet and I will shift for ourselves. There will be less work for her now that your mother has passed away. Indeed, over recent months, with Mary being cared for in Sheffield, we have discovered a new routine and when Harriet cannot manage, we can ask a girl in from the village to help her out.'

Mary-Ann frowns as she turns to hug her father. How thoughtless of her not to recognise that he will be lonely.

'Thank you for telling me this, Father. You are generous in allowing me to continue my education and I promise you I shall work diligently so that you won't ever be disappointed. And each weekend when we return, we shall plan to do special things together so all three of us will long for Saturday mornings.' She ends with a spirited laugh that tugs at her father's heart. Such optimism she has inherited from her mother, Elizabeth.

The winter was always going to be hard this year and even Christmas could not lift their hearts greatly, despite the efforts of the girls to decorate the house and to perform a newly created pantomime for the toy theatre. After so many Christmases overshadowed by illness and death, Joseph finds it difficult to enter into the spirit of the occasion. They are grateful that Uncle Godfrey has invited them to dinner following the service on Christmas morning and the toy theatre is loaded onto the trap to entertain the family afterwards.

Among her presents Mary-Ann finds one from John-Henry, an embroidered green velvet purse containing a silver sixpence. Beside it is a tiny hand-written note: *A beginning for the future.* How absolutely odd, she thinks. She has not presumed to send a gift to him and is embarrassed by his generosity and thoughtfulness. Blushing, she accepts the gentle teasing from her father and Frannie. She shrugs off their insinuations that she has found a place in the young man's heart. Inwardly she glows with pleasure and waits impatiently for a private moment when she can pick up her pen to express her warmest thanks. In the meantime, as the trap clatters its way homewards from Uncle Godfrey's, she sits huddled under shawls, composing and re-composing her reply.

Joseph hunches over the reins, his leather hat pulled down against the December cold, and over the journey reflects on the sadness of the year. May the next decade bring better times for his girls and perhaps also for himself.

CHAPTER 43

1860 Spring

Joseph found the winter particularly taxing. Snow and the frozen ground made it hard to attend to the chores essential to keep the farm running smoothly over the coming year. Ditches that needed clearing to allow melt water to flow into the ings, could not be dug out before the snows arrived and he feared flooding across the already water-logged land. Mending fences was impossible with fingers too frozen to handle tools and he watched the cattle in the mistle chew their way through his stock of fodder, praying that it would last until they could be turned out into the spring meadows.

The short days were worst of all. He was out before sunrise to supervise the milking and again in the late afternoon as the lads swilled the floor clean by lamplight. He helped roll the milk churns into the dairy in the hope that the roads would be clear the following morning to make their promised deliveries into Doncaster.

The loneliness of the long evenings closed in on Joseph. Now that it was just him at the farm during the week, Harriet would make him a hearty breakfast to set him up and at midday he would sit down to a steaming dinner to keep him going until evening. Soon after Christmas, Joseph became uncomfortable having the girl work late at the house and bade her leave a simple plate of bread and cheese and a small pot of soup. As long as the chores were done, she could leave late afternoon before he arrived back.

Now it is well into February and already he can feel spring in the air. The days are lengthening and he is hopeful again. It is his nature to be so. Among his farming friends such a trait is a rarity. Years of disappointment have trained farmers to be cautious, to expect the worst and to be pleasantly surprised if stock thrives and crops flourish.

Midweek, he rides over to visit his brother Godfrey following the loss of yet another of his sons. At Christmas, Joseph was shocked to see Robson changed from a strapping nineteen-year-old into a consumptive shell that struggled for breath. Sadly, his death early in January came as no surprise.

They walk the fields and talk of farming matters: what has been sown, what prices to expect at the fat-stock sales. Both men try to avoid talk of family but cannot. Godfrey stops and faces his brother.

'How is your life now, Joseph? You don't look rested. God knows I've had my bad times of late but at least I still have my wife and my remaining children to sustain me. How do you manage with the girls away at school? Can you bear to be alone in that house?'

Joseph continues walking ahead. He has tried not to examine his feelings so needs a few moments to consider his answer and addresses his reply to the bleak fields before him.

'At this time of year, it is hard, especially with this weather. Even the weekends, when I have my girls, the time with them is so short. I just let them prattle on about their studies. I pray that with what they learn they will have the chance to …' He is about to say 'improve themselves' but that implies that the lives that he and his brother's family lead require improvement. 'The chance to see something beyond Doncaster.'

'Nancy is worried about you being lonely, and wishes to invite us all to supper one evening. Would you come?'

'That is kind of her and, were it just family, I would welcome it. As for a wider circle, in truth I have no appetite to meet up with people I know little or not at all. And if it were a Saturday evening, I regret that is reserved for my girls.' Godfrey nods ruefully. It will be easier to prise a winkle out of its shell than to bring Joseph out among company. Privately, he believes his sister to be too manipulating. Of course, Joseph is young enough to father more children, but is it something his brother desires at his age?

Nancy, ten years his elder, has always mothered Joseph and proves to be persistent. As the spring advances and after a few family suppers, she arranges occasional card evenings for farming friends including the Cockins. On one occasion, a Friday evening early in April, she extends an invitation to include Joseph and, purely to make up the pairs, she asks another member of the Cockin family to join them, Maria, an unmarried lady already known to her brother.

Joseph examines his cards, slightly irritated that Nancy is turning the evening into a conversation piece, but means to be polite.

'So, Maria, you have been away from us for some while. I believe you have been travelling. Did you stray onto the Continent?'

'Good heavens, by no means,' Maria protests moderately in her deep velvety tones with only a trace of local accent. 'I would love to go to Paris but it is being dug up all over the place. Apparently, Napoleon the Third intends to do away with the old streets and form a network of boulevards. It all sounds rather grand, but for a future visit, I fear. No, there is too much unrest in other parts so I restrict myself to visiting friends in Scotland and most of all in London where I was at school.'

As Joseph prepares to play his first card, he realises that the Maria he has known slightly over the years has hidden depths and reminds himself she comes from a well-to-do family. It is she who owns half a dozen cottages and the Old Hall in Bentley, once the workhouse, now turned into a fine residence and let out to a family. He recalls her advice when they sought a hotel for their visit to the Manchester Art Treasures exhibition. An experienced woman of substance, self-sufficient. For the rest of the evening, he devotes his attention to the cards and only responds when spoken to. He is tired after a day in the fields and wonders if the effort to wash and dress up is worth the candle. He returns to his empty home, strangely dispirited. He looks forwards to his bed and tomorrow he will drive into Doncaster to fetch his girls.

Father and daughters sit at the dinner table as Harriet serves up a chicken and ham pie. Joseph responds to Frannie's enquiry about his past week and for want of anything else to talk of, tells of the previous evening's card party. Frannie is delighted that at last he has been among company and asks who was present. Mary-Ann ponders a while then probes:

'Miss Maria Cockin, which one is she? There are so many Cockins in Arksey, I lose track. Is she the one in her twenties, daughter of Mr George?'

'Good heavens, no,' chuckles her father. 'I've no idea of her age but I reckon she's not far off fifty.' The girls exchange glances. They have not heard their father laugh in over a year.

As spring unfurls and the first green blush appears throughout the hedges, on trees, over fields, the days grow longer and Joseph senses an easing in his mind. His sister's card evenings become a fortnightly event, despite the complaints of her husband, William, that he is now in his mid-seventies and needs an early night. Although Nancy invites other couples, Joseph's playing partner remains Maria Cockin. No great lover of card games, nonetheless, Joseph now looks forward to these evenings and the idle conversation that passes between the players. It is not demanding, other than concentrating on the cards themselves, and he finds himself at ease with the company. He will not admit such to himself but he is fascinated by Maria Cockin. She is slightly built, not handsome. Her dark hair is parted centrally and scraped back severely into a bun. He is mesmerised by her eyes which are slightly hooded and penetrating. When Maria Cockin turns her gaze onto him, he feels that she stares into his very soul. She is not a prattler, like his sister, and when she speaks it is as though she has considered the content and presentation of every sentence before it is delivered. No doubt her London education was of the highest quality. She can converse on matters national, international, even political, with a depth of understanding that is beyond Joseph. He reminds himself to read the newspapers more assiduously before the next card party.

The following weekend, Joseph ventures a suggestion to his daughters.

'It is time, I believe, that I should repay my sister's kind hospitality and offer to host a card evening here.' He pauses and sees he has their full attention. 'I am sure that Harriet could put together a suitable cold collation and it would please me mightily if you would help me host the evening.' The reaction is of speechless surprise. 'Of course, I do not expect you to partake in the card game,' he smiles. Reassured, the girls look at each other with raised eyebrows.

'Of course.' Frannie, ever the practical one, recovers first and quizzes her father as to what sort of food would be required. Mary-Ann waits her turn and asks innocently:

'Whom would you invite for this first soirée? Better that the guests be people you know well so that we do not feel obliged to put on a grand show.' Joseph is taken aback by his daughter's astute assessment of the proposed engagement. She is right.

'I thought that on this occasion it should be your uncle and aunt who have hosted me for some months, and …,' he hesitates, bearing in mind Mary-Ann's comments, '…perhaps your uncle and aunt Godfrey, keeping it family. Then, to make up the pairs, I suppose Miss Cockin.' His daughters exchange looks and, smiling, nod their agreement.

For the occasion, a girl is brought in from the village to help Harriet scrub and polish the house. Mary-Ann takes it upon herself to seek her Aunt Nancy's advice, then organises what delicacies will be provided through the evening.

The parlour shines in the lamplight and daffodils in vases dare to intrude with their freshly-cut scent and brash colour. Joseph is surprised how nervous he feels as they await the arrival of their guests. Mary-Ann looks so pretty in her new gown, long overdue as her body blossoms forth into womanhood. She stands beside him, consciously or unconsciously adopting the role of mistress of the house. Frannie cannot stand still and darts hither and thither adjusting this and that. She is so excited to be present.

Aunt Nancy is first to arrive, her husband, William still in the yard handing over their trap to one of Joseph's lads. Her eyes are everywhere and she is clearly satisfied by what she sees.

'Well done, Brother,' she pecks his cheek affectionately. 'Let's see what this evening brings.'

Last to arrive is Maria Cockin who has driven herself over from Arksey where she has her own home. Mary-Ann is in awe of a woman who owns a house, a pony and trap and is competent enough to drive it alone in the dark. She takes Maria's cloak and admires the quality of the cloth and trimmings. The London tailor's label says all.

Throughout the card game, played on a green baize covered table set up in the middle of the parlour, the girls sit aside on the sofa watching the interaction between the six players and listening to the idle conversation. When the players break for refreshments, the girls lead them into the dining room and help people to cold cuts, pickles and warm bread rolls laid out on the sideboard.

Maria thanks Frannie who is being particularly helpful and, as she takes a seat at the table, pats the empty chair beside her.

'Come Frannie, bring something for yourself and tell me about your school. I hear the Misses Legge run a fine establishment.' Frannie quickly complies and is all too happy to chatter about her favourite lessons. Mary-Ann, still supervising the serving of supper, overhears the conversation and is stung that Miss Cockin has not yet chosen to enter into conversation with her. She spots her father at the other end of the table and he, too, is observing the exchanges between Frannie and his new friend, Miss Cockin.

At the end of the evening, the traps are called to the front door, so rarely used in most farm houses. Guests pull on great coats and cloaks and there is the usual buzz of thank-you and farewell. Joseph is quite concerned that Maria is driving herself home at this late hour and offers to accompany her. She bows with a smile and a shake of her head and he reluctantly hands her up into her trap and watches as she competently steers her pony out of the yard, the twin lamps bobbing each side of the trap as they disappear down the lane towards Arksey.

Joseph turns to his daughters and smiles with satisfaction. One daughter beams back at him, the other is bemused.

CHAPTER 44

1860 Summer

Her last full day at the academy. Mary-Ann looks around the dining room. Across the table sits her dearest friend in all the world, although it is a strange friendship in some ways. Often Miss Hannah-Mary Willey can be just too direct, too harsh in her judgement and Mary-Ann wonders whether Hannah-Mary will miss her. The two weeks with the Willey family are assured for this August but what of the future? The future. That imponderable has hung over her since Easter when her father suggested that she needed to think beyond school days.

The conversation was difficult on both sides. For a while, Joseph had been considering what might be best for his elder daughter, fast approaching her seventeenth birthday. It was not a matter of money; he could afford another year of school fees. Instead, it was something that Maria Cockin had raised. On the alternate Fridays without a cards evening, she would invite him to supper at her home, sometimes with other guests present, sometimes just him alone. It was not only the excellent cooking of Maria's housekeeper which attracted him, Joseph also appreciated her conversation, her company. Although initially uneasy to be entertained by a lady alone, he reminded himself that they were both of mature years and that his presence would not compromise her reputation, especially with her housekeeper bustling in and out.

'Well Joseph, what are your thoughts for Mary-Ann? Is she to remain at the academy for another year? Should you not be thinking of introducing her to the wider world?'

He had looked askance at Maria. Of course, she was right but he was avoiding the matter for the time being. Perhaps this woman of the world might have an opinion.

'She could put that learning to good use, surely?' Maria has little time for those who idle away the days. 'Could she not work as a governess or at least give instruction to children requiring support? There must be people with such needs in these parts and that way she could continue to live at home, or at least not far away.' She left Joseph to ponder.

Easter is always a favourite holiday for Mary-Ann and Frannie. This year, as the early April sunshine warmed the earth, both girls relished the days spent at the farm, especially with new piglets squealing, scrambling to reach the sow's teats. Best of all were the newly born calves, licked dry by their mothers, wobbling up onto stick-like legs. Even Mary-Ann can be tempted out of the house to marvel at nature in springtime.

Her father drew her to one side and together they leaned on a gate overlooking the fields, the dikes, the wide cloud-filled sky of Yorkshire. Feeling his tension, she turned to observe him as he continued to look beyond.

'Lass, it's time to think about your future.' He paused. She waited with some trepidation. 'I know you're happy at Miss Legge's but next month you'll be seventeen and I'm sure you're anxious to move on, move forward,' he added, trying to be more positive. Still, she did not offer to help him. 'What are *your* thoughts, lass?'

She continued staring at his profile, a slight frown on her face.

'I have indeed been very happy at the academy and I am most grateful for that opportunity. I suppose it has opened my eyes to what is outside Bentley, even beyond Doncaster. Miss Jameson, remember she was my geography teacher, she is now in America. She has inspired me so much to look beyond.' Her father turned to face her, concerned that she has aspirations to cross the Atlantic. Mary-Ann smiled reassuringly. 'No, I am not suggesting that I should follow her, although I would love to travel to foreign places. Rather more, I wish to learn how to become more independent. Mother, that is my stepmother, showed us what is possible when she worked as a companion in Sheffield, long before you married. I know that it was because money was short for her family, but at least she did it and honourably too.' Her father nodded, glad to hear her speak positively of Mary. 'Maybe I too could work as a companion, perhaps somewhere locally to begin with, then, who knows?' She would not confess to her father that her ultimate aim was to find a position in Bradford, a more vibrant town where she would be closer to her friend, Hannah-Mary, and of course to John-Henry.

And now the time is come. Today she will travel back to Bentley, her trunk packed with schoolbooks and her uniform which, in time, will be passed down to Frannie. She looks forward to devoting the coming weeks to exploring what opportunities might present themselves to an educated young lady but, before she embarks upon the next stage of her life, she will enjoy two whole weeks with her best friend and be close to someone held especially dear to her heart. She blushes at the thought of John-Henry. Hidden amidst the schoolbooks in her trunk lie the letters which arrive weekly from Bradford, concealed within an envelope addressed to Miss Hannah-Mary Willey. Since they are recognised as written by her brother, Hannah-Mary receives the envelope unopened and retires immediately to a quiet place to slip out the enclosed envelope intended for Mary-Ann. Over the months the content of each letter has evolved from the factual to a softer tone where the young man writes not only of his daily life but also of his ambitions, of his dreams. Woven amidst his lines one might read that she also forms part of that ambition, that dream. She fears to hope.

The hallway is cluttered with luggage and girls rush around kissing and promising undying affection. Joseph shoulders his daughters' trunks onto the trap, shakes hands with both Misses Legge, waves cheerily to Hannah-Mary, awaiting a cab to the railway station, hands his two daughters up onto the trap and they are away. He remains silent, conscious that this might be an emotional moment for Mary-Ann. Suddenly she turns and touches his arm. She raises her voice over the clatter of hooves on the road.

'Father, from today please call me Marian. It is a frequent foreshortening of Mary-Ann and it is more modern. Will you do that for me please, Father?' Joseph is speechless with astonishment and simply nods. Frannie, already privy to the change of name, smiles to herself. So very Mary-Ann.

Over the coming weeks, Marian spends her days visiting family and former schoolfriends, intent on seeking a child in need of tutoring. Uncles and aunts are sympathetic but cannot help. The schoolmaster at Arksey prickles at the suggestion that she might provide any element of education lacking among his pupils. Elizabeth Barraclough wants to help and tries hard to warm to the girl, but cannot suggest any possibilities. She further irritates Marian by continuing to call her Mary-Ann, the name chosen by her dear lost friend, Elizabeth Addy.

One morning, the girls look up from their ever-present mending as they hear a horse and trap arriving in the yard. Frannie stands and peers out of the window.

'It's Maria Cockin. Were we expecting her?' She watches as one of the farm hands helps down the newcomer and she hastens to the kitchen door to make welcome. Marian sighs and gathers up the mending. She does not wish their visitor to inspect her needlework nor the old pair of drawers in need of repair.

'Good morning Miss Cockin. Is it Father you've come to see?' Frannie is shy but also direct. 'He's out with the sheep but I can send for him.' Marian appears in the kitchen and intends to move their visitor from the somewhat disorganised space into the now tidy parlour.

'No thank you, Frannie. It is Mary-Ann I've come to talk to.'

'Marian,' murmurs the elder girl. 'Why don't we go into the parlour, Miss Cockin? Can we offer you a cup of tea?' She remembers her academy training and stands tall and proud and gestures elegantly to the hall. 'Shall I lead the way?' Maria smiles stiffly in return and follows. Frannie takes this as acceptance of the offer for tea and busies herself with the kettle and a tray.

The voluminous skirts of Maria Cockin's outfit brush the doorway of the parlour and she chooses the sofa to best accommodate her gown. Marian notes the quality of the printed cotton and the detail of trimming. Deliberately, she takes the chair opposite, the one that is usually her father's. Maria notes this and without further ado, she comes to the point.

'Well, my dear, your father tells me that you are seeking a position as a companion or tutor. How successful are you thus far?'

Marian steels herself to show no emotion. How dare this woman come into their home and demand to know her business? Her mouth smiles.

'I have made enquiries among family and friends in the area, but so far without finding anything suitable. It's early days and I am sure something will turn up, ere long.' She is relieved by Frannie's entrance bearing a tray of tea things. Maria allows the interruption to play its course until all three are served. Frannie sits uncomfortably, unsure whether she is invited or not, but as neither Miss Cockin nor Marian has asked her to leave, she remains. Her sister shoots her a look of gratitude. Maria frowns slightly.

'I, too, have been making enquiries, on your behalf, of course,' she adds. She is no fool and is aware from the girl's stiff bearing that her interference is not welcome. 'Your father wishes very much to support your endeavour to spread your wings.' She smiles with as much warmth as she can muster. Mary-Ann, or Marian as she likes to call herself now, does not endear herself but for Joseph's sake she wants to ensure the girl finds a suitable placement.

'Do you know the Huttons who farm at Killam, over Cantley way? They are known to your Aunt Nancy. She is a friend of Mrs Hutton, a widow now, though I always thought she'd be the first to go. Ten children in twelve years; it's a marvel she survived.' A shadow crosses Marian's face with the memory that her own mother died after only two children. Maria does not notice. 'Frederick might be the eldest son, I'm not sure, but he is running the farm now. Quite sizeable, I believe, over 300 acres.' Marian does a quick calculation. Even bigger than Uncle Godfrey's farm. 'She has a daughter, most agreeable, I'm told, but she is delicate and no longer goes to school. Fifteen, named Charlotte, and in need of tutoring in the finer things in life such as drawing and music.' Frannie looks down at her cup. Neither subjects are her sister's particular forté. 'Would you like me to effect an introduction, my dear? Of course, we shall discuss it with your father first.'

Marian struggles with her rising annoyance and Frannie knows how much it costs her sister to smile politely, thank Miss Cockin for her solicitude and offer more tea. Maria calibrates the mood and puts her cup and saucer aside, thanks Frannie for the tea, Mary-Ann for hearing her out and rises in one smooth movement from the sofa before departing the room.

'No need to show me out, I know my way,' she discards over her shoulder as she sails on through the kitchen.

To Marian's great irritation (only because it meant Maria Cockin was right), she really likes Charlotte Hutton when eventually they meet. Mrs Hutton is kindly and the houseful of children, older and younger, remind her of the Willey family and the happy if chaotic times she enjoys there. It is agreed that she will spend time with Charlotte to work out what subjects best suit the girl, then she will start to tutor shortly after her return from Moor House.

'Well, Father, I think this arrangement will suit me well. I shall travel there on Monday mornings and return home Friday afternoons. So, as before, you will have both your chickens home to roost each weekend. What say you now?'

Joseph smiles broadly and makes a mental note to send a message of gratitude to Maria.

CHAPTER 45

1860 August

As Marian steps down from the train in Birkenshaw, Hannah-Mary waves her handkerchief and directs a porter to carry her friend's bags. Arm-in-arm, the two girls seek out the trap waiting to carry them up to Moor House and set off. Marian is struck by the change in Hannah-Mary after only a month apart. Is it the way she now dresses her hair, secured in a tight bun, or is it something about her bearing? Suddenly she seems quite grown-up. Indeed, Marian regards herself equally so to have made the railway journey alone, despite the fact that Hannah-Mary has already done so numerous times. Although full summer, the sky has clouded over and the two young women huddle together under a blanket. It is so good to be together again.

'Isn't it beyond wonderful not to be returning to the academy in September, not ever, ever again.' Marian shouts above the rattle of the trap and fast clip-clop of the pony's hooves.

'Indeed,' echoes her friend, 'and there's so much ahead of us.'

Being Saturday, the men of the Willey family return from work at midday. Dinner is subdued as the father is still seething from the failure of a business transaction that morning. Quietly, Hannah-Mary suggests that they escape for a walk. Wrapped in shawls against the sullen sky, the friends take a turn around the garden, hoping to find a quiet place to talk.

'You wrote to me that you have found a position. Do tell me more.' Hannah-Mary draws Marian to sit beside her on the wooden bench sheltered from the moorland breezes by an old hawthorn hedge.

Marian is not quite sure how to put the situation in the best light. If she considers the destiny of some other departing pupils, her new position is hardly auspicious. On the other hand, the alternative, that is to stay at home and play house, would be far worse and that outcome, she suspects, will be Hannah-Mary's lot.

'Oh, you know, it's not for the long term, but it will suit me for now.' She starts hesitantly but gathers enthusiasm. 'There is this girl, Charlotte Hutton. Her family farm is near my Uncle Godfrey's place. Her father died a couple of years back so her older brother is running the farm now. It's quite big, twice the size of ours, I'd say.'

'And what of Charlotte? Do you like her? Why does she need home schooling?'

'Oh, she is a sweet thing, just fifteen. Yes, I know, only two years younger than me. She went to the village school but her nerves are bad and she has missed lessons for the last year. She is so shy that it took a while for me to discover how I can help. Just imagine, Hannah-Mary, me educating anyone.' She ends on a nervous laugh.

'You silly goose, you'll be perfect,' comments Hannah-Mary earnestly. 'Because you found some lessons hard, this will make you a more sympathetic teacher. Lucky girl, I say.'

'Who's a lucky girl?' John-Henry appears around the corner of the hedge, cricket bat in hand. He is greeted by groans from the girls who shoo him away, his sister proclaiming that it is

Marian's first day and she is excused cricket for once. He looks bemused.

'Marian? Who's Marian?' He directs his question at his sister's friend, who blushes. Hannah-Mary snorts derisively.

'We are done with school now and we are looking towards a bright new future,' she pronounces and adds with a touch of sarcasm: 'Marian is a name much more of today, don't you think?' Her brother looks quizzically at her as though she were mad and turns to the girl he has always known (and held fondly) as Mary-Ann.

'Is that so, er, Marian?' He deliberately stumbles over the name, making it sound close to Mary-Ann. She blushes a deeper red.

'I, um, I like the name Marian and there are so many Mary-Anns,' she adds feebly. With lips pursed he nods.

'Indeed so. I'm sure we shall become used to the new name and after all, it is the person who is more important than the name, don't you think?' He ends with a smile, echoed by Marian, relieved that is done. He returns to his question. 'So, tell me more. Why is Marian a lucky girl?'

His sister chuckles and tells him all about the plans for the future. Curiously, he is less enthusiastic than expected.

'I see. You will be leaving your family, Marian?'

'Not at all. I shall only be away four nights each week and I'll be quite close to my uncle's farm.'

John-Henry nods absently and examines the handle of his cricket bat. Without looking up he pursues his enquiries: 'This brother who is now running the family farm, how old would he be?' Hannah-Mary knows her brother well and detects a harshness in his tone, betraying a degree of irritation.

'Oh, I'm not sure,' lies Marian, for the first time realising that she will be living in a household with an unmarried young man, albeit along with his mother. 'Possibly your age?'

That does little to assuage John-Henry's unease but he nods, shrugs and departs whistling.

The next two weeks follow the usual pattern but this year there is something indefinable which overlays Marian's visit. She is sensitive to it and those closest to her feel it also. Chief among them is Hannah-Mary who has guessed the cause. It is impossible to ignore the affection apparent between her friend and her brother. She is content at the prospect of a permanent link sometime in the future and sees it as her role to facilitate matters. Each evening after supper, she suggests to Marian a gentle stroll through the lanes, down to the moor or on to the village. Each time, as a throw-away comment, she invites John-Henry to join them – just to open any heavy gates for them. Mrs Willey watches over the top of her spectacles as they disappear from sight and glances over to her husband, fortunately dozing behind his newspaper. She, too, is content with the story playing out before her.

It is during one of these evening strolls, at the point where usually Hannah-Mary strides ahead to allow Marian and John-Henry to converse in private, that she appears to slip and turn her ankle. She reassures them that it just needs a short rest and fortuitously they are close to the church with a convenient bench. She waves them on impatiently and, reluctantly, they leave her, crossing through the churchyard to the gateway at the other side. As he reaches to unlatch the gate, John-Henry pauses and, instead, reaches for Marian's hands. She blushes but looks him in the eye. Her heart is racing, her breathing is shallow and she feels rather light-headed.

'Marian,' he pronounces her name deliberately, although he would prefer to remain with 'Mary-Ann'. 'I hope you will not find me presumptuous in speaking now as I wish.' She shakes her head even without knowing what he intends to say. 'You have visited our home for some years now and in that time I have watched you grow from a child into a young woman.'

Her cheeks remain pink and she drops her eyes. This declaration is not unwelcome but it is certainly unexpected. She is unsure how to react with modesty when she feels excitement mounting in her breast. Surely, he would not be so forward to speak thus unless … 'For my part I have had the advantage to observe you candidly, watch you at ease with my brothers and sisters, learn what makes you laugh, what makes you sad, even…', he chuckles, 'what you hate to eat.' She shares his joke as they both recall her repugnance for lambs' kidneys. He strokes her right hand. 'And in recent years this fair hand has penned such sweet letters to me.'

'In answer to your dear letters to me,' she whispers.

'Again, through those lines I have discovered so much about you. I hope that in the same way you have come to know something of me. You see, I am now twenty-two and although I work within my father's business, for which I shall for ever be grateful, I know that I wish to build my own future. There is a friend in Bradford, like me a wool-stapler, and together we plan to go into partnership. As yet, I know not where that business will take me, but I do know that there is only one person with whom I wish to share that future. Quite simply, I love you, my dear, and I would be honoured if you would agree to spend your life with me.'

Her hands fly up to hide her face, a reaction of shock. He fears that he has vexed her until her hands fall away and reveal a beaming smile.

'Oh, my dearest, you take my breath away. How could I fail to love the sweet kind soul that you are? I have known you as a friend and the best of brothers to my dear Hannah-Mary. During my visits I have observed you, too, and seen your kindnesses to your mother, your care for your younger brothers and sisters, your generosity of spirit.' Suddenly she remembers her position. 'Of course, we must speak to my father, but I am sure he will give us his blessing.'

Hannah-Mary becomes weary of awaiting the return of the pair and makes her way home, in no doubt that she has done the right thing. By the time they arrive at the house, the couple has decided to confide in only Hannah-Mary until John-Henry has spoken to his parents. If they agree to their betrothal, his plan is to travel to Bentley with Marian and to ask for her hand in marriage. He is sure that his mother will welcome her into the family but as for his father …

Joseph is alerted to the likelihood of such a request when he receives from Marian a letter asking if John-Henry might accompany her home and would he grant the young man the opportunity to speak with him. He turns over the letter, sighs and picks up his hat. A walk around the fields is what he needs. Frannie wonders what lies within the letter, written in Marian's hand. She is a patient girl and knows that her father will reveal all when he returns later. She bides her time and sets about preparing slices of boiled ham and a fresh loaf for tea. Marian will return on Saturday and Frannie looks forward to hearing about the happenings at the Willey farm, even if it makes her own life seem quite ordinary. Nothing wrong with ordinary, she muses.

Joseph meets the train at Stockbridge station and the two men shake hands, each measuring the other for the conversation to come. Both allow Marian to prattle on about the railway journey as they travel the short distance into Bentley.

After lunch, Marian takes Frannie upstairs to show her the bespoke gown she bought in Bradford, something quite simple but smart for when tutoring young Charlotte. Father and John-Henry disappear into the parlour and the door is closed firmly.

Frannie talks to Marian about her own two weeks around the farm, but her sister isn't listening, her mind elsewhere.

'For goodness' sake, Sis,' she explodes. 'Do you listen to a word I say? What is being discussed downstairs? Is he asking to marry you?'

Marian is taken aback that Frannie could be so perceptive let alone so blunt. At first, she blusters then, from shame for trying to mislead her sister, she tells all.

'Forgive me, dearest Frannie.' She throws her arms around her sister and holds her close, rocking her gently. 'Yes, John-Henry loves me and I love him.' She blushes deeply.

'Well of course, we all know that,' comments Frannie in her matter-of-fact voice. 'What is going to happen? Will you marry soon? What about tutoring Charlotte Hutton?'

'No, yes, that is we shall not marry for some time. John-Henry plans to set up in business with a partner on his own account, so he may need to travel for a while, which would not be ideal for the start of a marriage. He suggests we wait for a couple of years. Of course, we don't know what Father will say.' She looks hopefully at her sister. 'Will he look favourably on John-Henry, do you think? He has met him only a few times though he could not but admire him, surely? Frannie, I don't mind how long I have to wait; I simply cannot imagine marrying anyone else but him.' Frannie smiles, happy for her sister's good fortune to have found someone to love so soon.

A call comes from below: 'Mary-Ann, um, Marian, will you please come down?'

She is heartened by the cautious smile on John-Henry's face as she enters the parlour. Her father, on the other hand, appears serious but not unkindly so. She stands nervously before him until he waves her to the sofa. He indicates an armchair to John-Henry and stands before the empty fireplace.

'Well, Miss, this is indeed a surprise.' It was not, but he felt it warranted such an introduction. 'John-Henry has told me of his feelings for you and I am heartened to hear that you are held in such high regard. I would have expected nothing less. He has requested your hand in marriage and, although I do not underestimate the depth of his feeling for you…' Joseph cannot bring himself to use the word 'love', '…and he reassures me that his sentiments are reciprocated, I am concerned that you are only just seventeen.' He pauses and Marian's heart plummets. 'You have not had experience of the wider world and although I have no doubt that your feelings will remain steadfast, I would prefer that you wait a couple of years before marriage. John-Henry has told me of his intention to start his own business and I applaud his enterprise. No doubt though, he will wish to establish himself before taking a wife. However, I hasten to add that I would have no objection to your announcing an engagement to marry. In fact,' he adds emphatically, 'I would truly welcome such a declaration.' He chuckles at what he considers to have been a suitable speech for the occasion.

John Henry rises and smiles at Marian. 'I have no doubt that we are content to declare our love for each other now and equally are ready to prepare ourselves for marriage over the coming years.' He crosses the room and shakes Joseph's hand. 'Thank you, Sir. I shall not disappoint you, or you my dearest.' He turns to Marian. 'May I?' He looks to Joseph for permission as he takes her hand and on Joseph's nod, bends to kiss it.

CHAPTER 46

1860 September

There are smiles again at Killam. The Hutton family is enjoying an Indian summer. Windows are flung open to let in the musky scent of autumn before winter snaps tight shut. But it is Charlotte who makes them smile. After only three weeks of gentle but persistent encouragement, Marian has persuaded Charlotte to sing. At first it was a timid accompaniment to the confident voice of her new teacher, then a duet equally shared. Now she is off and away and, each time, her tones become stronger and more animated. As the household goes about its business, the piano strikes up and Charlotte lifts their hearts.

Nobody explained to Marian why her pupil no longer attends school. She knew only that the girl hardly spoke unless necessary. Indeed, during their first few days together, the conversation was very one-sided and Marian had to contain her exasperation.

'Please Charlotte, you must help me. I have been engaged by your family to advance your education. You are only two years younger than me and although you no longer attend school, there is much that you learnt before. Your arithmetic is more than adequate and I see from your bookshelf that you enjoy reading. My role is to help you with other subjects which will be of use to you in the wider world.' As she spoke the words, she realised that this was precisely the wrong approach. The 'wider world' is what Charlotte fears. That night, Marian lay in the small, sparsely furnished bedroom allocated to her and considered how to help her young charge to become more at ease with the outside world.

The following Saturday, back at the Addy farm, she waited eagerly for Frannie's return from the academy then handed her a list of text books she wished to 'borrow'. Her sister was shocked to be expected to steal a French primer, a book of traditional English songs and the drill book, the basis for the young ladies' regular exercise.

'I only want the drill book for the weekend so that I can copy down some of the movements. I remember many, but not all. You can return it on Sunday. The other books – nobody will notice that one has gone missing.' Frannie was still reluctant. 'Please, please. I need these books to achieve anything with Charlotte. It is too exhausting by half to sit and talk with her. I cannot tell you the time I spend in my room preparing for the lessons the next day.' Marian was appalled at the amount of effort needed to create the basis of just one lesson. She was relieved to think that in two years' time she will be a married woman and not have to consider life as a companion or governess. That would be too horrid.

Frannie is such a conscientious pupil that nobody questioned her walking into a classroom, picking up a book and walking out with it under her arm. Her sister was indebted and over the following weeks a sort of routine emerges where Charlotte is tutored in French, geography, singing and drill. For dancing, they call upon the elder Hutton daughter, Caroline. She is a gifted pianist and happy to display her skills as Charlotte and Marian (taking the gentleman's part) struggle their way around the parlour.

Each week a letter arrives for Marian. Previously, John-Henry would write to the Addy farm in Bentley, but has decided that his sweetheart may be lonely during the week and so addresses his letters to Killam. His sister, Hannah-Mary, takes his billet-doux to the village post office and wonders if the choice of destination is to make a statement to the Hutton family, specifically Mr Frederick.

As her trust in Marian grows, Charlotte is curious to know more about Marian's beau. How did they meet, when did she fall in love, isn't she just a little bit nervous about leaving home to marry? In responding, Marian is conscious that her protégée will struggle to find someone to love and marry unless she can be encouraged to escape the confines of her family.

In his turn, John-Henry enquires about life at Killam. What are the brothers and sisters like? What crops are grown there? What stock do they keep? Is it a well-run farm like her father's?

Truth be told, she does not really know. Although meal times with the Huttons are as boisterous as at the Willey farm, Frederick is friendly but finds idle chatter tedious. As he comes to know Marian over the weeks, he enquires about her father's farm. He is acquainted with her uncle, Godfrey Addy, and acknowledges that he has been a welcome source of advice since his father died. Marian warms to Frederick, a bear of a man with tousled sandy hair and infectious chuckle.

As Christmas approaches, Marian wishes to show the Huttons how much Charlotte has progressed and persuades her to create a musical soirée to entertain the family. Caroline is included to provide the music and younger brother, Christopher also joins in. After a couple of weeks of rehearsals, the date is set for the Saturday before Christmas. Reluctantly, Charlotte agrees to Marian's father and sister attending. For her, performing to strangers adds a frisson of fear to the occasion.

The parlour is decked with greenery. Candles replace the usual lamps to reinforce the Christmas atmosphere. Joseph and Frannie are welcomed by Mrs Hutton and Frederick and soon the two men are in close conversation discussing matters agricultural.

Marian observes them and is struck by how at ease they are together.

The entertainment is a success, not only in the warm reception from the onlookers, but also in Charlotte's confidence in reciting poetry and singing *Sweet Lass of Richmond Hill* accompanied by her sister. Marian feels great satisfaction that, even within a couple of months, the girl has made such progress. Frannie is thrilled to be invited to such an occasion and sits quietly making mental notes of how the decorations have been created and what food is provided afterwards. She stores this information for future use. Perhaps one day she might have the good fortune to find a farmer who seeks a homely girl, and she needs to be well-equipped to become a farmer's wife. But that is a long way off. Afterwards, she, Marian and Joseph huddle together in the trap and sing Christmas carols on the journey home through the cold starlit lanes.

Next day is Christmas Eve and the two girls take pleasure in decorating the small fir tree which yet again they have cajoled their father to cut for them.

'According to the ladies' magazines, it is all the thing. Our Queen has known of them since childhood and each year she has a tree decorated for her own children.' Joseph listens to Marian speak with authority and wonders what Elizabeth would make of this young lady with her modern ideas.

Frannie has created decorations to hang from the branches: baked pastry shaped into stars and covered with white icing; green apples looped in red ribbon; oranges studded with scented cloves; tiny bags made of satin off-cuts, filled with fudge, marzipan or butterscotch. As they stand back to admire their artistry, Frannie turns shyly to Marian.

'Would you mind if we bring Henrietta down to sit at the foot of the tree? I don't like to think we have forgotten her and she would look so pretty. Marian flushes, feeling a tinge of shame that her once adored doll has lain neglected for so long, encased in her original box at the bottom of her bedroom cupboard.

'Of course, you are right.' She speeds up the stairs and removes a layer of shoes that covers the carton in which Henrietta lies entombed. Unconsciously, Marian whispers softly:

'Forgive, my sweet. I have been so thoughtless and you have been so patient. There,' she cries, holding the doll aloft, smoothing her petticoats and skirt, patting the hair into place. 'You look as beautiful as ever. Come now, come and join our fun.'

Joseph, who has been banned from the parlour until the decorating is done, now stands silent in wonderment as he views the tree transformed. At last, a Christmas to be happy again. He smiles in anticipation of their extra guest at the table the next day.

It was the Sunday before his daughters returned home for the Christmas holidays when he broke the news. As they neared the end of their meal, he announced that he had invited Miss Cockin to eat Christmas dinner with them. The silence that ensued was not anticipated. He bridled at the lack of enthusiasm and curbed an instinct to remind his girls that he did not need their approval to invite a friend into his home. Immediately he felt ashamed at such irrational thoughts and was momentarily surprised by his defensive reaction. Frannie broke the silence, clasping her hands anxiously before her.

'Marian, we should discuss with Harriet how we can improve on what is planned for the meal. Miss Cockin is used to such fine food and we must not appear lacking in finesse.' Her sister stared at her, bemused that Frannie's immediate concern was about the meal itself. Personally, she had no concern at all for what Miss Cockin might expect served on her plate. Her thoughts whirled as she considered why on earth her father would invite that woman to eat with them on Christmas Day of all days.

Harriet took the news in her stride and by the time the girls returned for Christmas, the larder was stuffed with all manner of delicacies to set before the Addy family and their eminent guest.

On Christmas Day, Maria Cockin drives herself from church to the Addy farm and as Joseph relieves her of an all-enveloping cloak, Marian cannot help but gasp in admiration at the glorious gown beneath. The soft wool is woven in a rich tartan of red and green and the sleeves are piped in green to match the colour of Maria's eyes. Conscious of the admiration, not only from the girls but also from Joseph, Maria Cockin softens uncharacteristically and smiles warmly as, in turn, she takes each of their hands in hers.

'It is so kind of you all to invite me to share your Christmas dinner. I cannot tell you how much I have looked forward to spending this day with you.'

Marian flushes, and expresses her own welcome. She has decided: this is Christmas Day and it is her duty to make it a happy day for her father. Perhaps it will not be as painful as she feared.

The letter written to John-Henry after Christmas is packed with news: the success of Charlotte's soiree on Saturday; the decorating of the fir tree; Christmas morning at church then home to dinner with an unexpected guest. She writes candidly about her misgivings but reports that the meal was undeniably pleasant. Miss Cockin is a lady of independent means as well as spirit and enjoys travel. Marian comments on Miss Cockin's manner of addressing her and Frannie – 'in the same way she speaks to Father, as though we are grown-up.' She concludes on the subject, admitting that the lady is nicer than she thought. Marian ends, begging him to write quickly with news of the Christmas up at Moor House and she tells him how much she longs to see him again.

She last saw John-Henry in Bentley one weekend in October when he presented her with a token of his love, a silver ring designed with a love knot. The next day, after church, Joseph hosted a luncheon at which the betrothal was announced to close family. John-Henry was viewed by all as a delightful young man, someone with prospects, given his father's successful business in Bradford, and everyone was happy for the pair. It is planned for Marian to make a return visit to meet more of the Willey family but, for the present, the winter weather deters.

The reply comes by return of post and he writes of yet another freezing cold Christmas with icicles a foot long, everyone trying to avoid their father. With pleasure, she reads of his impatience to see her. He tells that in January he will move into lodgings in Bradford. He will be living with the Ackroyds, parents of his new business partner, Alfred. The news concerns Marian as until now she can picture him safe in the family home each evening. Now, during the week he will be living with unknown people. Of course, she trusts him, but the length of their betrothal, the distance between them, the infrequency of meeting add strain to what is already hard to bear. She must be strong.

The following Sunday, Nancy has invited her brothers' families to dinner after morning service. For the men, the topic of the day is the likely break-up of the Union in America. Various states are threatening to secede and the fear is that there will be armed conflict between those supporting and those against slavery. Already Lancashire's cotton trade is depressed thanks to the over-production of the last two boom years. Should there be a war, Heaven help the workers when stocks are used up and no more raw cotton can be shipped in. Overhearing the conversation, Marian is glad that John-Henry's future lies not in cotton but in wool.

Aunt Nancy's thoughts lie elsewhere: 'Tell me dear, did you have an enjoyable Christmas Day?' Marian senses a hidden objective and is cautiously vague in her response. Her aunt is undeterred. 'I understand that Maria, that is Miss Cockin, joined you for dinner?' The statement is presented as a question and she looks expectantly at Marian's face, which betrays nothing.

'Yes, indeed, Aunt. She is a good friend to our father and her conversation is always wide-ranging and informed.' This is not the response awaited by Nancy. Despite further probing, she discovers neither what her niece thinks of Maria, nor the opinion of her brother. Such an unexpected inquisition troubles Marian. It reinforces her contemplation of the prospect that perhaps her father is indeed developing an intimacy with Maria Cockin. During the ride home after dinner, as Frannie prattles on about the food and the company, she reflects on the prospect of her father re-marrying.

CHAPTER 47

1861 January

The January sky is flat grey. Frannie is returned to the academy and shivers in her schoolroom, weary from a sleepless night in the freezing cold dormitory. Joseph walks the frost-iron fields and looks skywards for signs of snow. On her first day back at Killam Farm, Marian is not in the mood for a week with Charlotte and the day is too drear for a walk when the two might share news of their Christmas Day. No alternative, back to studies.

Both welcome the interruption when called to dinner. No sooner than everyone is seated around the kitchen table, steaming plates fragrant with rabbit stew, Mrs Hutton begins quizzing. She is intent on discovering how the Addy daughters viewed their guest for Christmas dinner.

'Well, Marian, you had a visitor at table on Christmas Day.' Her statement forewarns the young woman that Mrs Hutton may already have heard her friend's side. She is cautious in her response.

'It was a pleasure to have Miss Cockin with us. She always has much of interest to say. That comes from her good fortune to have travelled, I suppose.' She smiles the topic back across the table.

'Indeed, Maria is a lady who always contributes much wherever she goes. I am sure your father welcomes her company.' Marian allows the comment to hang in the air and desperately seeks another topic to escape this interrogation. Why are people so interested in Miss Cockin? Do others suspect what is now becoming clearer in her own mind? Frederick diverts into questions about the Addy farm and she responds with a grateful smile. Did he do that purposely? More probably his interest lies not in idle gossip.

The winter months stretch ahead of Joseph and, as he trudges his daily round of the farm, he reflects that, come the really bad weather, it will not be possible to meet friends. Particularly Maria Cockin. He is surprised how often she comes to mind. Something she has said, a gesture, an exchange of looks, a shared understanding. He admits that in intellect she is by far his superior. Certainly, she is financially independent. Does this concern him? He enjoys her company and is surprised that at fifty-three he still feels a physical stirring. After John's birth, Mary made it clear that marital relations were out of the question. He acceded to her wishes but many were the times, as he lay beside her, that he longed for the willing embrace of his Elizabeth. Now, he is slightly embarrassed to consider such congress with Maria. Even at forty-seven and still a spinster, she would be a virgin, he has no doubt. Deliberately he breaks such a train of thought by summoning his dogs. He greets them vigorously, provoking excited barking.

Equally, Maria contemplates her friendship with Joseph Addy. Where might it lead? Where does she wish it to lead? She considers her options. Life as an unmarried woman does not trouble her. She has some means which allow her to run her own home, albeit modest. The absence of a man in her life has not been a disadvantage thus far. Perhaps therein lies her problem. In younger years there were one or two men who found her company pleasing. Initially she found this flattering. However, at the point where friendship might blossom into romance, she remarked doubts on both sides. She perceives that the strong sense of confidence in her own capabilities, instilled by her father, might prove a deterrent to most men. Perhaps that is why she now finds in Joseph, a mature man in his fifties, someone who has endured much travail and is very much his own man. She is at ease when they are together. Would she wish to forsake her independence through marriage? She sees in Joseph Addy a man who likely would be happy for her to pursue her own interests. Whether he would wish to travel with her, she is unsure, but that would not matter a jot, were he content to remain on the farm as she set off to visit friends or attend concerts. She is intent on travelling to London and also to Leeds for its newly-established musical festival. Perhaps Marian might like to come with her instead. She sees no appeal in becoming an old lady, alone with a cat. But what of Joseph? Would he contemplate marriage for a third time? If he married someone younger than her, he could still expect to have another son. That is out of the question as far as she is concerned, but even if a child were not his wish, would he expect his conjugal rights? Her years have not been so cloistered that she does not have some inkling of what could be expected. On occasions, her instincts have been aroused. If it were her duty to respond to Joseph, he is a fine figure of a man for his age and she does not shrink from the prospect.

By the end of January, Joseph has not seen Maria for a few weeks and, returning from market, he diverts his trap in the direction of her stone-built house. He walks up the path through her neat garden and knocks the door, conscious that curtains twitch at the cottage across the road. The housekeeper is surprised to see this unexpected visitor but knows he will be welcome. She bids him enter the parlour. A while later, possibly the time it takes to adjust hair and refresh an outfit, Maria joins him with a warm smile.

'Joseph, what a pleasure to see you.'

'I'm sorry Maria. It is ill-mannered of me to arrive without an appointment but ...'

'Nonsense, you are welcome at any time. And I have missed your company.' Joseph feels his cheeks flush with pleasure. She invites him to take tea and they sit either side of the fireplace where a sleepy fire is being encouraged to blaze up. As they wait for the housekeeper to reappear, they talk idly about the weather and the difficulty of travel, especially transporting his daughters to the academy and the Huttons' farm. Maria pours their tea and they settle back into their armchairs, the firelight brightening the early afternoon gloom. The conversation falters. Joseph realises he has created a situation that he had not intended, or if intended, perhaps not now.

Maria regards him calmly as he slowly stirs his tea. She notes the slight frown, the way he chews his lower lip. She sighs, realising that she must take the lead, and sets down her cup and saucer. Sitting upright, her hands now folded in her lap, she speaks gently but firmly.

'My dear Joseph, may I speak plainly? You and I have come to know each other over the past year and neither of us is unwise to life and what it brings. We are not young things with our lives ahead of us, therefore I believe we should be honest with each other.' Abruptly, Joseph sets down his cup and saucer, risking spilling the contents. What is coming next? Maria sees concern in his face. 'You have had the joy of marriage with two much loved wives but it has been God's will that they were taken from you. Joseph, a man of your age, still enjoying the vigour of the prime of your life, may wish to enter into marriage again, perhaps with a younger woman who could bring you a son. Nobody who knows you would deny you that possibility. It is the hope of most men to pass their name and heritage to a son. However…' At this point she hesitates but decides to continue. 'However, it may be that for you the prospect of another marriage could be to find a partner to bring you companionship, someone who can share whatever remaining years the Lord may allow. Were that the case, Joseph, I should consider it an honour were you to choose me.'

It is questionable who is the more shocked: she for proposing herself as his wife, he for hearing the woman he admires suggest he might take her to be his own. There is a long silence while they look at each other, then she drops her eyes, fearing that she has gone too far. He breathes deeply and takes to his feet. Her eyes remain fixed on her lap. Clearly, he intends to leave. Instead, he wanders about the room.

'Maria, what you say is true and I confess that I have considered the prospect of marrying again and, with God's will, to have a son. But truth be told, my faith has been sorely tested with the loss of four loved ones. I have no wish to endure such agony again. And yes, what I now seek is the companionship of a good woman with whom I can spend my remaining years, a woman I esteem and…' His voice falters and he blushes. '…cherish.'

Maria stands up slowly and offers him her hands. He steps towards her and takes both, such capable hands. She looks earnestly into his eyes. Will he accept her? He does not kiss her hands but presses them to his breast.

'My dearest Maria, it would be an honour to cherish you.' She smiles up at him and pulls his hands to her lips. Happiness will come from this union, she is sure, and the deeper feelings of love will take root and grow given time.

The poor weather and falling night hasten his departure but he promises to return soon. Until then what has passed between the pair will remain their secret. So much more to say, so much to consider.

*

As springtime brings more clement weather, the visit of the Addys to meet more of the Willey family is to take place. Frannie is most excited as she is yet to visit Moor House. Marian longs to see John-Henry and Hannah-Mary again but is nervous at the prospect of meeting the wider family. Joseph is confident that his daughter will be more than acceptable to the Willey family but, in any case, his mind is on his own affairs. During the past months he has been meeting with Maria to explore further their joint aspirations for life together. At present, so far as he knows, their secret remains undiscovered, but the time is nearing for them to reveal their true relationship. In fact, both are quite naive to think that nobody has guessed what lies behind their frequent meetings.

Marian is thrilled to be back at Moor House but, with so many people crammed into the farmhouse, she and John-Henry struggle to find a moment to be alone. Hannah-Mary, again, takes charge and calls Marian to join her in the garden, where John-Henry awaits his sweetheart. She withdraws to a discreet distance where she can divert interlopers.

There is an awkwardness between the couple, not visible earlier when, hand-in-hand, they were congratulated by uncles and aunts. Now, abruptly alone, there is so much to say but where to begin?

'You seem different,' John-Henry holds her at arms' length. 'You ...' He cannot find the right words. 'Grown-up' would be insulting to a young woman, but indeed, she has developed a poise unnoticed hitherto. Not unpleasing but a new face to the woman he loves.

'I trust that you approve?' responds Marian, somewhat coquettishly. John-Henry smiles although he does not like her playing the flirt. He changes the subject.

'Your letters tell something of your life at the Hutton's farm and you seem to be happy there.'

'Oh, it is not what I wish from life but for now it will do,' she replies carelessly. 'I find it tedious having to prepare for the next day's studies, although Charlotte is a pleasure to instruct.'

'And the family, they are good to you?'

'Yes, indeed, and as time progresses, I am coming to know her brothers and sisters. Her elder sister Caroline is very capable and is taking over the management of the household from her mother. Arthur is a year younger than me. He works on the family farm and is such a clown. He makes me laugh every day.' She chuckles.

'And the eldest son, Frederick is it, he runs the farm?' She is aware that John-Henry already knows this and suspects he wishes to pursue this particular thread. It amuses her to weave a narrative.

'Indeed, he does, and well from what I perceive. It is a much bigger farm than ours and I can see that it generates a good income for the family.' John-Henry would like to discover what evidence there is for this good income but cannot help yet ask more about the man.

'As eldest son, Frederick must be well placed to make a good marriage, in that case. A large farm, good income …'

'You are quite right, dearest. And to boot he is a fine-looking man with a pleasing temperament. He will be a good catch for anyone seeking to become a farmer's wife.' His spirits lift slightly with this last remark. As he struggles financially at the start of his own career, the presence of a man with such positive attributes in close proximity to his sweetheart has given him concern. He is too much of a gentleman to compel his betrothed to keep her promise were she to fall in love with another. However, his fears have been quelled by her comment that Frederick would be ideal for a girl wishing to be a farmer's wife. From what he has learned of Marian's aspirations, becoming a farmer's wife is the least. He smiles and lifts her hands to his lips.

'It is so good to see your family again. Your father also looks different. He seems cheerier than in the past.' Recollecting the sadness of recent years, he hastens to add: 'He was likely still adjusting to life without your stepmother.'

Marian wonders if she should confide in him and concludes that, as her future husband, he should be trusted with her misgivings.

'John-Henry, may I speak in great confidence? I have not wished to put my suspicions to paper, but I believe my father has intentions.' He looks startled. What intentions could she mean? She explains: 'There is a lady in Arksey, a rather grand lady, unmarried and slightly younger than him. First, they met at my aunt's home for card evenings. Now they meet at each other's house. Alone. She is the lady who spent Christmas Day with us,' she concludes emphatically.

'Ah yes, I wondered who she was and why she spent the day with you. Do you like her?' Marian shrugs a non-committal reply. 'So, you think your father intends to take her for his wife?' He smiles at the thought of his future father-in-law finding happiness again.

Marian nods glumly. 'I'm afraid so.'

'Would that be so terrible?'

'She would come into our home and change it. She would change my father, I know it. It would spoil everything.' Tears of frustration spring into her eyes, bringing a shadow to this happy day. Nonetheless, she finds relief to have expressed her concern of what might come to pass. Little does she realise just how soon.

CHAPTER 48

1861 Summer

Joseph takes his place in the front pew. The irony of marrying again in Sheffield does not escape him. True, it is a different church from that where he and Mary wed; this one built in the triumphant style beloved by the wealthy of the city. They say that the Master Cutler himself lives just down the road. Beside him sit his two daughters. Marian looks across with a reassuring smile that belies her true feelings. Her eyes wander around the church. What a barn of a place. She will choose to marry in the small Norman church where she was baptised, where her mother is buried. Indeed, St Phillips in Upperthorpe is a far cry from All Saints but it seems that Maria was adamant that she would not marry in Arksey, at the church where Addy and Cockin families have worshipped for generations.

'No, Joseph, please humour me. Try to understand that this is my first marriage and one that I had not expected at this time of life. It will be a significant adjustment for me, and also for you, but I am doing the right thing. Unfortunately, most of my family consider me rash and old enough to know better than marrying, be it you or anyone else. A wedding in Sheffield makes it easier to distance myself from my family, both geographically and emotionally. Only my dearest sisters, Elizabeth and Mary, have supported me and I am truly grateful to Mary's son, Joe, for suggesting St Phillip's and allowing me to reside with him in the parish for the reading of the banns.'

In contrast, the Addy family has welcomed their union. Godfrey and Nancy, Joseph's surviving brother and sister, are happy that there will be someone to care for him in later years. Nancy acknowledges that her friend, Maria, will not be compliant like Mary, nor a partner in the farm as was Elizabeth, but her brother is a good soul and deserves someone who will enliven whatever years remain. Maria will surely do that. Frannie is slightly in awe of her soon-to-be stepmother, but equally glad that her father may be happy again. She has worried about his lonely weekdays at the farm and has long considered abandoning her schooling in order to keep house for him. Now this decision is removed. Marian has mixed views. Like her sister, she has been concerned about her father's solitary life but she is unsure of Maria Cockin and her motives. At forty-eight, there is little chance of children. It is well known that, like most Cockins in the area, she is comfortably off, so she is not marrying for money. It is difficult for Marian to conceive of a marriage only for companionship and she remains suspicious.

The tiny congregation is dwarfed by the large church. On the left, the side reserved for the bride's family, sits Maria Cockin's elder sister, Elizabeth Gillot. Like Maria today, she married just short of fifty, and remains childless. Beside her sits the eldest Cockin sister, Mary, and her husband Joseph Bray. Both sisters have rejected the misgivings of their siblings and are here to celebrate the wedding of Maria, hitherto considered unmarriageable.

On the right of the aisle, behind Joseph and his daughters, sits Godfrey Addy flanked by his wife, Susannah, relieved that on this occasion his brother's marriage may be conducted within the law. The small group of Addys is supplemented by his older sister, Nancy, with her husband William Stacey. She has known the Cockin sisters for years and her friendly nods across the aisle are a precursor to the intense gossiping over Madeira wine at the wedding breakfast later.

The bridegroom eases his position on the uncomfortably narrow pew and gazes ahead at the tall east window, ablaze with the stained glass of memorial panels. The organ, high above the west door, has been playing quietly as the few guests gather but now the tempo changes, signalling the arrival of the bride. Joseph turns to look as the small entourage processes down the aisle. Maria, erect and elegant in a crinoline of dusky blue silk, takes the arm of her nephew, Joe Bray. In his early thirties, he is slightly built, with an earnest face and stooped shoulders, as befits a book-keeper. Following on, clasping a posy of pink roses, is Maria Broadhead, her cousin's daughter, at twenty-three fresh-faced and delighted to play her part in the day.

As Maria passes her bouquet to her attendant, Joseph steps forward and they exchange smiles. The parson embarks upon the service and Joseph follows the prompts and responses. He cannot help but recollect the two previous ceremonies, which followed the same words, and compare his emotions. With Elizabeth he felt pride that she had agreed to become his wife, and great anticipation for their future together. It was quite different with Mary. He recalls the apprehension, fear of discovery, the relief in having persuaded her to take such a risk, and his hope for children. As he turns to regard Maria, he feels no anxiety, equally no anticipation of great things to come, certainly not children. Instead, there is a sensation that his life will now flow inexorably forwards, like a river rebounding off the banks, streaming over obstacles along the way until it flows into the open yonder. His thoughts are interrupted as they move into the vestry to sign the register with their witnesses, Joe Bray and Maria Broadhead.

In her next letter to John-Henry, Marian reports on the wedding day. She was relieved that the weather remained dry as they walked from the church, past the Infirmary to the nearby home of Joe and Lizzie Bray. She tells John-Henry of her pleasure in seeing his sister, Louisa with her husband Will Addy, newly returned from America and accompanying Will's mother, also related to the bride. She would happily have spent the whole time quizzing them about farming in Illinois but Louisa seemed reluctant to expand upon the experience and Marian had the impression that it was not only the Civil War which encouraged them to pack up and return to England. Life out there, especially away from the cities, could be harsh. No place to raise their small children.

Marian does not write about the journey home from Sheffield. As their father and stepmother were spending a few days in Derbyshire, she and Frannie travelled back on the train with Uncle Godfrey and Aunt Susannah with whom they would stay a couple of nights. Despite the clatter of the carriages along the rails, the rocking movement induced sleep, a doze at least. With her eyes closed, Marian could pick up snatches of conversation between her uncle and aunt.

'… have his hands full …need some energy to keep up with her … good job she can fund her own dress allowance …' and so on. Marian tucked away what she heard. Exactly her thoughts.

Joseph and Maria return from their brief honeymoon. On their arrival at the farm, Harriet greets them, all afluster, anxious that the new Missus will not find fault with her work. Fortunately, the housekeeper who worked for Maria Cockin is of advanced years, so there was no question of her moving in with the new Mrs Addy, reputed to be a taskmistress who permits no slacking.

Maria Addy walks into her new home. The house tells its own tale. The decorations chosen by Joseph's mother were never altered by Elizabeth. Mary, who followed in her sister's footsteps, at first did not have the confidence and later could not find the energy to make changes. Maria wonders how soon she may tactfully enliven this home, stuck in an era some decades past. Perhaps this could be an opportunity to engage with her new stepdaughters?

They enter the marital bedchamber. Maria's eyes swiftly take in the simple but solid furniture and she smiles at her husband: 'Charming, my dear.' She is pleased to note the triple-panelled screen, clad in a striped grey and yellow brocade. Uninspiring but somewhere to undress with dignity. For her, that was the most difficult part of her wedding night in Harrogate.

Without the passion of youth but with the courtesy of maturity, Joseph waited a while downstairs in the hotel's sitting room, flittering through the newspaper, until he felt that Maria was safely abed. Back in their room, it was he who took advantage of a modesty screen and removed his best suit and under-garments before donning a newly-purchased night-shirt.

Maria pulled back the light bed coverings.

'It is such a warm night, I doubt we shall need these until the early hours,' she laughed, breaking the tension. And so, with humour and mutual respect, they spent their first night together, slowly and kindly discovering that passion is not the exclusive right of the young.

The morning following their return from Derbyshire, Joseph takes the trap to collect his daughters from Godfrey's. Maria spends the time wandering from room to room, considering what immediate improvements could be made and what might be part of a long-term campaign to enliven this dreary farmhouse.

She is in the kitchen with Harriet when Marian and Frannie enter and smiles warmly at both, offering tea and biscuits. Marian is relieved that they are not welcomed with a maternal kiss. She could not have borne that, and notes that her stepmother makes no move to provide the refreshments but instructs Harriet.

Frannie and Marian are still on holiday from both the academy and the instruction of Charlotte. In a week's time, Marian is to leave for Moor House so their stepmother is anxious to initiate her project forthwith. There has been no opportunity to discuss it with Joseph but time is of the essence. As they sit together at dinner, she raises the matter.

'Frannie, Marian, would you like to join me tomorrow as I wish to spend the day in Doncaster visiting various establishments of interest to me. It could be quite diverting for you to accompany me, perhaps?'

Joseph betrays nothing of his thoughts and he raises an enquiring eyebrow at each of his daughters in turn.

'Oh yes, please,' cries Frannie. 'That would be such a treat.' Marian uses the chewing of a piece of meat to provide thinking time. She quickly senses that to demur would be churlish.

'Indeed,' she hesitates to call Maria 'Mother'. 'What an excellent idea.' Her father looks relieved.

That night, in the privacy of their room, Maria broaches the subject of the shopping excursion. 'It is simply an opportunity for me to become acquainted with your daughters. I thought we might look to refresh the curtains in their rooms and they can see for themselves what is available nowadays.'

Joseph is only too aware that his home lacks the style of Maria's own house and he is perfectly content for her to make changes. He warms to her wish to closely involve his daughters in any alterations. A wise woman, he reflects, as gently he pulls her closer.

The next evening, returning from the fields, he is confronted with a table full of snips of fabric, swatches of wallpaper and sample sheets of paint. He laughs and delights in the enthusiasm with which the three women in his life debate the merits of the various patterns.

Pray let this be the beginning of better things.

CHAPTER 49

1861 August

Something has changed. Marian can sense it. This summer, John-Henry's family no longer treats her as a guest. Instead, she is now regarded as one of them and expected to do her share. Of course, Mrs Willey is appraising what sort of a wife she will make. Initially resentful, Marian nonetheless needs the approval of her future mother-in-law. Only Hannah-Mary realises what an effort it takes for Marian to be housewifely.

Today they have left such matters behind them and, together with Betsy-Emma, the friends are bound for Bradford and a day of shopping. Marian smiles at the excitement on the face of the fifteen-year-old as their train threads its way through the green Yorkshire countryside towards the soot-spouting mill chimneys of the town. Betsy-Emma is home from school and Marian is intrigued to hear of the education she receives at the Fulneck School in Pudsey, once attended by her older siblings. The boarders are both boys and girls, many from families living in the West Indies. To Marian, the religious overtones of the school's Moravian ethos sound stifling and she now understands why Hannah-Mary remained there for only one term, before rebelling and insisting on moving to a different school.

The two sisters seek new bonnets for the November wedding of their brother, Godfrey, by no means Marian's favourite person. They wend their way through the crowded streets and first make a beeline for an enormous drapery store, subdivided into smaller shops offering wares from elegant millinery to the silkiest stockings, from bales of colourful fabric to drawers of intricate buttons. The girls are in their element and test the patience of serving staff as they parade one bonnet after another. The day passes swiftly, interspersed with cups of tea and cake. Betsy-Emma wanders off and, after chastisement, is forced to walk between the older girls.

Their return home is delayed by a brief meeting of the lovers. John-Henry promised to leave his desk at five o'clock on the dot and they rendezvous at a teahouse close to his place of work. Seemingly, nearly every street has new buildings under construction for stuff and wool warehouses. These imposing buildings, some built in Italian Renaissance style, speak of confidence and financial success. The whole town feels more cosmopolitan, especially amidst the chatter of many foreign languages drifting across their path.

As John-Henry enters the teahouse, he removes his hat and scans the tables. The girls are already seated, a pot of tea on the table. Without reticence, Marian rises to meet him, adjusting her hat as it slips awry. The young man clasps both her hands in his. He takes the vacant chair beside her and a waitress is summoned to bring hot, toasted teacakes.

This is their first meeting since the spring and neither could wait until the following weekend when he would be free to return to Moor House. Marian brushes aside his polite questions about her journey from Doncaster and quizzes him about his life in Bradford. He starts to talk about his work but she quickly tires of that. Her interest is elsewhere.

'Tell me about the family you lodge with. Are they good people; do they feed you well?' Her exploratory questioning is simply a cover for her real concerns.

'As Alfred and I are now in partnership, he suggested I should lodge with his family. It's a modest home, very close to where Alfred and I work, and the Ackroyds are kindly people.'

'So, does Alfred have brothers and sisters too? Are they pleasant enough?' Only Hannah-Mary realises why her friend is exploring this route: to discover if there are potential rivals for his attentions.

'Oh yes, two nice girls, one still at school and the other, Sarah, she's about my age and she helps keep house. The place is as neat as a pin. Mother would be more than happy with the state of my room and the fine meals they provide.' Marian has no doubt that Mrs Willey would welcome such a diligent home-maker as Sarah. She feels a pang of jealousy.

As Betsy-Emma rattles on about their day in Bradford, Marian observes her fiancé, smartly dressed in a linen jacket befitting the summer weather. He makes a fine figure and she glows in the knowledge that he has chosen her to be his wife. Nonetheless, she would like to know more about this Sarah Ackroyd but hesitates to return to the subject and thus reveal her insecurity.

The following Saturday afternoon, Moor House reverts to the noisy scramble of people that Marian enjoys. John-Henry is back from Bradford with brothers, Francis and Godfrey. His bag full of washing is whisked away by the housemaid and, after refreshments, he takes Marian for their favourite walk across the fields behind the farm. Betsy-Emma and Hannah-Mary tag along behind as chaperones. After a while, the two girls find a suitable spot in the sunshine, protected from the lively breeze. Each has brought a book and they are soon deep into their stories. The betrothed couple note this tacit abdication of responsibility and in turn find a well-placed stone wall which radiates the absorbed heat of the sun. It warms their backs as they sit on Marian's crocheted shawl spread over the grass.

John-Henry takes her hand and puts it to his lips. She shivers with a strange sensation that inclines her to move closer. She takes his hand to stroke her cheek then pulls it to her own lips. She intends her mouth to merely brush the soft hairs on the back of his hand but in doing so is overcome by an uncontrollable thrill. She kisses down hard and long before pulling back with a start, appalled at what she has just done. She drops her eyes in confusion. John-Henry is also taken aback by this unexpected display of passion which has triggered a similar surge of feeling, a surge which must be mastered. He seeks to diffuse the rising desire and gently withdraws his hand.

'Next summer, when you visit the family, you must spend more time in Bradford so that you can help me choose a house for when we wed the following year.' She nods absently, feeling confused and wishing the two girls had not deserted her.

'It is such a long way off,' she whispers. So much could happen in between, she fears.

'In the meantime, there is another wedding to look forward to.' John-Henry tries to divert her thoughts and talks of his forthcoming role at his brother, Godfrey's marriage in November. Marian has not met the bride-to-be, Sarah, but wonders why she is marrying Godfrey. There is something about the older brother which disturbs her. Somewhat taciturn in nature, he has little to say to her, even when she ventures to make conversation with him. He has a bullying streak, evident in the way he teases the younger children beyond the point of fun, and she has seen him being unkind to the farm dogs.

Back in Bentley, Frannie is having a fine time of it. Maria consults her opinion at every opportunity. What meals does her father enjoy? What are the important dates for her calendar? Frannie is pleased that her new stepmother wishes to honour the memory of her mother and of Mary. As best she can remember, the girl writes out the dates of the birthdays and deaths of Elizabeth, Mary, Sophia and John.

The accounts books are in some disarray since Mary took ill. Bookkeeping was never Joseph's strength and now he sits with Maria who quickly picks up what needs to be done. For many years she managed her father's accounts until her brother took over the farm, so the basics are familiar to her.

Joseph soon recognises that although Maria is now married to a farmer, she is far from being a farmer's wife. She will not be seen at harvest time helping to bring out food for her husband, let alone for the hands. Harriet and the milk maids will be despatched to do that. Equally, organising the harvest home will be left to Frannie and Harriet. She will be there on the night but she seeks no involvement in such matters. Marian resents that this role, so much part of her own mother's life, is apparently beneath Maria Addy. Her sister, however, is in her element and becomes ever more loyal to her new stepmother.

There is no doubt that the farmhouse is gradually looking brighter. After wallpapering the girls' rooms and commissioning new curtains, Maria has progressed into the marital bed-chamber. Joseph is presented with two suggested styles of decoration. Frankly, he does not have much of an eye so consults his elder daughter. Marian is flattered to be asked and chooses the summery hues of the wallpaper with a green trellis decked in peach-coloured roses. Her stepmother is irritated that Joseph allows her stepdaughter to make the final choice, but keeps her peace. After all, she has Christmas in view and intends to put her own stamp on the celebrations.

The joyous occasion envisaged by Maria is somewhat muted by the news in mid-December of the death of the Queen's beloved consort, Albert. Shops feel obliged to temper their usual exuberant displays out of respect for the Monarch's loss. Balls planned prior to Christmas are cancelled. Not that such a decision affects Joseph and his wife, but it is part of the cumulative restraint that spreads across the country. Frannie is upset that the academy has withdrawn invitations to friends and family to attend the musical entertainment which pupils have rehearsed and now will perform only for each other.

'It is indeed a sadness, Charlotte, but at least we can see that even the highest in the land cannot escape from serious illness and death.' Such is Marian's comment to her young companion as they sit together putting the final stitches into samplers which will be framed for gifts. Embroidery is one of Marian's least favoured pastimes but the advent of Christmas speeds her needle.

As 1862 dawns, Maria looks back with satisfaction at her first Christmas of married life. This year the pine tree carried even more baubles, to the delight of her stepdaughters who carefully positioned each delicate confection of crystal purchased from a famous emporium in London. Under her instruction, the goose and all the trimmings were cooked to perfection and borne triumphantly to table to great acclaim. Joseph could not have been happier.

Now she transfers her attention to planning the coming year's activities. As she suspected, her husband will not accompany her on excursions up to Harrogate to take the waters, or across to Manchester to hear the fine music of Mr Charles Hallé's orchestra. The idea of visiting London is quite out of the question and each time she ventures to tempt him away from home, Joseph declines, pleading the farm as his excuse. As a long-time solo traveller, this deters her not one bit. She views it as an opportunity to broaden the experience of her stepdaughters. Come the spring, she embarks upon a programme of cultural adventures, one which the girls embrace with excitement blended with trepidation.

March sees their first excursion with a visit to a concert in Manchester. Both girls are thrilled at the prospect of the rail journey across the Pennines and to the overnight stay in the same hotel as on their visit to the Art Treasures exhibition four years ago when they first heard Mr Hallé perform. Frannie has no idea what it will be like to sit through a concert of three and a half hours but is curious to find out. Her sister is far more concerned about what she should wear at such an event. It is certain to be attended by the great and the good of Manchester and she wishes to look her best.

On the evening, overcome by the crush of people, both girls keep close to Maria as they step into the brightly-lit foyer of the Free Trade Hall. Maria knows her way and leads them to deposit their cloaks before leading them to their seats. As she gazes around the wood-panelled hall, amidst the hum of polite voices that fills the vast space, Marian adjusts the tiny hat balanced on her coiffure, elegantly dressed with the help of her stepmother. She nervously touches the silk rose at her bosom, a Christmas gift from her parents, clearly chosen by Maria. She seeks out young women of her age to compare her own appearance with that of the more sophisticated audience.

Frannie tries in vain to count the large number of musicians who crowd onto the platform. The moustachioed players, dressed in black tailcoats, take their seats and proceed to fill the hall with a cacophony as they tune up. Silence falls and Mr Charles Hallé walks to the front of the platform, bows to the audience and takes his position on the classically carved wooden podium. With a flourish, they are off and the girls are thrilled by the sounds that envelop them, ignorant of what they are hearing, simply delighting in the lively composition which opens their first real concert.

'Which was your favourite piece, Frannie?' asks Maria as they walk the short distance to their hotel.

'Oh, the first one,' replies the girl, by now quite tired and longing for her bed. It was a very long concert, to her mind. 'It ripped along and it was quite short.'

'And you, Marian?'

'It was when Mr Hallé sat at the piano and performed Mendelssohn's *Song without Words*. It wasn't just that he played so well; it stirred up all manner of feelings. I am sure the whole audience was equally enthralled.' Her stepmother is gratified.

'So, girls, we may come again in the autumn when the new season starts?' Marian's enthusiastic response contrasts with a sleepy nod from Frannie.

Slowly, slowly, Maria continues her scheme to shape the lives of the Addy girls. For the better, of course.

CHAPTER 50

1862 late spring and summer

London. She is going to London. Marian can scarcely believe her good fortune. It was on Easter day, the family sat around the dinner table, when her father announced that, to celebrate Marian's nineteenth birthday, she and Frannie would spend several days in London to visit the Great London Exposition. The intention was to broaden their education and to that end he had already obtained permission from Miss Legge for Frannie to be absent for a week in June. Maria would lead the party.

'Will you join us, Father?' Ever selfless, Frannie was concerned her father would be left behind.

'Nay lass. Much as I would enjoy such an adventure, the farm will be busy and I cannot leave it unattended for that long. It is my pleasure that both of you can see so much and I am indeed fortunate that you will be in the capable hands of your mother. She knows London well from her school days and visiting friends since.'

The days spent in the capital are crammed, not only with things to do, but above all with people, carriages, carts, horses, the new omnibuses. And the noise – street sellers, hooves and wheels on cobbled streets, itinerant musicians, to say nothing of the smells, mostly unpleasant.

They reach South Kensington and, as they step down from the omnibus where their full-skirted gowns emerge rumpled from the crush, the ladies stand in awe looking up at the building before them. The exhibition is housed in a massive structure with two huge glass domes, at over two hundred feet high, said to be the biggest ever.

Maria buys a catalogue and they sit at one of the tea stands deciding which exhibits to view. Much on show is of little interest. Not for them the locomotives, models of ships, armaments and agricultural machinery, although they marvel at the Australian Colonies flaunting their mining wealth in a glittering obelisk that represents their abundant gold. Instead, their attention is drawn to the furniture and smaller items for the home, particularly the designs of Mr William Morris which attract many female visitors. The art gallery is scanned briefly but their uncomfortable footwear encourages the party to sit beneath one of the domes, listening to a piano recital before a final cup of tea and the queue to take the next omnibus back to the centre and their hotel.

Intent on improving her stepdaughters' cultural appreciation, Maria draws upon her knowledge of art history gained during her expensive education. At the National Gallery in Trafalgar Square, she takes half a day to explain the significance of the collection on display, particularly the recently acquired Italian paintings of the Renaissance period. Marian finds the first hour of interest but then her attention wanders to the smartly dressed men who accompany sophisticated ladies of her own age. Are they suitors or members of the family? Surely, they would be chaperoned if the former. Can she imagine John-Henry taking her to an art gallery? At every turn, she makes mental notes of the clothes, the hats, the shoes she admires. Frannie stifles a yawn. She may be five years older since the Manchester Art Treasures exhibition but she longs for the tea room and a glass of sherbet.

Each day, they return to their hotel exhausted from walking; walking through museums and art galleries, walking along streets to gaze at the elegant clothes displayed in shop windows. They stroll in Hyde Park with the hope of seeing royalty pass by in landaus but all they see are red-coated officers cantering fine horses along Rotten Row, hooves spinning divots over the onlookers.

Marian pens a letter to her beloved each evening, enthusiastically listing the sights and trying to convey the thrill of being in the capital. Reading between the lines, John-Henry perceives that his future wife enjoys an adventurous spirit and is ready to try things unknown. That matches his own aspirations. The more he becomes immersed in the wool business, the more he realises that the world has much to offer. He suspects that she will never be the homely sort, like the girls where he lodges, but he warms to her enthusiasm and longs to have her at his side.

*

It is during her subsequent visit to Moor House that Marian realises the responsibilities she will be taking on as a wife. Over previous months, John-Henry has spent his evenings after work walking the streets of Bradford in search of a suitable place for them to live. It is too early to settle on a particular house but by the time Marian arrives, he has identified the area where they should live.

'Manningham is a pleasant neighbourhood, not too far from my business in the centre, and my brother and his wife have set up home there. Will you come into Bradford and meet me after work on Saturday? We can take some refreshment in that tearoom and in the afternoon, I can show you where I suggest.'

To save time, and Marian's feet, John-Henry engages a cab to drive them the short distance north-west of the centre. The horse trots away from the station, heading uphill along Manningham Lane.

'There are plans to build a theatre somewhere along this road. Won't that be a thing?' She nods. Having heard tales from her stepmother of theatre in London, this would be the next best thing. Soon the grime and smells of the industrial town centre fall behind them as they pass churches and schools and ride on to the leafier parts. The air is clearer in this neighbourhood but she is surprised to see how many houses have been built, all so close together.

'I thought we could view some of the properties I quite like and afterwards we are invited to take tea with my brother, Charles, and his wife, Matilda.'

Marian is somewhat daunted. She has no real acquaintance with Matilda and fears that she will not know the questions to ask, let alone how best to react to the answers.

They alight from the cab. John-Henry takes her hand, tucks it under his arm and off he strides, full of enthusiasm to show his bride-to-be just where he wants to set up home. They meander from one road to another until finally he swings her into a large close with houses built on all sides.

'I have saved my favourite until last. This is Hanover Square and from its name, I imagine there may be German families living here too. Charles lives not far from here and has German wool merchants for neighbours.' They move further into the close. 'So, my dear, what do you think? Would it not be the perfect place? No passing traffic, just the ticket to bring up a family.' Marian blushes at the suggestion of children but has to admit that he is right.

They walk slowly past the neat stone-built houses, one continuous terrace designed more as a horseshoe than the square shape the address suggests. The majority are three storeys high and each front door has a classically designed fanlight, topped by a carved stone canopy. Marian admires the distinctive windows with their pointed arched panes separated by elegant stone mullions.

'My preference would be for one of the larger ones as there would be a room on the top floor for a girl living in,' she ventures.

The lack of a significant private garden is countered by the extensive grassy island in the middle of the square. Today children are running about the small park with mothers and nursemaids seated on benches overseeing their play. It has a happy feeling.

'At present there are none available but I am watchful and the minute a house comes free, shall I ask for us to view it?'

'Indeed, my love. It would be such a pleasant setting for our first home, especially so close to your brother. Should we walk over now? It would be poor manners to arrive late.'

They turn right out of the square, walk a short way along the busy main road, past Victoria Street and turn right into Eldon Place. Facing them at the end of the road stand the distinguished houses of Eldon Terrace. Marian notes that Charles, the eldest brother, has already made his way in the world. Number 3, a large semi-detached house of buff-coloured stone, has an imposing pilastered front door, approached by a flight of six steps. As John-Henry rings the door bell, Marian stands at the bottom admiring the tall sash windows, three up, two down, each gracefully draped with velvet curtains. Her heart thuds at the coming ordeal. Is her gown of sufficient style and quality? She remembers that Matilda's family are the Tattersfields, blanket manufacturers, so monied.

A housemaid with a long white apron welcomes the anticipated guests and leads them into the drawing room where the pair are greeted warmly by Charles and his wife. Marian longs to stare about her to appraise the furnishings but her attention is drawn to the little girl who is running from chair to chair, tripping, falling and scrambling with peals of laughter.

John-Henry scoops up his three-year-old niece, Annie, but she squeals to be put down.

'Come, Marian, do sit, and forgive my daughter's misbehaving,' says Matilda, apparently now expecting a third child. She draws the girl to one side. 'If she continues to be this excitable, she will be up to the nursery to join little Henry,' she chides. Tea things are carried into the room, Annie is despatched upstairs, and soon the talk is all about houses and living in Manningham.

Marian contributes little to the conversation but is happy to listen and learn. Charles is eleven years older than John-Henry and works in partnership with his father at offices in Cheapside in the centre of Bradford. Inevitably the two men fall into talk of the trade and Matilda quizzes Marian about plans for the wedding next year.

'It will take place in October, well after the harvest is in,' explains Marian, 'and John-Henry is happy for us to marry at All Saints in Arksey, rather as his brother, Godfrey married Sarah at her church in Huddersfield last year.' She is curious to learn more about that wedding. 'Did you and Charles attend?'

'No, not I. It was a very quiet affair. Sarah's father died a while back so only her mother was there. Even Godfrey's parents did not attend. Mr Willey's decision at the last minute. Felt unwell. Fortunately, Charles and John-Henry could go with two of their sisters.'

'I have not yet met Godfrey's wife …' Marian lets the remark hang, hoping for Matilda's view but she avoids the question and reverts to her guest's earlier words.

'Is All Saints your family church?'

'Indeed, and where my mother is buried.'

'Of course, how unforgiveable that I forgot that your mother is no longer with us. May I ask how old you were when she died?'

'Only six and my sister only six months old. I hardly remember her now,' she blurts out, wondering why on earth she should divulge such thoughts to a relative stranger.

'That must be hard at a time like this. She would have been so proud of you and I am sure she would have loved John-Henry – everyone takes to him,' Matilda smiles gently. Marian nods, ashamed that her mother is rarely in her thoughts after so many years. She warms to Matilda and relaxes into easy conversation about family and life in Manningham.

'I'm looking forward to seeing John-Henry's sister, Louisa, next time I visit. By then she will have had her baby. I'm curious to hear more about her life in Illinois. What a brave thing for them to do, to travel out to America straight after their wedding and start farming over there. They must have wonderful tales to tell.' Marian's enthusiasm is picked up by the brothers who leave off their conversation to join in.

'Not all happy tales,' comments Charles drily. 'It was pretty basic when they arrived and I think they both struggled with the conditions. Having two babies in quick succession must have been hard for my sister. No friendly local midwife to call on. The outbreak of war was the decider and the family was glad to see them return. Father was persuaded to find a job for Will in the wool trade and they seem settled now.'

Later, a cab is summoned to return them to the station and, as they approach the city centre, John-Henry steals a kiss.

'One step closer, my dearest, one step closer.' Marian squeezes his hand in response. Yes, indeed but, strangely, she feels that Manningham may be only the first step.

CHAPTER 51

1863 Spring

Maria opens the small leather-bound box. She has finished the accounts for the month and is putting the desk to rights. Joseph leaves the book-keeping to her but still uses the bureau for all manner of things, from useful lengths of cord to bundles of letters which she suspects he would keep private. She has opened and closed various drawers to tidy away odds and ends and discovered a green leather jeweller's box. Lifting the lid, she recognises the piece as a mourning brooch and hesitates only a moment before lifting it from its velvet cushion. Not particularly handsome, she reflects, though such things seldom are. She identifies in the woven lattice the silver strands of Joseph's hair and assumes the brown tress must have come from Elizabeth. As his third wife, Maria has never felt that her husband was so deeply attached to his second.

She turns the brooch over and the engraved gold case reveals the name, age and date of death of Elizabeth Addy. Fourteen years ago. Turning it face up, Maria considers the significance of the brooch. Why has she not seen it before and why does it lie alone out of sight? Aesthetically, the piece holds no charm in Maria's eyes. It is cumbersome and burdened with sentiment, something to be worn by a woman, not a young girl, and then only on a garment of substance, one that would do it justice. She speculates whether Joseph has already offered it to Marian. She sighs, sad that Elizabeth did not live to see her daughters grow up, and packs the brooch away once more. Such is fate. One woman's misfortune is another's opportunity. No point in dwelling on it. Other things of greater import and she needs to consult Joseph on the wedding preparations.

Marian is grateful for her stepmother's help with the arrangements for the autumn wedding but has her own ideas. Her dress is already in preparation and is being made by a Doncaster seamstress to a design taken from one of Maria's ladies' periodicals. Mindful that All Saints, Arksey would be chilly in October, she has chosen a gown of white brocaded silk with long, tight sleeves and a modestly high neckline. The bodice will be decorated with a flattering off-the-shoulder deep lace flounce and end in a deep vee at the waistline. The voluminous skirt consists of three descending layers of the silk, each trimmed with a double layer of ruffle, and all three gathered up in two flounces to reveal a simple white silk petticoat. On order from a London establishment frequented by Maria is a floor-length lace veil, a wedding gift to her stepdaughter.

'There is a shortage of heirlooms among the Addys,' she comments to Joseph without judgement. 'Let this become one.' Marian is overcome by such generosity and writes as much to John-Henry. In the post a few days later comes a letter from his mother offering the gift of a pale blue and soft grey Indian shawl to keep her warm in the church. Marian is thrilled to accept and, as well as writing her thanks to her future mother-in-law, she sends a note also to Hannah-Mary, expressing her deep gratitude for the thoughtfulness of such a gift.

Hannah-Mary writes back: 'Although ashamed to say it, I am full of envy. The Indian shawls to be had in Bradford are simply exquisite and I was delighted to help my mother choose one for you but then wished to keep it for myself. There, what a thing to admit to a friend.'

Marian misses Hannah-Mary greatly and besides the longing to be married to her darling John-Henry, the thought of living closer to her dearest friend promises an even rosier future. She has felt somewhat lacking of companionship in recent weeks. Charlotte Hutton is now eighteen and really there is no longer an excuse for her to have the pretence of further instruction. During the last year Marian has seen her protégée blossom and Charlotte's family is grateful for the confidence she has encouraged in the younger woman.

In May, the Addy family celebrates Marian's twentieth birthday and John-Henry accompanies his two sisters, Hannah-Mary and Betsy-Emma, to a family luncheon in Bentley. Maria seizes the opportunity to question him about the house they have chosen to start married life.

'I don't know Bradford well but I hear that Manningham is a pleasant enough area?' In fact, she knows that it is more than pleasant but is keen to draw out this very nice young man.

'The house is in exactly the road we had chosen and when I knew it was coming vacant, I spoke to the landlord and secured it straightaway. There are some decorations to be undertaken but he has allowed us to select the wallpaper and paint colours so it really will feel like ours by the time we move in.'

Maria admires his positive approach to life. From her conversations with Marian, she has heard a detailed description of the house which will certainly suit this young couple setting out in life. Nonetheless, she recognises that both will find the house and surroundings cramped compared with the farmhouses where they grew up.

The summer flies past with preparations for furnishing the new home and of course the arrangements for the wedding day. Marian is meticulous in her planning, incorporating much of what she has admired in the weddings of others. Her three bridesmaids, sister Frannie, Betsy-Emma Willey and Aunt Nancy's daughter

Eliza, all have been fitted for their matching gowns which will be of silk grosgrain in a fetching shade of apricot trimmed with cream piping. Her posy will be of cream silk roses as the choice of fresh flowers in October will be limited.

The evening before the wedding she feels completely calm. The Willey family has arrived safely in Doncaster and are staying at the hotel where the wedding breakfast will be held. She enters her bedroom where her gown hangs from the picture rail. In the half-light of dusk, it takes on a ghostly form which makes her start in surprise. In the second it takes to recognise the dress, she is reminded of her mother. For so long she has steeled herself against sentimentality. From the day she stepped into the academy in Doncaster, she has had to preserve a protective shell. Her mother is no longer there to provide a loving arm, an encouraging word. Of course, her father loves her but expressing that is not part of what he could ever be. Tonight, she misses her mother. If only she could have met John-Henry. In the fading light Marian sighs and draws the curtain against the dark.

The next morning the house comes alive at an early hour. Even though his men are perfectly capable of feeding the stock and milking the herd, Joseph needs his routine. Betsy-Emma and Eliza arrive full of excitement and with Frannie are ready to help Marian into her gown before arranging her titian coiffure and veil. Maria enters the room and surveys the scene with a critical eye. She suggests some firmer pinning of hair and veil, adjusts the fall of Frannie's skirt then smiles her satisfaction. It is time. She and the bridesmaids leave in the first carriage, with Marian and Joseph to follow on ten minutes later.

Father and daughter stand in the parlour, he beaming with pleasure. What a beauty she has become.

'Your mother would have been so proud of you. You've turned out a grand lass and your John-Henry is a good man.'

Marian basks in his pride and takes his hand. She struggles against showing emotion.

'She is in my thoughts too, Father, and I shall remember her as I follow her path down the aisle.'

'This may not be the moment, my dear, but I have always had in my mind that this would be the day I gave you the memento of your mother which I had made all those years ago.' Joseph pulls from his coat pocket the dark green leather box. He opens it and offers her the brooch. To his disappointment, she recoils.

'Sorry Father, not today. Please keep it for now.' Seeing that he is hurt, she hurriedly adds, 'It is too heavy to wear with this gown and I would hate it to become lost. Please put it somewhere safe, just until …' Her words tail away. She hates the mourning brooch. It is the last thing on earth she would ever want to wear.

Within the cool of All Saints, as the bridal pair go forward to take their vows, Joseph recalls the day that he knelt at this same altar with Elizabeth. How proud she would have been this day. John-Henry's family, seated in the south aisle pews, have time to admire the small ancient church with its beamed barrel vault roof and imposing carved wood pulpit which is dominated by an elaborate tester to project the voice of the parson to the farthest corner. Mrs Willey has been informed that it stems from the mid-seventeenth century and during the signing of the register, the over-awed lady imparts this knowledge to her irritated husband.

At the wedding breakfast afterwards, the bride's father speaks very briefly, unaccustomed as he is. The groom's younger brother, Francis, delivers a witty and warm welcome to Marian as she joins the Willey family, and everyone ignores that his father constantly checks his fob watch and that his elder brother, Godfrey, has drunk too much and is found later in a side-alley fumbling with one of the serving girls.

Frannie observes what is happening around her. At fourteen she is becoming a young woman but still enjoys the simplicity of life at school with her friends, and weekends at home with her father and stepmother. Will she miss Marian? Of course, but six years is a big gap to span and really, they are very different people with little in common. Will she ever meet a John-Henry? She doubts it and would not seek to. The Willey family may live on a farm but they are far removed from the farming families she has grown up with and feels comfortable among.

Marian and John-Henry will spend tonight at the hotel before leaving tomorrow morning for a few days in Harrogate. As the local guests leave, she feels tired and regrets that they have chosen to spend their first night together at the same hotel as his family. Sensing his wife's anxiety, John-Henry passes round the word that they will retire early to prepare for the long journey tomorrow. Joseph and Maria take their cue and say fond farewells to the young couple. It will be some while before they see Marian again as after Harrogate the pair will return directly to Bradford where their new home awaits.

Hannah-Mary hugs her friend, now her sister, and whispers words of encouragement in her ear. This moment has been much discussed by the two women and Hannah-Mary is curious to hear of the secrets of the wedding night. Mrs Willey kisses her daughter-in-law and smiles anxiously. She too was hopeful on her own wedding night but reality soon struck home and she knows all too well the peril of a demanding husband. However, John-Henry is in her mould and will respect his wife and treat her well.

At the turn of the staircase, the couple pauses to wave at the smiling family. As Marian sweeps the faces below, her eye is taken by the stare of her brother-in-law, Godfrey. His eyes are fixed on hers and a smirk plays over his lips. She shivers.

Mrs Willey need not have feared. John-Henry is wise enough and sufficiently in command of his emotions to recognise that a blend of nerves, inexperience and tiredness would not make for a successful first coupling. His proposal to lie side-by-side, holding hands, quietly recollecting the best of the day, may not have been what his bride expected, but the deep sleep which soon overcame her ensured she was relaxed and ready for his welcome approaches of the early morning.

CHAPTER 52

1864 Summer

At the Bentley farmhouse, Joseph Addy holds his first grandchild, just hours old. The baby boy is red with rage at the light, at the noise, and his arms are swaddled tight. The grandfather has been entrusted with the child while the mother is tended by the midwife and her sister, Frannie. Walking slowly up and down the landing, rocking the child, he turns to his wife, Maria, and chuckles.

'What a grand little lad; our Mary-Ann has done us proud.' In the emotion of the moment, he reverts to his daughter's given name, forgetting her preference for the more elegant Marian. 'Nor has she kept us waiting long. It took my Elizabeth four years to conceive Mary-Ann and another five with Frannie. Mary, on the other hand …' He pauses and reflects that discussing the fecundity of his two deceased wives was probably inappropriate, given that his middle-aged third wife likely would remain childless. Maria, without a maternal bone in her body, allows his discomfort to reign for a few seconds before laughing and stroking the baby's tiny nose.

From outside comes the noise of the yard: the clatter of milk pails, the skitter of hooves on cobbles as cows return to the field. A grand start to a summer's day. The sound of a pony arriving in the stable-yard announces the return of the lad bidden ride into

Doncaster to catch the next post with news of the birth. Letters were despatched to the child's father, still at work in Bradford and not expecting the baby for at least another week. Having dissolved his partnership with Alfred Ackroyd shortly before their marriage, John-Henry set up in business on his own account and now works all hours possible to become established.

Maria is particularly gratified that her stepdaughter chose to return home to Bentley for the birth of her first child. She has no illusions that her own presence played a part in the decision, knowing only too well that there is only one woman wanted at a childbirth and that is Elizabeth Barraclough. Now in her fifty-third year, the midwife has lost count of the babies she has eased into this world, Marian and Frannie but two of them.

The birth was not particularly difficult, as these things go, though Marian would take issue with that view. Certainly, she was calmed by Elizabeth Barraclough's quiet voice urging her on when all her strength had deserted her; though, as well as the intense pain, she was equally disconcerted by the distress on her sister's face. A good farmer's daughter, Frannie has witnessed the birth of many animals, from kittens to calves. She had heard the anguished mewing of the cats and the bellows of the cows. When it came to her sister, Frannie was shocked at the length of the labour.

Frannie now opens the bedroom door and beckons them in. Marian, still pink from the exertion, lies propped against fresh pillowcases, and a crisp clean sheet is all she needs for cover in this summer heat. She opens her arms for the return of her child, her wonderful little boy. Joseph bends low to transfer the baby and leans forward to kiss her brow.

'Well done, lass. A grand little lad. John-Henry will be right proud.'

'He is so perfect,' whispers Frannie, now recovered from the travail of the early hours of the morning. She has passed the stage of elation and now feels desperately tired.

'Does the boy have a name yet?' Ever practical, Maria wants to commission a needlewoman to embroider initials on some clothing already prepared for the baby.

'Alfred, Alfred Willey,' pronounces the beaming mother. At which point young Alfred produces cries remarkably strong for such a tiny thing and Elizabeth Barraclough ushers everyone out of the room as she prepares to help the new mother into the mixed blessings of breastfeeding.

By the time John-Henry arrives next day, Marian has grown in confidence and, with help, now presents the picture of contented motherhood. He brings with him Mrs MacDonald, the nurse engaged to support Marian through the early months. The capable Scots lady takes over, and Frannie marvels how this quietly determined body bends all to her will. The baby responds to her immediately and Marian gratefully accedes to her every wish.

Within a week the little family is ready to return home to Manningham. Family and friends process through the farmhouse, bearing gifts for the child. Marian is still feeling weak from the birth but John-Henry has energy and enthusiasm for them both. He has never been happier.

As they pack for the journey, Joseph finds Marian busy in the nursery and seizes the moment.

'We shall miss having you both with us, my dear, and we shall come up to visit soon. In the meantime, another matter. You will remember how on your wedding day you said it was not the appropriate time to take the brooch I had made …' Just as last October, he reaches into a pocket and withdraws the jeweller's box. Marian's heart sinks. Why raise it now? She has so much to do, she is tired and Alfred needs feeding. She has to put an end to this.

'Father, please forgive me. I know how much that brooch means to you, but I cannot take it. If I did, it would be deceiving you and it would remain at the back of a drawer. I shall never wear it. I never could. I am so sorry but I do not want it.' Her tiredness makes the words tumble out unadorned. She hears callousness in her voice and is ashamed. Already emotional, she bursts into tears.

Joseph, initially shocked by her outburst, hesitates then pulls her to him. She feels his whiskers tickle her cheeks and draws back, contrite to have hurt his feelings.

'Mary-Ann,' again he lapses into her given name, 'I had no idea you felt that way. When I had the brooch made, your mother was not long in her grave. When she died, your Grandma Addy clipped a tress of her hair for me to keep and pass on to her daughters. The fashion then as now was to create a piece of mourning jewellery: a brooch, a pendant or a ring. I just thought a brooch would be a way to preserve her hair and remembrance. You were only six years old but had recollections of her so I thought that you, more than Frannie, should have it. But I thought wrong.' He walks to the window and looks out over the roofs of the stable and mistle, away over the big sky towards the Wash.

Marian drops her head in dismay and returns to packing baby clothes into a carpet bag. What was said could not be unsaid. Her father nods with understanding and, without a word, leaves the room. Nothing further is discussed and nobody else is aware of what passed between father and daughter. The next day Joseph and Frannie accompany the little family to Stockbridge halt and, as farewells are exchanged on the platform, Joseph takes Marian to one side.

'Don't fret, lass. I'm not angry. Your mother wouldn't want you to take the brooch against your will. But look, will you have this instead?' From his pocket he brings a white handkerchief and unwraps an oval silver locket. 'I gave this to your mother on our betrothal and I know you have admired it in the past.' He proffers the keepsake which holds locks of her and Frannie's hair, and she takes it with tears in her eyes.

'I shall cherish it all my life, Father. Thank you from my heart.'

He kisses her cheek. 'God bless you.' Their whispered words are drowned out as the locomotive steams noisily into the station. Father and daughter are at peace one with another.

*

Number twenty-six Hanover Square is a neat little house. Quite large enough to start married life, Marian told herself. And yet … She grew up in a spacious farmhouse living with only her parents and at most two siblings. In comparison, this terraced villa in Manningham feels claustrophobic. She dares not reveal her feelings to her new husband since she did view it before they wed, even chose new wallpaper and curtains. That would have been the moment to speak. Now she must hold her peace.

It is during the daytime, with John-Henry out at business, when the walls seem to close in on her. With no garden at the rear of the house, to breathe the air she must walk out onto the central green, overlooked by the lace-curtained windows of her neighbours' houses. She misses the true air of Bentley and open spaces where she grew up. She tells herself that in time she will become accustomed to Bradford, tainted by the smoke, smells and clamour of mills and railways and so many people living on top of each other.

Now that the Scots nanny has flown off to her next charge, Marian is exhausted and frets at the time it takes to do anything, even with the help of Susan, their young house maid. John-Henry encourages her to take the baby out and spend time with his brother Charles's wife, Matilda. Instead, despite the distance,

Marian prefers to meet his sister, Louisa. She admires how she copes with three young children without appearing distracted. Furthermore, she is curious to hear more of their life during the four years they were pioneering out in America, although the reality was less appealing than she imagined. Louisa's portrayal of life in a newly-built Illinois township, where life revolved around cattle and pigs and was quite devoid of refinement of any sort, reminds her that the grass is not always greener on the other side of the fence. It was especially alarming to hear of their abrupt departure once the country was riven by the horrendous war between the North and the South. The journey back to England, Louisa pregnant with their third child, must have been a nightmare and one which had preoccupied the Willey and Addy families until they were safely landed in Liverpool.

Occasionally, she travels down from Manningham into the centre of Bradford to drink tea with her sister-in-law, Hannah-Mary. Marian wonders how this old schoolfriend keeps sane when most of her days are spent at Moor House with only the company of her mother and younger siblings. But on this day, she has news of a visitor.

'A friend of Louisa and Will is coming over from America and will stay with them in Bingley. Sounds rather a character,' she comments dryly. 'His name is Sam Edwards. Born in the Welsh Marches. Farming family. Worked all over: New York, California, in gold mining, silver prospecting, farming of course. His older brother has been out there for some time and is settled with a house and a hardware store.'

'My,' says Marian, suddenly alert. 'No mention of a wife?' Hannah-Mary shrugs that she does not know. 'I wish I could be there when he tells you all about his life. Though perhaps best not tell your father. He wasn't happy that Louisa was whisked off to America when she married my cousin and was only too pleased to have his fears borne out when they returned because of the war. Your Mr Edwards doesn't sound the steady sort that your father would approve of, even though you are the next daughter in line to be married off,' she teases.

Hannah-Mary frowns. There is nothing for her father to approve of, for heaven's sake. Edwards is a friend of Will and Louisa; nothing to do with her.

What indeed does Miss Hannah-Mary Willey make of Mr Samuel Edwards when eventually they meet? After an intensive ten days visiting family then travelling through the industrial parts of England, having seen more than enough of the appropriately named Black Country and equally smoke-besmirched Sheffield, he is spending some time in Bingley. Once refreshed, he will finish his business in further manufacturing towns then head back to Liverpool for his return transatlantic crossing.

Hannah-Mary has invited Marian to join her in the expedition to Bingley. Alfred is deposited with his Aunt Matilda's nursery nurse for the day and, after a short rail journey, the two friends arrive to be greeted by a house full of noisy children all keen to show off their exciting visitor. Louisa ushers her younger children out of the room in the charge of her thirteen-year-old daughter, while Will presents Mr Samuel Edwards to his sister-in-law, Hannah-Mary and cousin, Marian. The stranger bows and Hannah-Mary nods briefly in return. Within the small parlour they sit in awkward proximity.

'I trust you have had an easy journey, Miss Willey,' ventures the man. Marian is immediately taken by the his accent. She expected to hear that soft lilt of people brought up in the Welsh Marches but reflects that he was little more than a child when he emigrated and clearly his drawl indicates the influence of people from many different countries. She continues to observe Hannah-Mary and Mr Edwards as they exchange pleasantries. She likes what she sees. He must be in his mid-thirties and his well-tanned face is framed by a full beard and neatly trimmed hair showing a hint of grey at the temples. The conversation flows on to what it is like to live in California and they are all relieved to hear that a degree of order has now been established in that region, once renowned for its lawlessness. Marian is struck by the man's restless manner and muses that those who had the courage to emigrate and graft are the ones to benefit from the opportunities of the New World. From what she has read in newspapers, the hierarchy of social class is no deterrent to success, unlike in Europe and especially Britain. She detects a wistful note in Will's voice as he quizzes his friend about business opportunities. He made it clear on their return from Illinois that were it not for the war between the North and South, he would happily have remained. However, probably as well to be back safe in Yorkshire, Marian reflects. His face has an unhealthy pallor and she remembers her father's words of concern for her cousin's health.

Marian enters into the conversation, eager to discover for herself what life might be like for families living out in California. Certainly, the climate seems most appealing although she suspects that may be offset by a lack of culture. An hour passes quickly as the questions flow and their guest is happy to talk at length about his business and his aspirations. As the visit concludes, he turns to Hannah-Mary to help with her shawl.

'I leave in a few days but it would give me great pleasure, Miss Willey, if you and Mrs John-Henry would be kind enough to show me something of Bradford, were you free to meet me there tomorrow? Perhaps we could break the day with dinner somewhere acceptable to you both?'

Hannah-Mary casts a doubtful look at Marian who smiles broadly.

'What a splendid idea, Mr Edwards, Hannah-Mary and I would be delighted.' It is decided. Furthermore, Mr Edwards insists on accompanying the ladies as far as the railway station and their train back to Bradford.

'Well, my dear,' exclaims Louisa to her husband as the three disappear down the road. 'That sounds promising don't you think? How do you see my sister settling into pioneer life?' Will shakes his head. He cannot see it happening.

But Marian can. The following evening, she sits opposite her husband as they share a light supper at home. She is tired and really not hungry after eating in town with Hannah-Mary and Sam, yes, they are to call him Sam. John-Henry is intrigued to hear that the man is to visit Moor House the next day and meet his parents.

It is the end of October before Marian hears from Hannah-Mary how Sam Edwards was received at Moor House. In the meantime, John-Henry has heard muttered comments from his father which were far from encouraging.

'I liked the man,' Hannah-Mary opens frankly. 'Nice enough looking, though weathered, I suppose you would call him. He probably spends much of his time outdoors and the summers there are much hotter than in Yorkshire.' She goes on to recount how, originally, he had travelled west, sometimes in wagon trains, sometimes by stage-coach. 'His elder brother had gone out earlier and alone in the 1849 gold rush. Once their mother died, Sam sold his horse to pay his passage and travelled out to try America for himself. It seems that he never settled in one place for very long. I can't recall everywhere he's been but distance doesn't seem to worry him. Did you realise that to get here from California, he has to travel by boat down the west coast to Panama, cross the isthmus then take a ship up to New York and on to England.' Marian's eyes grow wide with amazement.

'So, why was he over here? Why did he go back when there's a war on over there? Did he talk about the war?' Marian considers the man foolhardy.

'Most of California is on the side of the North. They have been against slavery from when the state was formed years ago.

But he did say that on the boat travelling down to Panama City, their baggage was searched and they had to give up their guns during the voyage.'

'Guns?'

'Of course. And it's not just the Confederates they have to defend against; there are always the native people.' Marian's jaw drops. What a wild place to live.

Hannah-Mary continues. 'There's been family business to settle over here in Oswestry and he has been buying goods for his brother's store.'

'So, what did your parents say about him?' Implicit in the question was what did Mr Willey think of him.

'Mother took to him straight away but you know Father, he barely tolerates people who aren't family and not always even them. I don't suppose we shall see him again.'

'Will you write to him?'

'I'll reply if he takes the trouble to write to me.' So, not totally dismissed, thinks Marian.

John-Henry half listens as Marian tells of his sister's encounter but he is too preoccupied, worried by a matter he cannot discuss, one he hesitates to share even with his wife. It concerns the troubling behaviour of his older brother, Godfrey.

Late summer, John-Henry became aware that nobody in the family had seen Godfrey's wife, Sarah for some time. After questioning Hannah-Mary during her recent visit, he was disturbed to hear that neither she nor her parents had seen Sarah and her young son for over a year. He thought it strange that when his elder sister, Elizabeth, married James Walker at St Peter's in Bradford, there was no sign of Sarah and the boy and only weak excuses from his brother. Knowing Godfrey of old, he fears no good lies behind this.

Chapter 53

1864 Autumn

John-Henry preferred not to worry Hannah-Mary with his own suspicions. Godfrey's attendance at his father's office had been erratic and on numerous occasions led to angry words from John Willey. Furthermore, his brother frequently smelled of drink. Since childhood, Godfrey had shown a propensity to bad temper. Several months ago, when Charles announced that his partnership with his father was to be dissolved and that he would set up on his own account, this occasioned an unpleasant outburst on Godfrey's part. Whether he suspected their father of providing the seed-corn for the new venture or whether his brother's rage was founded on other frustrations, John-Henry could not tell, but the display of anger, accompanied by chairs being overthrown, was disconcerting at the least.

Not long afterwards, John-Henry is busy at his Cheapside office when his clerk enquires if he would receive Mrs Godfrey. John-Henry is surprised but welcomes Sarah. She explains she is come into town in the hope of seeing her husband.

'Good to see you Sarah but I am sorry, I don't know where Godfrey is. I think he must be travelling. I haven't seen him for a few days.' He watches her pale beneath the brim of her hat and as he bends forward to offer a comforting hand, he is shocked to see a livid bruise below her left eye. Sarah is no shrinking violet and he views her as a woman of strong character, although pleasant enough. Now she looks crushed.

'I too have not seen him for several days. There was an argument and he left, but not before …' Her voice fails.

'Did he hit you?' Reluctantly, she nods. 'Has this happened before?'

'Indeed, many times.' John-Henry recoils in consternation.

'The first time he knocked me down, I was newly pregnant with John. The following year he dragged me by the hair and beat me with his fists. He has hit me with a poker, with a chair, and a few months back he threatened me with a knife. I fear for my life and what would become of my child. Now he has gone and I do not know when he will return. For now, my mother has come to Dudley Hill to keep me company.'

His mind races. Should he find Godfrey and confront him? Discuss it first with his brothers, Charles and Francis? They must try to keep this scandal from their parents. He paces the room in silence and as he calms, he realises the futility of trying to reason with Godfrey. The only safe solution is for her to leave Dudley Hill with her child and her mother.

'You must go home at once then pack a bag for you and John to travel with your mother to Huddersfield tomorrow morning.' She hesitates, clearly afeared that Godfrey might return that very evening. He would be enraged to discover his mother-in-law present. There is the matter of the money he owes her. John-Henry suggests a solution.

'Hannah-Mary is in Bradford shopping and we planned to meet at mid-day. Sarah, you must permit me to explain your dilemma and I shall ask her to come and stay the night with you all at Dudley Hill. May I do that? On the chance that Godfrey returns this evening, he would not dare hurt you with our sister present.'

Wearily, Sarah leans back in the chair and covers her face with both hands. She is driven by desperation.

'Thank you, John-Henry. Were your brother as good and kind as you.'

Next morning, Sarah with her mother and two-year old son, accompanied by Hannah-Mary, depart their comfortable home for an uncertain future. The following day, John-Henry receives a letter confirming their safe arrival in Huddersfield. He now awaits the return of Godfrey to the family business.

Some days later, Godfrey is back at his desk but makes no mention of Sarah's disappearance. What does the man intend?

*

Thick, smoke-laden fog penetrates the houses surrounding Hanover Square. The gas lamps struggle in vain to light the roadway. Any remaining yellow leaves hang limply on the trees, awaiting strong winds to speed their descent. The greyness echoes John-Henry's mood and he has little appetite for the conversation to come. Evenings are drawing in and he welcomes the lamplight spilling from the front windows as he approaches home.

Later, with a light supper tucked away, John-Henry seizes the moment.

'My dear, I do hope you won't mind but I have invited Hannah-Mary to dinner on Sunday.' He knows that his wife will welcome any chance to spend time with her old schoolfriend, so presses on without a response. 'I value my sister's opinion and there is something I would like to discuss with you both.' Marian's eyes narrow. Indeed, she enjoys the company of her dearest friend, but detects a gravity in his words.

'Will you tell me now what it is we are to discuss? My word, but it sounds serious.'

Seated in the softly lit front parlour, John-Henry tells her of the dreadful happenings which have occurred at Dudley Hill over the last year or more. She hears of his shame that one of his brothers could behave so cruelly to his wife and cries out with relief that Sarah has escaped to safety at her mother's home.

'The matter I wish to discuss on Sunday is delicate. At present, only Hannah-Mary and I are aware of the situation. My brother Godfrey keeps his head down working for Father and refuses to discuss the matter with me.' He rises and paces the floor. 'Marian, I am appalled that a brother of mine could behave so disgracefully.' His obvious anger distresses her.

'So, your parents have no idea? Have they not questioned why Sarah and young John have not visited them; why they were absent from Elizabeth's wedding?'

'Indeed, but Godfrey spins a yarn and, because Hannah-Mary does not want them upset, she colludes in the deception and talks of seeing Sarah and the boy. Which she does, but not at Dudley Hill.' He shakes his head in sadness and gazes down into the blazing fire.

'And on Sunday …?'

'Hannah-Mary has told me that Sarah cannot continue like this and wishes their marriage to be dissolved.'

Marian takes a sharp intake of breath. She is aware that since the introduction of the new law some six years ago, it is no longer only the wealthy who can end an unhappy marriage, but she knows of nobody who has undertaken such a step. Maybe out of shame such matters are suppressed but, more likely, many women would prefer to bear the abuse in silence rather than face life without financial support and with their reputation tarnished, no matter how unblemished the reality.

Ahead of Sunday, her husband consults a friend who works in legal chambers in Bradford. Sworn to secrecy, the young lawyer has indicated to him what is considered the best approach for Sarah. Thus prepared, John-Henry presides over the Sunday roast and attempts to keep conversation flowing. His wife and sister have little appetite and want the meal over and the housemaid off and away for her free afternoon so that they may speak privately. They retire to the parlour where a sleepy young Alfred settles on his mother's lap.

'London? She will have to use a lawyer in London?' Hannah-Mary cannot restrain herself. 'She will get eaten alive by those dreadful legal men.'

'Nonsense, Sister. You have been reading too much of Mr Dickens. There are new courts set up to deal with the breakdown of marriages. She won't disappear into Chancery like the Jarndyces. It has to be London as that is where the experienced lawyers practise. Furthermore, it will be removed from Bradford and hopefully any scurrilous reporting in the local papers. My friend is helping me identify a suitable firm who can take her case. We cannot approach our family solicitor as no doubt he will be called upon to advise Godfrey.'

Marian hesitates to comment though she is not in the least surprised that matters have come to this. What an odious man. Her thoughts turn to the Willey family.

'Your father has to know.' Neither husband nor sister responds. They fear the consequences of his rage not only against Godfrey but against them for their deception. 'You are going to tell your parents, aren't you?' She looks disbelievingly from one to another. 'It is not possible for this case to go before the courts without their knowledge.'

John-Henry sighs. This is the real purpose of the meeting. How and when would be best to reveal the truth to the family.

'You are quite right, my dear, but …'

‘Marian, we have to keep this from my parents as long as possible.’ Hannah-Mary hastens to defend the case for caution. ‘It could take a long time to come to court, so why not wait until we absolutely have to tell them? They could do nothing to help in the meantime so why burden them with the worry and the shame?’ She does not add that she wishes to preserve the whole family from the wrath of her father.

Over the coming months John-Henry is frequently absent from the office, discreetly accompanying his sister-in-law to London to meet her lawyer. As Christmas looms, Marian begs to spend the few days of the holiday with her family in Bentley. She shudders at the thought of spending Christmas Day at Moor House, knowing what she knows. He agrees willingly as he too cannot bear hearing the web of lies spun by his brother.

*

The Addy family is delighted to have them all to stay, especially the grandson, now known as Alfy, who is much grown. Home from school for the holidays, Frannie at sixteen is now a young lady but retains a charming, natural way about her. She regrets, however, that she lacks the sophistication of her older sister.

‘Well, Sir, how has the farm been this year?’ John-Henry recognises that this is safe ground to start conversation with his father-in-law and has enough knowledge of his family’s farm to ask pertinent questions.

‘Not so bad this year, thank you, but there may be hard times ahead.’ As he anticipated, the polite exchange between Marian and his wife comes to a halt.

‘How so, Father?’ questions Marian, perfectly able to hold one conversation and listen to another.

‘Seems likely that the Cookes are going to sell up, or at least get rid of much of their land. I reckon the young Sir William is more interested in his businesses in London than bothering with his estate and tenants up here. The flooding and draining over the centuries have been an expense for his forefathers and I suspect he has had enough. William Mellows, the valuer over from High Melton, has already been to have a look round, assessing our buildings and land.'

'Yes,' interrupts Frannie. 'Father allowed me to take Mr Mellows and his son Joe around the fields, so he could get an idea of the size of it.' Marian raises her eyebrows enquiringly at the thought of her younger sister already taking on responsibility. Maybe the son was a further attraction?

'So, what would you do, Father?' His daughter calculates that at fifty-six he is strong and healthy and could farm for years.

'I've been making enquiries, don't you worry. William Mellows knows a lot about what's available or coming up for rent. I respect and like the man. I've known him for many years. He farms much more land than I do and we meet occasionally at the fat-stock shows where he is a judge of some standing. There's possibly something over Cadeby way but it's not a problem for today. Time enough to start planning next year.' He looks to his wife to back up his pragmatism but Maria is not happy at the prospect of having to move house, should the farm be sold from under them. Such is the fate of the tenant farmer. Quietly, she is glad of her own income to cushion her old age.

After a quiet but very happy Christmas, tears are shed by the two sisters as Marian, John-Henry and young Alfy depart for Bradford. Like many people who take family and friends for granted, Marian has only realised in the last year just how fortunate she is to have a kind and generous father, a loving sister and a stepmother who does not try to replace her birth mother, now only a distant memory, but seeks to broaden the world of both her stepdaughters. It is her that Marian would have taken into her confidence, to share her fears for her sister-in-law and the impending divorce, but she dares not go against John-Henry, who has sworn her to secrecy.

CHAPTER 54

1865 Spring

Awaiting their return to Hanover Square is a note from Sarah Willey to say that the divorce hearing will take place on the seventh of January. Fortunately, on this occasion she does not need to attend court. Over the coming days, frequent exchanges of correspondence between John-Henry, Sarah and her London lawyers ensure that the facts supporting her case are as strong as could be. As expected, the first hearing is a formality and the next is set for a date in April.

'So long to wait,' murmurs Marian. 'The strain will be so wearing for her.'

'Godfrey's legal advisors need time to respond. It is the law. I just hope that in the meantime my brother will not seek her out and put pressure upon her to withdraw her suit.'

Now is the time to break the news to his parents and family, but first he needs to inform Godfrey of his intention. It will not be a pleasant affair.

Nor is it. Having insisted that Godfrey should attend a meeting at his father's office, John-Henry takes him by the arm and leads him into the sample room with bales of wool laid out for inspection. Here they will be alone.

'What is this about?' questions Godfrey impatiently. 'We have a meeting with Father in five minutes.' The two men stand facing each other, both tense with anticipation.

'Perhaps you will not wish to be part of the meeting once you understand what is about to be discussed. It is your choice, but now that the court has heard your wife's petition and the hearing is set for April, you can no longer keep this disgraceful affair from the family. It is my intention to tell Father today.'

Godfrey's breathing is now heavy and from the look of him he would as like as not take a swing at his younger brother. His jaw is set but, instead of striking out, he turns on his heel and strides across the floor. At the door he pauses.

'Do what you must, damn you. I don't intend to stay. All you know is what that jade has told you. You didn't have to put up with her nagging and complaining. Some wife!'

The door slams after him. Shocked by the outburst, especially the slur against Sarah, John-Henry pauses to gather his thoughts then, with trepidation, walks down to his father's office. John Willey sits glowering behind a large desk. He is already in a bad temper. Who is John-Henry to take it upon himself to summon his father to a meeting without an explanation? Next to the window stands younger son, Francis, and seated across the desk his oldest boy, Charles. Banging around with cups of tea is Hannah-Mary, who has come into Bradford to give John-Henry support. All turn towards him as he enters the room. He clears his throat and waves away the teacup proffered by his sister.

'Thank you all for coming so promptly. I have something of importance to share with you.'

'Wait. Godfrey isn't here yet. He's always late for everything,' his father snaps.

'It is to discuss Godfrey that you are all come together so I shall come swiftly to the point. I am saddened to inform you that our brother has behaved very badly towards his wife and in consequence Sarah is taking him through the courts to obtain a dissolution of their marriage.'

John Willey first looks uncomprehending then roars with rage. 'I knew she was a wrong'un,' he explodes.

John-Henry shakes his head in disbelief and continues. 'I have waited thus far to delay as long as possible the pain which you now undoubtedly feel. Mother has been at the forefront of my concern and I leave it to you, Father, to deliver this dreadful news. Hannah-Mary has been privy to the affair from an early stage …' He ignores the father's growl at his daughter. '… and she has been able to provide support to Sarah now living safely with her son at her mother's place in Huddersfield.' He pauses to accept the teacup and his father rises from his chair to lean across the desk.

'You, Miss, you dare to scheme with your brother behind my back.' Hannah-Mary bites back her response.

Her brother defends her. 'Hannah-Mary and I have taken it as our responsibility to minimise the consequences for our family and are guiding Sarah through a legal maze. As the law has changed relatively recently, the expertise in this case lies in the capital, so she is being represented by a firm of London lawyers, as is Godfrey by another.' His father looks up, horrified at the prospect of legal fees at London rates.

Slowly, the questions emerge and John-Henry explains the shameful litany of abuse suffered over the years by Sarah. He points out the advantages of using a distant lawyer, not the least to try to contain the level of gossip which a divorce will provoke. Charles and Francis are clearly shaken by the suffering of their brother's wife and especially at the prospect of the family name being dragged through the mire. Initially, nobody voices their inner thoughts but each is aware of Godfrey's temper and predilection for alcohol. Slowly, shame gives way to anger and the brothers' voices are raised in condemnation of his fecklessness. John Willey slams his fist on the desk and demands silence.

'Quiet, all of you. Do you want the rest of the firm to hear our business? This will damage our name, maybe even our company. For now, we must keep our views within the family and not discuss this shameful affair more widely.'

'What are you suggesting, Father?' Charles rises angrily from his chair. 'Are we to allow our good friends and neighbours, to say nothing of our business associates, to think that we condone and support our brother? I for one will not allow anyone to believe that I shall have anything further to do with Godfrey. To me, he is as good as dead.' His father goes red in the face as the choler mounts.

'I do not doubt that when the facts are known generally, he will be ostracised from polite society, but he is my son and if he is to find God's path to forgiveness and redemption, his family must stand by him.' He surveys his children and as no response surfaces, he stands and moves unsteadily towards the coat-stand. 'I cannot stay any longer. I need to return home to speak to your mother. Heaven knows what it'll take to settle her hysterics. Hannah-Mary, you will accompany me.' She helps him into his coat, grabs her own and with a desperate look towards John-Henry, follows her father through the door.

John Willey reveals the family's disgrace to his wife in his own particular way. Hannah-Mary sits anxiously in the dim hallway, ready to fly to console her mother. She hears raised voices, loud cries of distress. After half-an-hour her father emerges scarlet faced. He barely casts her a glance before reaching for his great-coat, hat and boots and, without a word, sets out amidst drizzling low cloud to inspect his land.

'Mother?' Hannah-Mary ventures, pushing open the oak door into the low-ceilinged parlour. Mary Willey, not yet sixty, suddenly looks older. Her daughter sits beside her on the sofa and waits. Mrs Willey regards her, clearly hurt.

'So, you have known of this for some time yet chose not to inform your parents?'

'John-Henry and I sought only to protect you from Father's anger and to save you from pain. It was always our intention to tell you when the time came.'

'And what do you think of the matter, Hannah-Mary? Does the fault lie entirely with Godfrey?' Hannah-Mary is angry that her mother could doubt the validity of Sarah's claims of abuse. Surely, she would not wish to defend her son against such dreadful accusations. Brusquely she explains the story in greater detail and recounts her visits to her sister-in-law in Huddersfield.

'And what of the child? Who will look after young John? What if she loses her suit? Does she lose the child too? Can you imagine your brother being capable of looking after his son alone? Dear Heaven, he will end up living here and much as I love the little lad, I am too old for such things. It will be you and Betsy-Emma who …' As the enormity of what lies ahead finally strikes Mrs Willey, she starts to weep. Hannah-Mary finds it curious that it is the fate of the child which is first in her mother's concerns. What becomes of Sarah, even of Godfrey after the scandal of their divorce comes to light, seems not to worry her. Maybe that too will hit her in time.

The news percolates through the family though, by agreement, only to spouses and no further. The matter is not discussed openly at Moor House but Godfrey's siblings gather in small groups to whisper their shock and pose questions. Shortly comes word that the court hearing has decreed that in April there will be an in-person hearing of the evidence from both parties. Mrs Willey is horrified at the prospect that her son will have to appear before a judge to defend his wife's accusations. Will there be newspaper reporters allowed into the hearing? Will the awful details be revealed to every Tom, Dick and Harry by Grub Street hacks?

Unfortunately, the family's scandal becomes news even before the hearing in London. Despite his sons' urging him not to, John Willey insists on going to court against Mrs Quarmby, his daughter-in-law's widowed mother. His case, as the plaintiff, is one of trespass and is presented to the West Ridings court. At the time of Godfrey's marriage to Sarah, he gave them one hundred-and-seventy-five pounds worth of furniture. After hearing of the breakdown of the marriage, he was told that the house was unoccupied and discovered that most of the furniture had been removed. Furious to have lost what was his, he asked Mrs Quarmby if she knew where it had gone. No, was her response. Would she return it? Nay, not so.

The counsel for the defence explains that the wife is suing for divorce for cruelty and adultery. John-Henry and Charles, sitting in the public gallery, wince for what more might be disclosed. Their father stands stubbornly resolute as he is asked the devastating question:

'Have you not heard, sir, that one cruelty is that of communicating a loathsome disease?' There is a gasp around the court and John Willey turns red. For once, his voice is hardly discerned.

'No.'

The counsel continues, implying that it should be Godfrey Willey in the box, not his father, but he dares not appear. It seems his mother-in-law loaned him one hundred pounds against a bill of sale and as it has not been repaid, under the conditions of the bill she has the right to enter the house and repossess the furniture and more. The defence lawyer explains that after 'young' Willey absented himself from Dudley Hill, Mrs Quarmby moved in to keep her daughter company then they decided to leave, take lodgings elsewhere and remove their furniture. Shaking his head, the judge turns to counsel and asks why could this matter not be settled out of court? Accordingly, after a brief consultation with their clients, the judge announces that the case is dropped, greatly to John Willey's fury and his family's relief. The damage is done however, and the story lies for all to see in the next edition of the *Bradford Observer*. For weeks, Mrs Willey refuses to leave the house even for church, so great is her shame.

The family agrees that the April hearing in London should be attended by John-Henry and Charles. John Willey cannot bear that his son, whatever he might have done, be abandoned by his family. Whilst John-Henry is clearly advising Sarah, Charles must be seen to be supporting Godfrey and, if not altogether comfortable at the prospect, he understands that any report back to his parents must be accurate and unbiased.

Nobody, though, is prepared for the ferocity of the cross-questioning, especially by Godfrey's barrister against Sarah. He implies that she provoked her husband into his 'chastisement' and that she has admitted that she deserved some of the consequences of his 'understandable' lost temper. Fortunately, Sarah's barrister responds robustly and interrogates Godfrey, asking if he had known that his wife was three months' pregnant with their only child when he struck her and knocked her down in May 1862? What crimes had she committed to warrant being dragged by the hair and struck with his fists in 1863? Things must have come to a pretty pass in 1864 for his violence to become more frequent. In the February he hit his wife with a poker; in May he hit her with a chair and kicked her. Finally, in July last year, during an argument when his wife accused him of adultery, he threatened her with a carving knife, using offensive language. What, he appeals to the judge, could the poor woman do other than to remove herself and her child out of harm's way?

Much of what is disclosed, especially in such dramatic tones, is new to Charles and he regards his brother, Godfrey, with distaste. He has not come to know his sister-in-law that well but nobody deserves such treatment. He exchanges looks with John-Henry who shakes his head sorrowfully. What a shameful state of affairs.

Separately, the two brothers return north: Charles accompanying but hardly speaking to Godfrey; John-Henry with Sarah as far as her mother's. The following day, the two men meet at their father's office and recount the minimum detail necessary and explain that the judgement will not be announced until November due to the need for the case to be evaluated.

CHAPTER 55

1865 - 1866

The summer heat stifles Marian and she longs for the gentle breezes of her father's farm. A letter from Frannie informs that she will leave Miss Legge's academy for young ladies at the end of this term and her future is to help her stepmother keep house. That will be welcome to Maria, muses Marian. That extra pair of hands will allow her to travel more. Her father seems very happy in this his third marriage but she knows he is most content at home with his land, caring for his stock. His more cosmopolitan wife must need travel with friends or not at all.

Before responding, she tentatively suggests to John-Henry that it would do her and Alfy good to leave Manningham and spend a few weeks in the fresh air of Bentley and so it is that in July her husband accompanies them both on the railway journey to Stockbridge station. Frannie greets them with the trap and before long Alfy is crawling over the parlour carpet, being fussed over by his grandfather.

Joseph Addy is concerned to see the lines of worry on the face of his son-in-law but keeps his counsel, aware that the divorce case is taking its toll on the Willey family. When John-Henry leaves the next day to return to Bradford, Marian walks with him out to the trap.

'Please make sure that you eat well, my love. I have instructed Susan on what to cook for you in my absence.' She strokes his cheek and fine set of whiskers. 'I shall write to you every day so that you miss nothing of Alfy's progress. He will blossom here in the country.'

John-Henry kisses her soft lips and smiles. He will miss his family but the coming days will allow him to make up for lost time and devote attention to re-building his business. The war in America has finally ended after four long years and that must provide opportunities for the wool trade, opportunities for him to grasp.

Marian enjoys the attention of her own family and relaxes while her sister takes good care of young Alfy. Indeed, she regards Frannie with new eyes. The girl has lost none of her girlish enthusiasm but has developed a natural grace which enhances her rather plain features. A party is held to celebrate her seventeenth birthday, attended by a number of young friends including Joe, the fresh-faced son of William Mellows, the valuer who farms out at High Melton. Unfortunately, Marian cannot enjoy the party to the full. She feels off-colour but nonetheless is pleased to see signs of close friendship between Joe and Frannie.

Towards the end of the two weeks, Marian feels decidedly delicate and the smell of food nauseates her. She is again with child. This time her immediate reaction is not one of elation. A combination of the sickness and the memory of the discomfort and pain of her first confinement tempers any joy at the prospect of a second baby. As John-Henry arrives to collect his family, Marian strives to maintain an appearance of normality.

Back in Hanover Square, she hands her son to Susan, then lies fully clothed on the bed. She hears John-Henry's tread on the stairs and feigns sleep. He withdraws to allow her to rest. Now the tears may roll free. She forces herself to change into her nightgown then, beneath the sheets at last, she sinks into a deep sleep. Tonight was not the moment to reveal her news.

The prospect of an addition to the greater Willey family scarcely registers beyond the female members, so much attention being directed towards the forthcoming divorce judgement. By October, the tension has mounted to the point that everyone who can, avoids John Willey as he storms at those daring to contradict him. John-Henry visits Sarah once a month to ensure she is managing. Her father's legacy has now come into its own and she and her son are able to get by financially as nothing is coming from Godfrey.

The men of the family immerse themselves in matters of business though Godfrey is rarely seen. Whatever the outcome of the judgement, there will be significant costs to be covered. Godfrey smarts under his wife's refusal to allow him to take his son home to Dudley Hill. He rages that she permits him to see the boy in Huddersfield only once a month and then only if accompanied by Hannah-Mary. He must curb his anger lest his sister report it to the family.

On the tenth of November 1865, the judge decrees the marriage is dissolved on grounds of cruelty and adultery with women unknown. He awards Sarah costs. Neither party attends court, and only John-Henry from the family. As expected, the case is disclosed at length in newspapers in London and throughout Yorkshire.

The *Express* of London reports how, after asking a servant to remove a tray, Sarah was knocked to the ground and repeatedly abused over subsequent years. The *Morning Post* and the *Sun* cover the trial briefly. To the family's shame, Godfrey is described as a dissolute character. In Sarah's home town, the *Huddersfield Chronicle* runs a detailed piece on the eighteenth of November laying out the whole sorry story and including the claim that Godfrey only married for her money and said that 'to kill her would be a trifle'. Mrs Quarmby triumphs at the report that the judge described her son-in-law as 'a very bad character indeed'. The same day, the *Leeds Times* discloses that Sarah benefitted from a legacy of four hundred pounds from her deceased father but, on reaching her majority, she sought to protect it from her husband after experiencing his cruelty. All is laid bare. The family's shame is complete.

It is a subdued Christmas at Moor House and John-Henry feels honour-bound to accept his mother's invitation, nay, plea, for him to bring his family to lighten what otherwise would be a gloomy festival. Marian, now heavily pregnant, reluctantly complies, dreading the bitter cold and likely snow on that hilltop, but knowing that next year, with two children, a visit would be even more difficult. Alfy provides a distraction but his grandfather is indifferent to the child. Nagging at the back of the old man's mind is the fact that he has no idea what Godfrey is up to nor how he is finding money to live.

*

Early in the new year, Louisa Addy invites her sister, Hannah-Mary, and Marian for tea at her home. Marian is large, her baby expected in February, but Louisa is positively enormous.

'The doctor has told me and Will that this time it could be twins,' Louisa explains with not a little fear in her voice.

Marian commiserates: 'I believe that there is a history of twins in Will's family though not on the Addy side. I seem to remember that your mother-in-law has twin brothers. Didn't Will once live with the Cockin twins, even worked for them?' She trails off, unwilling to progress further and reveal the mystery within her own family.

'Go on,' urges Hannah-Mary, curious to know more.

'Yes, do.' Louisa waves her to continue. 'I know already something of Will's family history.'

Marian wishes she had not started down this path, uncertain how much Louisa knows.

'My father's older brother, George, never took to farming and worked as a butcher. He married a girl from a good family, Hannah Cockin, related somehow to my stepmother, Maria. Whether she thought he would do well for himself, being a member of the Addy family, I don't know, but after Will was born, things went badly and she left Uncle George, taking her son with her. They went to live on the farm run by her brothers.'

'Yes,' acknowledges Louisa. 'It was a difficult time for Will. He loved his father but was only allowed to see him at his Grandma Addy's home. Isn't that the house where you grew up, Marian?'

'Yes, but all this happened before my parents were even married. And I wasn't born until the year before Uncle George died. How old was Will then?'

'Just fifteen. It was a dreadful thing.' Louisa hesitates but Hannah-Mary is curious and urges her sister on. 'Marian probably knows the details better than I do.' She looks hopefully at her sister-in-law, who continues:

'I was never told by my father but Elizabeth Vazin, as she was then, she knew everything about our family, and said that Uncle George was found dead in our barn. It was my mother who discovered him. She'd gone looking for eggs. Apparently, there wasn't a mark on him. As it was an unexplained death, the doctor called the coroner and it was recorded as a Visitation of God. That's what they write on the death certificate when they don't know.' There is a silence: Louisa reflecting on the effect that must have had on her husband as a youngster; Hannah-Mary pondering if such a short life is hereditary or down to dissolute living.

'Had he been drinking?' The question escapes. Louisa looks horrified.

'Nobody has ever said so.' Marian feels this the most diplomatic response and keeps to herself recollections of Elizabeth Vazin's version of events.

*

By the end of January, it is apparent that Godfrey has no intention of paying Sarah's legal costs and her lawyers have no option other than to press for payment. On the eighth of February the *Bradford Observer* announces for all the city to read that Godfrey Willey is bankrupt. Over the ensuing days, his father and brothers go about their work, facing every business acquaintance, tacitly challenging them to comment on the matter. Nobody does. Perhaps it bears testament to the reputation of the Willey family and the way they conduct business that those who know them simply reflect that there is always one black sheep in the family. Or maybe nobody wants to get on the wrong side of John Willey.

As Marian's confinement nears its end, John-Henry cannot afford to pay much attention to such matters. He is conscious that although their first child was born without complications, that is no indicator that the second will follow similarly, and he senses his wife's unease as her time draws close. Susan is under strict instruction to call him home, should he be at his office when the moment comes. In the event, Marian's pains start in the middle of the evening and her doctor is summoned to attend. This is John-Henry's first experience of childbirth close at hand and he is dismayed by Marian's cries. He busies himself with Alfy who is woken by the disturbance and sings nursery rhymes to distract the child and himself. It is in the pale glimmer of dawn that he hears a weak cry and his wife is now silent. He waits anxiously and shortly the doctor emerges smiling.

'You have a son and your wife is well, though very tired.' His nurse appears bearing a bundle of cloth surrounding a pinched little red face. John-Henry is over-joyed. Two sons. And Marian safe.

She is lying back on the fresh pillows, her face still flushed from the exertion, when her husband enters the room cradling their baby son. He beams and bends to kiss her. She nuzzles the newly washed child that he places in her arms. She is so tired that she hears her husband's joy and pride as if at a distance. Of course, she is relieved that the child is perfect but feels a pang of disappointment not to have had a daughter. Not having been brought up with boys, she is not entirely at ease with them. Maybe next time, though please let that not be soon.

The birth of another boy is welcomed but within the extensive Willey family there are always new births, sadly also losses, and then life moves on. All too soon, however, attention returns to Godfrey who is appealing to the courts to get his bankruptcy discharged.

Yet again, it is the press which reveals the family disgrace and late in March the *Bradford Observer* reports the court case where Godfrey seeks to have his debt of nearly nine hundred pounds discharged. Despite the prosecution's appeal to the court that he is doing so in order to avoid paying the three hundred pounds owed in legal costs to his former wife, the judge declares that he can do no other than discharge the debt. The Willey family is shamed yet again but their son is triumphant in evading the payment to 'that woman' and declares that he will leave Bradford to seek his fortune elsewhere. The family is relieved. Only his mother is distressed.

CHAPTER 56

1866 - 1867

Since the spring, Joseph has been riding out to view land to rent. He is anxious to take the lead on other tenant farmers who, like him, will shortly need to find a new landlord when the Cooke family disposes of its estate. True, the new owners might be amenable and permit the tenants to continue farming fields that, in some instances, have been worked for generations but that's not for Joseph. He prefers to have first choice of land to grow his crops and rear his stock, land that is still owned by gentlemen and not by newly monied industrialists. He turns to William Mellows, with whom acquaintance has grown into friendship, and occasionally the agent joins Joseph to ride out and inspect land coming up for a change in tenancy.

It is not just the fields that Joseph must review. Even were they allowed to stay on in Bentley for a while, eventually he and Maria must find somewhere else to live and that is also influencing his decision. Mellows has indicated that a comfortable house is coming free in Sprotbrough so, after an initial visit, Joseph returns with Maria and Frannie to seek their opinion.

'Ah yes, I know this place. As a girl, I came here to visit the family.' His wife gives nothing more away as they rattle into the yard. A lad comes to hold the pony while Joseph hands down first

Frannie then a more cautious Maria. A middle-aged woman, newly widowed, opens the door to them and, after expressing his condolences, Joseph thanks her generosity in allowing them to view the house before she vacates it.

'How very cosy.' Embarrassed by the situation, Frannie is anxious to say something positive for the sake of the widow. In reality, she is struck by the comparative smallness of the house. Maria does not comment, instead slowly walks into, around and out of each room. Nothing escapes her. However, she is blessed with a good imagination and although smaller than their place in Bentley, the rooms are light and could be decorated to her taste, her latest taste. Furthermore, there are outbuildings to house the farm workers and, apart from when Marian brings her little family, they hardly constitute a large household.

Sprotborough, situated close to the north bank of the Don Gorge, is a pretty village and is dominated by the grand hall, where the baronet and his lady abide in solitary splendour surrounded by a retinue of butlers and other servants. Already, Frannie has calculated that High Melton is within walking distance, something that young Joe Mellows also comments on when he and his father call to hear Joseph's decision.

'Why Frannie, you could be living just down the road from us if your father agrees to take it.' His open enthusiasm encourages her to think that perhaps he might have a soft spot for her. Now to convince her father to reach a decision soon, before any other tenant does. She needs not worry; Joseph and Maria both recognise opportunities and soon the agreement is concluded. He will continue to farm some of Cooke's land over at Bentley and once crops are harvested for the last time, some fields will be relinquished and replaced by those in nearby Cadeby.

Marian reads of her father's decision in a letter from Frannie who is unable to disguise her delight at moving closer to the

Mellows' estate. In recounting the news to her husband, she admits sadness at the loss of her childhood home.

'It was the last link to my mother, do you see? Although I was only six when she died, I remember her sitting with me in the nursery and singing me to sleep.' John-Henry nods with understanding. His own family has lived at Moor House for generations and he cannot imagine it otherwise. However he knows that Marian is struggling to cope with the new baby, named Joseph-Henry in honour of his maternal grandfather and father, as well as the lively two-year-old Alfy. This time, the nurse has stayed with them for an extra month to allow his wife to regain her strength.

So, for the last time, John-Henry takes his family down to Bentley for the summer. Marian remains there for three weeks, basking not only in fresh air and the occasional day of hot sunshine but also in the bliss of being indulged by her family, even her stepmother. Maria ensures that she has time alone to rest and has bought the latest novels for her to read in the afternoons. Her father happily hoists Alfy onto his shoulders and the two head out, over the fields, fields that the boy will not recollect in years to come.

It is Frannie who notices first. Not strictly true. Marian realises it but wishes to deny it. She cannot face the smell of ham frying at breakfast and remains in her room until plates are cleared away. She tries to pass it off as being lazy but cannot fool her sister.

'Marian,' Frannie smiles brightly but feels a flutter of disquiet. 'Could it be that …?'

Marian lets fall the pretence. 'Yes,' she snaps. 'Another baby. Every year, another baby.' She dissolves into sobs. 'I feel like an animal. It is exhausting. Of course, I love my boys. I love my husband. But this is so hard.'

Her sister hesitates. As a farmer's daughter she is knowledgeable about procreation and the whispered conversations with schoolfriends at the academy have increased her awareness. However, she has always struggled to reconcile this knowledge in context with people she knows.

'I suppose if you are to perform your wifely duty, this is the consequence. There is nothing to be done,' Frannie ventures.

'I can hardly refuse John-Henry, can I? Of course, if I am tired and feeling unwell, he does not force himself upon me, but he is a good husband and it is something that he needs. Haven't we seen what happens in a marriage when a man satisfies his needs elsewhere?' She shudders. Frannie nods glumly. It is the woman's lot.

Upon their return to Manningham, Marian's condition is soon perceived without the need for explanation. She doesn't try to hide her dismay and John-Henry is inclined to share her view. The house in Hanover Square is becoming smaller by the year.

'It will be a girl, this time, I'm sure of it,' he encourages. She is less optimistic.

In an attempt to brighten her mood, Marian arranges to meet Hannah-Mary in town at their favourite tea shop. If she hoped to find sympathy from her sister-in-law, she is disappointed.

'Another child? Well, that's the role of the wife, isn't it?' was the only comment made. In any case, Hannah-Mary is not interested to hear about the mundanity of Marian's life. She has news to impart.

'Sam Edwards plans to visit us again in November,' she pronounces. Marian looks puzzled.

'Has he written to you since he was last in England? Wasn't that two years ago? You never said.'

'Indeed. He wrote to me as soon as he arrived back in Ione and we have exchanged correspondence ever since.' She sounds quite matter of fact as though it were an everyday thing to send letters thousands of miles away, letters which take weeks to arrive.

'Where on earth is Ione? What does your father say?'

'It's in California but a long way in from the coast, towards the mountains. His brother has a supplies store there as the town lies on the main road to the goldmines.' She observes Marian's frown. 'It isn't a shanty town, you know. There's a school, flour mill and a Methodist church too.' So, not God-forsaken, thinks Marian. 'As far as my father is concerned, he is unaware of the exchange of correspondence. He writes to me at Louisa's address.' She smiles at the neat deception.

'So, why is he coming to visit this time?' Marian asks, feigning innocence.

'Why, to see me, of course.' Hannah-Mary frowns as her friend laughs. 'No, really. He has not said as much but I believe he wants me to go with back with him. Well, to marry me first.'

Marian stares unbelievingly at Hannah-Mary who appears put-out that anyone should be astounded at such a suggestion, forgetting that nobody has been privy to the correspondence exchanged over the last two years. Sam's letters have revealed a sufficiently good level of education and his ambition to emulate the success of his older brother, John. If he has not yet made his fortune, it is not for the want of trying as he moved across the country working and prospecting. On the other hand, his health has been challenged by the harshness of the life over there which tends to influence his mood adversely on occasions.

'So, what work is he doing now?' ventures Marian.

'He works with his brother in the store,' snaps Hannah-Mary defensively. 'And he owns his own house,' she adds, to lend weight to his credentials. Marian nods thoughtfully.

Sam Edwards arrives in late autumn, with its short days and persistent mist not the most cheerful season to be visiting Yorkshire. He stays again with the Addys in Bingley and Hannah-Mary visits him there or they meet in Bradford. Anxious to get to know the man who is paying court to his sister, John-Henry insists on inviting the couple to Sunday dinner. Marian is fussed by the suggestion and engages Susan's younger sister to keep the boys fed and amused upstairs.

Already, she has misgivings about the whole affair. Louisa has sent her a note indicating that their visitor is manifesting signs of low spirits between meetings with Hannah-Mary. Apparently, John Willey has made it clear to his family that he has no intention of having that man in his house again and it will be the worse for Hannah-Mary if she continues to see him, someone who works 'in trade' and without any family of substance. Protesting was to no avail. Her father was convinced that any man who went out to seek his fortune in America would have to be a 'murderer' to survive. Such harsh criticism only hardens Hannah-Mary's resolve. She just needs time.

In the event, John-Henry is pleasantly surprised by the lack of bluster and swagger one often finds in the 'colonial' types who leave British shores to travel in search of opportunities in foreign lands. He listens as the man, just shy of thirty, speaks frankly about the country he has chosen: the uncompromising terrain, the extremes of climate, the demanding work and the diverse people who came through adversity from all points of the globe, people who, like him, are prepared to graft to make something of their lives. John-Henry feels admiration for Sam's tenacity and grit and is inspired by the sense of adventure he conveys. Marian, on the other hand, sees nothing in this description that matches her own expectations of life in America, but begins to understand why her good friend is attracted to the no-frills life portrayed. Nonetheless, beneath the tanned good looks of their visitor, she detects a more sensitive side and could well believe that left alone in times of adversity he would struggle.

Hannah-Mary has little to say following his departure. After the antagonistic reaction of her father, the prospect of Sam returning to see her seems slight, but she is determined to pursue this friendship. As she prepares for yet another family Christmas at Moor House, she looks about and asks herself: 'Is this all I shall ever know?'

CHAPTER 57

1867

John-Henry's prediction was correct. The baby is a girl and Henrietta Willey makes her debut the following spring. There is no question in her mother's mind about the name, although she cannot admit to her husband that the treasured doll, still boxed in tissue paper, also rejoices in the name of Henrietta. Her secret.

He is enchanted by this little lady who soon learns to hold his gaze and chuckle. In the coming months, Marian also falls under the spell of her daughter, destined to be the prettiest, cleverest child imaginable, or so her mother believes. Dreams are what Marian must cling to as her life becomes dominated by the needs of her growing young family. She is sure that John-Henry has no idea how utterly draining it is, even with a nurse, to cope with the constant demands of her two young boys. She is convinced that neither she nor Frannie were so full of energy or so boisterously loud. She wants to invite Frannie to help her once the nanny departs, and her suggestion is greeted with pleasure.

'Please let me come,' writes her sister. 'Now that we have moved into the house in Sprotbrough, our sainted stepmother is driving us to distraction with all manner of decoration work. Why this could not have been undertaken before we left Bentley, Heaven only knows. I need to escape for a while. Please allow me to play aunt?'

John-Henry is delighted to have his sister-in-law to stay. She has a calming effect upon his dear wife who is finding the pressure of three children quite overwhelming. The two women take every opportunity to escape the confines of the house and to walk up to the wealthier and leafier parts of Manningham. Frannie happily cradles her niece while holding tightly onto Alfy's reins, whereas Marian pushes little Josh in the wicker baby carriage shared among the sisters-in-law. This three-wheeled transporter is still quite a rarity and it certainly makes life easier.

Frannie is curious to understand her sister's situation and amidst the chatter introduces occasional searching questions.

'There is plenty of room for a nurse to live on the top floor with Susan? From what I have seen over the last few days, you need more help.'

Marian does not reply immediately and makes a play of adjusting the sun shade to protect the eyes of her second-born, now called Josh by his elder brother.

'It's not just the space that is the problem. It is the cost too.' She notes her sister's questioning eyebrows. Her loyalty to her husband has prevented her discussing such matters before, but she needs to tell someone of her concerns. 'Things have been somewhat difficult of late, financially that is. I have never told the family but two years ago, while the family was embroiled in the divorce case, John-Henry had to go to court to give evidence in a bankruptcy case. One of his clients, a major wool spinner, owed him an awful lot of money. Sadly, we were one of many who never received a penny due to us. It hit us badly and we are only just starting to get back to where we were. But things are looking up a bit now,' she adds brightly, perhaps too brightly.

As Frannie hastens to commiserate, Marian cuts across her, regretting having disclosed their problems. 'Enough of that. Do tell me more of your new life in Sprotbrough.'

Her sister shifts Henrietta to the other arm and seeks a low wall where they could rest a while in the sunshine and watch the passers-by. Alfy takes the opportunity to climb onto his mother's knee and peer into the baby carriage with the intent of prodding his sleeping younger brother.

'It is working well enough, I suppose. Maria – did I tell you she wants us to call her that now? – she is making wonderful improvements and Father is perfectly content with her changes. You know, it is good to see the two of them together. I'm pleased he has found such an excellent companion. They are both getting to know people in the village, mainly through the church. Father was honoured to be invited to become a church warden at St Mary's. It is a lovely little church; really old, of similar age to All Saints. And, as you would expect, Maria is busy helping with the less fortunate of the parish.'

Alfy wriggles from his mother's knee and turns his attention to his baby sister. Frannie watches him offer his forefinger to be grasped in Henrietta's tiny fist. She relishes the moment.

'As for me, I sometimes feel that I am in the way, not that either of them would even think that. To be frank, once the house is settled, there is not so much for me to do and I feel I should think of my future.'

*

Harrogate? Maybe London? Maria Addy is delighted that her stepdaughter wishes to venture further afield. She has marked Frannie's restlessness since the move from Bentley and even the attentions of William Mellows' boy, Joe, has not lifted her spirits.

Anxious to act before the girl changes her mind, Maria contrives a visit to an old schoolfriend now living in widowed splendour in a smart villa in Harrogate. Early in September, Maria and Frannie travel to the growing spa town and settle into a small but comfortable hotel.

Jane Cavendish benefits from the fruits of her late husband's labours in the City. On his retirement, he and his wife moved up to Yorkshire, county of his birth. Within a year he was dead of heart disease and his widow stayed on. And on. Now a pillar of Harrogate society, she enjoys her life there, even if her health could be better. She welcomes her visitors with tea and cake.

'My dear Frances,' she addresses Frannie. 'What good fortune you have in your stepmother, dear Maria. We were so close at school in London and that friendship has endured these many years since.' Curious to learn more of the Addys, Mrs Cavendish proceeds to tease out the story of Frannie's family.

'And Marian; how old was she when she married?'

'Just twenty. She is married to a lovely man and has three children, with another one due next year.' The two older women exchange a glance. Frannie cannot discern whether it is one of regret for having no children of their own or out of sympathy for a woman who is a perpetual baby maker.

'And you, my dear, would you want children one day?'

'Oh yes indeed, Mrs Cavendish. I love visiting my sister and spending time with the little ones. But that is for the future.'

'Of course. But tell me, is there a beau in your life at present?' Maria shoots a look of censure at her old friend. It is impertinent to ask Frannie such a question though, truth be told, she is intrigued to hear the answer.

'Oh no, not really.' So, a half *yes*. 'There is a young man who has become a good friend but I couldn't really call him my beau.' Frannie's cheeks burn with embarrassment and Maria interjects to steer the conversation into safer waters.

'Joe Mellows is a pleasant enough lad who comes to the house occasionally with his father who is agent for the land that we are farming now. The Mellows are well-regarded in the area, just like the Addys,' she reminds her friend.

The next day, Maria and Frannie explore the town and accompany Mrs Cavendish to take tea in the Spa Rooms. The surrounding tables are full of chattering ladies, mostly dressed smartly even though not always in the latest fashions, notes Maria. Many acknowledge her friend as they enter.

'Well, lass, how did you find the social whirl of Harrogate?' asks Joseph when his daughter and wife return home.

'Grand, absolutely grand. And it was very kind of you to take me.' Frannie pats the arm of her stepmother. Maria nods and quietly continues her benign plotting. Perhaps there might be an opportunity for Frannie up in Harrogate. Next day a letter is penned to Jane Cavendish.

*

In Hanover Square life is not so blissful. Marian's morning sickness is dragging her down. She is angry that despite still breastfeeding Henrietta, she has fallen pregnant for the fourth time. How was that possible? She has no appetite and her daughter is hungry for all the milk she can provide. She can bear no longer to look in the mirror. That wan face cannot be hers. She looks haggard. And the noise. There is always noise. One or other of the children will be shouting with joy, with rage, for food, for attention. The nurse has been re-engaged and Susan grumbles that the older woman takes up too much space in the attic room – and snores.

John-Henry works long hours since he is intent on expanding his business, especially the growing exports to the United States. When at home, he does his best to amuse his sons, mainly to relieve his wife. He witnesses the toll that the children take on Marian, and now regrets this fourth pregnancy. Perhaps he should talk with his old schoolfriend, now a respected doctor, who has long since advocated the cause for 'voluntary motherhood'. Four children should be enough for any family and financially there is no prospect of moving to a larger house.

Marian views the coming Christmas with despair and insists that they remain in Hanover Square for the festivities. She cannot face the prospect of travelling while pregnant. John-Henry is content with the decision and looks forwards to creating the magic of Christmas for his children: Alfy, three, Josh, two and baby Henrietta. In the meantime, Hannah-Mary comes to visit and Marian seeks distraction in quizzing her about the lovelorn Sam who, last heard, has departed California and travelled to the other end of the world.

'So, there clearly is no future with Sam, now he is gone even further away?' she suggests.

Hannah-Mary sighs. She no longer knows what to think. His letters were full of darkness even before he set out on the long and tedious journey to New Zealand.

'I really cannot tell. He wrote to me before he departed, saying that he much regretted having left California, yet there he has no close friends and doesn't seem to be able to settle. He even described himself as a Wandering Jew. As for marriage, he fears that he has nothing to offer me, neither fame nor fortune. He knows too well that my father does not approve of him and although I am legally of age to marry of my own will, were I to do so, Father would cut me off financially and that would not do, would not do at all.' She shakes her head emphatically. 'But in any case, he is no longer in New Zealand.'

Marian looks startled.

'Already he has visited New Zealand and left? Was it so awful there?'

'Probably not. He planned to live there and find employment so ended up travelling around the place, mainly on foot, but found nothing to please him. After three months he decided to return to America. Frankly, I do not know how he can bear these long sea voyages. Apparently, this time he was en route for Wisconsin but met up with someone now settled in Illinois and so stayed on there. Wasn't that where Will and Louisa lived?' She doesn't wait for a response and continues, while pouring more tea. 'It seems that he has bought some land there and is working for someone else in a dry-goods store.'

'I see,' is all Marian can say. Not the dependable sort, is what she thinks. Her friend shrugs.

'Well, life goes on. I am twenty-four and there is still time for making decisions. It isn't just Father who would be unhappy with a marriage based on such shifting sands. Now though,' she abruptly changes the subject. 'What are your plans for Christmas?'

The two women reminisce about the toy theatre, once the centre of Christmases past. Marian hopes that it survived the move from Bentley to Sprotbrough and lies safe somewhere in her father's attic. She would like to create plays again when her children are old enough to appreciate them. Hopefully there will be no more babies. The thought of future pregnancies beyond this one quite depresses her spirits. Hannah-Mary, recognising that many children require space and money and, ever the practical, comments:

'There are devices, you know. You place them inside where the baby comes from and that traps the, you know ...'

Indeed, Marian did know but was unaware of such devices. How has Hannah-Mary learned of such things? What would John-Henry think? It is hardly something she could discuss with him. But to carry on like this every year …

CHAPTER 58

1868 - 1870

In June the following year the pregnancy comes to full term and she is delivered of yet another son, Ernest. This baby is smaller than her previous three and Marian is reminded of her half-sister, Sophia Elizabeth, who never thrived and departed after only three months. Her usual anxiety following the birth of all her children is redoubled but she dares not voice her concern to John-Henry. Their preferred nurse is not available and her Welsh replacement takes no pains to hide her disappointment in her new charge. Ernest cannot latch onto his mother's breast and cries constantly. The nanny insists on a bottle in order that the lad may thrive.

Marian hates the exhaustion which overcomes her with each pregnancy and regards the nurse with distaste. While grateful that she is spared the night-time feeds, she resents another woman taking her place. She is out of sorts with her children, her husband and herself.

During the week, John-Henry is happy to escape to business and face the challenges of the wool trade. His office is part of a Renaissance-style building decorated with a Greek-key frieze and balcony, also home to Bradford's Chamber of Commerce. Every Monday and Thursday he makes his way down Cheapside and around the corner to the Wool Exchange where he is a member, a position of significant prestige. This centre of the universe for Bradford's wool merchants and manufacturers was opened only the previous year at a magnificent shindig for the great and the good, attended by John-Henry, Charles, Francis and their father. Like all others in the wool business, he is fiercely proud of this distinguished building of local sandstone which sits triumphantly on its triangular island in the centre of the town. Built in a style described as Venetian Gothic, it stands three storeys high and its tall clock tower, topped by a squat spire, is particularly admired by those local merchants of Flemish origin as reminiscent of their homeland. This is where agents, brokers and other middlemen meet with manufacturers, some of whom continue the old practice of renting piece rooms to display their wares. Here John-Henry, like others in his family, discuss contracts and the deals are often sealed verbally. The word of a Member holds good, it is said.

His business in the United States is growing year on year and he has developed good contacts with agents in major cities such as New York and Philadelphia. In idle moments, his mind wanders beyond the bounds of Bradford to the New World where opportunities lie. He was envious when his sister, Louisa, went out to Illinois with her new husband to start farming life from scratch. Would Marian be prepared to try a new venture? When they were courting, he thought so. Now, however, there is something lacklustre about her. Is it solely due to the children? Women are made to bear many children so long as their health holds good. Not that he particularly wishes more than four. He is spurred to meet his medical friend.

How best to broach the subject with Marian? The conversation with the doctor was enlightening and now that he is in full grasp of the facts and even has the address of a nurse trained in such things, John-Henry is anxious to put matters in hand. Since the birth of Ernest, he has refrained from marital relations, first out of concern for his wife's health and then out of fear of conceiving a fifth child. In any case, Marian is usually already asleep by the time he has changed into his nightshirt.

Eventually he chooses an evening when she appears a little less fraught. He has rehearsed his words but fears he may appear clumsy. They are both seated in the front parlour and he moves to join her on the sofa.

'Marian, my love, you appear much better this evening. I hope that you are regaining much of your strength since the birth.'

She looks up from her book, surprised that he should express concern for her health. For a while they have hardly exchanged words other than to talk about the children. *Does he wish to resume marital relations? Please, no, not yet.* Perhaps she has snapped too much of late. To her frustration, his expression of sympathy is all that it takes to tip her over the edge and she feels tears flow.

'My dear Marian,' John-Henry wipes her cheeks with his handkerchief. 'Will you do me the kindness to hear something I need to say? I cannot bear to see you so distressed and I fear that I am to blame.' His wife frowns and shakes her head. 'Yes, Marian, it is because of my love for you that you find yourself in this ... way. This fourth child has drained you of strength. It cannot be God's will that you and your child suffer so. There has to be an end to it.' The words come out more abruptly than he intended and she looks horrified. 'Please let me explain. I have spoken with a doctor who specialises in such matters and it is perfectly possible for you to enjoy what is being called 'voluntary motherhood'. That means that you, yes, *you* will choose to bear a further child or not. There is a device which is simple and painless to use which creates a barrier to prevent future pregnancy. He has recommended a trained nurse who can explain it all to you. Please, Marian, will you consult her? I cannot bear to see you so drained, knowing that I could do something to prevent this in future.'

Marian is pink with embarrassment that her husband has raised such a personal matter but harks back to the conversation with Hannah-Mary. There has to be a better way than each year a new baby. She relaxes against his shoulder, to avoid his eye. How typical of John-Henry to be so caring.

'I have heard tell of such things, though I feared that you might be against anything that prevents God's will.' Her husband protests but she carries on. 'I will gladly visit the nurse your friend recommends, especially if,' she hesitates, 'if it will mean that you no longer turn away from me as we lie together. I may be tired but I have missed your arms about me, my love.'

Marian's subsequent visit to a medical clinic, discreetly located in a leafy part of Manningham, is a success. She feels adventurous to be taking steps to manage her own body, her own future, in the knowledge that her husband considers it the right thing to do. With the renewed attentions of John-Henry, her low mood all but disappears; his attentions now welcomed as an expression of shared love without the fear of consequences.

The only cloud in her life is baby Ernest who will not gain weight no matter how much she and the nurse tempt him with the bottle. His siblings regard him with caution, sensing that the little chap is far from robust. Meanwhile, his sister, Henrietta, continues to grow and enchant her parents and brothers alike. Her mother delights in seeing the girl's progress although fears her becoming spoilt.

It is early in the new year that concern for Ernest deepens. He begins to teethe which reduces his defences and when, in January, his two brothers develop colds, it is not long before he shows signs of illness with a cough that racks his tiny body. The doctor visits but despite the syrups recommended, there is no improvement. One evening, Marian cannot bear to hear the coughs interspersed with pitiful whimpers and chooses to sit with him up in the nursery through the freezing night, gently rocking his cradle before the fire, sometimes cuddling him on her lap, trying to persuade him to take nourishment. It is nearly six o'clock and still dark when the nurse comes in to relieve her.

Ernest has fallen asleep in his cot though his breathing is rasping. Marian is slumped dozing in the low nursing chair. A gentle touch on the shoulder rouses her and reluctantly she rises for the nurse to take her place. She will take an hour or so in bed, before the other children wake, in the hope of gaining some strength. Her husband is already risen in preparation for work and he pulls the counterpane around her shoulders.

She is asleep when the nurse calls John-Henry. There is a change in the child's breathing, a change she has witnessed before. Susan, already awake and setting the fires to warm the house, is sent immediately to fetch the doctor. John-Henry wakes his wife, urging her to come quickly as Ernest struggles for breath. And so together they watch their eight-month-old son slowly drift from this life. Marian sobs quietly as she holds him in her arms for the last time. How could God be so cruel to take this little soul, still innocent as the day he was born? John-Henry stands apart, confused and shaken by the loss of his child. Only the arrival of the doctor rouses him from this daze and he concentrates on the formalities which must now proceed.

The announcement in the *Bradford Observer* is short and tells their world that the Willey family has suffered the loss of a son. Such a simple statement, but nothing can convey the depths of grief at 26 Hanover Square.

Frannie hastens to Manningham. Marian is beside herself with grief. The three children cannot understand why Mamma keeps to her room and, despite Frannie's best attempts to amuse them, they clamour for their mother. Their aunt swathes the boys in caps and mufflers and marches them around the snow-covered roads endeavouring to expend as much energy as possible.

Despite John-Henry's protestations, Marian blames herself for the death of their baby. Should she have forced herself to eat more before his birth? Poor mite carried no weight at all when he was born. No wonder he succumbed so quickly to the bronchitis.

Unlike Marian, Frannie has no recollection of the death of her baby sister, Sophia, but remembers clearly the despair in the house when her brother, John, died aged only four. Such a grand little lad. Older now, she can recognise the immense pain felt by her father to have lost his only son.

That sadness is reawakened when she returns home to Sprotbrough and her parents. Joseph shakes his head sorrowfully.

'It will take them many years to come to terms with the death of a child, no matter how many others she has. Sometimes God's Will is hard to fathom.'

Frannie suspects it very unlikely that there will be more children born to that household. She turns to preparing her outfit for church next morning and looks forward to the possibility of seeing Joe. She wonders if he has missed her company and, like her, looks forward to spring with the return of warmer weather and their walks along the canal towpath.

And so, the year passes. Frannie's friendship with Joe Mellows grows at a gentle, shy pace and from time to time, she accompanies Maria to shop in Doncaster and visit Mrs Cavendish in Harrogate to eat cake.

Spring brings another visit to Moor House by Hannah-Mary's overseas friend but no indication of acceptance by her father. Joseph and Maria settle further into the Sprotbrough community.

John-Henry's business continues to grow while his younger brother also Francis branches out, ending the partnership with his father, and promises to achieve great things in the world of wool. His mother, however, worries that he is now thirty and still without a wife. Hannah-Mary is busy helping her younger sister Betsy-Emma prepare for her December wedding and pushes to one side the notion that soon she will be the last unmarried daughter. Marian struggles to overcome her low moods and masks the loss of Ernest by concentrating her attention on

Henrietta, adored by her two older brothers, for the time being at least.

Occasionally, the Willey family wonders as to the whereabouts and goings-on of Godfrey. He chooses not to attend Betsy-Emma's wedding nor to join the family for Christmas. He continues to work within the wool business but without any particular base and nobody is quite sure where he lives. However, true to form, he does not remain invisible for long and in the following February yet another scandal threatens the family. John Willey receives a shocking message from his lawyers; his son, Godfrey is being held by the Bradford police charged with the rape of a young woman earlier in the week. The old man summons Charles, John-Henry and Francis to his office and the three brothers listen aghast to what their father recounts. His voice betrays his anger and his hands tremble with rage. The lawyer, also present, outlines the bones of the matter and promises to do his utmost to obtain their brother's release on bail the next day.

'What sum do you believe will be required?' John-Henry braces himself, knowing that the family will need to contribute towards the surety.

'It depends on the magistrate, but it could be around two hundred pounds.' His audience groans at the amount to be raised. Each mentally considers how easily they might free such a sum, or at least a significant share.

The next evening, Saturday, the twenty-sixth of February, the *Bradford Evening Telegraph* yet again broadcasts their shame to the world. The women in the family are instructed not to read about the court hearing but how could they not do so? If all their friends and acquaintances will have read the sordid details, how could they not be prepared for their next appearance among polite society? Marian's eyes grow wider as the story unfolds on the page and by the time John-Henry returns home to Hanover

Square, weary, angry and ashamed, her questions come tumbling out and reluctantly he answers.

'How did he come to know this Margaret Anne Bibbey?'

'It seems that she is the sweetheart of one his friends, Tom. They had met a few times.'

'What sort of a baggage is she, unmarried with one child already and another on the way? What was Godfrey doing at her parents' home? The newspaper says that the details of what he did to her are unfit for publication. Did they …?' Her husband nods. 'Well perhaps she was willing. It says that she didn't report it for a few days. Do you think her man found out and she had to bring charges to hide her infidelity?'

'I have no idea, Marian, but either way, my brother has behaved abominably yet again. A man of his upbringing should not take advantage of a girl of eighteen no matter what her circumstances. And we shouldn't judge her. Lives are different for people of her background. The fact remains, my brother was brought before a packed court today and will be held in gaol until the second of March when he can apply for bail. The family may have to stand surety for him. We have no idea what he is worth these days.'

After church the next morning, Marian and John-Henry acknowledge the parson briefly, nod across to Francis and Charles, attending with Matilda and the children, then hasten their way home, eyes downcast to avoid the gaze of other members of the congregation.

Three days later, Godfrey is released by magistrates on bail of one hundred pounds on his own account with two others putting up fifty pounds each. His father and Charles stress to him the imperative of preserving their money by not absconding before the Assizes in Leeds, scheduled for eleven o'clock on the twenty-eighth of March.

Ahead of the hearing, the *Leeds Times* reports the Borough Court proceedings so far.

'Willey had visited her house before in company of her sweetheart, Tom and once alone. When he entered on the forenoon of the day named, she was alone and soon he made improper overtures to her which she rejected. He bolted the door and she tried to leave. He then proceeded to extremities then committed the capital offence. She said she had neither torn his whiskers nor clawed his eyes, but declared that she screamed a little and made what resistance she could. At first, he offered her half a crown and she said she would tell Tom, his friend. She told her parents but it was a few days before it was reported to the police. He was committed to Leeds Assizes, kept in police cells as bail refused until bail was raised on Wednesday.'

As with the divorce case five years earlier, the older brothers, Charles and John-Henry volunteer to attend the Assizes to support the Willey family name, if not especially their wayward brother. They sit in the public gallery while their barrister tears apart the charges laid against his client. Miss Bibbey presents a miserable picture at the end of the cross-questioning and whether Godfrey is guilty or not of the violation of this young woman, in the eyes of the Grand Jury, there is insufficient evidence and the case is thrown out.

John-Henry will never forget the look of betrayal in the eyes of the girl and the barely concealed triumph behind the face of his brother who steps free from the court. The three brothers travel back to Bradford in silence and Godfrey is scarcely acknowledged when he takes leave of Charles and John-Henry in the city centre. Their father is waiting in his office to receive news of the outcome. Grim-faced, he nods to his sons and immediately sets off to Moor House to tell Mrs Willey that her son will not be going to prison.

CHAPTER 59

1870-1871

Although Mrs Willey convinces herself that her son is not guilty, others are less sure. Meanwhile, the rest of his family has to endure veiled comments among the Bradford business community. The married brothers, Charles and John-Henry, keep their heads down, their lives focused on work and family. Their younger brother Francis, now known as Frank, is already building a successful company and has moved into a handsome house in Oak Avenue, close to the public park newly created by Bradford Corporation after acquiring Manningham Hall and its grounds at a generous price from wealthy mill owner, Samuel Cunliffe Lister. Furthermore, Frank is becoming increasingly involved in the West Riding Artillery Volunteers with its battery established in Bradford. In uniform he cuts quite a dash and it is his mother's hope that ere long he will meet a suitable young lady.

*

It is after Sunday dinner when Frannie's stepmother announces that she has received a letter from her friend in Harrogate. Jane Cavendish has reached that stage in life where some activities are beyond her and, to counter the onset of loneliness, she seeks company. Far from wanting someone of a similar age, she prefers the stimulus of youth and invites Frances to live with her as a paid companion. Maria marks the look of surprise on Frannie's face.

'Jane is a cultivated woman with broad interests and liberal ideas. Whomever she chooses will not only widen their horizons but benefit financially. She is generous in both spirit and pocket.'

Joseph looks at his daughter, who does not respond. He has no wish to see her leave home but fears that her life is becoming too narrow. Furthermore, he is unsure whether her friendship with Joe Mellows will lead to anything. There is something of brother and sister about their relationship.

'You don't have to reply today, Frannie. Sleep on it and write your reply tomorrow.' His daughter nods and smiles at her stepmother, knowing that Maria has her best interests at heart.

The afternoon brings watery sunshine and Joe comes calling. She wraps up warm against a fresh breeze and the two set off for a turn around the village. After their usual exchanges, she tells him about the letter.

'Harrogate? Never been there. Are you thinking to accept?' His voice discloses no indication of his thoughts.

'It's a very fine town, Joe. There is a lot of building going on and many people are moving there. It is certainly livelier that Sprotbrough.' Immediately she regrets her implied slur on the village and seeks to make amends. 'Life here is fine for those with families growing up but living with Father and Maria is …' She is unable to put her feelings into words without sounding ungrateful. She is happy to help with household chores but once they are finished the days drag.

'Aye, that I understand. At least I have my work on the farm during the day and of an evening there are lads of my own age that I can knock around with.' They walk on in silence, each with their own thoughts. When they reach the lock, they pause to watch a narrow-boat navigate between the open gates. Joe looks at her shyly. 'I would miss your company if you choose to leave.' It is what she hoped to hear.

'That's kind of you to say, Joe. I feel the same but I believe that now is the moment for me to explore a little and Harrogate is hardly the back end of the world. What's more, I shall be coming home regularly so we'll be able to meet then. And we could write.' She notes his enthusiasm wane at this last suggestion. Like many lads, writing letters is not a favourite past-time.

Within a month, Frannie has moved in with Mrs Cavendish at her house in High Harrogate and is settled into a new routine of shopping, promenading and taking tea. The days are not demanding and her employer, for that is what she is, has a wealth of anecdotes from her long and interesting life. Every third weekend, Frannie returns home or travels to Bradford to stay with her sister. During the intervening weeks she writes to her parents and Maria replies. She also writes to Joe and he responds eventually, his letters full of apologies for his tardiness and likely spelling errors.

Life in Harrogate has its rhythm and although her days are full, she misses Joe. The letters they exchange reflect their growing attachment, strengthened by their encounters in Sprotbrough. Visits to Manningham to see Marian and her family become a rarity as Frannie prefers to return home and meet Joe during her free weekends. To her relief, in late summer, Mrs Cavendish suggests her companion might enjoy spending a few weeks back at the family farm.

Although a busy time for country-folk, this is the season for agricultural shows and Frannie accompanies her parents to see the parade of livestock, scrubbed up for the occasion and led by stockmen in freshly laundered gowns. The proud owners are anxious to take the prize for the best horses, sheep, pigs, cows or beef cattle. Joseph Addy relishes such events and the chance to meet up with his old friends, not only William Mellows but also George Mann, farming over Scawsby way, and other farmers, once fellow tenants on the Cooke's estate. Frannie is quietly proud that Joe's father is one of the judges in the fat-stock competitions, a role he performs at several shows around Yorkshire. More importantly, she glows with delight when Joe appears and asks her father's permission for them to walk together to explore some of the display rings as well as the stalls dotting the field.

The show is crowded and the grass underfoot uneven so Joe offers Frannie his arm. He guides her among the throng of people, everyone intent on enjoying their day in the sun and watching the county's finest animals led around the parade ground.

'It's grand to have you home for more than just a couple of days,' he confides, his open face beaming with smiles.

Frannie laughs. She feels ridiculously happy to be walking beside him, her arm resting on his. She wants this day to last for ever.

'Yes, indeed. I enjoy my time with Mrs Cavendish. She has been more than kind and I mix in society that I would never have found in Bentley or Sprotbrough, but there is much to bring me back home.'

'So, you miss me then?' he ventures with a cheeky grin.

'Not in the slightest,' she retorts with a look that belies her meaning. 'Of course, I miss you. And you know that very well.' She wants to stand on tiptoe and kiss his cheek but knows that would be far too forward for a young lady. Instead, they continue in a comfortable silence.

He takes her to the ring where the Shire horses are being trotted round, their besuited grooms running at speed to keep up with these gentle giants, mains intricately plaited and freshly washed leg feathers flowing like pennants. On his father's farm he has been given responsibility for managing the breeding of their own working horses and he wants to see for himself the difference a good pedigree brings to the form and movement of these powerful beasts.

Already, Joe yearns to breed a line of stallions which one day will win the champion's cup at this very show. He has other dreams, though, and now pictures Frannie at the centre of his future. She would make a good farmer's wife. She understands the life, has picked up no airs and graces from her schooling or her time in Harrogate. Above all, she is a kindly body and he is at ease with her. He looks about him and surveys the crowd. Farming lies behind the faces of landowners, tenants, farmhands, dairymaids, butchers, millers, farriers and so many others who depend on the land for their livelihood. For him, it is a life he has grown up in. Whether he would have chosen it, he is unsure. He is certain, though, that if he is to win Frannie's hand, at least with her father's blessing, he must make a go of it. At present he works the family farm while his father goes about his valuation business, but everyone recognises that William Mellows is the boss. If only he could get a tenancy on a farm of his own, somewhere to develop his talent for horse breeding. It would take time, but then he would have something to offer this sweet girl. For now, he must hold his peace. Time enough to reveal his dreams when he has made his way and achieved something to tempt Frannie back from Harrogate.

*

As autumn progresses, there is concern in the wool trade that the growing conflict between France and Prussia will have a serious impact on business. John-Henry and his brothers increase their focus on North America and the opportunities there. They develop their contacts and establish agents in major cities to expedite trade with this fast-growing market.

Christmas approaches and the ladies of the Willey family look forward to shopping in Bradford, now stocked to the gunnels with all manner of goodies. Hannah-Mary will be in town for a dress fitting and invites her sister Louisa to travel in from

Bingley. She arranges for them to meet with Marian at a favourite hotel where they may enjoy a quiet luncheon. Both married ladies are delighted at the prospect of such a jolly occasion unencumbered by young children. As the meal progresses, conversation turns to finding a husband for Hannah-Mary, now twenty-seven. Despite her protests that she is perfectly happy, she admits that life at Moor House can be tempestuous, particularly with her father.

'I hate the way he talks to Mother, always picking on her and belittling her.'

Louisa nods, remembering how it was before she escaped and wed.

'When he was in a temper, we all kept our heads down. No point in trying to defend Ma as he would only turn on me too and I'd get the lash of his tongue,' she sighs. 'It must be hard for you now being the only girl still at home.'

'I'm glad to get away as often as I can. Frank invites me to stay with him in Manningham when he needs his big sister to act as hostess for his supper guests. I arrived there last night and intend to stay a couple of days. Tomorrow he is holding an evening for some of his regimental friends and wives. It is quite diverting but I find all the unmarried officers of little merit. Quite annoying in fact. So, as for finding me a husband, please do not fret yourselves. Life is good and I have little to complain of.'

'Hmm,' muses Louisa. She is curious to hear the latest about Sam. 'What news from America?'

Hannah-Mary shrugs the question away. The letters keep coming, Sam is working hard, running his dry-goods store and appears to be moving into banking, giving out loans to his Illinois neighbours. No sign of another visit to England, but who would wonder, given the huge effort and cost involved. And for what? In any case, she is still unsure if that is where her heart lies. Marian fills the silence.

'Hannah-Mary, do you remember the stories that our geography teacher used to tell of her brother in America? I believe that she went out to join him eventually. How wonderfully exciting that might be?' Marian, despite loving her husband and children, still yearns to travel but is yet to cross the Channel let alone the Atlantic. That evening she recounts the conversation to John-Henry. He is bemused.

'Hannah-Mary is a woman with her own mind. She will not accept second best, which is why she has rejected suitors thus far. I liked her Mr Edwards but she would need a guaranteed base before taking such a big decision.' He pauses to reflect further. 'Mind you, Marian, America is the place to be. So much opportunity in that young country.' She takes note. This is the first time her husband has shown the slightest inclination for travel.

*

Winter time in Harrogate is as grey as in any other part of Yorkshire but Mrs Cavendish does not stint on coal and Frannie enjoys a warmth which she has rarely known at home. Society does not stop for inclement weather and the season is filled by musical soirées and card afternoons. No matter how blustery the day, the two women are content to wrap up in their cloaks and take the air. Out of gratitude for her friend's kindness, Maria insists that Mrs Cavendish returns with Frannie at Christmas to partake of the family celebrations at Sprotborough. The lady is happy to comply, especially as it will give her the opportunity to inspect Frances's young man. The meeting occurs over the holiday when the Mellows hold open house. The Addy family and their guest walk up to the large farmhouse and are warmly received. It is with satisfaction that Mrs Cavendish observes Joe: polite, not badly looking and with a robustness that she prefers in a man. After she and Frannie return to Harrogate following the festivities, she gazes at her young companion and wonders how long she will retain her services. She reassures herself that Joe needs to feather his nest first before he can contemplate asking for his sweetheart's hand.

The topic of weddings is rarely far from the minds of any family with marriageable sons and daughters and by the following spring, the matter is a source of speculation also within the Addy household when they gather in Sprotbrough for Easter. Young Alfy is to stay a week with his grandparents and the lad arrived yesterday accompanied by his aunt who travelled from Harrogate to collect him from Bradford. Joseph is happy to have his oldest grandson to stay, even though it stirs sad memories. At six, Alfy is now a little older than his own boy, John, when he died. He pushes the memory away and turns to question Frannie.

'So, tell me more about Hannah-Mary's beau. He sells pots and pans, does he, this American?'

'No, Father. Well, yes, but much more than that. I believe he has a hardware store in a town in Illinois. That's the state where cousin Will lived when he and Louisa went off pioneering. It was a rough place to start with but I think it's far safer these days. And he's English, not American, born near Oswestry.'

'What a strange state of affairs,' muses her father. 'You say that he is a friend of my nephew?'

'Will and Louisa got to know Sam when they travelled out to live in America. I suppose that on a longish voyage you spend quite a lot of time with people. They liked him a lot.' She turns to Alfy to explain. 'Mr Edwards travelled all across America, from east to west, in a wagon pulled by bullocks and they had to fight off the native people.' The child's eyes grow wide. Joseph quickly changes the subject to enquire about his nephew.

'How are things with Will? Marian wrote that he is none too well. What's his line of business again?'

'He's a wool merchant now, Father, like nearly everyone in that part of Yorkshire. Louisa worries about his health and she has her hands full now with yet another lad born since the twins. Yes, I know, six children now.' Although Frannie doesn't share her sister's aversion to a large family, when the breadwinner suffers poor health, perhaps forbearance might be advisable.

'So, what's up with him? Let's hope he won't follow his father. My poor brother, George, dropped dead at forty-one and nobody knew why.' Conscious of the flapping ears of a little boy at her side, Frannie shrugs, unwilling to discuss further.

As planned, on the following Saturday Marian and John-Henry arrive with Josh and Henrietta to stay the night and spend Easter Day with her family. At his daughter's request, Joseph has found her toy theatre and his wife has dusted it down so that the next generation may discover the delights of story-telling. Marian is thrilled and, with Frannie's help, they guide Alfy's small hands and read aloud the voices of the tiny cardboard characters that dance across the stage.

John-Henry looks on and feels gratitude that life gave him a wife with imagination and curiosity to be the mother of his children. Now that she is no longer burdened with constant pregnancy, her energy has returned and she brings enthusiasm to all their lives.

Later, Frannie introduces him to her friend, Joe Mellows, and he takes an immediate liking to the fellow. Down to earth, speaks plainly, no doubt trustworthy. Frannie deserves a good man. Together with Joseph, they talk about sheep and the price of wool and complain about this and that, as is the way of farming men.

CHAPTER 60

1871 - 1873

New Year's Eve and Joseph rests his gloved hands on the frosted five-barred gate. The moon rises to illuminate a light dust of snow on the sleeping fields. Not a bad year on the whole, he reflects. Not grand, but not bad. The farm has turned a good penny or two, certainly sufficient to keep him and Maria comfortable and give work to his men.

At sixty-six Joseph has no concern for his own advancing years. Although still capable of working alongside the farm hands, he is determined to get out when things become too much. He has no intention of dying in harness. For some time, his older brother, Godfrey, has not enjoyed good health and decided a while ago to retire from farming and settle in his wife's home town of Pontefract. His sister Nancy, widowed some five years back, now seventy-one and still farming with one of her sons, is none too well. Joseph knows that when his time comes to step down, Maria will want to move closer in to Doncaster.

With the passing of another year, he reflects upon his good fortune: the gift of his daughters, his three lively grandchildren and a companionable wife. As for 1872, he has no doubt that tomorrow will bring good news to welcome the year. Young Joe Mellows has asked to meet him in the morning and Joseph can guess the reason.

After greeting Joe at the front door, Frannie calls her father and disappears up to her room. Maria, by arrangement, is busy in the kitchen discussing meals for the coming days.

'Bring yourself in, lad,' Joseph beckons the young man who is trying hard to appear at ease. They enter the compact room where Joseph keeps his ledgers and books. Closing the door causes a tendril of smoke to escape from the meagre coal fire. Joseph wafts it away and offers a cup of tea.

'No, thank you Sir. I won't take up too much of your time.' At that, Joe pauses, his opening lines, rehearsed along the way, momentarily escaping him. The older man smiles encouragingly. 'You will know that I've become very fond of your daughter, Mr Addy.' Joseph nods. He recalls the day he asked Widow Hall for Elizabeth's hand, but that was so much easier given that the poor woman viewed Joseph not only as a good son-in-law but also as the potential saviour of her farm. 'Over time, I've come to believe that she, too, has the same feelings for me. Frannie has such a kind nature and shares my love of farming …' He loses his way then spills out his request. 'I would be honoured to make her my wife, Sir, with your permission.'

No flowery words of praise for his daughter, no reference to her fine upbringing and education, muses Joseph. Just that he loves her and wants to be with her, to marry her. How different from the more cultivated conversation when John-Henry came asking for the hand of Mary-Ann, but the older man identifies more closely with this lad, someone who lives for the land and what it can bring forth. He hastens to set Joe at his ease.

'Let's see now. At present you live at home at High Melton and work for your father, helping to run his farm?'

'Indeed Sir. I have worked his land ever since I was a young lad. Farming is what I do.'

'Frannie tells me you're a year older than her, so twenty-four thereabouts?' Joe nods, knowing what comes next. 'So, what would be your plans for you and your wife? Would you live at High Melton with your parents or try to get a cottage?'

Joe sits tense on the edge of the chair. His plans are mainly in his head but he is sure that his father will see him right.

'I have talked with my father about the future and he agrees that in time I should try to get a tenancy of my own, something small to begin with, but somewhere with enough space to breed Shires – they're my real love. I've no doubt he will help me find a suitable farm. Until then, my family's home would be big enough for me and my bride.' Joseph considers how Frannie would fit into the Mellows household and decides she would make a good go of it. How could any family resist such a gentle soul as his daughter?

'Well Joe, you know that I am honoured to count your father as a friend. I've watched you over the years to know that you've been brought up in a respected, honourable family and that you'll take care of my daughter to the best of your ability. Yes, lad, I am happy to give my permission for you to wed Frannie.' He stands, thrusts out his hand and clasps that of the relieved young man. 'Mind though, I suggest we announce your betrothal shortly and look to hold the wedding in the summer of next year. It takes that amount of time for the womenfolk to prepare. Now, off you go and tell her the good news.'

At the end of March, spring flowers brightening the hedgerows and gardens, the two families host a bit of a do to celebrate the betrothal of Joseph Mellows and Frances Addy. Marian takes her sister to one side and hugs her tenderly.

'You have found such a dear man and I know you will be very happy together.' Privately, although she is fond of Joe, Marian cannot help but consider him, well, so very rural. But then, that is where Frannie will be happiest, she reflects. It's a good thing we're not all the same. Henrietta pulls at her aunt's skirts, begging to be her bridesmaid as she will be six next year.

Already the older women are sitting, heads together, considering the details of next year's wedding. Maria, who can hold her own with Mrs Mellows any day, is parrying with her own thoughts, while Jane Cavendish, invited down for the occasion, proffers the nuptial customs of Harrogate society. She is relieved that Frannie has agreed to continue as her companion up until her marriage, no doubt wishing to save as much as possible of her remuneration. From what she sees, the prospective groom does not seem to have great prospects, but it's not for her to comment.

And so, the year progresses and each time Frannie returns home to Sprotbrough, she is bombarded with suggestions, all well-meant, which urge decisions. The general consensus between the families is that a June wedding would be most suitable, and mid-week to avoid the many agricultural shows where Joe's father would be called upon to judge. Joseph is torn between her marrying at Arksey, where he and her mother wed, and St Mary's in Sprotbrough where he is now a church warden. During supper one evening, he reveals his thoughts, hopeful to get a decision. Maria sits quietly, conscious that Mrs Mellows is champing at the bit to get arrangements in place. Frannie has other ideas.

'Would it pain you, Father, if I chose neither? I don't know the church here and Arksey no longer has a connection to my life. It is a distance, I know, but Christ Church in Harrogate has become very important to me and I have made many friends among the congregation. The vicar there is kind and I am sure he would be happy to conduct the ceremony.'

Joseph struggles to conceal his disappointment. Maria is mentally calculating how many hotel rooms they will need if the two families have to travel north for the occasion.

'Well, lass, it's not for me to say.' He looks towards his wife in hope of guidance but receives only a hard stare which he cannot fathom. 'It's not what I expected. Neither close to Joe's home nor yours.' He gathers that Maria does not wish to be drawn into the conversation. 'Is Joe happy with your wish?'

'When I explained my preference, he just shrugged his shoulders, and said what makes me happy makes him happy.'

Despite herself, Maria interjects: 'Has he told his parents yet?'

'I've no idea. We have a good eight months until next June so there is no rush is there?'

Joseph supposes not and suggests that she and Joe have a conversation with the Mellows and then tell him the date they have in mind so that the process might begin. He would like to be a fly on the wall when Joe's mother gets the news. Secretly, he is quite proud that Frannie will make a stand and that won't do her any harm when she comes to live under the same roof as her future mother-in-law. Joe may be easy-going, but he doesn't inherit that from his mother.

Jane Cavendish is delighted that Frances wishes to marry from her house the following June. Without a daughter of her own, she intends to offer to pay for her young companion's wedding gown. She knows that the girl is careful with money and would likely restrict her choice within a tight budget. It will bring Jane great pleasure to see Frances finely dressed on her special day.

The seasons change and in September, Joseph is saddened by the passing of his sister, Nancy. He was very fond of her and had already become somewhat of a mentor to her elder son, William Stacey, now farming in Cantley following the death of his father six years ago. Over the coming years, this relationship will flourish further.

Marian and John-Henry's three growing children remain quite sufficient within the confines of their house in Hanover

Square and both parents are relieved that the chosen method to limit their family has been effective.

Like the rest of the Willey family whose lives are bound to the woollen industry, John-Henry is suffering from falling prices and profits and each month sees yet more business associates hit by bankruptcy. Even the money that the mills invested in machinery to increase production and reduce manpower cannot protect the industry from the competition of the French all-wool worsteds now challenging the home market. Added to that, the British do not seem to be able to match the quality of dyeing and design of the imports. Only someone as wealthy as mill owner, Samuel Cunliffe Lister, can shrug off disaster and rebuild, literally, his business. Last year's catastrophic fire destroyed his Lilycroft Mill but now a new and finer mill is under construction on the same elevated site with the promise of a magnificent chimney to outstrip even the stack of the Lumb Lane Mill which dominates Hanover Square.

John-Henry is glad that his two sons are not yet of an age to enter the workplace. Instead, they have their education before them. He plans for the boys to attend the new Bradford Grammar School which has emerged out of the City High School, built by Jacob Behrens from frustration with the poor quality of education then available. Behrens was one of the many European immigrants who became successful wool manufacturers and merchants, the latter congregating in the business area of Bradford known as Little Germany, and brought with him not only an acute business head but also a sense of duty to the community. John-Henry's own next-door neighbours in Hanover Square are of German and Swiss origin and without doubt they have added vibrancy not only to the business but also to the culture of the town.

Frank, with his insurmountable energy, is powering his company further, and old John Willey grudgingly admires how this son can balance a twelve-hour working day with involvement in Bradford's commercial aspirations, the appeal of the Artillery Volunteer Corps and his love of fox hunting. No wonder that there has not been time to seek a wife.

'Why cannot our Frank find time to meet a suitable girl?' laments his mother. 'I just want to see him settled before I die.' Her husband rolls his eyes heavenwards in despair at his wife's silliness. He foresees his son going on to make an even greater fortune than himself. In the meantime, a housekeeper should suffice.

Another year begins and for Frannie the next six months will be taken up with preparations for her wedding day. She is thankful to be living in Harrogate, for the time being distanced from her future mother-in-law. The prospect of starting married life under the same roof as Mrs Mellows disturbs her but she reassures herself that Joe will ensure all will be well. So far, though, there is no sign of a small farm to rent and he will have to continue working for his father until that happens. Thank Heaven she gets on with his sister, Anne, whom she has invited to be principal bridesmaid, if only to keep Henrietta under control.

Jane Cavendish guides her young friend, for she has never regarded her paid companion as her employee, and together they select the design and fabric for the wedding gown. Frannie is grateful for Mrs Cavendish's generosity but insists on a style that is modest in appearance and cost. Together they choose a silk faille, a fabric more finely ribbed than grosgrain and one which will crease less than silk alone. In ivory, it will suit Frannie's complexion. The bride-to-be rejects anything with a full bustle but accepts a more modest one which falls to a slight train. The jacket-bodice covers a flat-fronted skirt which in turn is draped with an apron-type overskirt. A discreet trim of lace is all the decoration Frannie will allow.

'Dearest Jane, this will be the most beautiful gown I have ever worn and I will never forget your generosity.' As she thanks her benefactor, she cannot help but think that, although she loves what they have chosen, when will a farmer's wife ever have cause to wear something so magnificent again? Her careful nature regrets this expenditure and who knows in future when such money might be needed.

CHAPTER 61

1873 Summer

A few days before his younger daughter's wedding, Joseph retrieves from his bureau the small, green leather box which over twenty-four years has harboured the mourning brooch. It holds all that remains of his first wife, Elizabeth. He examines the piece, fashioned from gold and enamelled with black scrolling. First, by the light of the window he views the lattice of silver and brown hair preserved under glass, then he turns it over to read again the inscription:

Mrs Addy

Ob: Jan: 3 1849

Æt: 39

He closes the box and puts it to one side, ready to be packed for the journey up to Harrogate. What will be Frannie's reaction when he presents it to her as guardian of her mother's memory? He is sure that she will be pleased, nay honoured, to receive this memento but he must prepare an answer to her likely question: why was it not given to her older sister on her marriage? He must find a suitable explanation, one which will not reflect badly on Marian. His own deep hurt at her rejection of the brooch must be suppressed.

His wife has managed to discover the travel arrangements of the Mellows' party and engineered her own railway itinerary to get them into the Harrogate hotel a good couple of hours ahead. She wants Joseph, as father of the bride, to take the lead and to be seated at ease in the hotel lounge ready to welcome the incoming guests. On the day, she is already changed from her travelling clothes and refreshed just as Mrs Mellows sweeps in with her party, still dusty from the journey. Frannie is to come over to the hotel later and take afternoon tea with her parents and the Mellows. It will be the last time that she will see Joe before she walks down the aisle tomorrow.

As afternoon tea is served in the elegant lounge of the newly built hotel, members of the wedding party assemble. Frannie fusses around each newcomer and hopes that once there is a sufficient crowd, she and Joe can escape into the conservatory to share some moments alone. Marian and John-Henry arrive with their three children. Alfy, soon to be nine, glumly contemplates a room full of straight-backed women, each gripping a fine-china saucer in one hand and the handle of its partner cup in the other. He knows better than to move off the upright chair where his father has placed him but fidgeting his legs is a natural reflex. Josh, just seven, finds it hard not to wriggle and has opted to sit on the floor, partially screened by his mother's full skirts. A restraining hand from time to time will keep him in check. No such hope for Henrietta, however. She is so excited that tomorrow she is to be a bridesmaid. Her ivory satin dress already hangs upstairs in the bedroom she shares with her mother. She hops from one foot to the other and follows Aunt Frannie around the room, saying hello to anyone who will listen and explaining that she is six-years old and will be a bridesmaid tomorrow. She knows she is pretty and, although her brothers ignore her, strangers always smile and pat her head. Her father fears for the years ahead with a young madam like this.

Joseph calls Frannie to his side and rises as she approaches. He leads her quietly away from the chattering group and it is he who takes her into the conservatory which, despite the abundance of glass, is cool thanks to the plants and the spray of the small fountain. He draws her to a bench and reaches into his pocket for the jeweller's box.

'Well lass, you are looking very fine today and no doubt tomorrow even more splendid. How proud your mother would have been.' He pauses and swallows hard. He didn't expect to be taken by the emotion of the moment.

'Oh Father, would that I had known her, even for a few short years. All I have are your memories.'

'It is for that reason, Frannie, that I would like you to have this memento of your dear mother. It is right that you are the one to own it and to wear it. Marian has her memories, but you do not.' He opens the box to reveal the brooch and hopes this daughter will appreciate it. Frannie gasps. She has heard of the brooch but never seen it before. She has been curious but was always too shy to ask about it. Her father removes it and turns it over so that she can read the wording on the back. As she smiles and starts to thank him, his heart lifts and he interrupts her.

'It is not a dainty piece and possibly better worn on heavier clothing rather than a summer gown, so please do not feel obliged to wear it for now. If you like, I shall hold it for safe-keeping until you are returned from your honeymoon and you can look forward to wearing it come the autumn, maybe.'

His daughter reflects a moment. 'Indeed, it would be better worn on more substantial fabric than silk, but I think I have an idea. Please let me have it now. It is only right that my mother should be close on my wedding day.' She is grateful for his thoughtfulness and puts her arms around his neck for her cheeks to be tickled by his soft grey whiskers. What good fortune to have a loving father who has always kept alive the memory of her mother through all his own difficult times.

The next day as Jane Cavendish helps her dress, Frannie reveals the brooch to her friend. Together they fashion an inner pocket within the bodice of the wedding gown and as Joseph walks her up the aisle of Christchurch, the spirit of Elizabeth Addy joins them, embodied in the brooch nestled unseen at Frannie's breast.

Later, as everyone settles back replete from the wedding breakfast, all agree that it has been a very fine occasion. Nothing fancy, but the star of the day was Frances Elizabeth Addy, now Mellows, who enchanted everyone with her simplicity and sheer happiness. For Jane Cavendish this is a bitter-sweet day, the day she says farewell to her companion, the friend she has regarded as a daughter. Returning home that evening, to a house still showing signs of the morning's disarray, she feels that chill of a mid-summer's evening when the sun is clouded over.

For Joe and Frannie Mellows the coming days spent on the coast at Whitby are a time of exploration and discovery. Alone at last, both unsure how to behave within this great adventure, they revel in the moment. For Joe, Frannie is the sweetest girl and he can scarcely believe that he has won her. His young wife, though considered unsophisticated by some, is already wise enough to savour this time, knowing that when they arrive at High Melton, life will change yet again.

*

Marian returns to Hanover Square with her family and the day-to-day demands of squabbling children. The boys defend their baiting of Henrietta with the excuse that she is impossible to play with, largely because she is girl. Henrietta flounces off to sit with her dolls on the green opposite the house and pretends she does not belong to her family, something hard to ignore when Alfy and Josh bring their ball game ever closer to her precious children.

John-Henry comes home early from business with worrying news of his brother-in-law, Will Addy.

THE MOURNING BROOCH

'Frank tells me that Will has been working over at Bakewell and has been taken seriously ill. He received a message from Louisa that she is on her way from Bingley and together they will travel down to Bakewell.'

'What ails him? Is it his heart? Do you remember that his father died suddenly? Just dropped dead in the barn. Only forty-one. Will can't be much older than that now. I remember your sister being so relieved when he passed that milestone. Poor woman, she must be out of her mind with worry, and the new baby not yet a year old.'

Late that afternoon, Frank has managed to bring Louisa to her husband's side in a neat little guest house in the market town of Bakewell. Will is in terrible pain and his body blazes with fever. His thick wavy hair lies damp against the pillow and his once bushy beard has been clipped short. The attending doctor pulls Frank to one side and silently shakes his head. He suspects a perforated appendix so surgery is now too late to save him. Other than alleviate the pain and fever, there is little else he can do.

Will has been staying at the guest house for the week while visiting local sheep farmers to discuss wool sales. The room is clean enough but not large. Frank withdraws briefly to the nearby Rutland Arms to book rooms for the night for himself and his sister. On his return, he finds her at Will's bedside. A nurse appointed by the doctor sits observing her patient who is dosed with laudanum. Occasionally his eyelids flicker open and the look of fear and despair wrenches even the heart of Frank who considers himself strong in times of adversity. As Louisa struggles to hold back her tears, all too aware that soon she will lose the man she loves dearest in the world, Frank's thoughts turn to her future as a widow with seven children ranging from fifteen years down to eleven months.

It is he who carries out the formalities when Will finally slips away and he who next day brings Louisa home to Bingley.

The modest house is brim-full with children who, other than the oblivious baby, stand in fearful silence as their distraught mother enters leaning heavily on the arm of Uncle Frank.

Marian observes the strength of the Willey family as it comes together to support its own. The funeral is attended by Louisa's father, on a promise to his wife not to repeat his belief that he never approved of his daughter's choice in husband, and by her brothers apart from Benjamin, presently unwell, and Godfrey who is still in disgrace. These brothers come fresh from a quickly convened meeting to discuss her financial situation, at least in the short term. Joseph travels to Bingley to attend the ceremony out of respect for Will's father, his long dead brother, George, and to represent the Addy family, knowing that Will's mother, Hannah, has insisted on going to the church along with Louisa, the only two women present.

What greater sadness than to see your child die before you, reflects Marian as she sits in a reception room at the hotel where the rest of the womenfolk attend the arrival of the men for the wake. She tries to work out the relationship between her stepmother, Maria, and Will's mother, both of the Cockin family, but gives up confused. She reproaches herself for such inconsequential thoughts when the burning question is how on earth will Louisa survive alone with all those children to keep? John-Henry has intimated that the family will have to come to his sister's aid and although Marian would not see her in penury, she fears that her husband's business is not thriving quite as well as hoped.

Louisa is not the only child Mrs Willey worries over. Her youngest, Benjamin, now twenty-two, has been ill for some weeks and the day following Will's funeral, she and Hannah-Mary travel over to Little Horton to visit him. Only a couple of miles from Hanover Square, Number 8 Claremont is a substantial stone-built house befitting the position of retired worsted manufacturer, William Monies, one of John Willey's friends happy to provide lodging for Benjamin while he trains in the wool business. Even Hannah-Mary is shocked to see the state of her brother, his face pale and drawn and, clearly, he has lost much weight since last she saw him. Mrs Monies seeks to reassure Mrs Willey but to no avail.

'No, no, I won't hear of it. We must get him home and I would like our own doctor to see him.' Despite remonstrations that the local doctor is highly regarded and has been visiting Benjamin every few days, Mrs Willey insists that he be brought up to Moor House the very next day. Hannah-Mary questions whether moving the patient would be advisable in his condition but she is slapped down by her mother. The following day a carriage arrives with Hannah-Mary and John-Henry to assist their youngest brother, now so frail.

Sadly, not even their own family doctor can define what lies behind the young man's decline but he prescribes tinctures and suggests that the constant care of his family will contribute greatly to his recovery. Within days there is a change but dramatically for the worse. Hannah-Mary speaks with the doctor out of earshot of her parents.

'Do you not know what is wrong? He has no fever, no pain but he seems to have given up the will to live. Were he a woman, I would say he be love-sick. I cannot persuade him to eat, no matter what tempting food I prepare.' Embarrassed by his inability to help, the doctor simply shakes his head with regret.

At the beginning of August, Benjamin is carried to his burial on the shoulders of his brothers, Charles, John-Henry, Frank, Richard and, yes, Godfrey too. The last is shaken by the loss of his youngest brother even though, with fourteen years difference, they had not been close. Afterwards back at Moor House, Mrs Willey is conflicted by her deep grief at the loss of her youngest child and a curiosity to know what Godfrey is doing with his life. She has heard that he is living in a modest house over at Undercliffe, east of Bradford, and is desirous to know whether he lives there alone. Unsurprisingly, her husband is so angered by the presence of this son who has disgraced the family name that she dares not seek him out for a private word. She whispers to Hannah-Mary to undertake this mission on her behalf and, after rolling her eyes in exasperation, her daughter slips from the room in search of her wayward brother.

CHAPTER 62

1873 - 1875

Godfrey stands in the garden, cigar and drink in hand. Awkwardly alone, he intends to leave his parents' house as soon as possible. Of course, he does not expect the welcome of the prodigal son, so the froideur of his father and brothers comes as no surprise, but he thought his mother would have greeted him more warmly when the men returned from the grave. Warily, he watches Hannah-Mary's approach.

'Well Sister, how are you? Not escaped them yet?' Hannah-Mary ignores the jibe and wafts away the cigar smoke with an impatient gesture.

'Mother wants to know where you are living these days, and how you are managing.' As ever, straight to the point, unsmiling.

'I'm over at Undercliffe. I found a nice enough house in a quiet row and there are views over the moors. But what of you? Has that man from America given up?'

Hannah-Mary snorts dismissively. She has no intention of discussing her private life with Godfrey and needs to probe further.

'How do you manage? Your washing, your meals? Got a housekeeper?'

'Not a housekeeper, but a woman who comes in and does.' Hannah nods thoughtfully and pursues her line of questioning.

'What news of your boy? How old is John now, around ten?'

'Something like that. No, no news. His mother lives over Golcar way now and makes it difficult for me to see him. The Custody of Children Act allowed her to keep him only until he was seven but,' he falters, 'I've had much to do so no time to make other arrangements but I shall insist that he is to go away to school very soon.' Hannah-Mary nods. Just as they all suspected: abandoned his boy as well.

'And business …? Do you come across your brothers in your dealings?' She knows full well that he does not.

His rambling answer indicates he has wool business here and there but then he draws the conversation to a close. She reckons there is little more to be gained, nods a curt farewell and turns on her heel to report back to her mother. Godfrey takes his leave, speaking only briefly with his sister, Louisa, seated apart from the rest of her family and looking positively dazed from the loss of a beloved husband and dear brother within a few weeks of each other. Indeed, Hannah-Mary was surprised that her older sister had come but supposes she needs to be among them all. Bingley is too far from the rest of the family and the Willey brothers are intent on bringing her to live closer to them.

*

Besides family concerns, as the year progresses, John-Henry has other worries. By the autumn, a serious financial situation has arisen in the United States after banks and railway companies fail as the railroad expansion bubble bursts. Europe is also facing challenges, particularly in the newly-formed German Empire, and the Austro-Hungarian economy is staggering after the crash of the Vienna Stock Exchange in May. Repercussions are being felt all over Europe, and France is on its knees having just finished paying reparations after their disastrous war with Prussia. Money is tight everywhere and sales of wool within the British market cannot compensate for export losses. He fears this depression will last some years and, as the middle man between farmer and wool manufacturer, there is little he can do to improve matters.

For Marian, any thoughts of moving to a larger house must be set aside and she has serious conversations with Susan's successor, Martha, on how to manage the household budget to better effect. The seventeen-year-old kitchen maid is terrified of losing her position and is determined to make ends meet.

*

Over at High Melton, Frannie learns a different rhythm of family life; a life with her new husband shared with his family. Although they have a couple of rooms to themselves, meals are taken together with her in-laws including Joe's two older unmarried sisters, Elizabeth and Ann. Frannie gets on with the sisters well enough but is wary of old man Mellows, now in his late sixties and not as affable as her own father. Dealing with her mother-in-law is like walking on egg-shells and she misses the uncomplicated life she led with Jane Cavendish in Harrogate. How could two women of a similar age be so different?

In the privacy of the tiny sitting room adjacent to their bedroom, Frannie tries to draw from Joe how best to please his mother but she soon realises that he is unaware of any problem. As the last son to remain at home, he is indulged by his mother and sisters alike. When it comes to love-making, she is conscious of the quiet of the big old house and that the flexing of the bedsprings must be heard by all. Joe claims that his parents are hard of hearing but she is not convinced and finds it difficult to relax into his arms. If only they could find a little place of their own. Maybe that would come with the birth of a child but at this rate, that could take a while.

In fact, it is the next spring before an opportunity arises: a farm of some 170 acres at Cadeby with a modest house attached. William Mellows ensures that news of the upcoming tenancy is restricted and so it is that Joe's application is accepted with the surety of his father.

'That's splendid, lass,' says Joseph Addy when his daughter calls round with the news. 'Joe knows that land and it will do you nicely.' For some time, he has worried about Frannie living in the Mellows household. William might be one of his friends, but that mother …

Making a home of her own is just what Frannie is made for and, with the help of the Mellows' two housemaids, she sets about cleaning and brightening up the two-storey farmhouse located just outside the village. The money Joseph presented to the pair upon their marriage can now be spent on pieces of furniture, and his wife, Maria, keeps finding lengths of material which might suit for curtains somewhere in the house. Frannie is grateful for everything. Joe's father didn't pay him much while managing the family farm and it will be some time before they see a return from their own farm. Things will be tight for a while but Frannie never complains and, like all farmers' wives before her, gets on with life and takes over managing the hens and the sale of eggs.

Marian asks if she may visit and Frannie swings between eagerness to see her and an acute awareness that her home is not and probably never will be as grand as that of her sister. In the event, their meeting provides an opportunity for an open exchange, possibly the frankest conversation they have ever had. Afterwards, Marian would reflect that the two had rarely been alone for any length of time since they were children. The six years age difference, although less apparent now, still makes her feel protective towards Frannie.

'There is so much you will be able to do here,' Marian ventures, looking around the sparsely furnished rooms.

'Yes, of course, in time.' Frannie hesitates and sighs. 'But you know farming, there is no guarantee that the crops or the stock sales will bring in what you hope. Joe has started breeding Shire horses on his own account, but he has yet to make his name.' She marks her sister's frown and adds brightly, 'But we shall manage just like everyone has to.' Unsaid are her thoughts: *unlike you and John-Henry with his established business.*

Marian wanders over to the window looking out onto the farmyard where chickens stalk and scratch. Should she share her own position, out of sympathy with her sister? Would it be disloyal to her husband?

'Yes, Frannie, we have to manage, but it isn't always easy, not even for us.' Her sister raises her eyebrows in surprise. 'Business is not good. We depend a lot on exporting our wool and the overseas markets have crashed. You are fortunate to have a lowland farm and can mix livestock with crops, but for the upland farmers dependant on their sheep, times are hard. I am lucky to have Martha to help me. She may be young but when she shops in the market, you can be sure she bargains the best price. And together we can put food on the table that belies the frugality of the ingredients.'

Frannie is astonished. She always thought that membership of the Willey family ensured a comfortable living. Now she knows otherwise. She, too, speaks more frankly.

'If it weren't for Father, I don't know how we would have managed over the past months. He has loaned us a bit to buy some dairy cows, just to get us started.' She reflects that perhaps her sister has no knowledge of the loan and swiftly adds, 'But we shall pay it back as soon as we can.'

Marian waves away the protest. She does not begrudge her father helping Joe and Frannie and knows he would do the same for her.

'You are at the beginning of your new life, Frannie, and this is an exciting time, even if a bit frightening. I am ahead of you and now have my life planned out as a mother of three children, living in a nice enough part of Bradford but constrained financially and, to be honest, I once had dreams of travelling. I cannot see that ever happening now. We don't even travel up to London let alone onto the Continent, though in recent years that has not been possible with all the troubles over there.'

'Yet you have a good husband and three wonderful children, Marian. Maybe you will have more? Isn't that what is expected of us, to stay at home and raise children?'

Marian throws up her hands in horror. 'No, no more children. We have taken care of that.' Her sister frowns in misunderstanding. 'I take precautions so that I don't have to bear any more children.' She is conscious that her voice has risen to a strident tone and softens her words. 'I am sure you will want many children, but three is enough for me. I hated the confinements and I'm afraid that I find children so overwhelming.'

Frannie nods in understanding. She has seen the situation that cousin Will's widow, Louisa, finds herself in with seven children and no father to support them. For herself, the prospect of a large family is far from daunting. Having grown up almost as an only child, especially when Marian was away at school, she does not want a child of hers to be lonely like that.

Months later, as she prepares for her first Christmas in their new home, she recalls the conversation with her sister. For a few days she has struggled to get out of bed of a morning before retching into her chamber pot. She knows the signs. She is with child and could not be happier.

Early in the new year, Joe and Frannie announce proudly that their first child is expected late summer and Joseph is ashamed to note that the news brings him even greater happiness than when Marian announced her first confinement. Somehow, he feels more protective of Frannie than he ever did of her sister. Was it because she was only a baby when her mother died? He does not try to understand but that is how he feels.

Less good news arrives at the end of February; the Willey family is stunned to hear that Godfrey has taken another wife. After hearing the bare bones of the story from John-Henry, Marian arranges to meet Hannah-Mary in the centre of Bradford.

CHAPTER 63

1875

A delayed Hannah-Mary arrives at the hostelry opposite Bradford's magnificent town hall, built just two years earlier. She is clearly in a bate.

'Father insisted on coming with me into Bradford then took for ever to get ready. He really is too bad. We are obliged to wait on him, hand and foot, and all he does is shout at everyone. Poor mother is run ragged.'

Marian seeks to calm her friend by ordering their meal and chattering on inconsequentially. Hannah-Mary will have none of it. She knows why they are meeting.

'So, what has John-Henry told you of this marriage?'

Marian smiles wryly at her sister-in-law's directness which over many years she has learnt to tolerate. 'Just that Godfrey married last week, in church, and Manchester Cathedral of all places. How can that be? He is a divorced man.'

'Precisely so. It appears that he presented himself as a widower and nobody took the trouble to check the veracity of such a claim. Maybe his new wife doesn't know of his past or, to keep face, chose to conceal the fact.'

'Who is she? Someone from round here?'

'Not at all. A Mrs Elizabeth Hulme, a widow from Rochdale. An innkeeper. Imagine. Nine years his senior,' Marian's eyes grow wide as she calculates in her head. Fifty, no wonder John-Henry avoided further explanation. She can only imagine his father's view of the matter. 'Mother wept when she heard, which only made Father all the angrier. Nobody knows ought about her family, when her husband died or whether she already has children of her own. At least at that age it's unlikely she will be having any with Godfrey.'

'Has anyone informed Sarah? Is their son aware he now has a stepmother?'

'I think the lad is away at school, so possibly not. He doesn't see anything of his father anyway.'

Marian shakes her head then considers the positive side to the news. 'At least there will be someone to support him as he grows older, although it is questionable whether an innkeeper is the ideal spouse for someone who likes his tipple,' she chuckles. Hannah-Mary does not respond and stares gloomily at the plate of soup that has just arrived.

'I have received a letter from Sam.' She allows the statement to hang in the air and Marian pauses, soup spoon raised, awaiting further news. Instead, her sister-in-law engages with her own plate. Marian determines not to ask further and they take their soup in silence. When Hannah-Mary has finished, she places the spoon neatly at six o'clock on the soup plate and stares balefully at Marian.

'He is coming over in May.' Still no word from Marian, who simply raises interrogative eyebrows. 'He intends to speak to my father again.' From the flat tone of voice, Marian cannot work out whether Hannah-Mary is uninterested that Sam is returning to ask for her hand or that she holds out no hope that she will receive her father's blessing. At thirty-one she is of age and legally does not require her father's permission; however, with

Mr Willey's approval would come his financial support too. Marian does not envy her position. By now she should be married with several children. Childbirth at any age is dangerous but even more so the later one starts.

*

When Sam Edwards arrives in Bradford a few months later, he makes his first call to Louisa Addy, now established in a neat house in Grosvenor Terrace, equidistant from her brothers Frank, Charles and John-Henry, and close to an excellent school for her seven children. She is touched that Sam should visit and weeps as he recalls his memories of his friend, Will. Nonetheless, she recognises that this visit to England has a purpose and she is anxious to support this lost soul who seems destined to travel in search of a future just beyond his grasp.

'Please tell me how I may help you, Sam. I presume you are here again to see Hannah-Mary?'

'Indeed so, Louisa. She is the one constant in my life yet she is not in my life. Despite our infrequent meetings, I feel I have come to know her so much over our years of writing and I am convinced that she is the only woman who could carry me through whatever life brings. She is a fine woman, Louisa, strong-willed, I acknowledge, but you know from your time living in Illinois that life in America requires women of strength, of stability.'

Louisa listens patiently to Sam's outpouring and balances in her mind the picture he paints of her sister and the one she knows of old. Yes, strong, stable, all of that but … so difficult at times. However, it is not her place to disabuse this man of his ideal. He has wandered the world long enough and now he is in need of a wife and mother to his future children, one who will cope with the knocks and set-backs of living in a new country where social niceties scarcely exist and people of your own sort are rare. For Hannah-Mary the time has come to leave Moor

House otherwise she will live and die a bad-tempered spinster. In the meantime, the family accepts that she bears the full brunt of her father's irascibility and her mother's despair. Louisa, despite her penurious situation following her husband's early death, resisted the invitation to live again at Moor House under her father's roof. After years of Will's liberal fathering, her children could not be exposed to John Willey's tyrannical outbursts. No, Hannah-Mary must marry Sam and that very afternoon she would rouse support to ensure it happens.

The following morning, refreshed from a good night's sleep at his Bradford hotel, Sam walks through streets lined with the latest examples of current taste in commercial buildings, each seeking to outdo its neighbour. Past the Wool Exchange, he turns into the narrow Piece Hall Yard and climbs Piccadilly towards the Bradford Club where John-Henry and Frank are members, along with all the leading names of the town's wool establishment. Built not ten years earlier and emulating the Randolph Hotel in Oxford, the Venetian Gothic club dominates the corner of Manor Row and Upper Piccadilly, and lies just minutes from the offices of the two wool merchants in Duke Street and Cheapside.

Sam enters through a portal guarded by granite Corinthian columns. John-Henry comes out to greet him and they join Frank upstairs in the elegant dining room. Sam notes that his companions are acknowledged by other smartly dressed gentlemen also engaged in breakfast. After he has outlined the adventures of his journey from Towanda in Illinois, crossing from New York first-class on the *City of Berlin* into Liverpool, the brothers steer the conversation towards their sister. As previously agreed, John-Henry opens the batting.

'It is over ten years since you first met Hannah-Mary and we know that in the intervening time you have travelled much and your business enterprises have been extensive.' That was his polite way of saying 'sporadic'. 'During that time, you have maintained a long correspondence with our sister and we understand that your friendship has developed significantly. It is some six years since you were last here and it would be presumptuous of us to speculate the reason for this visit, but should it be to again ask her to marry you, you will forgive us if we, who care deeply for our sister, should wish to understand your position.' John-Henry smiles then addresses his plate of kippers.

Sam expected nothing less. He is all too aware that the history of his travels and enterprises would not present well to these two immaculately turned-out wool merchants with their neat houses and places of business in just the right part of town. Over the years, his letters to Hannah-Mary have revealed but one part of his story and he certainly has no plan to disclose the reality to her brothers.

'I shall not deny that the years in America have been hard, especially during the War of the Rebellion, and without my brother, John, I am sure I could not have kept going. You both have your roots here but for me, since having left England so young, I have had to live a life without stability in a country where opportunities arise at every turn. One has the choice to stick with what one knows or to take a chance and run with it. To take the latter course is easier if one is unencumbered by a wife and family. That is what I have done for the last ten years and sometimes it has gone badly for me but at present it goes well.

'It is not the Englishman's way to reveal his sentiments but the first time I met Hannah-Mary I knew she was the woman I needed for the life I have chosen. Indeed, she is strong-minded and not a bit sentimental, but I have no doubt that she would be steadfast in supporting me.'

Now it is the turn of Frank to explore the detail of 'at present it goes well'.

'Quite, quite.' He dismisses Sam's analysis of his older sister, doubtful that the man is truly aware of just how strong-minded she can be. 'Would you be kind enough to tell us more of your business enterprises and where you are living now?'

Sam has rehearsed the details, fully expecting to be giving this explanation to Hannah-Mary's father, not her brothers.

'After exploring New Zealand – well enough but not for me – I settled in Towanda in Illinois where I bought a piece of land and worked in a dry-goods store for a regular income. A couple of years later I bought out the store plus the entire stock of dry goods, clothing, boots and shoes, and separately bought eighty acres of farm land. That was the year I last came over to see Hannah-Mary. I had hoped she would agree to come back with me and help me build up the business and the farm but either her father was still against it or maybe she just didn't have a fancy for that sort of life.

'Back in Towanda, business continued well. You may not know it but many small towns have no bank and over time I built up a steady income by loaning out money. This allowed me to extend my land by a further one hundred acres, then the following year, eighty more.' He imagines the brothers totting up his capital reserves.

'What do you farm on this land?' John-Henry seeks the full picture.

'I don't. I lease it out and let someone else do the farming. However, my business goes well, I have travelled to England in a first-class cabin this time and I believe that I am now financially in a position to offer marriage to Hannah-Mary.'

'So, Towanda would be your home together?'

'Not particularly.' He notes the brothers' surprise. 'John has now settled in Santa Barbara on the California coast. The climate there is much kinder than that in Illinois and it would be my intention to sell up the store in Towanda and invest on the West Coast.'

'And Hannah-Mary is aware of all this? And happy to join you?' John-Henry feels uneasy at the suggestion of his sister marrying and moving to an unknown and unsecured future.

'She knows that I regret leaving California and that I plan to join my brother, John. Only when I have spoken to her later this morning will I know whether she wishes to follow me.' He smiles frankly at his inquisitors. 'And even if she agrees, will she do so without the blessing of your father?'

Frank exchanges a meaningful look with his brother. 'You are to visit Hannah-Mary this morning at Moor House, I believe. Our father is due at my place of business in,' he checks his pocket watch, 'an hour's time. John-Henry and I will talk with him. If our sister wishes to marry you and to travel to the other side of the world, we shall see to it that there is no impediment from our father.'

Although the paths of father and lover cross somewhere between Bradford and East Bierley, the two men do not meet and Sam knocks on the door of Moor House with unexpected confidence.

The meeting between father and sons does not run smoothly. Who thought it would? But, by dint of reasoning and argument, John Willey eventually concedes that he does not really need to keep Hannah-Mary at home while he has a wife to run around after him. He is impressed by the sound of the land holding and ownership of a store. Its location is of little interest to him so the brothers do not mention the possibility of a move to California.

As for Hannah-Mary, she greets Sam with a mixture of emotions. Despite the years of telling herself that she will never have her head turned by a man, the arrival of Sam's letters always stirs feelings not quite of elation but certainly of pleasure. To have the man now sitting opposite in her family parlour creates a warmth within her but equally she feels slightly out of kilter, fearing she might lose control of the situation. The tone of the conversation is friendly and she is genuinely interested to hear more of his life out in Illinois. When he asks after her life and family, she realises just how narrow is her world compared with his.

In anticipation of his visit and its likely purpose, she has already analysed her opportunities. If she remains at home, she is destined to become an old maid tasked with caring for her elderly parents and, God forbid, her father if her mother dies first. The prospect is not appealing. On the other hand, to accept his offer of marriage would be a step into the dark. Yes, it would be a marriage of her choosing, and Heaven knows, there are still plenty of women today who marry a man on their father's wishes. Does she really know Sam Edwards just from reading his letters? Plenty of women marry a man with whom they have only ever met in the company of others, so who really knows their husband until they are wed? If she held sufficient money of her own to pay her return passage to England, that would be her safeguard should their union prove insupportable.

'Dear Hannah-Mary, let me be clear. You have won my heart and I trust that you believe that during these years apart, I have been constant in my love to you alone. I believe that I can now offer you a good home and the fine future you deserve if you will be my support in achieving great things. Will you be my wife?' He kneels before her and opens a small black velvet box to reveal a gold ring studded with precious stones.

Hannah-Mary has no grand speech prepared but knows her own mind. Although she is not yet aware of the outcome of her brothers' meeting with her father, she is confident that they will carry the day and that there will be no objection to the betrothal. She nods her acceptance with a smile and bends forward for Sam to kiss her.

CHAPTER 64

1875-1876

The Willey family shares a collective sigh of relief. Hannah-Mary is to wed Sam Edwards next year and in doing so will escape the confines of Moor House and the ill-temper of her father. Her mother is relieved that her last remaining daughter has found a husband, but she views with despair her own future, left to her husband without the distraction and support of Hannah-Mary. We all have a cross to bear, she reminds herself, but is convinced that hers will bring her to an early grave.

Marian is delighted that Hannah-Mary will marry and although sad at the prospect of losing her friend to a life across the ocean, she feels a pang of envy for the coming adventure. She reflects on the bravery of those willing to embark upon a new life overseas. At least Hannah-Mary will be with Sam and his brother's family, well established in the ways of the new country.

*

September sees the arrival of Joseph William Mellows, named after his father and paternal grandfather, as is the right of a first-born son. Frannie is relieved that the birth went well as far as such things go and Joe is as proud as Punch to take the boy into his arms. The following day, Joseph Addy walks over through the early autumn sunshine to inspect his latest grandson. Another little person, with tiny fingernails and button nose. How Elizabeth would have loved to meet him, the son of the child she cherished for only six months before she was taken. For Joseph, the ache of losing his first wife will remain for ever.

In the coming months, Frannie proves to be an instinctive mother and, on the occasional visits to Cadeby, her sister is quite envious of her natural capability. True, the house is slightly dishevelled and Marian has to bite her tongue when she sees how their house-maid runs the kitchen and speaks to her mistress in a too familiar way. A respectful distance is required, she believes, so that everyone knows their place. Frannie seems happy with her life and welcomes everyone with open arms, especially her nephews and niece who have grown up so quickly. Marian is exhausted by her two boys. Alfy, now eleven, and Josh, at nine, are both keen scholars, something to be thankful for in boys, she acknowledges, and their love of the sports field is to be encouraged, if only to burn off their energy. As for eight-year-old Henrietta, who dotes on her new baby cousin, something will have to be done and soon. Marian cannot recall being so wilful at that age, even though she did grow up almost as an only child, given the six years' difference between her and Frannie. No, boarding school is what that young lady needs and she must put her mind to it ere long. The Doncaster academy where Marian was schooled cannot be considered as the younger Miss Legge died a few years ago and the older, more rotund Miss Legge has sold the place on.

Henriette is oblivious to such plans and there is but one ambition in her head: to be chosen as one of the bridesmaids to Aunt Hannah-Mary when she marries next year. On the few occasions she meets her aunt, she braves the prickly reception to stress how well-behaved she was for Aunt Frannie's wedding two years ago. And she will be nine next year, and taller, and … But Aunt Hannah-Mary brushes her aside, not the least interested in discussing the details of her forthcoming wedding day with anyone, least of all a frivolous child. Really, children should learn their place.

When Hannah-Mary meets Marian alone, shortly before Christmas, she allows herself to be quizzed about the future. In truth, it provides the opportunity for her to face and voice her own thoughts. Furthermore, she realises that this friendship will be greatly missed when they are separated by an ocean and a continent, though will not admit it.

'Where exactly will you live when you first arrive in Santa Barbara?' Marian starts to tease out the details of Hannah's new life.

'His brother and wife have a home large enough for us in the short term and then we can look together to find something of our own. Sam is anxious that I help make the choice.' Marian nods approvingly. John-Henry similarly consults with her, or appears to, but not all wives are so fortunate. However, as the conversation progresses, she gathers that much of Hannah-Mary's future is uncertain and begins to fear for her friend.

*

Christmas was always destined to be special this year – for Hannah-Mary her last in England perhaps for ever; for Joe and Frannie Mellows a first-born son to add meaning to the festival. For Joseph Addy, however, Christmas Day sees not only a gathering of his daughters and their families around his table, but also an announcement. He waits until everyone is stuffed with plum pudding and even the children are quiet.

'I am right glad that this year we could all be together to celebrate Christmas. I have been fortunate to welcome into my family two sons-in-law who not only take great care of my dear daughters but who also enrich our lives with their presence and of course their children. A man cannot ask for more.

THE MOURNING BROOCH

'Today I have something to tell you all.' The adults stiffen in anticipation and even the children stop wriggling, aware that something serious is about to be imparted. 'You will recall that three years ago, my dear sister, Nancy, died, and was followed the next year by my older brother, Godfrey, having attained his allotted three score years and ten. Next year I too will reach that age. My brother had already recognised that farming is not for old men and had given over the farm to his son then moved to Pontefract, where he enjoyed at least a few years of retirement before his death.' Joseph notes the frowns of concern on his daughters' faces. 'Not that I am suffering from ill health, but Maria and I both agree that we want to enjoy some years of retirement together so I intend to give up the farm in the new year and we shall move elsewhere.'

There is a moment of silence while his words are absorbed. His wife observes the reactions. His daughters are speechless. They knew this day would come but they forget that their father is getting older. John-Henry seeks to dispel the tense silence.

'I am sure you will not be sorry to say goodbye to early morning milking, Father.' A chuckle around the room lightens the mood.

'A sensible decision, Father,' adds Marian hurriedly, anxious to support his plan. 'People don't realise just how hard farming life can be.'

Frannie tries to envisage her father without his fields and cannot conjure up that vision. She remains silent.

The conversation switches to where the couple might move. Already Maria has had some thoughts. No, they would not return to Arksey or Bentley, but there are some very nice places over in Balby, close enough to visit Frannie and her family and also to get into Doncaster.

After the visitors have left and the housemaid has cleared up and gone home to her family, Maria sits quietly with Joseph in the parlour, savouring the peace and the smell of the logs burning in the hearth. The flames and crackle of the fire are mesmerising.

Maria speaks softly: 'Will it be hard to walk away from your fields?'

'No, my dear, not this time. I have farmed this land for only a few years. It was hard to leave the farm at Bentley. I grew up there and as a boy with my father walked his fields. That was very hard.' He turns to her and strokes the back of her hand. 'I get tired these days and I want to spend more time with you and my grandchildren. With the railways we can do a spot of travelling. Maybe to the coast, maybe up to Scotland. Even up to London.' Maria laughs. She knows that he would hate London and loves him all the more for thinking it would please her. She looks forward to finding a new home for them to end their days, please God a long time hence.

By the spring of 1876 Maria has found that new home, Oak Field House in Balby, a small village mid-way on the road between Conisbrough and Doncaster. The practicalities of the move are surprisingly easy. Having no son to inherit his tenancy, Joseph simply gives notice to quit and by the summer he and his wife are settled into a comfortable house, located not far from the church of St John the Evangelist, both built a few decades earlier. Here he can become part of village life, spend his mornings reading the newspaper, potter in the garden and take leisurely walks through nearby farmland where he can cast an experienced eye, assessing the progress of crops and the health of grazing cattle. Maria manages to get him to Harrogate but he insists on staying at the hotel he knows rather than at the home of her friend, Jane Cavendish. She does find the occasion to travel to London but not with Joseph, as expected. Her stepdaughter, Marian, makes a good travelling companion and in any case, Maria's help is sought in finding a suitable academy for Henrietta.

Armed with a list of educational establishments for young ladies and a hotel booked for two nights, the ladies travel to London with great expectations. Maria has called upon the knowledge of her former schoolfriends, now with grandchildren at varying stages of education, and letters have been exchanged with four suitable academies located across the capital. Marian tries to mask her excitement at being in London again. John-Henry enjoys travelling with her to explore the city but it is a costly and therefore rare event.

Marian's benchmark is, of course, the Doncaster academy she attended, and she knows too well not to be seduced by the effusive welcome in the headmistress's study. She insists on seeing the sleeping and washing arrangements for boarders before requesting sight of some exercise books. Geography and French are subjects chosen for deeper interrogation. At one school, in Kensington, the girls are beautifully groomed and polite but there is a listlessness in their eyes. Marian knows that Henrietta needs discipline but she has no wish to have her enthusiasm for life crushed out of her.

As Maria and Marian enjoy their final supper before returning north the next day, they review their notes. Fortunately, the most expensive establishment is deemed too authoritarian. Eventually, they agree that it is the Stella House Collegiate School in Dartmouth Park that has taken their eye. With space for only a dozen boarders, the school nonetheless doubles in numbers with its day girls. The headmistress, a Miss Sutton, seems well-bred and the teacher of the French language is a native of France, essential for Marian who once struggled with the subject.

Back in Bradford, Henrietta has no idea of the real reason for the trip to London, and is eager to hear what her mother did and when could they all go up to see the sights together. John-Henry listens to his wife's white lies as she describes a visit to Grandma Maria's friends, and awaits her private disclosure of the details of the schools. Marian remembers with horror the cold of her first winter in the dormitory at Miss Legge's Academy so they agree that next spring, when Henrietta is nearly ten, would be the best time for her to start. Far better for the girl to enjoy springtime in London. Hampstead Heath is but a short step from the school and would allow for health-giving walks in the sunshine.

In any case, Henrietta's head is full of only one thing and that is the imminent wedding of her Aunt Hannah-Mary and, joy of joys, she is to be a flower girl on the big day. She has tried so hard to be well-behaved over recent months and now she is to be rewarded with a pretty new gown and matching shoes. If only she could share her excitement. Her brothers simply roll their eyes and cover their ears once she starts talking about it and sigh with relief when she flounces off in high dudgeon.

For Marian, her concern is less about the role of her daughter in the forthcoming wedding ceremony, and far more about the wisdom of the marriage at all.

CHAPTER 65

1876

In early July, Sam Edwards travels by train cross-country to New York and takes ship for England and his awaiting bride. He is invited to stay at the home of his future brother-in-law, Frank Willey, an arrangement to keep him distanced from the bride's father. Ahead of the wedding, he accompanies Hannah-Mary to meet the parson who will preside on the day. The Reverend Welbury Mitton, the first incumbent at St Paul's, Manningham, knows well those members of the Willey family who live locally and worship at his church – Frank, Charles and John-Henry.

As they advance up the incline along St Paul's Road, rising cliff-like before them stands the chancel of the church, built in early-English Gothic style some thirty years earlier. Beyond, the tower and 140 feet high spire present an equally imposing structure. Sam groans inwardly; not the modest church of his home town in the Welsh Marches. His fears are dispelled by the warm reception offered by the Reverend Mitton and he accepts the clergyman's offer to show off his church. Sam is taken by the fine stained-glass windows, particularly the rose window in purple and turquoise above the west door and the lancet window showing Christ enthroned, designed by some modern-day artist whose name means nothing to him. Some Italian called Rosetti, he believes.

After a brief homily on the joy and sanctity of marriage, during which an irritated Hannah-Mary grips the side of the pew, they discuss the details.

'It is best for Hannah-Mary to explain our wishes,' leads Sam, knowing that this will be his only contribution to the ensuing conversation. He has only been in town for a few days and it has quickly become clear that decisions regarding hymns, readings, music, flowers and bells had already been made. He wasn't fussed and was happy to agree to it all.

'And finally,' concludes Hannah-Mary, 'the bells.'

'Ah yes,' the vicar shuffles and nods, awaiting her comments.

'I understand there is only one, so we shall not have bells, nor even one bell. To my mind it will sound like tolling at a funeral and I'll have none of it.' The vicar hesitates to contest her view but defends his lone bell. He disappears to the left of the chancel, grasps a single bell rope and tugs vigorously to produce a merry sound, albeit of one note. Hannah-Mary shrugs and concedes it will do.

In the days leading up to the ceremony, there is much afoot at Moor House. Is it not enough to prepare for a wedding without the extra work of packing trunks to be shipped across the world? Hannah-Mary's trousseau contains not only gowns and under-linen for summer but also for winter. She is limited to what she can take but with natural Yorkshire economy, she has no intention of having to buy more than absolutely necessary at the other end. She has had to restrict the amount of monogrammed table and bedlinen which she may transport and is much aggrieved to be forced to confine her books to only three. As they will be at sea for some days, she has to pack everything in layers in order of need. Her head spins with the effort to concentrate and her temper deteriorates accordingly.

To the disappointment of Mrs Willey, the couple can meet only in Bradford but even she recognises the wisdom of avoiding a confrontation between Mr Edwards and her husband. Frank's house is well ordered, as one would expect of a bachelor with a good housekeeper, and there are no children about the place, well-behaved or not, to distract from conversation. Sam recognises the great strain afflicting his best-beloved and makes allowances for Hannah-Mary's somewhat curt responses to his questioning. No doubt she will relax and return to herself once we are on board and under sail, he reassures himself. On the single occasion she is accompanied by her mother, he is able to observe his mother-in-law to be and reflects that if his future wife might be as agreeable as Mrs Willey, he would be blessed. He is unaware that his wife-to-be considers her mother to be weak.

Marian is delighted when her friend asks if she might stay at Hanover Square the night before her wedding. It would be closer to St Paul's and Hannah-Mary has no wish to stay at the best hotel in Bradford along with her parents. Alfy and Josh are despatched to stay the night with Uncle Charles around the corner in Eldon Terrace so that she can have a bedroom to herself and space to be attired the next morning. Henrietta is disappointed that Aunt Hannah-Mary is not to share her bedroom but makes up for it by darting in and out with all manner of questions. Her aunt makes a mental note to give birth only to sons if daughters can be as silly as this one.

Eventually, Henrietta in bed, the house descends into calm and Marian sits on the bed as her sister-in-law potters around setting things in order for the next day.

'How do you really feel, my dear?' For once Marian adopts the direct approach so beloved of Hannah-Mary, who immediately stops and straightens, flexing her aching shoulders.

'Really?' She pauses and considers her reply. 'Frankly, I shall be pleased when tomorrow is over and we are on our way to Liverpool. I cannot be doing with all this fuss and it will be a relief to leave Moor House. Mother weeps and father storms and she weeps more. Whatever America brings, it must be better than that.

'Sam loves you deeply and will take great care of you.' Marian tests the water. She has no doubt of Sam's devotion but wonders if it is truly reciprocated.

'Hmm, I've no doubt that will be his intention.' Hannah-Mary stops and Marian reads doubt in the pause.

'Surely, your love for him will provide any additional strength he might need?' Even she cannot ask outright if Hannah-Mary loves the man she is about to wed.

Her friend looks her full in the eye, shares the weakest smile and responds: 'Time will tell.'

Early the next morning a message arrives from Mr Willey. He has had a bad night due to an uncomfortable bed, a noisy room and indigestion, and although he will attend the wedding, he does not have the strength to walk down the aisle with his daughter and instructs John-Henry to take his role. The family breakfasting in Hanover Square receives the news with equanimity. Hannah-Mary is indifferent and her brother professes he will be proud to give her away. That settled, everyone hurries off to complete their toilette and dress for the occasion.

A small crowd of onlookers stands at a respectful distance on the corner of Church Street as the carriages arrive and expensively dressed gentlefolk descend and process up the short path to be welcomed by the Reverend Mitton. Sam Edwards sits in the front pew, staring forward. His eyes linger on the carvings of the Gothic style arches behind the altar. This is the moment he has desired for over seven years. So, what is that sensation in the pit of his stomach? Not nerves. He has faced more unnerving situations than this. Doubt? That is nothing new. His whole life has been beset by doubt. It is not the first time he has felt this and will not be the last. He has chosen this path and now will step up and step forward. As on so many occasions before, there is now no alternative.

To Henrietta, under the watchful eye of older bridesmaids, the day is simply splendid and, although she would not ever say so, even more beautiful than the wedding of Aunt Frannie. She marvels at the composure of the bride, though surely, she should smile more? A pity that Mrs Willey continuously dabs at her eyes with an increasingly sodden handkerchief and the girl wonders why old Mr Willey ever came in the first place since at the reception he hardly speaks to anyone and sits alone clasping an untasted glass of wine.

Afterwards, John-Henry and Marian accompany the married couple to the railway station and help them with their hand luggage, the large trunks already despatched to the Liverpool docks. It is only as they lean in to kiss farewell that Hannah-Mary realises what Marian has long feared; this could be the last time they will ever see each other. Is it the tears in Marian's eyes which arouse a similar response in her own? Sam warms to this hitherto unseen display of emotion and draws his wife to him. He is her guardian now and is proud to be so. Let not the Willey family fear for her future as Mrs Sam Edwards.

John-Henry links arms with his wife as they watch the couple board the train and take their seats in the First-Class carriage furthest from the smoke-belching locomotive. Marian holds a white handkerchief to her nose so not to breathe in the noxious fumes from the coal-fired furnace that will power the train towards Liverpool. The sadness felt moments before has been overtaken by an overwhelming longing to match her friend's courage. To her surprise, she wishes herself on that train, travelling into new territories, into the unknown.

By her side, John-Henry finally admits to himself that his sister's readiness to emigrate and embrace a new life has stirred an unexpected yearning. Wool is needed throughout the northern hemisphere. Already he is doing business with Canada and the

Americas, so why not test the waters over there and see what life brings? As they stand waving at the departing train, he smiles at Marian. Might she also share this spirit of adventure and in a few years consider a new life together in the United States of America? His heart quickens with the thought.

THE END

ACKNOWLEDGEMENTS

Many years after inheriting the mourning brooch, I was curious to know who was the woman named on the brooch. My cousin, Keith Smith, came to the rescue having researched our Lancashire farming family back several generations. He identified Elizabeth Addy. Then it was my friend, Hilary Jauncey, who took up the baton and delved into the internet to track Elizabeth's descendants. Many were the triumphant emails exchanged late in the evening when yet another piece of the jigsaw was discovered. Even as BOOK ONE was reaching completion, Hilary continued searching and finally found that which had been so elusive: the location of the Addy farmhouse in Millgate, Bentley, still visible in a 1952 aerial photograph before being demolished.

Over the years, my research took me from my Midlands home up to Doncaster and the surrounding villages of Bentley and Arksey. Jean Baldwin, a member of the Bentley with Arksey Heritage Society, gave me valuable information about the Addy and Cockin families, together with a photograph of Maria Cockin, Joseph's third wife. The superb www.arkvillhistory.blogspot.com produced by Alison Vainlo provided invaluable information about gravestones and the history of the two villages.

The area around Bentley was sliced by major railway lines during the period of this novel and I am grateful to railway buff,

George Morley, for his help in understanding what these changes meant for the region.

As the story progressed to Bradford and the business of its wool merchants, I was helped by the tireless research of my friend, John Cole, who revealed unknown facts and characteristics of some of the people of the story. The California element emerged initially from sharing family trees on Ancestry with the late Sam Edwards, a descendant of one of the wool merchants, and later, his brother, the author, Selden Edwards, who provided me with valuable diary excerpts of the original Sam Edwards, which paint a picture of life in California and of the Willey family back in Bradford in the late nineteenth century. It amazes me how intrepid so many were to cross the Atlantic in steam-sail ships to make new lives for themselves in the United States.

In preparation for BOOK TWO I have needed to understand the worsted wool business and John Cole pointed me towards those with special knowledge: Dr Pete Maw, Lecturer in Eighteenth Century History at the University of Leeds, who kindly explained overseas trading issues; Dr Derek Barker, Bradford historian, who helped with maps and knowledge of the industry of the region in the late nineteenth century.

Due to the COVID-19 virus I was prevented from visiting Bradford until I had almost finished BOOK ONE and I am grateful to my Yorkshire-born friend, Margaret Royle, for accompanying me on my first visit when local tour-guide, Nigel Grizzard, conducted us around the locations where the main protagonists lived and worked. A special thank you to Sharon and Robert Light in East Bierley who showed us Moor House, where Robert grew up, and explained what the 1632 farm looked like before development. Thanks also to Amjid Khan and family who welcomed us to see the home in Hanover Square, Manningham, where Marian and John-Henry Willey lived for around fifteen years. Gratitude also to Reverend Father Stephen Dickinson and his church warden, Ian Wilkinson, who showed us the interior of All Saints, Arksey, built around 1120, and explained the changes made in 1868 by Sir Gilbert Scott. A beautiful medieval church and central to my story.

I have tried so hard to be accurate and present an authentic picture of the period but if there are 'Routemaster' errors, I apologise. Equally, I have endeavoured to treat the 'real' characters with respect. The 'real' people represent probably ninety-five per cent of the characters and I do not know what they actually thought, said and did.

Finally, I would like to thank the following for their encouragement over the fourteen years it took to develop and write the first part of *The Mourning Brooch* and for their eagle-eyed proof reading of the book: Sandy Bradley, who also designed the cover, Sally Hamwee, Hilary Jauncey, Judy Ponsford and Margaret and Les Royle.

This book has been a labour of love. The research is compulsive and already I am deep into discovering much about the textile trade of Philadelphia to where the story moves in BOOK TWO. Sadly, thus far I have not been able to contact the only two living direct descendants of Elizabeth Addy's two daughters, that I know of. Perhaps one day …

I only ever met one person in the story of the mourning brooch, my godmother, Dorothy Walker, and her story is yet to be written, but, through my writing, I have been inside the head of every character on every page, every step of the way.

Autumn 2021

Jean Renwick

ABOUT THE AUTHOR

Jean Renwick started creative writing after she retired, following a career in public relations, and had spent three years at the University of Warwick and in Venice attaining a Masters in History of Art. She had long wanted to write a novel based on the inherited brooch but decided a course in creative writing would be beneficial first. Instead of starting *The Mourning Brooch*, she opted to write something quite different and so, *The Mahler Five* emerged and was published in 2016. Seated in a concert hall where Mahler's famous Fifth Symphony is being performed, five people listen to the music, their minds wandering to the big issues facing them. All are connected but they don't know this until the last chapter.

She lives in the West Midlands within easy reach of the City of Birmingham Symphony Orchestra and Stratford-upon-Avon with its RSC. She is active in fund-raising for the arts. A linguist, she travels mainly within Europe and continues to study to improve her German and Italian.

Printed in Great Britain
by Amazon

86857493R00298